Hardyville Tales

When "Don't Tread On Me" meets
"For Your Own Good"

Claire Wolfe

ISBN 13: 978-0-9846222-0-7

Cover illustration by Claire Wolfe

Backwoods Home Magazine
PO Box 712
Gold Beach, Oregon 97444

To Oliver Del Signore and Pat Taylor.

Without them, this book wouldn't be.

Claire Wolfe

Acknowledgements

At various times, and in various ways, a lot of people helped create the columns that eventually grew into this book. Some of those folks I know "in the real world," and some only as online nyms.

I couldn't have done it without all the following people: Oliver Del Signore, Joel Simon, Charles Curley, Wes (aka The Rocket Scientist), the Chivalrous Gun Guys of The Claire Files/Mental Militia Forums (especially Dave Polaschek, Ian, Chris, Slidemansailor, and Thunder), and the clever online gamers of said forums (especially Phssthpok, penguinss-careme, velojym, pagan, ShortyDawkins, septihol, Gloryroad, Mr. Dare, securitysix, A Nonny Mouse, Harleqwin, and Janis).

Special thanks to W.G. and family, who allowed themselves (in slightly edited form) to become vital citizens of Hardyville.

Every writer should kiss the feet of the proofreaders who save us from ourselves. In this case, those honors go to Oliver Del Signore, Darrell Anderson, Rhoda Denning, and the prefers-to-be-anonymous E.B. Tnahk ewe moor then eye can sayy.

The Del Signore family just keeps on earning credits. Special award of merit goes to Cathy Del Signore for demonstrating what a determined woman can do, even when bound hand and foot.

Tom P. gets special thanks for answering a question that earned his alter-ego a journey to Hardyville.

And if you like the fractured pink toilet, you owe it all to ZooT aLLures.

Last but never least, thank you to the *Backwoods Home Magazine* crew for printing most of the original columns and publishing this book. Thank you, Dave, for publishing *BHM* and putting up with me all these years. Thank you, Lenie, for eternal charm and supportive-ness. Thank you, Lisa, for being an always-patient author liaison. Thank you, Annie, for letting me watch you grow up and now for being one of my patient bosses. I owe a special salute to my favorite poet and *BHM* writer, John Silveira, from whom I stole mercilessly in the creation of Hardyville and its people. Thank you to everybody at *BHM* who helped get this book into print and into your hands.

Once upon a time...

... there was a town called Hardyville. Truth to tell, it wasn't much of a place. It was short on Wal-Marts (0) and popcorn-plying multiplexes (0). "Fashion" consisted mostly of Carhartts and cowboy hats. Entertainment ... well, there wasn't much, unless you consider do-it-yourself late-night singing among the patrons at Bark's Tavern to be Great Art. The nearest freeway passed about 200 miles away—and kept right on passing.

Hardyville did have three bars and five churches (or was it five bars and three churches?) and one ... er, "young ladies academy" presided over by the watchful madam ... er, I mean, headmistress, Miss Euphemia Fitz. It had a grocery store, one incredibly bad restaurant, and a proud civic monument in the bronze-ish and bird-doo-covered figure of the Statue of the Drunken Cowboy. It also had one unattractive tourist attraction (more about that later). But it didn't have a single sign of what people in the real world might have called civilization or culture.

It was just one dusty intersection with one lone stoplight, a few encircling residential streets, a fair number of surrounding ranches, and a whole lot of nothing. All this nothing was (and I should add, still is) located in a red-rock valley 600 miles west of the precise geographic middle of nowhere.

Hardyville was also—from 1997 to 2007, on and off—located on the Internet, first on a news site which shall remain mercifully nameless, and then on the website of *Backwoods Home Magazine*.

Tens ... maybe even dozens ... of readers flocked to visit Hardyville whenever it appeared. Given the town's absolute lack of conventional appeal, you might ask, "Why the heck would anybody do that?" But as you'll see, there are reasons—about 1776 of them—to want to be in Hardyville.

Hardyville has one really, really great thing: some of the most smart, cussed, stubborn, independent, clear-headed people you'd ever want to meet.

And Hardyville *doesn't* have one really, really awful thing most of the rest of the world is saddled with: too damn much government. Partly through an accident of geography and history, and partly through sheer determination, Hardyville managed to scrape its way into the twenty-first century almost entirely without politicians, bureaucrats, or any of their Evil Spawn. (And those it had, it dealt with, as you shall see.)

Hardyville is, in other words, what America once had a chance to become—and didn't.

So if you love freedom, perhaps you'll excuse a little high-desert dust and a lack of strip malls. Hardyville may be your kind of place.

But...

Hardyville, being part of the real world, even if a pretty out-of-the-way part, isn't immune to outside influences.

Hardyville went undiscovered by the rest of the world for many years, even though some darned writer named Claire did her foolish best to publicize the place. During those years, Claire (for whom I completely deny all responsibility) mostly wrote stand-alone columns that appeared once a week or twice a month. Those columns gave mere mini-glimpses of Hardyville. Sometimes they told mini-stories. Other times, they just used Hardyville to make some political point. (Yeah, that wasn't very nice, but the news junkies liked it.) Sometimes those stand-alone columns encouraged readers to get deeper into preparedness, think for themselves, and maybe even kick a little bureaucratic backside.

Four of those stand-alone columns—updated and expanded—are included in this book as an introduction to Hardyville-that-was.

Then (go ahead and blame that fool writer), Hardyville got discovered. By people from outside. People were so used to governments that operate on central planning, command-and-control, and tax-and-spend that they honestly couldn't believe society could exist without politicians, bureaucrats, 4,000-page regulations, and SWAT teams to force everybody to be orderly.

At that point, the old stand-alone columns gave way to multi-episode stories, which *Backwoods Home* publisher Dave Duffy was kind enough to print on his web site.

Four of those multi-episode stories—also updated and expanded—make up the main part of this book. Their purpose? Well, just to entertain. If they also edify just a teeny bit, or make you laugh, or encourage you in these dark days, all the better.

So what happens when the immovable objects of freedom and sheer, bloody stubbornness are slammed by the (so we are taught to believe) irresistible forces of faux-democracy, bureaucracy, and a whole army of other -ocracies and -isms?

Read on and you'll soon know...

NOTE: Because they appeared on the Internet, the original versions of these columns and stories often used hyperlinks to other web sites to explain details and sometimes just to amuse. I've expanded and revised the work to incorporate some of the material that was originally behind those links. But for people who'd still like to know more, I've included a section of key URLs (web addresses) in the back of the book.

Partial Cast of Characters

With emphasis on the residents of the Independent (and that's an understatement!) Town and Valley of Hardyville

Nat Lyons — Octogenarian rancher and descendant of the founders of the Hardyville. Informal community leader and dauntless bronc-buster, Nat can still gentle a horse or up-end the pretensions of a city slicker and walk away barely limping.

Carty — Former U.S. Marine (yes, I know; there are no former Marines), one tough dude, and another descendant of the town's founders. Although neither he nor Nat would be caught dead (or alive) participating in city government, the two of them make up the informal and entirely voluntary leadership of the citizenry.

Dora-the-Yalie — A thirtysomething escapee from yupscale suburban Connecticut. How she ended up in Hardyville is yet to be revealed. But to say she has never quiiiiiite adjusted to the culture of the place would be an understatement. She tries, though. She really does. And we try. We really do.

Bob-the-Nerd — Aka Bob Murakami; Hardyville's one-and-only computer geek.

Mrs. Nat — The lovable town grandmother. She appears in the flesh early on. By the time the main stories begin, she has died of cancer, but she lives in our hearts.

Will, Monique, and **Christian Goodin** — Newcomers to Hardyville. Owners of Goodin's Second Time Around Shop. They may be new residents, but they've been living The Hardyville Way for many years, even though they lived it mostly in Milwaukee.

Marty Harbibi — A local rancher. Also an obnoxious, know-it-all idiot. But our obnoxious, know-it-all idiot.

Janelle-the-Waitress — Formerly a harried server at the Hog Trough Grill and Feed (the worst restaurant in the known universe, which specializes, as the story opens, in the worst coffee in the known universe), Janelle and her husband now own the place. So she gets to be a harried small business person, which isn't necessarily an improvement.

Charlotte Carolina and members of her family — They're not from around here, but they find the road to Hardyville. Or rather, various roads.

The Young Curmudgeon — A youthful, usually drunken, mostly silent hermit of mysterious origins and a multitude of bad attitudes and habits. "Mudge" as he is sometimes known, lives in a squat made from a large steel culvert somewhere on the Lyons ranch. His wretched habits sometimes come in handy. When he isn't unofficially destroying things, he officially drives the community's only bulldozer.

Miss Euphemia Fitz — Who runs the "young ladies academy" just outside of town, next to the gambling palace. The young ladies in question include Scarlett, Domina, and Spike.

His Excellency The Honorable Lord High Mayor Pickle — A politician. 'Nuff said.

Etc. — Various members of the hoi polloi, the rabble, and the riff raff. In other words, the free, the proud, and the stubborn of Hardyville.

Newcomers — They tend to wear Birkenstocks and try to make you do things "for your own good" or "for the good of all." This is not welcome news. But is it as bad as it seems?

Claire — A stunningly mediocre writer who bears no resemblance whatsoever to yours truly.

Claire Wolfe

PART I:

A visitor's guide to Hardyville

Four quick, introductory glimpses into The Hardyville Way

Movin' to Hardyville

To reach Hardyville, you must grind your way up to Lonelyheart Pass, then slither on ice into the Great Brown Valley. If you know where to look, you'll find the ghost town of Lost Fortune crouched at the foot of the grade. But this time of year, it's best not to stop. From Lost Fortune, count 4,387,004 sagebrush bushes and you'll find yourself at the one-and-only stoplight in the middle of nowhere—Hardyville.

Half a block north, drop in at Hardyville's center of hot cuisine, the Hog Trough Grill and Feed. That's where, on this gray and snowy day, I found Dora-the-Exile-from-Yale staring in consternation at a menu.

"Is this chicken or steak?" she grimaced.

"What?"

"This." Pointing. "It says chicken fried steak. Well, which is it? Chicken or steak?"

"Mystery food," I shrugged. "Try it. You'll hate it."

She gave me that east-coast-martyr-to-hummus-and-arugula look, then turned back to the menu in search of something edible by her standards. She wouldn't find it. In Hardyville, you adapt to chicken fried steak or stick to your own kitchen.

Pretty soon Nat-the-rancher ambled in from the feed side of the operation, plopped some horse wormer on the table, and folded himself into one of the Hog Trough's slightly uncertain chairs. Nat's old and pretty grizzled. But he wears a cowboy hat even older and more weathered than he. The hat is the wonder of Hardy County and it stays firmly on his head through all waking hours of the day. I even once saw him keep the hat on as he took a back flip off a green horse and landed in cactus.

"Hey," he greeted me. "There's the lady who's making Hardyville famous in that newspaper column. Not too famous, I hope. Don't want a lot of strangers movin' in."

"Don't worry. I'm telling everyone that Hardyville and all you guys are imaginary."

"I feel imaginary sometimes," sighed Dora, still scanning the menu in hopes of locating a vegetable.

"Imaginary, huh?" Nat mused.

"Yeah, but strange thing; I still get a lot of requests from people who think they want to live here."

"You think they really do? Want to live here, I mean?" Nat scratched his whiskers.

"No. They just think they do. Most of 'em would run screaming bonkers out of here if they stayed more than a week. They imagine they want a picturesque life in some pictur-esque town filled with rugged individualists. But not many want to *be* rugged individual-ists, or even slightly inconvenienced individualists. Soon as they really understood in their bones that the nearest Wal-Mart is 93 miles away ... that they have to fix their own radiators ... that they might make the equivalent of $10,000 a year here if they're lucky ... and that the Hardyville One-Plex is going to play *Finding Nemo* clear into the next century—pfft! gone!"

"And once they realize there's nothing to eat except ... um ... Rocky Mountain oysters," added Dora. "By the way, what are Rocky...?"

"You don't want to know," Nat and I rushed to assure her.

"Well, you two are both born city girls," Nat went on. "And you're doin' okay here."

"Yeah, but in my case, it's simple," I answered. "I'm stubborn enough to put up with anything for the sake of being left alone and having some breathing space. Hardyville's about as good as it gets for that. End of story."

"Well, I miss concerts and libraries and ... oh, a lot of things," sighed Dora. "I even miss freeway gridlock, sometimes. But I'm getting used to it."

"You already got used to the snow plowing," I agreed.

Dora blushed. When she first moved to Hardyville she famously violated the modern Code of the West. She moved onto a scenic little acreage half a mile past the sign that said, "Road not plowed beyond this point." Then, come the first snowstorm, she went howling into what passes here for the county road-maintenance office, reminding them that since she lived there now, they'd darn well better not "forget" to plow for her.

True, they weren't plowing her road. Just like the sign says, M'am. And they couldn't see any reason to deplete their tiny road maintenance budget now, just because some snooty college girl from Connecticut never learned how to read.

Unlike many notorious California folks—or New York folks—or Denver folks, for that matter, Dora got it. She shut up and started trading with a local rancher—Nat. He plows, she delivers home baked bread. Dora learned. But too many transplanted folks would just sit and whine about the lack of services until they finally got what they wanted—and got our taxes (of which, actually, we currently have none) launched into the sky. Or they'd leave, sniveling all the way to the coast about how we benighted rubes failed to appreciate their Bountiful Efforts to Improve Our Community.

You see, that's what I mean when I say Hardyville is a state of mind. It's not where Har-dyville is that matters. It's *how* Hardyville is.

Hardyville is independent. But in this world, that means The Hardyville Way entails some sacrifice. (Though it really isn't sacrifice, of course, if you gain more than you give up.) Hardyville is out of the Big Brother eye. But that also means it's far away from a lot of what you might call conveniences. Hardyvillians help their neighbors. But that also means they expect their neighbors to help others—and help themselves. You may find charity here, but you'll damn well never find an "entitlement." You'll find those comforts you make for yourself and those friends you win and keep with your own steadfastness.

You'll find courage here. But you'll need your own courage if you want to be respected. You'll find virtue and vice and every good and bad trait that's found among human beings. But unless somebody trespasses against you, you'll just have to accept the way they choose to live their lives. In return, others will give you that same great boon. And boon it is, be-lieve me.

Unfortunately, too many people think freedom is some sort of gift that should be given to them, free and *gratis,* world without end, amen. But those same people are usually all too willing to wrench freedom away from others in the name of some "greater good." *That* is definitely not The Hardyville Way.

If you honestly want Hardyville, and all the cranky, troublesome, but spirit-filling inde-pendence it implies, then don't bring your dependencies and demands to Hardyville. Don't bring them anywhere else you go, for that matter.

You want to live in Hardyville? I tell you the secret, then, that Hardyville is as real as it is imaginary. It's at least as real, and as much a part of twenty-first century America, as Atlanta or Minneapolis. More real than Los Angeles, Washington, DC, or Aspen, Colorado.

How do you get there? If you can't find Lonelyheart Pass, you can start in the direction of Hardyville by thinking about the way you're living now. Are you racing like a little maze-rat, just to keep yourself in fancy toys? Do you fantasize about independence while tying yourself to every tax-funded service available? Are you living vicariously, via televi-sion? Do you choose to spend your days in a little gray cube? Is your mind in a little gray cube? Are you giving your freedom away to every diktat spewed by some gov-o-crat, be-cause you're too risk-averse to declare that your life belongs to you? Have you put your kids in day care, soccer, and gymnastics, more than in your life? Do you hate your life, but somehow never manage to take real steps to fix it? Are you using people—or being used by them—instead of having honest relationships? When it comes right down to it, do you choose convenience over independence? Do you choose the status quo over the uncertain-ties of happiness? Do your deeds fail to match your words, your hopes, and your ideals?

Then you're not on the road to Hardyville. If you want to be on the road to Hardyville, turn around.

Oh yes, Hardyville exists. And no, it isn't a quaint throwback to the past. It isn't some nostalgic remnant of nineteenth-century Americana. It's as modern and accessible as any other place, in its own way. But it's too inconvenient for contemporary tastes.

Most people will never make it anywhere near Hardyville. Even—maybe especially—most people who say they want to. Hardyville, like freedom, will remain the province of a few who give enough of a damn to put up with the inconveniences, or who care enough to change their hearts and lives for a more fulfilling, but somewhat risky, life.

And so we sit around the table at the Hog Trough—Nat who got born here, Dora who's a refugee, and me who's too plain stubborn for what elsewhere passes for the good life. Just the three of us and a few more hardy Hardyvillians.

The Hog Trough is kind of empty, truth to tell, now that winter has driven the outsiders away from Hardyville's one unattractive tourist attraction. And the food ... well, I'd rather suck on horse wormer. As the snow drives down from Lonelyheart Pass, shutting us off even more tightly from the outside, I know Dora and I are thinking of all the advantages we lack.

No stock exchanges, sushi bars, frequent fliers, or FBI agents. No bureaus, block grants, or cheerleaders for Barack Obama (or any other politician, right, left, or out-of-bounds). No major leagues, no Junior League, no malls, boutiques, department stores, or mega-corps. No Red Robin, Red Lobster, or Whoppers. No rush hour with choppers reporting traffic-on-the-nines. No Versace, Gucci, Ralph Lauren, or Donna Karan. No personal trainers, credit jewelers, street gangs, liposuckers, homeowners associations, post-modern architecture, deconstructionist intellectuals, PC committees, or Lexus dealers. No arbitragers, executive producers, multinational millionaires, multi-level marketers, or media stars. Ronald McDonald, Bill Gates, Hillary Clinton, Ralph Nader, Martha Stewart, Lindsay Lohan, Dr. Phil, and Dr. Laura are all somewhere, far away, beyond the forbidding hills. We are on our own here.

It's a bleak life. But somehow we will survive.

17

Claire Wolfe

How Hardyville got its One Unattractive Tourist Attraction

Spring showed up temporarily last weekend, bringing the first tourist of the season. That means—months before I intended—it's time to tell you about Hardyville's One Unattractive Tourist Attraction.

Hardyville, as you may know, is a one-stoplight, many-horse town that's home to two farm implement dealers, three bars, five churches and the aforesaid Attraction. It pains me to have to talk about The Attraction, because this means I must also confess that Hardyville once had something that plagues the rest of the world: politicians.

Politicians and The Attraction go together like rats and plague.

It all started when a dead philanthropist from the City bequeathed Hardyville his collection of genuine wax imitations of Old West people. You know—life-size figures of Wild Bill Hickok looking bored while being shot by a department store dummy. This collection had been in a warehouse since 1939, when such things went out of fashion. But the dead rich guy left them to Hardyville, absolutely, completely free—provided someone in town would "provide suitable housing."

Well, after much hemming and hawing and inspection of these wax haunts in their distant, dusty warehouse, the owners of the Hog Trough Grill and Feed offered to set Calamity Jane and Billy the Kid and the like around the edges of their restaurant. I guess they reasoned that the ugly old things couldn't disturb people's appetite any worse than the Hog Trough food did—and maybe the glassy-eyed statues would be so distracting nobody would notice the gristle, fat, and general tastelessness of the cuisine.

Other business people who might have had space available opined that, in this age where beeps, boops, and bright lights are the big draw, perhaps the most "suitable housing" for these cobwebby caricatures was right where they were, in that dusty warehouse.

That's where the politicians come in.

"But this is our chance to Put Hardyville On the Map!" protested Mayor Pickle in capital letters. "We can Bring People from all over the World, to View this Unique Reminder of

18

Our Western Heritage." He deplored our lack of Civic-Mindedness, and snorted down his long nose at the prospect of housing such Greatness in a mere private restaurant.

The city councilmen nodded their heads in agreement—in particular, Councilman Branch did.

You see, Councilman Branch just happened to have some "suitable housing" to sell the city—a big brick building right at the main intersection of Liberty Avenue and Freedom Way. Price: $269,000. His fellow politicians voted to buy the building before most Hardyvillians knew what was happening. Several months later someone dug through the records and discovered that Councilman Branch had himself bought the property for $97,000 only a few weeks earlier.

The steam from that revelation was just blowing away when Mayor Pickle announced that a mere $100,000* of city funds would be required to renovate the building to "Make it Ideal for This Fine Collection of Priceless Americana."

How could we argue with that? Well, we would have argued with it, except that the city council voted in secret to spend the money.

It was about this time that Rocking T Western Wear at 512 Main Street, the only clothing store for 45 miles, shut its doors. Seems cowboys couldn't afford new clothes like they once used to. Wonder why?

Well, the city fathers decided to let the bids for that "mere $100,000" renovation in five stages—downstairs, upstairs, roof, landscaping, then signs and displays. But when Mayor Pickle presided over the Grand Opening of the Bids for the All-Important Downstairs Display Area of the New Museum, the lowest bid, just for that one-fifth of the project alone, was $172,534.

People wondered where the politicians had gotten their "$100,000" figure. Particularly since that was a bit before Bill Clinton's magical "100,000 policemen," "100,000 teachers," and 100,000 girlfriends. I guess Hardyville politicians were just ahead of their time.

Anyway, by the time they trimmed a few items out of the wish-list (new price for downstairs: a mere $143,562) and got that part of the work underway, the Hardyville Hideaway Restaurant, only competition for the Hog Trough, had also closed forever. Not as many people can afford to eat out these days, so it seems, even what with working two jobs. Wherever does that money go?

Well, that particular group of councilmen lasted through the reroofing ($43,000) and landscaping ($79,344), before being replaced by a whole new slate of reformers campaigning on Fiscal Responsibility. (Mayor Pickle was re-elected, but that's because Hardyville always has a Pickle for a mayor.)

19

The new councilmen spent a week or two making noises about "cutting waste." Then they went out and got a Federal Farmer's Home Administration low-interest loan ($243,556) for the upstairs renovation and an Emergency Grant for Inner City Beautification ($37,892) for signs and the like.

When angry people showed up at the next city council meeting, the puzzled poly-tick-ans protested, "But it didn't cost Hardyville anything! IT WAS FREE GOVERNMENT MONEY!"

They said that. I tell you the truth. They really did. And some clods actually believed that although Hardyville could somehow make the people of Poughkeepsie and Paducah pay for our "free" pleasures, Pittsburgh and Portland would never in turn put their paws in Hardyville's pathetic pockets.

But then the new councilmen halved the town's snow-removal and road-maintenance budgets so they could hire Sindee-Lee Pickle at $75,000 per year to manage the museum. It wasn't because she was one of those Pickles, they said (Of course not!), but because of her Vast Experience as Assistant to the Assistant Manager of the World-Famous Museum of Barbed Wire, in the nearby Territory of Wyoming.

So, there we were. By then, Joan's Sew-It Shop had gone out of business—quilting and dressmaking supplies being more expensive than the ready-made imports—and The Quik-Mart had closed, due to the street being in such bad condition customers couldn't get into the parking lot. That left Pickle's Groce Mart** (yes, that Pickle's) the only place in town to buy off-the-shelf food.

"But," you might say, if you're an optimist, "at least you got a tourist attraction out of it." Well. ...

The cost overruns on the new museum went hand-in-hand with a predictable series of construction delays. And meantime, those ugly old wax dummies (and no, I don't mean Hardyville's city government) still sat in their cobwebby old warehouse.

Seems as if, about that time, there was a fire next door to said cobwebby warehouse. It wasn't in the warehouse, mind you. Just nearby. But wax ... heat. Well, you know how it goes. The cosmetic result was, shall we say, not pretty.

Unfortunately, in their enthusiasm to Bring Visitors From Around the Globe in Capital Letters, Hardyville poly-tick-ans had let slide a few details, like whether the town or the estate of the dead philanthropist was responsible for the insurance premiums while the dummies were in storage. (Hint: It wasn't the philanthropist's estate.)

I doubt that, in real life, handsome Wild Bill ever envisioned himself looking quite so much like Freddy Krueger. And even though Belle Starr was no beauty in her day, she probably never looked that ... well, run down.

"This was an Unforeseeable Catastrophe," Mayor Pickle pronounced, "for which No One Can, Of Course, Be Blamed. However, after an Exhaustive Search The City Fathers of Hardyville have located an Artisan Formerly of the Famous Madame Tussaud's in London. For a mere $345,000, he will come Right Here to Hardyville and Perform his Work in Our Beautiful New Museum, Rebuilding the Wild West Right Before the Very Eyes of Our Many Astounded Visitors. Think of the Oppor. ..."

At this point, I will tell you what we did. First thing, we got a citywide initiative on the ballot, abolishing the whole city council, for good and all. Some folks spoke of nooses. But we decided that, for now, mere abolition was less likely to draw outside attention.

Second, a bunch of ranchers convoyed down to the City, loaded up the dummies (the wax ones, that is), hauled them to the Glorious New Museum, stuck 'em here and there, then broke out the beer.

Third, Sindee-Lee Pickle was sent back to her promising career in Barbed Wire.

Fourth, using donations from the few business people left in town ($723.11), we installed one of those coin-boxes in the museum like they have in Europe, where you stick in a Euro or whatever to operate the lights for x-minutes. We leave the doors unlocked all the time, and anybody who cares enough can just walk in there, pay for his own damn lights, and stare all he wants.

We found a quarter in the box this weekend. That's how we know a tourist was here. We figure at the peak summer rate of ten visitors a day the museum will be paid for in just 32,000 years—if the electric rates don't go up.

The talk of nooses eventually died down, although an interest in knot-tying as a hobby seems to have taken curious hold among the more politically aware Hardyvillians.

Oh, we kept Mayor Pickle. But as part of the same initiative that did away with the city council, we reduced his responsibilities to one and changed his title. Now, in his new capacity as Omnipotent Potentate and Plenipotentiary of the Principality of Hardyville, he fulfills his function by delivering a Grand Oration at the annual re-dedication of the statue of the Drunken Cowboy (just west of the empty storefronts on Main Street). He is also occasionally heard to Proclaim something Official, though no one feels much obligation to keep track of his Pronouncements and no obligation at all to obey. His wife made him a purple robe, and someone donated a crown from an old high school play. He seems quite happy. And most of us are kind enough not to make snickering references to Emperor Norton.

But you know, the next time you're tempted to try to persuade me that poly-ticks can be reformed, or that there's some magical means we just haven't yet discovered to elect "honest" people, or that one more letter or petition will turn some tax-sucking, oathbreaking blob into a human being with a conscience—don't. Just don't. Because here in Hardyville, we've learned exactly what politicians are good for. Fertilizer.

———————————————

* All prices given in U.S. dollars, aka Federal Reserve Notes or FRNs—even though that's not what Hardyville actually uses most of the time.

** Yes, of course it should be "Grocery" mart. But the "ry" fell off the sign years ago and nobody ever bothered to replace it.

The Law in Hardyville

Since getting rid of politicians, the people of the small, mid-nowhere town of Hardyville haven't had much truck with laws, either. In fact—except for a few details about being nice to each other at the stoplight—here's our entire law code:

TITLE I
A. Do unto others as you would have them do unto you.
(1.) When in doubt, leave them the heck alone.
B. Do unto yourself as you would do unto others.

That's it. The entirety of our formal, written laws. We find this perfectly clear—especially when compared with, say, the U.S. Code, or even the implementing legislation for the World Trade Organization or the specifics of Obamacare. But for the benefit of people just moving in from some coast, or who spent too much time in government school, we hand newcomers an explanation sheet like this:

THE CODE OF HARDYVILLE
Dear Newcomers to Hardyville:
Welcome. We know you'll find our town a pleasant place to live and raise your family. We are very easygoing around here. You'll quickly discover that we don't ask you to live by many of our own rules; we just expect you live by your own. We realize that, coming from a different cultural and political background than you'll find in Hardyville, some of your principles might be quite different than those of your neighbors.

That's why one of our few laws says, "Do unto yourself as you would do unto others." You might wonder what this means in your own life. Well, that's up to you, but here's a sample:

1. Those individuals who wish to ban, tax, or regulate the personal health or social habits of others will be expected to provide legal certification that they have absolutely no destructive or annoying habits of their own, of any nature. In the tradition of pure democracy, the definition of "destructive or annoying" may be

23

determined by any two or more Hardyvillians, as long as they outnumber the person practicing the habit.

2. Anyone advocating the notion that all people have "rights" to housing, welfare, food, a job, medical care or anything else that has to be provided by hard-working people will be expected to provide any or all of the above, on demand, personally, to anyone making the claim for it. After all, to do otherwise would be denying that person his or her "rights." Of course, if you believe "society" is supposed to pay for these "rights," you are welcome to recruit all the parts of society who agree with you, pool your pennies, and guarantee any right you wish to anybody who demands that you give it to them.

3. Anyone who advocates asset forfeiture without due process is expected to place an identifying sticker on his or her vehicle so that the Hardyville police will know who they can stop next time they're short on donut money. Our friendly officers will cheerfully supply you with an absolutely free new "I love forfeiture!" sticker for your next vehicle as they tow away your present one.

4. Anyone who believes guns are evil should be sure to request a response by an unarmed policeman during any 911 emergency. (Hardyvillians, please note: Out of respect for cultural diversity, neighbors are asked not to use firearms to defend the homes and lives of people who have philosophical objections to the possession or use of guns.)

5. Any Hardyville residents who want government to ban anything on the basis that "nobody needs" such and such (e.g. "nobody needs a firearm"), will be expected to submit to quarterly inspections of their possessions by the Ad Hoc (and yet to be established) Hardyville Citizens Committee, Subcommittee to Determine Personal Need. Any items the committee does not deem "needed" (to be determined solely by the committee's standards of the moment) will be surrendered. This includes, but is not limited to: sports cars, valuable collections, excess cash, plasma TVs, fancy audio systems, designer clothing, gift cards from elegant shoppes, and other items not required for the basic maintenance of life. It's not really our idea of good government, of course. In fact, we think it's a terrible idea. But if you honestly believe any item should be banned and/or confiscated just because, in your view, people don't "need" it, we're sure we can find people to help you achieve this goal in your personal life, and we're sure you'll be thrilled to be relieved of all your "unneeded" items.

6. Supporters of affirmative action are expected personally to surrender their jobs to any member of any politically popular minority who expresses an interest in the position, no matter the qualifications of the person making the demand.

7. Those advocating bans on any non-coercive recreation practiced by others (e.g. drugs, sex, gambling) will be expected to give up one of their own pleasures for each item or activity of which they wish to deprive other people.

8. Persons proposing or supporting projects "for the good of others" or "the good of society" will be expected to participate cheerfully—and endlessly—in any projects their fellow Hardyvillians propose for their own good. Although we don't generally make a practice of thinking of such projects, we are, after all, human. Thus we're all capable of dreaming up things we wish others would do. If you believe in forcing your "good" on others, we're sure you'll be enthusiastic about complying with everything everyone else imagines is good for you.

9. Anyone endorsing the view that all products of European, male-dominated culture are oppressive to women, people of color, and people holding "intuitive," rather than "limited, linear" worldviews are expected to do the following:

a) Refrain from crossing all bridges, which are the product of the most linear, and therefore most limiting of sciences, mathematics and engineering.

b) Do not travel in any conveyance using either wheels or an engine for motivation.

c) Avoid entering any building whose construction is beyond the technological level of a brick hut.

d) Do not use iron or products containing iron, the most oppressive of white male metals.

e) Do not subject yourself to the use of modern medicines or medical technologies.

f) If taken to court, do not attempt to prove your innocence, as the concepts of logic and proof are inherently oppressive.

g) Most important, do not claim the protections of the Bill of Rights, including that of free speech. This document was not only composed by Dead White Males, but it was conceived, written, and ratified by that most evil of all DWM classes, that of hypocritical slaveholders. Therefore it is of no value at all and will naturally be shunned by all right-thinking persons who hold your worldview.

Finally, anyone wanting the U.S. government to force American citizens to fight wars at which the defense of the U.S. is not at stake will be expected to volunteer for front-line infantry service. All of Hardyville will hold a party to celebrate your departure.

That's it. A few very simple, common-sense rules which we know you will find consistent with your principles. Welcome to Hardyville. And always remember: ideas have consequences.

———————————————

NOTE: The Code of Hardyville was drafted with the assistance of Charles Curley. Mr. Curley hastens to add that he is not a lawyer and that—having been taken to court by the Bar Association in his state for alleged unauthorized practice of law—he is one of the few Americans who possesses a court order proving he is not a lawyer.

How Hardyville Fell Off the Map

The promise of a sunny day and an early-season barbecue had lured us optimists out to the Lyons ranch. A sudden spring blizzard, unpredictably twisting from its predicted path, drove us indoors and threatened to maroon us.

So there we were, a few select Hardyvillians huddled around the hearth with the extended Lyons clan—families that had trekked to the ranch from as far away as Pocatello, Republic of Idaho, and Two Guns, Arizona. Some of the Lyons' extended family members were even from that most foreign of all places, The Big City.

The real reason for the gathering was Mrs. Nat. It was time to give the generations one last warm memory of her. A year ago, she had been fat and sassy. Well, more like fat and grandmotherly in the way you imagine the greatest grandmothers to be. Now, despite the best efforts of Doc down at the drugstore, Mrs. Nat lay reduced and faded. Still, she had enough left of her to snuggle the latest great-grandbaby against her bosom, there in her recliner beside the blaze.

We had talked ourselves down to a nub, with Mrs. Nat mostly listening and a ravening pack of children rampaging through the doublewide. Now it was late and even the most boisterous kid-beast was settling down. The last pocket-sized game-thingy had beeped its last boop. The last "Did too!" "Did not!" had been settled. And it was so quiet we could clearly hear the crackling of the fire and the howling of the wind outside.

Just as some of us were wondering whether the storm would soon let us wander home to our beds, one little Lyons piped, "Grandpa, tell us a story!"

Another quickly added, "Yeah. Tell us about how Hardyville succeeded from the union."

"Seceded," snipped my favorite Lyons grandchild, Tessa, (and the only one of the mob whose name I could ever remember) with all the superiority of her 13 years. "But yeah, Grandpa. Tell that one." Suddenly aware of her adolescent dignity, she added, "The little kids need to hear it."

Nat protested that everyone already knew that story, practically by heart. And that it was getting late. And so on. It looked for a while as if he wasn't going to give in to the clamor.

But when Mrs. whispered, "Oh please, Sugarpie," Nat's resistance melted. We all leaned a little closer as he began.

"You all might have noticed," said he, "that Hardyville is inside of, but not exactly part of, *these* united States of America. Or mebbe I should say *those* united States. You might wonder how that came to be.

"Well, to understand that, you have to go all the way back to when Hardyville was founded."

"Seventeen-seventy-six!" a six-year-old shouted.

"That's what the sign at the town limits says. And that date marks the spirit of Hardyville for sure. But the truth was, the actual town came some 20 years later.

"It all started with Hezekiah Lyons, my great-great-great ..."

"...Great-great-great-great!" recited the children.

"Absolutely," agreed Nat with an impish smile. "He was great. I remember him real well." That silenced the children, who didn't know what to make of this new twist.

"It all started with stubborn old Hezekiah and a neighbor of his called Sean Brendan MacCarty." At this, everybody glanced at Carty, who sat a little straighter in the chair where he perched, cleaning Ma Lyons' household sawed-off shotgun.

"Even before the War of Independence was over," Nat continued, "We could see that the ideals of freedom were being sold out—if those ideals had ever been all that appreciated, anyhow. The men who spearheaded the revolution—men like Patrick Henry, Samuel Adams, and Thomas Jefferson who promoted the ideals of freedom—were being pushed aside by money men like Robert Morris and the worst, most slimy, evil, grasping, lying, deceiving villain of all ..."

"Alexander Hamilton!" the children chorused in tones that they might have used to say "Darth Vader" or "Lex Luthor."

"And why was he so bad?" Nat asked.

"Because he wanted big, strong, all-powerful central government!" the small Lyonses answered.

"And he lied about it," one of the older and better-read ones added. "He and his Federalist friends wrote all kinds of stuff claiming that their government could never get big and tyrannical because it would be held back by checks and balances."

"Right," nodded Nat. "By the time the big-government boys pushed through their illegal Constitution, we knew trouble was ahead. The promise of a Bill of Rights to be added later persuaded some people that everything would be okay. But those old Lyonses and Mac-Cartys knew that the big-government people would never let words on paper, even real pretty words like in the Bill of Rights, stop them for long."

"So Hezekiah, Sean Brendan, and a bunch of their neighbors and clansmen decided the best thing was to get out.

"Now the Lyons clan was pure English to the roots. We'd lived around Philadelphia and in Rhode Island for generations. Our ancestors were the kind that the do-gooding Pilgrims pitched out of their Plymouth and Massachusetts Bay Colonies for heresy. Our kind were believers—but most of all, we believed we didn't have no business shoving our religion down everybody else's throats—whether that religion be Puritanism, like it was originally, or government worship, like it is today. We believed in freedom as a matter of principle.

"Sean Brendan MacCarty and his people were a different kettle of kippers. They were just off the boat from Scotland, Ireland, and the wild north border country of England. Those people were fighters born and made. Every Scots-Irish son of a ... every man, woman, and third cousin of 'em considered every outsider to be a potential enemy or ally, but never a friend until shared hardship or shared blood said otherwise. They didn't believe in anything but family and being left the heck alone by everybody else.

"Still, we Lyonses and those MacCartys and O'Quinns and Wallaces had more in common with each other than we did with the likes of Alexander Hamilton, who wanted this whole amazing, anything-goes, it-takes-all-kinds land to be controlled by a bunch of ..."

Nat spat into the fire as if getting rid of a bad taste. "...Poly-tick-ans. From a big swamp on the east coast."

"So first, we all packed up and moved off to western Pennsylvania. At the time, people figured that part of the world was pretty much the frontier. You might get clubbed to death by an Indian out there. But Hezekiah and Sean Brendan figured that since the poly-tick-ans weren't coming out to protect the settlers against the Indians, they might also not come out to collect taxes and impose their east-coast city ways."

"Ha!" Shouted one of the rowdier boys, who'd heard this story before. "Hezekiah was wrong!"

"Yep," Nat sighed. "Ole Hezekiah was wrong. Before we'd been in western Pennsylvania three years, in came George Washington with an army bigger than any he'd led in the war, along with that evil bas ... tax-lover, Hamilton. They were gonna squeeze our money out of us or kill us, one or the other. So we had to head on out even further—although first we left a few tarred-and-feathered taxmen in our wake.

"A lot of people like us were already headed further west at the time. Some went deeper into Kentucky and Tennessee, some headed into Ohio. But we could see that everything in the east was soon going to be swarmed over by that bunch of tax-or-axers, so we picked up our muskets ..."

"Hey, hold on," Carty interjected, "It woulda been Kentucky long rifles by then. Best darned military weapon of its day—and We the People had it during the war, while the British 'superpower' didn't. And that matters because of all those people who now say that We the People shouldn't be 'allowed' to be as well-armed as the gummint. At the time of the Revolution, we were better armed than gummint of the king—and we kept those arms and used 'em to help open the west."

"Well, mebbe. Guess you're right on that," Nat nodded. "Fact is that Hezekiah, Sean Brendan, and our pals would have taken rocket-propelled grenades and C4 explosives, if we'd had 'em—people's militia weapons to fight against foreign invaders and domestic tyrants. But we took what we took 'cause that's what we had and this time we decided to head far, far ..."

"Far, far, farrrrrr," echoed the children.

"...far west," Nat agreed. "The history books don't tell it and we don't want 'em to, but the Lyons-MacCarty party ventured out farther, farther, farther, than any east-coast English folk had ever done. Sometimes we was helped by the local Injuns and French trappers and such. Sometimes we had to fight the Injuns and the French off—though that surely wasn't our p'ferred method. We'd rather of had every other free person on our side. Sometimes we traded. Sometimes we suffered. Sometimes we died.

"Sometimes," he admitted with a glint, "we resorted to dirty-dealin', theivin', and con-nivin'. But always in a good cause. And ..." here he waited for the children to supply the key detail.

"Only against gummint targets!" it came.

"Right." He wagged his index finger at them sternly. "Always be honorable with honor-able people. Remember that. Never fail. But when you meet a man—or a woman—who not only wants to take your hard-earned money by force, but wants to use it to run your life the way he wants it run ... you do what you gotta do. Just like Hezekiah and Sean Brendan. Will you do that? Promise?"

The children all nodded solemnly.

"Well, we did what we had to do. We made it across Ohio and across places that were nameless then but that eventually became Indiana and South Dakota and like that. Finally we reached what looked like the rear entrance to the hairy assh...armpit of hell. That suited the Scots and the Irish just fine. Places like that make good bolt-holes, and bolt-holes is what those old rebels've always liked. My English type ancestors preferred grass and nice groves of trees. But even us English thought that mountain range and what might lie be-yond it looked like a pretty good place to be left alone for a long, long time.

"We sent a scout ahead to locate a livable spot somewhere out there in all that nothing. Then we camped and waited. And waited."

"And waited and waited and waited!" the children chorused.

"When we finally realized the scout wan't coming back, we followed his trail straight into the middle of all that nowhereness. At the top of a pass, we found what was left of our scout, all dried out and dead of thirst. But the bony fingers—by then I guess you'd have to say they were more like fingery bones—on one hand were pointing straight into a red-rocked, sagebrush-filled valley. We figured that had to be our kinda spot."

"Hardy Valley!" the oldest children shouted.

"'This is the place,' ole Hezekiah declaimed. Or was that that Mormon guy? I forget. Anyhow, we figured we'd finally found someplace that wouldn't instantly attract a pack of poly-tick-ans looking for a bunch of easy tax payers to suck dry. So we hung our musk ... set up our howitzers and laid our razor wire, so to speak, among the greasewood bushes. And there we settled.

"And time passed. And nobody noticed Hardyville in this spot where no European-folk were expected to be. We didn't have gold mines or great ports or scenery. Or anything any-body else wanted. So other European-type folk, when they finally came, just kinda walked around us without spotting us. And that, of course, suited us just fine. The Shoshone, the Arapaho, and the Crow knew we were here. So did some other tribes. But by then them poor Injuns had figured out it wasn't a real good idea talkin' with wandering white folk, so they kept our secret—and kept on trading with us.

"Still, over time we gradually welcomed more and more like-minded neighbors who wandered in from the east—and later from the west. A few, like the Murakamis and the Harbibis came directly to Hardyville as they discovered the place. Others moved into the adjacent Republics of Montana and Wyoming. They settled the Kingdom of Deseret and the Idaho Territory. Some knew our secret, but they didn't talk much. A lot of those folks were outcasts who had secrets of their own, and anyhow, communications weren't so good back in those days.

"And then, slowly, we got word about distant happenings. Secession. And soon after that, war. They called it 'civil war.' But there was nothin' civil about it. It was never more than the powerful north-east coasters doin' what they always did—tellin' everybody else how to live. The states had built the fed'ral gummint for their own purposes, or that's what the Hamiltonian propaganda said. But now that selfsame fed'ral gummint meant to rule them from Washington—and it did. Not just in the south, but everywhere. It dragged those south-erners back in. And in the years afterward, it tightened and tightened its fist. On everybody. North, south, east, west. Everybody. Except Hardyville."

The children were hushed, horrified as they always were by the violent coup against the states and the people. Until one small voice of a child raised in the Big City ventured, "But grandpa, my teacher said the war was to free the slaves. You don't think people should have slaves, do you? If Hardyville is for freedom, shouldn't we have been on the feral gummint side?"

"We never had any slaves here. Can you imagine such a thing? And we sure didn't collect or pay some tariff, which is the other thing they keep saying that war was about. And we'd come this far to get away from all that everybody-else's-business minding. So why would we get involved in that mess on anybody's b'half?"

"'Sides," Carty shrugged. "Funny thing. Every other civilized place on the planet got rid of slavery around then, sometimes with some local violence, but not in one, single case did they do it with a war. If it was really about slavery, we're the only country that had to kill 600,000 people and destroy our whole form of gummint to do it."

"But you can bet," Nat said to the still puzzled kidlet, "that a bunch of individual Hardyvillians sent contributions to help operate the Underground Railroad to help slaves escape from their masters. And some claim that members of the MacCarty clan acted as conductors and stationmasters on that railroad, helping those that most wanted to be free help themselves. That's the way it has to work, you know. Freedom's not something any outsider can hand you. Or force on anybody by shooting or bombing."

Nat continued, "Other than that, we watched, sad and shaking our heads. We saw the ruins of war and the worse ruins afterward. We watched as the fed'ral gummint went from being war conqueror to pretending to be everybody's glad-handin' 'friend' an' rich uncle—handing out tons of money that it had never earned (but that it printed by the trillions of dollars), making promises it never meant to keep, and always taking a little more control, every year, every day.

"Most of our neighbors fell for it. They elected—Lord forbid—federal poly-tick-ans. They held out their hands for fed money, too greedy to see the strings. Too blind with their love of gummint to see that it was no more than a little bit of their own money coming back to them.* Eventually, the whole country went completely crazy and would put up with darned-near anything, even the meanest brutality and the craziest mis-management of their own personal lives, for love for big gummint.

"Only Hardyville, with its Whiskey Rebellion-soaked, stubborn-cuss heritage, held out. We didn't take stolen money—by which I mean taxes—and we didn't allow our own to be stolen. We didn't tell anybody else how to live, but we didn't let them tell us, either. We just kind of hunkered here, ourselves alone. Mindin' our own business. And nobody noticed.

We 'succeeded' without doing any big, dramatic 'secession.' And we disappeared into American history.

"Today ... There's just ... a gap. Cartographers brush at their satellite photos and think we're a flyspeck. GPS systems report that they're approaching the South Pole when they come near us. Compasses ... well they ..."

"Oh, Sugarpie," Mrs. Nat interrupted in her little whispery voice. "Now, don't go filling their heads with nonsense. It's not like that. It's not anything supernatural. It's just plain common sense. Like slaves on the Underground Railroad, you have to want to be here before you can get here. When you do want to, you'll find the place. Until then, no map will do you any good.

"And long after I'm gone," she added wistfully, "a few will be finding their way here. Count on it."

---

* Astute readers might notice that the dratted author of these pieces occasionally contradicts herself about Hardyville's relationship to the outside political world. For instance Nat claims Hardyville never took federal money, but clearly the town's ex-politicians once did while preparing the Unattractive Tourist Attraction. Other questions remain, for instance, about whether Hardyville ever used Federal Reserve Notes (FRNs) or always kept to its own gold and silver coinage, how much (if any) government the locals ever tolerated, and how much the town's economy is dependent on the outside world's.

The author would probably claim that these "issues" arose because the tales of Hardyville developed over 10 long years in two dissimilar venues. The truth is she sometimes forgot what she was talking about or changed details to suit the circumstances of a given story. Either a) inconsistency is part of Hardyville's charm or b) it'll all make perfect sense someday when The Great Hardyville Novel arrives to stun the world (and the *New York Times* bestseller list) with its brilliance and absolute, total consistency.

Claire Wolfe

PART II

Tales of Hardyville

These longer stories tell what happened when people from outside,
most with a very non-Hardyvillian viewpoint, began to settle in Hardy County

Claire Wolfe

THE COUP

Invasion of the Outsiders

Chapter 1
Return to Hardyville

It was the coffee that made my head snap.

I should have noticed something earlier, on my long drive down from the Hilltop Hermitage. I had been away from town for many weeks, on a silent retreat amid the mysterious monks, nuns, and assorted seekers, mystics, misfits, and weirdos of the Hermitage. I expected to be a changed person on my return—or at least a slightly discombobulated one. But I never expected *Hardyville* to change.

I mean, why would it? But it did.

I should have paid attention to the wide new driveway curving back into the junipers to some unknown destination about 20 miles above town. Twenty miles is practically on your own block as they measure things in these parts. But I barely noticed that mysterious new driveway—which soon enough would become important to us all.

Closer to town, I should have noticed Carty, Nat, Marty, and some of the other guys crawling around the roof of Hardyville's one rather mangy gun range, swinging hammers. Improving things. Things that had sat happily unimproved for years. I mean, we like our gun range, but it's not exactly a country club or the kind of place where rich dudes show off their $6,000 engraved Belgian shotguns. Nobody ever really cared if the roof over its shooting line was pretty.

But no. I didn't notice. Not me. Riding down from the hermitage after a two-month contemplative retreat I was too blissed-out to pay attention to any potential impediments to or enhancements of the Hardyville Way. I drove all the way into town without spotting a thing, got home after dark, and hit my own familiar pillow without an inkling of what was to come.

The next morning I wandered out for breakfast, still oblivious.

At least I should have noticed the fern in the brass pot beside the door of the Hog Trough Grill and Feed. The *living* fern. That was something that had never been seen in all the history of Hardy County.

But no. And no again. Only the coffee finally woke me up.

I blissed my way into the Hog Trough in the early morning. I sought a small side table for solitude, and after the briefest possible exchange with Janelle, who owns the place with her husband, I stuck my nose into my trusty old ThinkPad laptop and stared mindlessly at whatever happened to be on the screen. It could have been a pro-wrestling match, for all I cared. Or a politician making promises. My supposed preoccupation with the computer was only a leave-me-alone signal to the rest of the world. Then...

Siiiip.

Oh my god.

Oh. My. God.

The coffee. It was actually ... good!

I jerked to attention, practically giving myself a lapful of caffeine. Belatedly, I gazed around. There was not only the death-defying fern. Not only the brass pot with an elegant Asian character on it. There were cafe curtains in the windows. And gold leaf writing on the windows.

And outside...

There was a brand-new Prius hybrid parked on Liberty Ave. — and dwarfing that, a Hummer. Gaggingly trendy little fabric banners fluttered from our street lamps. Several storefronts were newly cleared of cobwebs.

And some unfamiliar guy with a crane was chaining up and preparing to haul away the Statue of the Drunken Cowboy.

Our Drunken Cowboy. Hardyville's proud monument to civic indecision and cultural nose-thumbing. Our pride. Our joy. Our target of many juvenile pranks. The embarrassment of church ladies everywhere. THE notable marker of our not-so-thriving downtown-if-you-can-call-it-that.

Leaving my coffee, I dashed out to see what the heck was going on. At that early hour, the street was usually deserted. But even so, by the time I got out there, a small throng was starting to do what throngs do. Except that this was two throngs, with obviously different viewpoints.

One mini-throng contained familiar faces, cowboy boots, and Carhartts. The opposing throngette was made of strange faces, natural fibers, and—uh oh—Birkenstocks. This throngette was filled with people who ... well, who look like the kind of people who demand that *you* save the earth while they drive gas-guzzling SUVs to their vacation homes in Aspen.

"What the *&^%$#@! are you doing?" somebody on the cowboy-booted side demanded of the young man with the chains in his hands. The young man, who had been about to apply said chains to the upper regions of our very own bronze dipsomaniac, hesitated in his work and looked nervously from throng to throng.

The young man merely shrugged and looked bewildered. But a tall, skinny Birkenstocker triumphantly waved a piece of parchment and crowed, "Orders of Mayor Pickle!"

The cowboys hooted derisively. I started sputtering and in language my grandma wouldn't have used even if her bloomers had been caught in the agitator. I said something you could loosely translate as, "Surely you jest, my good man."

He didn't jest.

"Orders," the young crane operator confirmed.

"But the mayor has absolutely no &^%$#@!ing powers!" I raved. "His only job is to wear a purple velvet robe and a cardboard crown and show up whenever something needs Proclaiming! He can't tell you ..."

"Well, Proclaim is what he did. It says right here," the chief Birkenstocker read, holding the parchment in front of his nose, "Whereas the Statue of the Drunken Cowboy is a Negative Influence on Our Vulnerable Youth ... and Whereas alcohol is Known to Cause Problems During Pregnancy and Other Crises in the Administration of Public Health ... and Whereas Said Statue creates a Retrograde Image of our otherwise Clean and Progressive Municipality, thereby hindering Vital Civic Development ... I, Mayor Delbert Pickle, Hereby Proclaim ..."

Lord, it sounded just like an April Fools' Day column I once wrote, where I filled my fanciful version of Hardyville up with do-gooders. Except this time it wasn't our own native mob of easily derailed and largely imaginary do-gooders. These were real people, strangers to town, or at least strangers to me—and their side of the throng was growing faster than ours.

The chief Birkenstocker finished his reading and someone behind him laughed in the direction of the cowboy-hatted crowd. "Too late, people. You can't fight city hall."

Whoever these Birkenstockers were, and wherever they came from, it was painfully apparent they didn't know their Hardyville.

You can't fight city hall? Sorry, guys. You're about to learn what it's like to be in a town that not only fought city hall but beat city government into powder with its bare hands, sowed the soil under city hall with salt so it could never grow again, tarred and feathered its former denizens (all but one ornamental mayor), sent them all off to Taxachusetts and the People's Republic of California, buried city hall at the crossroads with a stake through its heart (well, figuratively speaking, anyway), and danced a dance of drumming triumph on its grave. You can't &^%$##@!ing fight &^%$#@!ing city hall???

We'll show you how we fight city hall.

I will discreetly draw the curtain on what happened next. Let us just say that it involved firearms—albeit never fired—and several shocked and quite disillusioned Birkenstock-clad believers in the holy powers of democracy (even if in their case, as in most real-world cases, it was more like sneak-ocracy). And when it was over, the Drunken Cowboy remained, bottle lifted jauntily as if he were cheering the spectacle of his defense.

Thereafter several large members of the cowboy-hatted crew went off to give Mayor Pickle a wake-up call.

But who were these strange new people? And what was going on?

Stepping back onto the sidewalk to re-enter the Hog Trough, I noticed something else brand new. A black family was headed down the street toward me.

Now Hardyville isn't big on prejudice. Our bottom-most belief is that every individual deserves to be judged only on his or her own individual merits, and that leaves no room for giving a damn whether somebody is black, brown, yellow, white, or green with purple polka-dots. As long as they honestly love their own freedom and respect everybody else's, they're good. But purely as an accident of timing, location, and the fact that we happened to draw more hillbillies than normal, our version of "ethnic" never got much past a Murakami or a Harbibi.

But around the corner from Freedom Way, came a middle-aged man and woman—attractive, down-to-earth types, and a teenage son wearing well-worn athletic shoes and moderately baggy jeans.

The man's face lit when he saw me. I stopped, stunned. "Will?" I asked, "Will Goodin?"

Pretty soon, the various Goodins and I were surrounding each other in that happy but awkward little state where you're not sure whether to give somebody a big hug or just hang on to dignity and shake the person's hand. I had never exactly met any member of the Goodin family, but I knew Will by activism, reputation, and the wonders of digital photography. This was the man who ... well, I'll tell you another day about Will's Great Inner City Computer Project ... but suffice to say he did something governments are always promising to do but, after a few million dollars have disappeared into bureaucratic pockets, always fail at. He got inner city kids to labor in exchange for rehabbed computers and taught them a lot about technology at the same time.

"You guys. In Hardyville! On vacation?"

"No, we're living here now," smiled Will's wife Monique.

Will nodded. "We're renovating the secondhand store over there. Just bought it."

I looked over and saw at least one de-cobwebbed storefront and felt glad. Some things would still be in good hands.

"We just couldn't live in the police state any more," Monique sighed. "That's what America's turning into out there, especially in the cities. We had to get out ... and where else for people like us but Hardyville?"

Where else, indeed? If Will could perform miracles with kids in the inner city, he'd surely be a blessing to the youth of Hardyville. And Monique and Christian along with him.

"Uh ... it seems funny me asking you. But I've been away. So speaking of people like us, and people not like us ... who were those ...?" I waved a hand in the direction of the departing do-gooders.

"Claire," said Will, "We're not the only newcomers. It seems a whole lot of people are getting sick of living in the weird no-rights world out there. And thanks to somebody writing too much about Hardyville, this place has been discovered. By all kinds of people who don't like their lives in the outside world or especially who don't like the politics there. Left, right, libertarian ... all kinds."

"Unfortunately," Monique sighed, "A lot of them are bringing with them half the things they say they want to escape. And a lot of them ... well, they may not like the politics out there, but they have pretty fixed ideas about how to run the world, and they want to begin with Hardyville."

"But don't worry," Will hastened to add, seeing my face drain white, "Some are people like us."

People like us. I looked down at Christian Goodin, about sixteen but small for his age. "If this is a rude question, please feel free not to answer but ... um ... still no social security number?"

He and Will both shook their heads. "Nope," said Christian. "Haven't had a government number since the day I was born and don't intend to get a government permission slip to live and work. Ever."

"And now we're in Hardyville where we don't have to. Where we still don't have to, no matter what some people say."

I grinned at the Goodins. And they smiled at me. And I thought, *You know, maybe not all these new people and their changes are going to be too terrible.*

But as I looked in the direction of the retreating—but not beaten—Birkenstockers, I knew that nothing around Hardyville would ever be quite the same from now on.

Hardyville, meet the real world.

Chapter 2
Banners

Banners. Innocent little Banners. Trendy, dippy, artsy-fartsy, and no doubt ecologically sound banners created from sustainably grown ... whatever. Fluttering over the main streets of Hardyville. Over Liberty Ave. and Freedom Way.

They fluttered from lamp-posts up and down our pocket-sized business district, waving their message of yuppie prosperity and aggressive civic improvement in the early morning light.

Have I ever mentioned exactly how much I hate do-gooders? What C.S. Lewis had to say about them was right on. Here's what he thought of their ilk: "Of all tyrannies, a tyranny exercised for the good of its victims may be the most oppressive. It may be better to live under robber barons than under omnipotent moral busybodies. The robber baron's cruelty may sometimes sleep, his cupidity may at some point be satiated; but those who torment us for our own good will torment us without end, for they do so with the approval of their own conscience."

Banners. Faugh.

"But Claire," I hear you saying, "get some perspective. You're making a ridiculous fuss over a few cute, harmless decorations. What, are you paranoid, Claire? Bigoted?"

Right. Decorations. Harmless? No. They're the first virus that enters through that tiny bit of torn skin. They're the first spider mite of the horde that's eventually going to conquer every one of your houseplants. They're the first ATF agent who enters your door at midnight, bringing behind him murderous oblivion of the police state.

Anyhow, you already saw what that sort of civic-betterment thinking led to the morning after I came back from the Hilltop Hermitage.

But how did they get here? Not the banners, I mean. Those people. The kind who move to a place (presumably because it's better than where they were before) and immediately start improving, and then reforming it beyond all recognition.

That's what I was wondering as I passed the cafe curtains and the stylish bronze vase at the entry to the new, improved Hogge Troughe Grille and Feede. I was relieved (even if grossed out) to note that some of the gang had begun using the vase for a spittoon.

Just before I opened the sparkling clean glass door and stepped inside, I spotted Marty Harbibi, sleeping in his pickup truck next to the Statue of the Drunken Cowboy with a Mossberg 12-gauge in his arms. Marty, of all people, our local blow-hard, actually taking it unto himself to guard our one-and-only landmark. I was impressed. He's still an idiot. But he's our idiot.

"We just need to give them a little time and education!" somebody was arguing as I walked into the steamy cafe.

"Yeah, give 'em the kind a' education you get from a load of birdshot in yer backside!" somebody else hooted.

"Yeah. Or from the application of tar plus feathers plus rail in equal portions."

"We need to give them a chance," Dora-the-Yalie said, quietly but firmly. Then she paused to let the next line sink in: "Like you gave me." True. Dora in Hardyville is like an orchid growing in a patch of cow dung. But we love her.

Or at least most of us do. Did. Or something. Suddenly, it appeared that a lot had changed—not only in the form of newcomers, but in us. And that maybe our famous tolerance was only skin deep—and a very thin skin, at that.

"Well, I don' know, Dora," one of the ranchers muttered under his breath. "We let you in and look at the kinda people you brought us." His companion snickered. Dora couldn't hear the remark, but she could feel the atmosphere. When she'd spoken about giving the newcomers a chance, it was as if a Muslim had stood up the day after 9/11 and defended "towelhead terrorists" to a crowd of TV-watchin', sittin' down at the barber shop, VFW-goin' Bush voters.

This hostility was something new.

Dora fell back against her chair, shocked by the contempt radiating at her.

Nat Lyons wasn't present that morning. But Carty was there, dominating the room as he always does with his big-bald-Marine-ness. But today he wasn't saying much. I slipped into the chair beside him at the vast round table in the center of the room.

"How the heck did all this happen?" I wondered aloud. "I mean, I was gone only two months and when I left everything was peaceful. And normal ..."

"Well, it's as much your fault as Dora's," he said, taking a swig of coffee and grimacing at its tastiness. (Being a military man and a long-time patron of the Hog Trough, he'd gotten used to the old used motor-oil coffee and obviously wasn't adjusting well to the sort of coffee you'd serve to the Seattle set.) "Probably more your fault."

I held my tongue. No point arguing. People were inevitably going to blame me for exposing Hardyville to the world.

"But why? Why here, why now? Why would anybody like the Birkenstockers come here when Hardyville is everything they don't want?"

Some of the other guys took a break from arguing about the best temperature for applying tar and turned toward Carty and me. "Well, them people with the funny shoes that're gonna turn out to be cactus-toed sandals aren't the only newcomers, y'know," one of them explained.

"Yeah," I agreed. "I also saw some old friends of mine from Milwaukee. Good people."

"Right. All kinds of people showed up here. For all kinds of reasons. Some pretty good. Some, well ..."

"Problem is," somebody else sighed, "they're gonna bring in with 'em everything they said they wanted to leave behind. Taxes, whines, demands, regulations, rules, laws, and law enforcers. Sure as God made little green taxpayers, it's gonna happen. Hell, already happenin'."

Carty slowly shook his head. "I guess they came because everything—the whole mess out there in the world—finally got so bad. Torture and warrantless wire tappin' and war and war and more war no matter whether they elect an R or a D. Inflation, taxes, regulations, and too damn much gubmint. Mebbe somethin' just reached critical mass. But left, right, or otherwise, they're here. Like it or not."

"And why should we not like it?" Dora insisted, working up her courage. "We're about tolerance, remember? We're about encouraging a 'big tent' of freedom seekers, even if that means we have to put up with some things we don't always like. It means we want diverse people to live in freedom, and we'll dialog and interact with them instead of closing ranks like a bunch of boys in a treehouse. Right?" She glared around defiantly.

Silence.

Carty broke the tension. "Well, the fact is, we can't keep people out if they want to live here and property owners want to sell or rent to them. Y'all know that. Now they're here. So, we need a plan for dealin' with the stuff that pushy crowd of 'em's tryin' to pull."

And he, of course, was just the man to have one.

"First," he said, "we make up a duty roster for guarding the Statue of the Drunken Cowboy. At least one man on guard 24/7, armed with nothing smaller than a .40 S&W, 12-gauge, or—if you're takin' rooftop duty—.308. Once we've got the statue covered, then we mount a pre-emptive strike on their next likely point of attack, which is ..."

But at that moment, Nat bolted through the door as fast as his bowed octogenarian legs would carry him and demanded, "Have you seen what's goin' on at city hall?!"

We all looked up. Come to think of it, I'd noticed lights and a handful of cars down there when I headed for the Hog Trough. But nobody pays attention to city hall any more.

"Well, you better get down there, pronto. Them new people's up to no good."

As a man (and woman), the patrons dashed out of the Hog Trough Grill and Feed, waving our promises to Janelle to pay for breakfast upon our return. We exploded out onto the sidewalk and prepared to storm Hardyville's long be-cobwebbed toilet-seat of our former government.

But it was too late.

They were boiling down the steps of city hall, maybe a dozen Birkenstockers and a handful of more standard middle-class sorts. And they were grinning like the spotted owl that ate the snail darter.

As they came toward us the tall Birkenstocker who'd been in charge at the attempted statue removal waved a sheaf of papers over his head.

"Hardyville," he announced, "has finally entered the fringes of civilization. We now have ..." he flourished the papers at us, "a government."

Yep. That's what he said. A government. By some of the people. For some of the people. On the neck of anybody that happens to be in the way.

We staggered to a halt, late-comers plowing into the Hardyvillians ahead of us. Before anybody could choke out, "We have what?!" Chief Birkenstocker went on, smarmily.

"Oh, I'm sorry. You didn't know about our meeting to re-establish a proper civic structure for Hardyville? How strange. The time, date, and purpose have been clearly posted for the last three days in the city hall rotunda where absolutely everyone could see them." He smirked. "The people—that is, the people who are sufficiently concerned enough to undertake their civic responsibilities—have spoken."

"You can't do that," I protested.

"Oh, but Ms. Wolfe," the Birker smirked. "We didn't. You did. It turns out that, back when you people threw your little fit and got rid of the town government ... well, you didn't get rid of the town government at all. The original town charter still exists—and it provides for city government.

"The people of Hardyville," he went on, waving a hand toward his own companions, "chose city council members to fill the offices that you left vacant, but never abolished. We'll be in office until the next regularly scheduled elections, in 2016. You can vote us out then if you don't like us."

At that moment the flapping of one of the new banners caught my eye. It was just an ordinary decorative banner, as disgustingly cute, trendy, and environmentally correct as all the rest. But in that instant the famous Hardyville wind chose to snap through it. The little banner rattled and snapped in response.

Funny, I thought. It didn't look much like a battle flag.

Chapter 3
Make My Day

No, we didn't shoot them. I'll end that bit of suspense right off the bat.

True, many hands slapped holsters. You could hear the leather being smacked and the snaps snapping in the speechless silence that followed the chief Birkenstocker's announcement that he and his fellow conspirators—v*ters—had inflicted a "legitimate" government upon us. Never mind that "we the governed" had never consented.

But no. In that breathless moment between shock and revolution, for whatever reason, we did not plug their all-organic, 100-percent natural fiber, sandal-clad carcasses. Nor did we ventilate the yuppie-looking matrons and matroneurs (or whatever else you call the male equivalent) who seemed to be in cahoots with them.

In that half-an-eyeblink of decision-making, we looked to Carty, towering over us in his bald, brawny authority. And we waited just long enough for him to say, in his best Dirty Harry style:

"Go ahead ... govern us."

The Birkers faltered a moment in their moment of triumph. They knew they were being defied, but they did not grok exactly how.

But Hardyvillians did. The tension in the air deflated like a Bush-Obama administration lie. Some of us started laughing. Snaps snapped back into place. The slaps on leather were good natured pats for an old and comforting friend, the sidearm. As the Birkers stood there with questions in their eyes, the locals drifted back toward the Hog Trough Grill and Feed (even if it was now the Hogge Troughe Grille and Feede and served food you could actually eat).

Make no mistake. A cloud of anger hovered in the air as we strolled away from our new would-be masters. But it was leavened with amusement.

Imagine it. Governing a Hardyvillian. Just exactly how do you do that?

I guess I should stop and explain here just why we treat v*ter as a cussword and why we take the phrase "consent of the governed" a little more literally than you might out there in the real world. And why we could walk away laughing from the newly-and-duly consti-tuted "legitimate" government of Hardyville.

Whenever a bunch of people get together and v*te on what *other people* should do, the *other people* in question just become ... victims. Or suckers. Or cows to be milked. Or however you want to put it.

Some of the better men who were around at the time they set up the U.S. federal govern-ment tried to structure it so that there were some guarantees that the "out crowd" couldn't be trampled too badly by the "in crowd." That's what the Bill of Rights is about—protect-ing unpopular people's natural-born rights to believe as they wish, speak their minds, de-fend themselves, and not get totally mauled when hauled before the might of the state's so-called justice system. The Bill of Rights is supposed to protect the "little people" against the might of the v*ting masses and protect the "little states" against the might of the feral gummint.

But sorry. Even that well-intentioned protection is bogus. In the end, when you're talking politics, might always makes right. Or at least, it makes more might. And no matter how you structure things, no matter how noble your intentions, some little faction always ends up gaining control and using raw force for its own ends. You can say all the pretty things you want about the nobility of government, it is always and everywhere used as a tool for ruthless power factions to hammer powerless factions with.

So in Hardyville, we hold to the idealistic—yet eminently practical—philosophy that "if I haven't personally consented, I'm not about to be governed."

Philosophy? No, I'm wrong to call it a philosophy. Philosophies tend to go all wobbly when they run up against reality. In Hardyville, it's just a way of life. Tried. True. And not likely to be surrendered lightly.

Back at the Hog Trough, where Janelle-the-Owner awaited us with our breakfast tabs in hand, we mostly just decided to ignore our new civic tyrants.

Yeah, let them "govern us." It'd be about like trying to govern the Gands—the patiently, pacifistically stubborn followers of Gandhi—in Eric Frank Russell's great old science fic-tion story, "And Then There Were None."

The governators couldn't ruin our way of life as long as enough of us stubbornly fol-lowed our own consciences. Still ... we knew we'd better keep an eye on 'em. And that these newcomers now possessed the tools to make things dangerous.

"Need a volunteer to go to all their meetin's," Carty told us. "Somebody that can observe accurately, take notes, report back. And not get trigger happy," he added.

They looked at me. No way. I wasn't going to torture myself sitting through a bunch of government meetings. Bob-the-Nerd? Nah, he'd get lost in an online game of chess on his laptop and forget to listen to the meeting.

"I'll do it," Dora-the-Yalie declared, standing up. She gazed defiantly around the room, all too aware of how many people considered her to be a part of the problem.

Amid an undercurrent of muttering, Carty questioned her, "How do we know you'd give an honest report? How do we know you wouldn't just report about us to them?"

She took a breath. "Because," she said, "I learned to trade homemade bread to Nat for snow-plowing my road. Because I learned that independent people make good neighbors. Because I am a Hardyvillian. Just. Like. You." Her eyes scanned the room, firmly, insistently demanding trust. Most of us gave it to her. The few skeptics wouldn't meet her eyes.

"Go for it," said Carty. "Report back immediately after their next council meeting."

Dora appeared for a moment as if she were going to snap back at his peremptory tone. Then she took a deep breath and nodded. This was clearly not a time to argue amongst ourselves.

And so it was that Dora became our right-in-the-open spy and brought back the first news from the land of King George III ... I mean the Hardyville city council.

———————————

"Not much actually happened," Dora reassured us the next week after the first meeting she attended. She was the center of our attention as she sat sipping her French-vanilla flavored coffee (a new item on the the Hog Trough's "barista" menu). "Everybody mostly just talked."

We snorted. It figured.

"They talked about making a law to tell the bars what time they have to close." (Hardyville bars close only when—and if—the owners feel like it.)

We snorted.

Dora went on. "But they couldn't decide whether it should be midnight, one a.m., or whether they should outlaw liquor altogether." More snorts.

"Then they talked about the problem of our lack of government schooling. But they couldn't decide whether we needed K-5, K-6, a middle school, a junior high, or a high school first. Some wanted a school board to approve homeschool curricula. But they couldn't decide ..."

"Right," said Carty. "But what did they actually *do?*"

"They set up some committees to study the feasibility of ..."

"DO, I said," Carty barked. "What did they DO?"

"Well," she blurted in a rush, "they did all agree on one thing. One thing they'd need to do before they could carry out anybody's plan."

Uhoh.

"They passed a tax."

The silence was thick as Ben Bernanke's skull.

We were not surprised. Oh no, of course we were not surprised. But now we knew the name of the specific demon our new neighbors had evoked upon us.

In Hardyville we believe that there is only one legitimate way for a "legitimate" government to raise money for itself: Hold a bake sale.

Well, that's not strictly true. A yard sale, a door-to-door collection, or a guy dressed in an Uncle Sam suit standing next to a big red bucket outside a Wal-Mart (if we had a Wal-Mart) all are perfectly admirable ways for a "legitimate" government to raise money to do whatever it needs to do. It could even sell subscriptions. Really. To magazines or to its own services, either way.

The second a government shoves its hand into your pocket without your specific individual consent or tries to order a peaceable person to "comply" with some rule or another that you didn't specifically agree to, then—*voila!*—that quick, it isn't legitimate any more.

No consent, no governing.

There can be no such thing as a "fair" tax, either, no matter how many naive fools hope there can. Because every single tax in the known universe is nothing but protection money: We take your money and use it however we want. If you shut up about it we won't hurt you. If you protest too loudly or refuse to pay—*WHAMMO!*

No matter how much they wrap it in the flag, that's what all taxes amount to. Nope, no honest person would operate like that. Nosiree.

You can draw your own conclusions about how many "legitimate" governments that leaves on this over-governed planet. But while you're pondering that, we had a dilemma.

Now we not only had to ignore the self-elected government of Hardyville. We had to ignore them in some specific fashion.

"Um ... does the charter give them any authority to do that?" somebody asked. "I mean, were the Hardyville forefathers so dumb as to allow anybody to tax anybody without a v*te of the people?"

Nobody seemed to know the answer to that question, since none of us even remembered the charter existed until the Birkers waved it at us. Anyhow, it didn't much matter. Legal, illegal, or otherwise, we were going to resist anything the new "duly elected city council" ever did.

"What kind of tax?" we asked Dora.

"Just a small sales tax. Five percent."

Mutter mutter mutter, rhubarb, rhubarb.

Dora went on. "It may not be as bad as it sounds because there are exemptions for ..."

"Time," said Carty ...

"... and they say rebates will make it less regressive ..." said Dora ...

"...for the monkeywrenching," Carty went on ...

"... and that nobody will have to do any paperwork except a few store owners," Dora concluded.

"... to begin," Carty ended.

Nat rose and nodded in the direction of the Hog Trough's door. "And," he said, "don't forget the smugglin', neither. This is gonna be fun."

And out he walked with the spring of great, youthful purpose in his octogenarian stride.

Chapter 4
First Target

Pickle's Groce Mart was the first to collect the new sales tax. Yeah, you could figure that. The Honorable Lord-High-n-Mighty Mayor showing some *noblesse oblige* to his new city council. And maybe getting himself money to add some gold embroidery to his purple robes.

And yeah. The tax even covered groceries. Our pack of Honorable Officeholding Idiots believed the tax was made more "fair" if they applied it to everything, then issued monthly rebates—aka welfare checks. (Some folks are just weird, taking money out of people's pockets, then giving it back with the other in the form of a government check. Or maybe they recognize a cagey way to make everybody dependent on government.)

But I'm forgetting myself. Sorry.

Goodin's Second-Time-Around Shop was the first to resist. The Goodins were accustomed to living in the real world, where persons of the freedom-loving persuasion have to be tough or get buried. The Goodins were tough. Never, they said, would they work as anybody's tax collector. Never, they said, would they personally pay the tax.

The rest of us mostly just did what Hardyvillians do every day: ignored our new "legitimate government" like we ignore every other government. Well, except Nat.

Nat quietly went off and set himself up in the smuggling trade. Since no self-respecting Hardyvillian would shop at Pickle's any more, he started hauling his flatbed hay trailer to the Big City and bringing back bulk groceries. From then on, any old-timers who needed a can of beans or a jug of cider just headed out of town to the Lyons Ranch.

Of course our new ruling class-wannabes knew what Nat was up to. But what could they do? They knew if they messed with the honored descendant of a town founder, they'd have the wrath of Hardyville on their necks. Besides, Nat's ranch is just honeycombed with backroads and hideyholes. Even old mining tunnels. Anything could happen out there. Goods could be snuck in. People could disappear, if it came to that.

So what could our newly self-elected governing class do, then? Stop the customers from going out there? It's not like our governators had money to set up highway thugpoints between Nat's ranch and town to catch all the tax-resisting shoppers. We hadn't given the new "government" any money and weren't about to. Hardy County's two old deputies weren't about to risk their skins on any such thing, either. And—heaven forfend, it's not like the Birkenstockers were about to put their own stone-washed denim-clad backsides on the line. So people just kept going out to Nat's, buying what they needed, then driving their goods back into town with nobody—and everybody—knowing.

The newbies, well, they shopped at Pickles and paid their taxes. (Mostly, that is. You've no doubt noticed, even out there in the real world, that those who most ardently wish taxes and regulations upon others aren't always terribly keen to pay those very taxes or follow those very rules themselves. Even some of the noobs made their way out to Nat's to save money.)

The Birkenstockers and their allies might not have had a clue what to do about Nat. But, being government supremacists, they knew that they had to do *something* to scare us into line. That, after all, is the basic function of gummint.

And there, right in front of them, sat the peaceful, but nay-saying Goodins. How very, very tempting.

Dora—our spy at the Birkermasters' meetings—reported the key conversation about the Goodins, which went something like this:

"But we can't target them—they're black. It would look like we were, um, targeting them."

"But that's the beauty, don't you see? These Hardyville rednecks are insular. The Goodins are new. The Goodins are people of color. We can crush them as an example to scare other business owners into compliance and none of these bigoted rednecks will interfere. It's elegant."

Well, okay, the conversation might not have gone exactly like that. I'm paraphrasing so wildly I probably need a parachute to land in safe conversational territory. But that's what their decision meant, translated from poly-tick-speak into actual English.

But did I mention that Our Beloved Leaders didn't want to get their personal, well-scrubbed hands dirty with guns and things? No, this was to be—or at least to begin as—a battle of bureaucracy, a war of lawyer-words, an assault of ordinances rather than ordnance.

First, the Birkers fired off a bunch of tax assessments and demand letters to the Goodins. Week by week, the Goodins owed the city gummint more. Taxes. Interest. Penalties. And for all I know, special surcharges to keep the mayor's wife's Persian cat in Fancy Feast.

The Goodins never batted an eyelash. They just kept on doing a nice, taxless business. Used the demand letters for insulation, I suppose. Or a bed lining for their friendly, slobbery Newfoundland store-dog, Spooner, who soon became a favorite of us all, despite his tendency to slime everyone who walked in.

And you can bet a lot of people walked in. People who might not have given a second look to a second-hand store started patronizing the place. So many did that Spooner's slobber glands probably had to go into overdrive to keep up all the greetings.

Town life went on, as normal. The judges announced the winners of the annual Hardy Awards from our Freedom Film Festival. As usual, everybody ignored their pronouncements. Life went on. We waited and non-cooperated.

Next came the attempted regulatory nightmare. Suddenly, nothing about the Goodins' building met the Birkers' new fire code. Expensive repairs were demanded, under threat of ... well, you get the idea.

No, of course the Birkers didn't send an inspector to Goodins' shop. We still hadn't given 'em the money—nor did they have the *cojones*—to do warrantless searches. (Anyhow, the building had naturally been certified safe by the private inspectors the Goodins hired when they bought the place.)

And the Goodins just kept right on fixing up and selling used goods, especially computers. By now Will and his son had spiffed up a whole wall full of second-hand systems, exactly the sort of thing for low-tech ranchers and retirees, as well as young kids just buying their first machines. Business continued to improve nicely. And that was aside from the food smuggling the family was doing on the side, competing with Nat.

Monique Goodin, with an eye for fine foods, brought bulk herbs and spices from the Big City (and beyond!), packaged them under her own "Monique's Uniques" brand, and sold them. Her fine, fancy foods theoretically competed with Nat's more down-to-earth grub. But it was more like *vive la différence* than "cut-throat competition."

The Birkers escalated. They resorted to dirty tricks. Goodin's Second-Time-Around was suddenly inflicted with broken windows, spray-painted insults and threats. Not obvious government-supremacist threats, no. Not "Pay your taxes or else!" They sprayed nasty things like "N-word go home!" and "We don't want your kind in Hardyville!" to make it look like the abuse and threats came from us alleged rednecks rather than from them. But the faux threats didn't fool anybody.

Then, of course, the governators offered to "protect" the Goodins from the hateful threat of our non-existent racism. And in so doing, they noted that security required sacrifice from everyone ... like collecting and paying that sales tax so they'd have the resources to protect the innocent.

You see? That's what it always comes down to with governments.

Carty and his kids—and their friends, and their friends—showed up to replace the Goodins' broken windows and paint over the faux-racist graffiti. And the Goodins just went on. They sold. We bought. And we petted big old Spooner (who always laid right next to the counter), wiped the drool off ourselves as best we could, and went on with life.

Nobody wanted bad blood—either literal or figurative. Most, I think, hoped we could teach the high-falutin' newcomers a lesson in peaceful—but hardly passive—resistance. Show 'em how things could be done in a voluntary community.

Considering what happened next, though, a lot of us wondered afterwards that maybe we should have followed that first impulse to reach for our guns.

————————————

"Why the hell didn't you warn us, Dora? Whose side are you on?"

"But I didn't know," Dora insisted with honest tears in her eyes. "I went to all their public meetings, I told you everything I heard there. But ..."

The previous night, Hardyville had slept in innocent ignorance. The Goodins and Spooner took their well-earned rest at home. And the Birkenbastards had backed a truck up to the Goodins' loading dock, smashed in their storeroom door—and cleaned the shop out down to the last 1970s-vintage VHS machine and computer mouse. Then they boarded up the store, padlocked the front door, and posted a civil asset forfeiture notice. Everything the Goodins had worked for had been neatly—and "legally"—stolen.

No, I don't think it was Dora's fault. We're talking about government supremacists, after all. Those people always have ways of enforcing their will. Sure Dora sat in on the Birkers' public meetings. But why would they tell her what went on in their private "personnel matters"? And one of those "personnel matters" was that they hired the city council president's 23-year-old nephew—a kid with a long history of burglary convictions—to be Hardyville's police chief. He and his friends had done the dirty deed.

"What did they hire him with?" you ask, given that most Hardyville residents had never given them any revenues? Well, turns out that was all too easy—so easy we completely overlooked it. No, it wasn't Dora's fault. It was our fault. And the Birkers'. And indirectly the fault of millions of our snoozing American neighbors. Because just like in the real world, the Birkers decided to finance their new "legitimate" law enforcement by letting the cops keep proceeds from stolen loot.

It's called "civil asset forfeiture"—though it's the exact opposite of civil or civilized. Here's how it goes: Some government enforcer claims he suspects a "crime" is being committed—in this case, tax evasion. (Never mind that, in a free world, tax evasion is damn near a duty, not a crime.) Anyway, said enforcer confiscates the alleged criminal's worldly goods. The government keeps the goods—or the money they get from selling them.

Nobody is ever charged with a crime, because that would mean the government had to actually *prove* the alleged criminal was guilty. Nope. Instead, the person whose stuff was stolen is just expected to slink away. Probably it would cost him more in legal fees than his stuff was worth. Maybe confronting the cops would only get him in more trouble. And— here's the lowest blow of all—IF the person decides to attempt to go to court to get his stuff back HE has to prove that *his possessions* are not guilty of a crime.

Impossible you say? Impossible it is. You can't prove a negative, and the very idea that you should have to go to court to prove that your computer or your car didn't commit a crime is nutsoid, for sure. But it's based on a neat little trick of Medieval "justice" that blamed cats and rats and bricks for causing problems. And it works even better for the modern Medievalists who use it to fatten gummint wallets.

No surprise; out there in the real world, some 80 percent of folks who have their stuff "officially" stolen are a) never charged with a crime and b) don't even attempt to get their possessions back.

Sadly, that's the way "justice" works in real-world America today. But decent people— and that includes every long-time Hardyvillian, even down to idiots like Marty Harbibi and anti-social drunkards like the Young Curmudgeon—simply are too darned decent to think about perpetrating evil tricks like that. Being too decent to think of doing such nasties unto others, none of us were alert enough to think anyone might do such a nasty unto one of us.

So right under our eyes, the Goodins'—who had come to Hardyville because they thought life would be more free here—lost everything.

The Birkers congratulated themselves on their victory as they fenced the Goodins' goods and shared the take with their new police chief.

Then they waited for newly terrorized respectful town businesses to start handing over tax revenues.

They didn't understand that Hardyville had not yet begun to fight.

Chapter 5
Arms and Arguments

Well, the first thing that happened was that the new "police chief" left town.

I don't know exactly how he left town. Did he hightail it off to live for a while on his confiscated loot? Did he enjoy a vigorous ride on a tarry rail? Or did he perhaps get no farther than the Hardyville Pet Cemetery (strongly suspected also to be the cozy retirement home of the only IRS agent who ever ventured into town)?

That remains a closed book.

The second thing that happened is that the padlock on the Goodin's store was mysteriously blown off with a 12-gauge. Doors were repaired. About half the confiscated merchandise mysteriously reappeared—and Will and Monique Goodin were back in business.

This time, there was always a discreetly armed customer on the premises—even at 3:00 a.m.

Carty and his impromptu militia saw to it.

Much coffee flowed from the Hog Trough to the night shift at both the Goodins' store and the Statue of the Drunken Cowboy. The restaurant stayed open crazy hours to serve a watchful populace. We hung out there so much we even started getting used to the new Seattle sort of brew. Coffee that didn't taste like radiator rust. What a concept.

Everybody was involved, it seemed, in looking out for the Goodins. Understand, it was no act of charity, but a simple matter of protecting the property rights of all Hardyvillians—starting with a family of the bravest and most vulnerable. If we let them fall, sooner or later, we'd all fall.

Everybody was involved, that is, except the Young Curmudgeon, who as usual went his own drunken way. And Bob-the-Nerd. Oh, he was with us at the Hog Trough, sucking up the new coffee at all hours. But he remained bent over the old Toshiba laptop muttering darkly about deadlines and occasionally mentioning a client who was threatening to "shoot the software engineers and ship the product, whether it was ready or not."

And Nat ... well, he was just out there on his ranch, building a smuggler's empire. He seldom came to town at all these days.

But the rest of us ... we were in the battle of nerves, no matter where it would take us.

The financial blow to the Goodins was hard, even after the return of all the merchandise that could be rounded up. But people made up for that. Besides getting even more customers than before, and quite a few donations of gold or silver pieces, they suddenly found themselves the recipient of mystery cash in far more substantial amounts. *And* they soon began receiving an even more interesting series of gifts—a number of weapons of a sort most free Americans are no longer "allowed" to possess.

Y'see, some things about Hardyville never change.

In Hardyville, as I'm sure you know, there's no such thing as the government "allowing" anybody to own any kind of weapon. So it's true that the sort of firepower showing up at the Goodins' back door wasn't all that unusual for us. Nearly everybody has an automatic fun-gun stashed somewhere in the back of a closet. Most carry some sort of sidearm everywhere they go. A few Hardyvillians have always gone in for esoteric military gear.

So the items the Goodins began to receive and accumulate in their now carefully guarded back room were nothing unusual. Just standard Hardyville armaments—that ordnance we always hoped not to have to use. But there was so much of it!

And even in Hardyville we don't often see 20 mm cannons. But there they were.

"Please," Dora pleaded as we clustered in the second-hand shop and pondered the source of the newly arrived mystery weapons, "don't be tempted to go that way. I beg you. Don't meet violence with violence."

We looked at her. For a moment, some of us sympathized. Heck, we didn't want it to go that way, either. We preferred to have our town and our hides—and for that matter, even the Birkers' hides—intact. If possible.

We looked down at the MAC-10 machine pistols, and beside them the sleek and elegant descendants of the Tommy Gun. We noted the "Have a nice day" inscription on the muzzle brake of the Serbu .50 BMG. We glanced at the big old antique Gatling gun sitting behind the back-room curtain. And the sturdy wooden boxes and plastic tubes of ... other things. Even as we admired them, no we did not want to go there. A few hearts even went out to Dora for her peacemaking.

Then she said, "After all, there's right on both sides. If you could only find a way to compromise with the new pe ..."

Compromise? Compromise? Did somebody in Hardyville really utter that word again?

Her remark fell like a George W. Bushism into a convention of English teachers. Still, she soldiered pacifistically on.

"You know it's true. After all, the new people are trying to do what they believe is good for the community. Even if you don't agree on details or methods, it would be better to seek common gr ..."

"Get out, Dora," growled Carty. "Get out of here right now. You're not on our side, if you ever were."

"Wait a minute," I protested as Dora stood there, too stunned for the moment to respond. "That's not fair. She's been doing her job, keeping an eye on the Birkers for us. We already know Dora's a peaceable, bridge-building sort. We can't exile her for being herself. Besides, we need her."

"We can exile her for not knowing which side she's on."

"Yeah. Precisely. And by doing that, we'll let her know exactly which side she's on. And what good'll that do us, having her go over to the Birkenstockers, telling all she knows about us?"

Carty started to argue, but a strong (if quavering) voice cut him off. Actually it cut me off. At the knees.

I had thought I was defending Dora. But ...

"Claire, I'd have expected it of him," she sniffed, pointing her aristocratic nose at Carty. "But not of you. You pretended you trusted me. You're still pretending it. But in the same breath you make it clear you think I'd tell strangers every private thing I know about my friends. You really think that, don't you? You think if I got mad at Carty and the few other ... bigots around here, I'd turn my back on all of Hardyville. That's outrageous."

She snatched her coat off the back of a chair and without bothering to put it on, stormed toward the door. In the entry, she turned.

"You people. I'm getting out of here. You're unfair. Every last one of you. But I'm not going to stoop to your level. I'm not going to go over to the other side. I'm just going to go ... home. Goodbye."

And out into the stormy night she swept.

It takes a lot to silence a group like us, but silence us she did. We just looked at each other. Then we looked at the guns and thought about the Goodins' mysterious benefactor. And Dora. And what she might do once she'd had some time to consider.

And what the heck we were going to do about this mess.

Chapter 6
Unexpected Developments

The fates answered some of our questions before we could even get in a little target practice. As is typical with gods, fates, and others of their tricksy ilk, the answers were as unpleasant as they were unpredictable.

Actually, that's not quite fair. Magical powers weren't required—merely the combination of the Young Curmudgeon and the 30th-cheapest alcoholic beverage that could be purchased at Grouchy's Guns & Liquor. But what came next could have been executed by Loki, Coyote, or Murphy.

In the dark of one night, Mudge smashed his latest beater of an old American zillion-ton pick-up truck straight into the Bon Mot ice cream store. The Bon Mot had opened recently and unseasonably. Our young rebel-who-can't-remember-his-cause—aided by about a tank's-weight of steel—closed the store. Mudge and vehicle plunged through glass and brick, through quaint little tile-topped wrought iron tables, into freezers, and ended up in inventory.

Mudge and his truck came out looking like a wedding cake as imagined by Tim Burton, all macabre whorls and bows of chocolate, strawberry, vanilla, and flavors more exotic.

But was it really an accident?

Shortly before the crash, the newcomer owners of the Bon Mot had leaped off the fence after the government raid on the tax-resisting Goodins. Thoroughly cowed by that sneaky midnight show of force, they became the first, after Mayor Pickle and his Groce Mart, to rush into city hall to pay the sales tax. In buying off the threat from the governing mob, they had incurred the quiet wrath of the ungovernable mob.

So could Mudge have done his dive into their premises on purpose? Or was it just the likker acting? Mudge, who was hardly known to be "political," said nothing inflammatory as our two old deputies, Emin Borgo and Tomas Castenon, dragged him out of the flavorful wreckage and hauled him off to the jail (a caged-off spare room in the sheriff's house).

Mudge just mumbled incoherently and tried to grab another hit of Gallo as the deputies cuffed him.

He was out next morning. Between Hardyville's generously contributed bail money and two dozen witnesses prepared to swear under oath that they'd seen the tax-collecting store jump off its foundations and smack into him, there wasn't much else Borgo and Castenon dared do to Mudge.

He may be an irresponsible drunken menace. But he's *our* irresponsible drunken menace.

While Hardyville's Bad Boy stumbled off to sleep it off, we wondered what our Mudge was up to.

We didn't have to wait long to find out. The very next night, Mudge, in a borrowed pickup of suspiciously unknown origins (because Mudge surely didn't have the where-withal to acquire another truck so rapidly) and bearing fake Republic of Montana license plates, plowed into another of the town's brand-new businesses, Sassy Frassy's Natural Hemp Boutique.

This time he came out smelling real pretty (or at least he would have smelled pretty to a police dog, which we didn't have; the Goodins' Newfie, Spooner, found him rather attrac-tive after both "accidents").

Yeah, everyone hated to see a hemp boutique go. That could have been an asset to Har-dyville. But some folks nevertheless found Mudge's "taxidents" all too amusing. And judg-ing by that truck, some Hardyvillian must also have helped make the accident less acciden-tal by contributing a vehicle.

Ugly. Destruction of private property. That's not the Hardyville Way.

But you see, "Sassy Frassy" was in real life Susan Pickle-Chutney—spawn of the mayor and recently also the preying-mantis-like mate to the son of Epperson Chutney, aka the chief Birker and head of the city council. Can you spell N-E-P-O-T-I-S-M? Do I have to tell you that she also collected and paid the sales tax? And got a variety of highly favorable business considerations in return?

Or she did until that moment of Mudgeness.

After that morning, Mudge remained in jail for a while, contemplating restitution. Be-cause restitution *is* the Hardyville Way—no matter how many people might be snickering behind their hands at the crimes and secretly viewing Mudge as some sort of chemical-soaked Robin Hood.

In any case, with Mudge locked away and the Birker's young criminal police chief mys-teriously missing, the storefronts of Liberty Avenue and Freedom Way were safe once again. For the moment.

Hardyvillians seemed to like the notion of going after the tax-cooperators, even if most weren't willing to risk their own Cowboy Cadillacs on the effort.

Shortly thereafter, it became difficult for the owners of the taxpaying stores to buy a pair of shoes (at a non-taxing store) or get a cup of Hog Trough coffee. Their mail got mis-filed at the post office. Respectable neighbors wouldn't speak to them. They were, in short, shunned.

Sassy Frassy and the Bon Mot, as if they hadn't already suffered enough, both got to deal with Hiram J. McCarty, an insurance adjuster with (do I need to say it?) a long Hardyvillian pedigree, who made the post-Katrina insurance Scrooges look like Lady Bountiful.

It's easy to imagine what he had to say to the offended store owners.

"Well now, I'll tell you the pr'cise value of ice cream with tire tracks in it. In November. Not a penny. Obviously, not one red cent. No reasonable soul would think otherwise."

And "Hemp? Well, heck, that's ditchweed; you can't tell me all those washcloths and wallets made of it were worth more than you'd get at Wal-Mart. B'sides, now they're all ruint, which makes 'em worth even less."

The store owners protested in vain. Eventually they would work their way past Hiram and get just compensation from both their insurance companies and from Mudge. But in the meantime, they were finding out that government wasn't the only body in Hardyville that could make life miserable.

And now, of course, Hardyville knew that even the generally apolitical Mudge was on the side of the angels. Which was kind of like having Godzilla on your side, a distinctly mixed blessing. It made everybody wonder what might happen after he got out and worked off his restitution (which, based on Hiram J. McCarty's figures, was going to amount to about $1.98—though in reality it was probably going to take Mudge the rest of his young days to work off the debt he'd incurred.)

What, you don't consider a drunken, destructive lout to be on the side of the angels? You don't think smashing through storefronts and plowing through praline is terribly angelic? You think it shows a certain disrespect for both private property and the rule of law? You don't think refusing to speak to your neighbor just because he cooperates with a wrong-headed gummint is angelic? You don't think making life miserable for collaborators is the sweetest thing in the world?

Well, you're right. I agree with you. Personally, I felt lost and out of control. Our real job, I thought, was to get our old Hardyville back. Attacking each other until the town fell down around our ears wasn't going to be a winner for anybody. Not speaking to our neighbors didn't feel ... neighborly.

Yeah, Sassy Frassy and the owners of the Bon Mot needed to learn that there is a price for collaboration. But wasn't it a lot more important to get the Big Message to the taxers themselves? I wanted to say to those taxers, "When you take money out of a man's pocket that he hasn't personally and freely committed to give, there is a word to describe you. In fact, there are dozens of words for you. Just check any thesaurus under the heading of 'thief.'"

And it doesn't matter one pile of beans whether the thief claims he's doing it "for the common good." As I said before, if you don't have unanimous consent, then you don't have consent.

But I digress.

I felt people were striking out at random and at the wrong targets. That we weren't being much better than the people we were opposing. And we were wrecking Hardyville's first chance in a long time at prosperity. The newcomers, whatever else they were or thought or believed or did, brought assets with them. Assets that had the potential to enrich the whole town—even, and especially, without anybody taxing them.

Carty just shrugged when I voiced my reservations. "Collaborators," he said, "are traitors. Would you rather we shot them?"

Sassy and the owners of the Bon complained to Mayor Pickle and the city council. Our August Rulers huddled in the private splendor of high office (albeit a slightly besieged and mostly unfunded splendor) and discussed how to contain the riff raff—e.g. us.

And I admit I worried about the riff raff myself. I worried both about what our new "legitimate government" might do to us and what we—meaning the long-time citizens of Hardyville—might do, ourselves.

So things stood. Those few businesses who were paying the tax were doing it under the table. They'd just bump their prices up enough to cover the cost and never use the word "tax." They were terrified of what hardcore Hardyvillians might do to them.

Those business people who didn't pay waited, watched, and hoped Carty's citizen patrols would be protection against whatever cretinous relative or college-brained lawyer "expert" the Birkers would bring in next to try to confiscate their assets.

A few, like Janelle at the Hog Trough, cheerily joined the Goodins in outright, but non-violent, protest. She hosed the spit out of the shiny new brass pot by the door and set it up as a kettle to collect "voluntary contributions to fund the new government of Hardyville."

Or maybe she forgot to hose the spit out. Anyhow, no coin was ever heard to ring into those brassy depths.

Now that was a form of protest I could understand. But was it going to be enough?

We had a standoff. For the moment. Few taxes were making their way to city hall. But the taxers showed no sign of backing down, either.

The riff raff thought of the guns in the back room of Goodins' Second-Time-Around, eyed the newly boarded-up storefronts, and went about their business.

But what their business was was another thing.

Chapter 7
Militia Mystery

Me, I fled to the Lyons Ranch. My excuse was needing groceries, which Nat was now bringing in from the sales-tax-free Republic of Montana. Really, though, I just wanted to get out of Hardyville. The tension and chaos were drilling holes in my brain.

Instead of getting a little relief, I got a big surprise.

First person I saw out there was the last person I expected. Dora was stocking the shelves, unfolding bulk cartons and lining up individual cans and boxes for sale. Our eyes met awkwardly before we both looked away.

Nat rescued us by wheeling around the corner at that moment pushing a hand-cart.

"Hey, Nat," I greeted him. "How's the smuggling racket?"

"Safer'n breakin' colts. Warmer, too, this time a year. Anything we can help you find?"

I noticed the "we" and looked at Dora, who pretended to be completely absorbed in canned peas.

"Nah. I'll find what I need."

Nat cocked his head and gave me an assessing look. "Hear things have pret' well gone to heck down t' town."

I sighed, relieved to be able to confess it. Yes, things had pret' well gone to heck in Hardyville.

Dora looked up, "We have to do something to stop this," she said.

"But not your way," I replied. "Not by compromising."

As it turns out, the next move was "their way." Without Dora to sit in on their meetings and tell us of the new town government's plans we didn't see it coming.

They hired cops.

Cops. Real ones. Not like our pair of old mostly harmless deputies. Not like that 23-year-old nepotistic thief. No, real cops—which in these days you know doesn't mean Officer Friendly. I'm talking spit, polish, and swagger cops. Armor-encased cops. Whack-em-n-stack-em cops. Paid for by ... oh, as we pieced it together afterwards, a couple of them were funded by the U.S. Department of Agriculture. (And no, I am not kidding about stuff like that. It really happens all the time.) A couple others came to us courtesy of a side of pork grant from the notoriously porky Department of Homeland (Achtung!) Security. One was inflicted via some other federal program to—you'll pardon the expression—enhance "community-based policing."

All their equipment was FBI and Pentagon-donated. We found out that. And they had equipment never before seen—or needed—in Hardyville. Facemasks and shields. "Non-lethal" crowd-control devices. CS gas. Tasers. Flash-bang grenades. And an array of weaponry that—almost—matched our own. Actually, they had some stuff we didn't have and would consider abhorrent—things like CS gas and monstrous crowd-controlling Active Denial machines, which are far too indiscriminate for anybody who cares about individuals and individual rights to use.

We didn't even see, until later, their phone-tapping gear and other bugging devices they brought with them. (They had to do that stuff the old-fashioned way, since HardyTel wasn't about to collaborate with them, unlike all those phone companies you're stuck with out in the real world.)

All that stuff I just told you about wasn't even the worst of it, though.

Nearly all of the new cops had been hired from the federal Bureau of Alcohol, Tobacco, Firearms, Explosives, Incompetence, Dishonesty, and Entrapment. Or. Get this. They were rejects from the ATF hiring pool. People not good enough to be the fedgov's worst, stupidest, most incompetent, most lying, most arrogant thugs.

Yeah. Scary.

We didn't know their background at the time. But eventually it was pretty easy to guess.

They didn't have much to do at first. What with Mudge already in jail and drawing up his restitution plan, there were no violent criminals to deal with. Anyway, these new cops weren't really the kind to risk their hides around actual violent criminals.

And what else? They couldn't figure how to enforce traffic laws; ours are rather ad hoc, you might say. More customary than actually written down.

They might have liked to bust some of us for smoking pot or cigarettes in public places. But that, too, was legal in Hardyville. They probably put their heads together with the governators to see if they could bust tokers under state or federal law and decided they'd never get a hotshot persecutor to take up the case of smoking one pipeful.

Gambling. Prostitution. Drinking at all hours. And of course, every gun under the sun, possessed and carried every which way. It was all here in our (formerly) peaceful little town and it was all legal. Always had been. And there wasn't a thing they could legally do about it.

Because our only law was The Code of Hardyville and the natural law that makes us all heir to life, liberty, and property. Beyond passing their sales tax, the Birkers hadn't gotten around to changing any of that yet. Maybe they were so busy bickering in committee about what laws their Utopia should have that they hadn't gotten around to actually banning anything yet. Maybe they simply hadn't comprehended yet how vast our lack of laws actually was. Or maybe they were smart enough to realize that if they did too much, too soon, they'd be toast.

So for now, there just weren't that many laws to enforce.

Of course, a lack of laws to enforce wasn't going to stop this gang for long. They were the kind who could hassle just for the sake of hassling.

Again, the tension in the air of Hardyville screamed like a feedback from the world's biggest, loudest microphone. The waiting was terrible. What would the Birkers' new enforcers do? Would we be ready for them? And would we live to tell the tale if we met their force (even their "non-lethal" but equally tyrannical force) with force of our own?

We were getting awfully close to bringing out the weaponry from the back room of Goodins' Second-Time-Around, and from all those other places we keep it. Just in case. And of course there was all that weaponry we already carried every day. The first cop to force some peaceable driver off the road or attempt to force "consent" for a warrantless search was likely to ...

But as it turned out, the Birkenstocker Brigade found something else to occupy them before any of that happened.

The cops' fancy electronic equipment detected "suspicious chatter" on the Internet, on Twitter, and on cellphones. Worse. This detected noise was soon revealed to be—horror of horrors—"terroristic chatter." They soon realized they had an entire, soon-to-be-violent conspiracy on their hands.

And the origins and destination of this deadly chitty-chat? Hardyville. Our very own town. According to gummint news releases, the "terrorist organization" at the core of all this e-chatter—which called itself the Hardyville Whiskey Rebellion Militia—was growing and plotting EEEEE-vil. This wasn't just Carty's little band of gun-totin' business guardians. No, this was serious. This was BIG.

And while the Birkers and their enforcers knew what it was and that it was up to something and getting bigger every day, they didn't know exactly who or where or what this deadly new militia group might do.

A militia? I hear someone saying incredulously. Isn't that so totally nineties?

Yep. So 1790s, as a matter of fact. But never obsolete. Town founders Jedidiah Lyons and Sean Brendan McCarty had both been officers in their local militias before they headed out to look for more freedom. So was every man of age in those days. So are some of us men and women today.

But in this particular case, when rumors of "the Hardyville Whiskey Rebellion Militia" reached us, many of us looked at each other, shrugged, and mouthed, "WHO???"

Hardyvillians—even the hardiest and most hard-core of 'em—didn't have a clue. The only militia most people knew about was the ad-hoc one Carty was more-or-less in charge of. *Surely,* locals thought, *if there was another militia around, we'd know of it.* But nope.

The new "chattering militia" was as much a mystery to most Hardyville locals as it was to the new band of enforcers.

But no problem. The new fed-funded cops now had a homeland security threat to investigate. And that's all that really mattered. It meant they left most of the rest of us alone (although I did hear they considered rounding up and "detaining" some notorious Outlaw writer; might have, too, except the town's only jail cell was already full of Mudge).

Carty, of course, appeared the logical guy to be running a militia. But the new cops took one look at His Shave-Headed Hugeness and decided to find a less muscular suspect.

Had they looked without preconceptions, they'd certainly have noticed that Bob-the-Nerd was a classic 97-pound weakling, ripe for being picked on. But in seeking a "militia-type," the cops weren't considering some over-caffeinated Japanese-hyphen-American software geek, muttering to himself about the client who was going to shoot him if he didn't make the deadline on time. No, the Birkers and their new enforcers wanted something more in the way of a beer-bellied, camo-clad, lily-white racist.

So Bob, tappy-tapping away at his Toshiba in a quiet corner of the Hog Trough, gave them one scary, stereotypical militiaman, then gave them another—as he had, in fact, given them the entire Hardyville Whiskey Rebellion Militia.

Yeah. That was the "deadline" he was working on. He was creating the new "threat" out of whole cloth—and less than cloth. Mere bits and bytes.

I helped him compose some of the ranting screeds. We went out and consulted Nat for proper explosives terms to include in the messages (Nat knows all about dynamite and more modern boomy stuff). Doc over at the pharmacy helped with bio-war words. Altogether, we made that militia look stereotypically scary to the sort of bigoted boobs who were monitoring our communications. Scary and threatening.

The target for our Imaginary Militia? The specific threat? What were "they" actually planning—or what was Bob pretending they were planning—to do?

Well, that was the beauty of it. The slavering monsters of our makeshift militia never named their target directly, of course. In fact, they never said there *was* a target. They never made the tiniest specific threat against anybody or anything.

They used only Hollywood-type code phrases, the kind movie directors imagine that some guy who lives on piss-cheap beer, Nazi literature, and the dulcet tones of the white-supremacist singing duo Prussian Blue would love. Bob's mystery communications were filled with code phrases like "blow away Eagles Nest" and "stomp the Snake Pit" and "light up Lucifer's Lair."

It wasn't our fault, it really wasn't, if the cops and their masters leaped to the conclusion: Target—city hall. We never threatened anybody. We only ... alluded. Vaguely, at that.

Nevertheless, the BirkerMeisters and their do-gooding matron compatriots were sure their very own lives were being threatened. They flew into the tiz of all tizzies. They'd have built a bunker, if they'd had the money. No doubt a small army of them started applying for more federal law-enforcement grants for all they were worth.

And the threats from the imaginary militia grew more threatening—if you were already of a paranoid enough mindset to see them that way.

And the tension grew tenser.

And the panic in high places got shrill.

All the cops and their weapons were deployed around city hall. Sandbags and concrete barriers went up in the street. For good measure the governators, loaning their own money to the city while waiting for grants to come through, purchased a few weapons for city hall like the ones found commonly elsewhere in Hardyville.

And yeah, they purchased a few firearms for personal carry as well. The mayor, after taking their photos and fingerprints, gave every member of the city council an official per-mit to carry. Mayor Pickle knew no such thing was necessary in Hardyville, but it made them feel better. And Mr. Mayor certainly felt better after collecting the rather large silver-coin "permit fee" off each of them.

And so, armed to the eyeballs and hunkered down behind walls and bodyguards, The People's Leaders, Glorious Product of Holy Democracy, waited for disaster. And (armed with our continuing stream of disinformation) their enforcers investigated. And investi-gated some more. The cops were always on the verge of "a substantial break in the case," as the *Hardyville Independent* reported, struggling desperately to keep a straight face. They reported the exact same near-breakthrough again the next week. And the next.

With a few exceptions, our attempted governators were too busy protecting their own precious backsides to bother hassling We the Ordinary Old People. Even better: Old-line Hardyvillians and new neighbors were both so busy watching the city hall drama we quit hounding and threatening each other. We actually started talking neighbor to neighbor—and discovered that most old-timers and a goodly lot of newcomers had more in common than we realized. They weren't all committed members of the "good for you or else" faction. Just as we weren't all hyper-defensive toward newcomers.

But would our new neighbors—those who hadn't obviously taken the governators' side—stand by us when "crunch time" came? We'd need to find out—fast.

Chapter 8
Hardyville's Finest

Most of our neighbors—those who hadn't rushed straight into government office upon their arrival in town—turned out to be pretty decent people once we actually started talking with them—and once they got over wondering whose business the local madmen were going to demolish next. That did take a while, I admit. And many of our own actions didn't help one bit. But we overcame.

Yes, we had our differences. But many newcomers really had arrived seeking freedom. Some just didn't know how to walk the walk after a life of creeping and cowering and complying with "the authorities" in the real world. Many other newcomers might not have agreed with every part of the Hardyville Way, but they didn't mean to disrupt it, either. Things had just gotten out of hand when one smallish group decided a place couldn't be a place unless it officially had "officials."

Once a core group of ordinary citizens on each side had established a tiny beachhead of trust, Carty called a planning meeting in the big back room of the Hog Trough. Even Dora made an appearance, though she sat silently against the back wall surrounded by a group of newcomers.

"Some of you may think you like our new government," Carty told the assembled mini-multitude. "And some of you know for damnsure you don't. But there's one thing we should all agree on. Pretty soon those cops of theirs are gonna get tired of freezing their butts off guarding city hall. The city council is gonna get tired of the cops always bein' on the verge of a 'major breakthrough' in the militia case. And just to prove they're worth something, those cops are gonna come gunnin' for you. And you. And you. And me. Ordinary citizens of Hardyville."

He gazed around. Some of his audience nodded; others—newbies, mostly—looked skeptical.

"Here's what you can expect. They'll find all kinds of ways to hassle you—from tryin' to force you off the road for some harmless traffic 'infraction' to bustin' you for perfectly legal guns, pot, sex, or gambling. When they come after us—and they will—we all need to be ready to handle things right."

"I'm ready," Marty Harbibi snorted, leaning back in his chair and patting his holster.

"Yeah, we may need those, too," Carty agreed. "A person's got a lawful right, mebbe even a duty, to resist unlawful arrest. That's a historic right, and hasn't changed just because police in the real world think they're above the law. Remember: cops got no more rights than anybody else. Even outside of Hardyville, cops probably aren't even constitutional."

He looked as if he wanted to spit. "Settin' up a government-supremacist paramilitary unit in every damn berg in the country—hell, that's just askin' for trouble."

"Yeah," somebody barked from the back of the room, "well we already got trouble and so far we haven't handled it real smart. So now what?"

"Now," said Carty calmly, "We let them know who's boss. But first we need to remind *ourselves* who's boss."

In the days that followed, we buffed up on dealing with cops. Old-timers and newbies alike watched the Flex-Your-Rights videos *"Busted: A Citizen's Guide to Surviving Police Encounters"* and *"10 Rules for Dealing with the Police."* We watched videos by Barry Cooper, the ex-cop who is now in the business of catching and helping people be safe from crooked cops. Then we practiced role-playing, taking turns being the cop and the cops' targets.

Many more sessions than usual were held out at the range, with some noobs getting the thrill of puncturing their first paper targets and popping at poppers. The snipers' nests on the roofs of several local buildings were repaired after many years of disuse. We held Bill of Rights Enforcement education. And jury rights education. And in general, we prepared.

Believe it or not, even long-time Hardyvillians needed some of these lessons. Yeah, we're tough and independent. But face it, here in The Town the Government Forgot (or vice versa) we're not used to having beefy paramilitaries try to force us to cower before them and obey their every bark. So these preps were good for us, too. (Although Marty just shook his head, patted his holster, and said all that yakkety-yak wasn't necessary.)

Many of the newcomers joined the rest of us in taking "that yakkety-yak" to heart. Mostly these were the folk who'd found Hardyville the old-fashioned way—by setting themselves in the direction of freedom. They understood the danger we faced. It's just that most of them were so used to cringing and obeying out there in the Land of the Free that they didn't quite have the hang of saying NO to cops yet.

Other newbies ignored the whole business. They knew that cops might hassle lowlifes. And minorities. But they just as blindly "knew" that cops would never hassle their lily-white middle-class selves.

Some—like Dora, no surprise—felt that certain forms of resistance were appropriate, but meeting force with force was not. "Better to be tried by 12 than carried by six," she said to some of her new friends, not realizing how sadly she was fracturing the meaning of that good old phrase. She figured it meant, "Don't fight back; it's better to argue against the cop in court than it is for him to kill you for resisting him." When of course it really means, "Fight like hell against any aggressive attack and worry about legal consequences later."

Sad.

So of course, the gentle and disbelieving folk were the ones who suffered, when it all came down to it—when Hardyville's new police officers finally got sick of freezing their toesies guarding city hall and decided to go out and start raising some hell. Law or no law; they had cop business to do.

The reception their en-force-ment got from different sorts of people was remarkable.

Case in point: Divorcee Charlotte Carolina, who'd just moved in with her brood of teen-brats out on River Road, ended up face-down in the roadway for failure to wear a seat belt. Never mind that seat belts are a matter of personal choice in these parts. The cops needed something to do—and the Democratic Government of Hardyville desperately needed revenue since hardly anybody was sending 'em any taxes. After she brushed the last bit of gravel out of her cheeks, she paid them for the privilege of getting back in her own car.

On the other hand, when Officer Bruto tried to pull over Doc, who ran the pharmacy and whose old Studebaker was usually chock full of drugs, Doc just calmly kept on driving. He also made a cell-phone call. And a few minutes later, two big old pickup trucks turned up and ran the cop car off the road.

Case in point: The couple who owned the Bon Mot—as if they hadn't already suffered enough—ended up spending the night in jail for operating without a valid business license. Never mind that no such nonsense was necessary here. Mayor Pickle showed up at the jail the next morning and sold them a license his daughter Susan had just run off on her computer; he pocketed another handful of precious-metal coins. But the Bon Mots were happy. They hung their "official" license on the back wall—the only undamaged wall—of their store and returned to rebuilding. (Although between the government and the anti-government they must have wondered just exactly how they were going to make any money.)

On the other hand, when a newly self-appointed "undercover vice squad" came snooping around Miss Fitz's Academy for Young Ladies, hoping to discover some whoring going on, Miss Fitz and the girls demonstrated to them (quite personally) that yes, indeed, there was some whoring going on. The girls sent the resulting photographs to the officers' significant others. And to the *Hardyville Independent.* Which cheerfully published them.

When the cops tried to bust Carty for open carry of a weapon ... well, they just didn't even try that, you understand?

Some newbs stood up for themselves, like the Goodins. But others took a non-resisting path, like Dora. Or they went on believing that the cops would never target them—until the cops targeted them. Then they weren't ready. They let the cops into their homes and vehicles, and of course the cops always managed to find something to take issue with. Then the offended homeowners or drivers sputtered. They blurted. They got angry. They cited lists of the important people they knew. They pointed out that they hadn't broken any laws, since there weren't any to break. They protested their angelic innocence. And paid their fines or prepared for their court dates.

———————————

Now, our new federally financed rejects from the ATF may have been dumb. But they weren't *dumb,* if you know what I mean. Their lack of cogitation didn't interfere with their survival instincts. Yes, they definitely came to hate certain Hardyvillians for their resistance (and no doubt many names went down on many "get later" lists). But like hearty self-preservationists everywhere, they avoided the "hardened targets" and went after the easy marks first.

But that choice had an unexpected consequence. Which ended up making some people in high places most unhappy.

Call it Birkers' Law: The easier the target, the more likely he or she is to be picked on. In our case, the easier the target, the more it was likely to be a government-compliant newcomer. And then comes the consequence: the more government-compliant the newcomer, the more likely that person was to be connected to somebody in the Birker circle.

I mean, think about it. These are the people who believe in hiding behind barricades while sending other people out to do their dirty work. People who expect privilege and who imagine self-defense can be delegated—which it never can be. So of course such attitudes also rub off on their sons and daughters and husbands and cousins.

The cops, being even newer than our governators, didn't know who was who, at first. They just knew who looked like an easy mark. Like somebody who might get huffy and puffy and make excuses, but who wouldn't kick gonads, pull a gun, or plot retribution.

Quicker than you could say "compliance," they were busting the chief Birker's nephew for underage smoking and a city councilman's mistress for driving without a license (another nonsensical item not actually required in Hardyville; but these cops didn't much care about that. They just knew their job was to bring in revenues and run up impressive arrest stats to justify their salaries).

The poor cops. You almost had to pity them. They tried to figure out which "miscreant" was connected with which VIP. They really did, those bumbling bullies. But when they hauled in the mayor's wife one day for jaywalking, the People's Democratic Government of Hardyville had had enough.

Straightening their spines, Our Glorious Leaders arose from behind the sandbags and concrete barriers around city hall and ordered their enforcing minions: "STOP THIS NON-SENSE RIGHT NOW! If you can't keep Hardyville safe from the threats of the Whiskey Rebellion Militia, then at least do something to stop other *real* lawbreakers."

Epperson Chutney, aka the chief Birkenstocker and head of the city council, pointed his finger toward Goodin's Second Time Around and said, "It started with those people. They refuse to collect sales taxes. They're still refusing—and they're still in business. I order you to stop messing with penny-ante offenders. Get those tax resisters and bring the taxpayers of this town into line."

And thus Hardyville got its first encounter with a SWAT team. It wasn't (do I even need to tell you?) pretty.

Chapter 9
After Midnight

We had no spies in their midst now. We couldn't be 100 percent sure who they'd hit. The Goodins? Yeah, that was a no-brainer. But home or business? And what about Doc's drug store, with all its laudanum and cannabis? Or maybe Carty. He was obviously stirring up trouble (as they saw it). They might figure the man they feared to face in broad daylight would look a little less formidable at 3:00 a.m. in his jammies. As long as there were six of 'em and a flash-bang grenade to wake him up, that is.

Who knew? In preparing, we had to cover a lot of bases and stretch our resources thin. Every adult was responsible for his own and his family's self-defense. But we were neighbors and community. We had to "hang together or hang separately."

We might not know exactly what was coming or when, but we knew something bad was heading our way when all our new cops suddenly quit trying to pull us over for doing 35 in a whatever-the-heck-you-think-is-sensible zone and went into long secret huddles inside city hall.

Didn't take too much to figure out that Sgt. Stedenko and Deputy Barney Fife were about to morph into "Hardyville SWAT" ("Stay tuned as officers raid wrong house and shoot a great-granny!")

The next few days and nights were tense. And exhausting. Eventually we would pay for letting ourselves get overextended and over-tired.

But we'll have to give Hardyville SWAT this much credit. When they finally hit, they did hit the right house.

And hit is the right word. Oh. My. God. Being SWATted is like a car wreck. Too fast for reaction. Yet at the same time, like slow motion. You grope upward from sleep. Muscles won't work. Mind struggles to comprehend. It's not just a car wreck you can't stop. It's a car wreck in a nightmare in a shattered mirror in a pit of quicksand. And it hurts. You can't imagine how much it hurts.

I know. I was there.

The first—the only—warning we got was Spooner's low "woof" as he rose from sleep. He roused us—we women who were camped out at Goodins' house with Monique.

I admit it: we had let our guard down after days and nights of no action. A bunch of us—Monique, her twin sister Martina, Janelle, and I—were more or less making a hen party and sleepover out of our guard duty while Will Goodin and some of the men watched over the valuable goods at the store. After gossiping and giggling, we'd all fallen asleep sprawled around the den, our firearms in backpacks, purses, or under piles of newspapers on the coffee table. Confident that our lookout down the street would give us plenty of warning if anything happened, we were out of it.

And so, we would learn later, was Marty Harbibi, the lookout we were counting on. Out of it, that is. Snoozing. By the time he came to and called for backup, what happened had already happened.

————————————————

Spooner chuffed, hearing something outside the house. We scrambled, groping in the moonlight for weapons. Spooner shook himself and padded from the den, through the broad archway into the living room to greet whatever new friend might be approaching the front door.

"Spooner! No!" Monique cried. She grabbed for her Kimber with one hand. Grabbed at—and missed—Spooner's collar with the other. I was slower. I was still groping for my Glock as Monique and Janelle rushed after Spooner.

Bam! Magnesium-bright light blinded me. A concussion kicked the breath from my chest. And another concussion and another. My ears rang. My head exploded with pain. What was up? What was down? I couldn't see. Couldn't hear.

Then, beyond piercing pain and the ringing, a shotgun blast.

And screaming that went on. And on. And on. And on.

"On your knees, M———!" Something like a lead pipe struck me in the back. I fell. Martina crashed down beside me, crying out as her head struck the coffee table.

You can't know. You can't even imagine. You think, in your fantasies, you're going to defend your home or go down in glory trying. Yeah. We thought so, too. Instead, we were laid out on the floor with boots, knees, and guns in our backs before we could get half awake.

All I knew was pain and confusion. A copper tang of blood stung my nostrils and ached in the back of my throat as some thug shoved me prone, yanked my arms behind my back and twisted my wrist into flesh-cutting plastic cuffs.

Martina struggled against her captor as he tried to pinion her flailing wrists. "Get off me!" She screamed, "Get your filthy hands off me!"

The cop grabbed her by the hair, pulled back hard, then slammed her head to the floor. "Shut up, you black b——!" He shoved his MP5 next to her ear. And laughed. "You ain't seen nothin' yet."

I wanted to call out for Monique, for Janelle. Where were they? I couldn't see them with my face smashed into the carpet and my eyes blinded with dizzying afterimages from the flash-bang. Where was our lookout? Where was anybody? Where was help? All I knew was that somebody was still alive because somebody was still screaming.

After what felt like hours but was probably only a few minutes, I heard a different kind of commotion. The endless screams stifled down to sobs. The echoes of gunfire stopped ringing in my brain. The shouting and cursing and threats ceased, now that everyone in the house was down—one way or another—and subdued. And gradually I became aware of other people in the room besides cops.

I risked lifting my head. A wave of nausea struck me. But no sticks or knees or muzzles or Tasers did. That was an improvement.

What I saw was surreal. The cops were posturing over Martina and me like armed roosters. There we were, two handcuffed middle-aged women with three ... four ... I don't know how many submachine guns and tactical shotguns pointed at us, fingers tensed around triggers.

In one of those strange moments, like laughing during a funeral, I remember hoping none of the ninjas got the hiccups.

But the surreal part was that they appeared to be posturing for the sake of ... yes, Our Glorious Leaders. Behind the stormtroopers, safely over by the wall, shuffled a half dozen or so of our Civic Dignitaries. It was like a little celebrity gallery, invited along for the display.

Just as, in the real world, SWAT cops liked to invite the media along to witness their toughness, Hardyville SWAT brought, in its wake, practically the whole class of governators.

As I held my head up and tried to control the spinning, throbbing, and flashing, I saw Epperson Chutney, chief Birkenstocker, peering eagerly. He was so excited he looked like he was about to have an ... no, sorry, I won't say that in a PG-rated book. Some of the other self-appointed celebs looked more dubious. Even shellshocked. Dan White, one of the city council members, looked ... well, white. And there was the mayor in his purple robe, looking vaguely, clashingly green.

———————————————

And then a voice like God's own thunder boomed in the night. "Drop it! Or we'll blow away every ninja-masked bastard here."

I peered over my shoulder, setting off another round of vertigo. But it was worth it. Carty, Marty, Will Goodin, and even the long-gone-from-town Nat stood in silhouette in the blazing, blinking doorway. Their Uzis and Mossbergs pointed straight at the MP5s and Remingtons of Hardyville SWAT. For a moment, everybody froze. Neither side yielded an inch.

Beyond the ringing in my ears, I don't think I ever heard such silence. It, too, went on forever as each side faced the other with fingers wrapped tensely around triggers. A long time went by.

Each side leveled equal armament against the other. Each was equally determined. Each equally adamant. Each equally sure the other *must* back down.

The world stood frozen as fate, and the fates alone, determined the next move. Who would live. Who would die. Whether freedom or force would reign in Hardyville.

Then sounds of struggle arose from the living room. One of the women rolled to her side. Monique. I could tell by the halo of black hair in the pulsing light from the doorway.

With hands still bound behind her back, she struggled to a sitting position. Defiantly, with tears streaking down her face, she glared at the home invaders. She looked around. Spotted something. She seemed to freeze briefly. Then she began to edge along the floor— straight between the opposing lines of armed men. Sobbing, she pulled herself awkwardly toward a dark, still body lying nearby.

All eyes flicked toward her goal. As we feared. One of our own lay bleeding.

One of the thugs twitched. The barrel of his gun tracked Monique. Carty's Uzi swung in his direction. Nat, Marty, and Will stared down the rest of the invading gang.

And still Monique inched along until she reached the bloody body on the floor. Then she let herself fall forward, laid her forehead against the dark form and wailed, "What kind of people are you? What kind of people?!"

———-

There are certain things civilized societies don't permit. The casual slaughter of innocents is one. The moment citizens discover that their government considers the death of innocents to be business as usual—mere "collateral damage" or tactical necessity—at that moment, all things should come to a halt.

At that moment—that very, precise moment—a deadly slide has started.

Truly civilized people will stop. They'll say, "Never again. Not one more innocent life will be considered disposable. We will not only stop this. We will stop the attitudes and actions that led to this—for the sake of all that's decent and just."

Uncivilized people will yawn and say, "What's on the other channel?" Or worse, they'll hope that the other channel will be playing a reality show in which face-masked cops kick down doors and throw people to the ground while screaming obscenities.

A society that tolerates that kind of thing—even once—is sliding downhill on gravel and broken glass.

You have to choose. One way or the other. If you make the lazy, ignoble, uncaring choice, you can't honestly call your society free. Or just. Or healthy. Because as Jesus supposedly said (and you don't have to be religious to get the implications), "Inasmuch as ye have done it unto one of the least of these My brethren, ye have done it unto Me."

We looked across the vast cultural divide, between the bristling lines of arms. We gazed over the body of the Goodin's dead Newfoundland dog—Spooner, friend to all person-kind—and we halted.

Thank all those usually tricksy gods and fates, we all had the sense to halt. To pull back from the deadly slope.

Birkers and yuppie matrons and old-time Hardyvillians might not have a lot in common. But most of us share a common human decency. On that, perhaps we all can build.

As Hardyvillians looked down on the bleeding body of Spooner the Newf, we chose.

"Back off," demanded councilman Dan White, waving frantically at the police officers. When they didn't immediately lower their weapons, he screamed. "Back off! Back off! I said BACK OFF!"

Behind their balaclavas, the cops' eyes flicked to each other, nervous, questioning. "Authority" wasn't backing up their authority. Their world didn't work that way. Governments were supposed to be on their side.

"BACK OFF!" White screamed, panicking when no one moved.

Still, the motionless silence dragged on.

"... Or I'll shoot you in the back," came a quavering voice from the kitchen. Christian Goodin, 16 and small for his age, stood there with a 12-gauge shotgun—leveled straight at a knot of black-clad enforcers. He had sneaked through the backyard from a friend's house when everyone on both sides was caught up in the chaos.

"NOW," ordered Dan White.

"NOW," ordered Carty.

The only sounds in the room were Monique Goodin's sobs as she nuzzled Spooner's bloody fur—and the metallic clatter of MP5 machine guns and tactical shotguns firmly thumping to the floor.

"Hands in the air," Carty ordered. The thugs hesitated again. They looked to Epperson Chutney for guidance. He turned away as if he'd never met them. Dan White ordered, "Do it!"

And hands began to raise as Hardyville gave the stormtroopers a taste of their own "compliance."

But at that exact instant ... the world rocked and rolled. The sky flashed white and red. The earth shook until it nearly kicked all those still standing off their feet. And kicked we the fallen right in our already jelly-like guts.

Chapter 10
Overthrow

It was city hall.

It was Our Hallowed Hall of Government that went gloriously, spectacularly BOOM at that fateful moment. City hall shook like The Big One under our feet. City hall blew as high as the stink of overripe congressional pork. City hall rained down in fragments on rooftops, pickup trucks, and the forever imbibing Statue of the Drunken Cowboy. That (fortunately vacant) building filled downtown Hardyville with more trash in 15 seconds than our Glorious Civic Government had produced in its long months of existence.

And you know what? City hall, when it blew, took the only copy of the Hardyville town charter with it. The charter—the sole basis for the Birkenstockers' government—was nothing but scraps and ashes.

Oops.

It really was an "oops," too. You might like to think (I'm sure the Birkenstockers did) that there actually was a Hardyville Whiskey Rebellion Militia and that it actually did target Our August Seat of Government in such dramatic fashion. But nope. How could it have been the Whiskey Rebellion Militia when that was nothing but a cyberfiction?

In the immediate aftermath, as the guys helped us to our feet and cut our bonds ... as they bound the hired thugs and led them away ... as everybody staggered around wondering what the heck had happened ... nobody knew how city hall had been reduced to splinters. or who had done it.

In the following days, suspicions were muttered, fingers pointed, and conspiracies considered. Everybody had a guess and a suspect. But nobody knew.

We asked the Rocket Scientist to investigate. The RS works in the Big City (not too much rocket science goes on locally), but he's a guy with strong Hardyville ties. He accepted the job, sniffed, poked through the ruins, tested both materials and hypotheses, and came to this conclusion: When the panicked Birkers laid in all those weapons and supplies for protecting themselves from the non-existent threat of us, they were paying with their own money. (The city government, as you recall, wasn't getting any.) They must've bought some bargain-basement dynamite—well aged.

"As you may know," says the Rocket Scientist, "dynamite is made from nitroglycerin mixed up with diatomaceous earth. Dynamite is fairly safe to handle as long as it's properly stored. Needs to be kept cool and dry, though. And most importantly, it needs to be used. Over time it will 'sweat.' By which I mean that the nitroglycerin—very unstable stuff—oozes out of it. The sticks appear wet. In extreme cases, the nitro will even pool in the bottom of the container. Sometimes it will crystallize. This is very very dangerous. That stuff can and will go off with little or no provocation."

Under Our Wise Leaders, city hall was kept at an ecologically sound 68 degrees Fahrenheit. But the dynamite was kept right next to a heater. And—touchy stuff that it was—that sweaty, irritable old nitroglycerine considered a spark from that heater to be more than enough provocation.

Bye bye city hall. Bye bye city government.

Can't say as we'll miss you.

The following week, as we sifted through the rubble, we found just one thing almost perfectly intact. We placed the cracked pink toilet bowl from the mayor's office on a pedestal next to the Drunken Cowboy. After all, given his perpetual boozing, he was likely to need such an appliance.

Then Mudge came in and bulldozed everything else on the former city hall property—officially, this time. People chipped in and paid him—though of course most of the cash went to pay his restitution to Sassy Frassy and the owners of the Bon Mot.

Maybe we'll build an indoor shooting range on the old city hall site. Or a public square with a (purely ceremonial, you understand) hangin' tree. Those decisions will have to wait. A lot will depend on who turns out to own that brand-new hole in the ground. Deeds were lost in the Big Boom, too, so we really don't know.

But in the meantime, we had a martyr to bury.

All attended the funeral for Spooner the Newf up at the Hardyville Pet Cemetery. All, that is, except for our six fed-paid, breaking-and-entering, dog-killing, property-destroying, woman-assaulting cops. They were crammed temporarily and uncomfortably into a jail cell built for one until we could figure out what to do with them.

Epperson Chutney, chief Birkenstocker and former head of our former city council, didn't show either. His face hadn't been seen much since That Infamous Night.

Carty, Nat, Bob, and Marty served as Spooner's pallbearers (and Marty didn't fall asleep on the job this time).

The Goodins stood in a teary huddle beside the grave, embracing each other tightly as another of Nat's hand-made pine coffins was lowered into the earth.

All Hardyville stood there, fighting tears. Yes, even most of our newcomers—the remorseful guilty ones, the merely bewildered ones, and the worried ones who'd come here for freedom and found something other than they'd bargained for. Dora came. She stood beside ex city council member Dan White, her fellow peacemaker, holding his hand. Our two old deputies came, looking comfortable and familiar, but probably wondering if we'd continue to contribute to their salaries, given the current mood against all varieties of professional enforcers.

Hardyville would heal. Hardyville would be okay after some fashion. But it would never be quite the same, and we all knew that. There were tensions and factions never seen before. Values clashing. Troubles lurking.

But for the moment we were united in common humanity and a conviction that, no matter what we might disagree on, not one of us would ever again permit a thing like what happened that night at the Goodins' house. Never. Not ever. Civilized people simply don't.

After the ceremony and a moment of silence, we began the walk back to our vehicles.

"I hope you learned your lesson," Carty growled as one of our blessedly ex council members walked past him.

She stopped. "Yes, we did. We were wrong," she admitted earnestly. "Those new police—they were inexcusable. And a sales tax was not an equitable idea. I don't know why we even considered it."

Before Carty could give his amen and hosannahs to that, one of the other council members walked up and, with a look of most abashed sincerity on his face, agreed.

"Yes," he nodded. "Next time, a property tax would be much more fair."

"And easier to collect."

And the two once-and-wannabe-future city councilors walked off arm-in-arm.

I suppose it comes as no surprise if our erstwhile gummint is a bit slow to accept its explosively "former" status.

———————————

But no. Don't worry. I'm not about to tell you another Terrible Tale of Taxation, Tyranny, and Travail. Not yet.

We went back to town and set about setting things right.

The Young Curmudgeon helped the owners of the Bon Mot rebuild their shattered and battered ice cream store. The rest of us pitched in, as well. Even Scroogish insurance adjuster Hiram J. McCarty relented and owned that even ice cream that had tire tracks in it was worth its insured value. And soon enough we were all enjoying a dish of hot apple pie with melting cinnamon ice cream on top, paid for fair and square with honest money and no dishonest taxes.

84

Sassy Frassy? Well, the tax-paying, benefit-guzzling Ms. Pickle-Chutney was on her own. She sold the bashed-in remnants of her hemp boutique to plump newcomer Charlotte Carolina, for a pittance. Then she left town with her dad, Mr. Honorable Mayor, and her weak-kneed husband (degraded spawn of Glorious Leader Epperson Chutney). It was the first time in history that Hardyville had been without a political Pickle.

Can't say as we missed them, either.

Carty and Nat made the members of Our Formerly Glorious City Council round up or replace the rest of the Goodins' confiscated store inventory. They made the cops pay, out of their own pockets, for the damage they'd done to the Goodins' house and to our abused bodies. Those cops were lucky the Goodins were willing to accept Federal Reserve Notes, which they could then exchange for gold and silver in the Big City. Most of us wouldn't have.

After that, a party of tried-and-true Hardyvillians escorted the cops to the borders of town and wished them a hearty farewell.

Nobody could replace Spooner, of course. Nothing could. But eventually a new Newfoundland puppy of most outstanding lineage, health, and temperament would be gently delivered into the hands of 16-year-old Christian Goodin.

Then there was that other "merchandise" in the back room of Goodin's Second Time Around. The firepower. The mysterious crates provided by the mysterious benefactor. What to do with all that?

"Keep it," said Nat. "On behalf of the town. We all might need it someday."

And on what authority did Nat speak? Well, he never did admit he was the man behind the "merchandise." But we couldn't help but notice that he didn't seem to have gotten a lot richer from all that smuggling he did during the sales tax days. And ... well, you know Nat. He's that kind of guy. He'll be our chief suspect in "illegal arms smuggling" forever. In the meantime, with Pickle's Groce Mart now broke and closed, Nat remained—temporarily, perhaps—our only grocer.

And where did that leave us? With new stores on Liberty Avenue and Freedom Way. New neighbors, still not quite easy with each other. A new pink porcelain Civic Ornament. And Epperson Chutney—former head of the former city council and—once he slunk back into view—still a defiant Figure of Authority.

But his attitude of entitlement was not to last.

"You can't get away with this," he snarled when a mass of Hardyvillians confronted him outside the Hog Trough hauling a lengthy six-by-six, a pungent bucket of hot, sticky black goo, and a goodly number of old pillows that shed feathers into the wintry wind.

"No," said Carty, calm as you please. *"We* can. *You* can't. When you set out to govern us, you forgot to get the one thing that matters—consent of the governed. *All* the governed. And for forgettin' that, there's a price."

The last I saw of the Honorable Mr. Chutney, he was running for everything he was worth up Liberty Avenue, headed for the mountains east of town. As if they had all the time in the world, Carty's boys loaded their supplies and themselves into the backs of a couple nearby pickup trucks and drove off in a leisurely fashion after the long-legged sprinter.

I stayed behind, not in the mood for a cold ride or a hot tarring out in the sagebrush.

I wondered what our future would bring. I wondered if Hardyville could continue to hold out against the pressures of the real world now that some of the real world had moved in with us. I wondered when—not if, but when—government would raise its stealing, slaving, gangstering head again and in what form. I wondered who would end up hating whom.

As I stood, I saw Dora's golden-blond head in the passenger seat of the Toyota Prius belonging to her new boyfriend from the old city council. Dora and Dan White sped west on Liberty Avenue, disappearing out of town without so much as a wave or a glance, the back of the car heaped with luggage.

I was alone.

Behind me the windows of the Hog Trough glowed warm. An aroma of fresh coffee— good coffee—wafted through the doorway as the swinging door bobbled in the wind.

Above me on the light poles, banners—now slightly tattered—flapped noisily. Banners. Yeah, that was what started it all. Insufferably cute banners of very unHardyvillian kind. They had been an eerie presentiment of "civic betterment" to come, the first sign that Hardyville had changed forever.

But you know, if you didn't think too hard about the people behind them, they really weren't, of themselves, all that bad. Kind of charming, really. Yeah, we could get used to them.

I turned and entered the steamy warmth of the cafe. Janelle looked up and waved from the table she was busing. "Menu, Claire?" she called across the empty restaurant.

"No," I said. "I'll just have a Latte Royale with whipped cream, shaved chocolate, and a grating of fresh nutmeg. And how 'bout two almond biscotti on the side?"

Yeah, some changes a person could definitely get used to.

Claire Wolfe

MONKEY-FU

In which we witness the transformation of Charlotte Carolina and learn how, with the help of a slightly mystical mystery man, the Carolina family found themselves on the road to Hardyville.

Chapter 1

In the Mirror

This is the totally true tale of how one family first set tires on the road to Hardyville. It begins in the direction of the rising sun, not far from where the powerful—and the consumers of power—gather.

———————————

Charlotte Carolina, bleary from sleep, peered at herself in the mirror and groaned.

She squinted to edit out her puffiness and sun-damaged skin. Taking a brush, she attempted to bring order to her morning haystack of hair—still as blonde as it was in her teens, thanks to the attentions of Lady Clairol.

After a few strokes, she laid down the brush, opened her eyes for an honest glimpse, and rasped at herself, "Face it. You're 39. You sag. You're past what Daddy called 'pleasingly plump.' You are," she continued mercilessly in her tobacco-thickened voice, "over the hill, underpaid, under-appreciated, bored, boring, used up, dried out, and ..."

"Mom! You didn't wash my purple blouse! I told you I needed my purple blouse today. How come you didn't wash my ..."

Charlotte closed the bathroom door, muting Jennifer's (no, remember, she wanted to be called "Paris" now) ...muting Jennifer's complaints.

She glared determinedly into the mirror again.

"I love my children. I really do." An affirmation. "I love my children. I love my children. I love my children." Noticing that her knuckles were white as she gripped the edge of the sink she stepped back and tried to relax. She gazed earnestly and offered her mirrored self some comfort. "The only problem is that you haven't had enough time with them these last couple of years. Everything would be all right if you just found a little more quality time to give them. It would."

She began applying makeup to her doughy face. That face. That body. They really weren't that bad, she assured herself. Certainly salvageable. A little more exercise. A month on another diet. Atkins maybe, this time. Yeah, that would do it. She'd start the diet next week. And exercise. Let's see, you could wedge that in between ...

"I'm leaving now, Mom." It was the voice of Tonio, her 17-year-old son, just outside the bathroom door.

"What time will you be home? I need you to ..."

But Tonio's footsteps were already receding. He probably had another "meeting" after school. What was it with his "meetings," anyhow? She would have a good sit-down with him. Find out what was preoccupying him. Soon.

In the meantime, she stroked foundation cream onto a face that, she thought, increasingly resembled a slightly deflated balloon.

Then, giving it up as a hopeless job, she turned away, crept out of the house, and walked down the driveway to attempt to start the old Ford.

Outside the sleek glass offices of CYACorp, a wiry young man waited and watched.

He waited as if his life's mission was to wait—with infinite patience. He watched as if his life's mission was to watch—with infinite observation. He stood so still as to be almost invisible among the hustling workers, who rushed from their cars with tense intensity and hunched shoulders.

An overage Ford Taurus squeezed into a parking space, smoke leaking from both its tailpipe and its slightly cracked driver's-side window. The plump, harried-looking driver stubbed out her cigarette, checked her lipstick and her bottle-blonde hair in the rear-view mirror, and emerged from the cockpit with a furtive look, fanning at herself as if to banish the odor of smoke. CYA had a non-smoking policy, even for employees on their own time.

The woman tugged at her too-tight skirt and fumbled her car keys. As she bent to pick them up, her purse fell from her shoulder, contents spilling on the ground. Several other women hustled by, none offering to help. Gathering her possessions, rising, then gathering herself as if about to perform some deed requiring more courage than she believed she possessed, the woman with the raddled complexion and the garish hair propelled herself past the security cameras, through the blank glass of the CYACorp's intimidating entrance, and out of the young man's sight.

Yes, Charlotte Carolina was the one, he thought. She needed him. She didn't know it, of course, and would have denied it had he been foolish enough to approach her and make that claim. But she needed him.

The Toad, bleary from drink, looked at himself in the mirror and saw that he was good.

"You are one handsome devil," he assured himself, though of course he needed no assurance. The fact of his wonderfulness was not only apparent to him, but to the adoring media of a nation.

True, he was a touch puffy around the jowls (around the middle, too, truth be told). But a little pudge was the price a man paid for a successful life of public service. Neither the jowls nor the unfortunate nickname "Toad" (the consequence of being Congressman Ted O'Day and having a one-time rival named Newt) kept him from doing his utmost for his country.

A few cosmetic defects didn't keep him from doing his utmost in the babe department, either. Or in the pocketbook. But those were just perks of the job. Every reasonable person understood that. Sure, once in a while you had to lay low while another hot-shot journalist went on a crusade about "corruption" or some political rival left his own mistress long enough to point fingers at you and yours. But it was all part of the game. Everybody in Washington knew that.

And, he reminded himself, picking up his razor and beginning to plow the facial furrows, the game is always played in a good cause. The ends justify the means.

And the ends were good. The Toad was absolutely confident of that. He knew, without a shred of doubt, that when he died—which hopefully would be many years from now and God-willing not in the arms of his latest love-bunny—the *Washington Post* and the *New York Times* would forgive his minor peccadillos and sing the praises of Ted O'Day, the Great Centrist.

Yes, that's what they called him when they weren't giving him amphibian nicknames. The Great Centrist—the man who could unerringly find the middle course between conservatives and liberals. He was legend. He could always find a way for both sides to achieve their goals, even when rhetoric said their goals could not be reconciled.

It was Ted O'Day who helped push the Medicare spending bill through Congress over the objections of right-wing political dinosaurs.

It was Ted O'Day who made sure the National Security Agency's warrantless wiretap programs got well funded over the objections of whiny left-wing civil libertarians.

Yes, Ted was the man who stood foursquare in the middle, bridging political gulfs like a Colossus. And always ensuring that everybody got something out of the deal.

In the face of the worst disagreements, The Toad was the man who could magically work the bipartisan compromise, seeing that every side got something it wanted out of every bill. More money? An expansion of a favored agency? A new regulatory power? More enforcement? Harsher fines and sentences? Ted was the moderate's moderate who could ensure that each side gained and no one ever really lost. Well, except a few wing-nuts and throwbacks, people who didn't matter because they had no political clout.

It was The Toad who had seen to it that the Pentagon got its slice of the "No Child Left Behind" law—giving the liberals their latest round of school reform and conservatives their military recruiting, all in one tidy package. Not to mention a few billion more over time for his good friends on K Street, the ever-growing community of free-spending lobbyists.

The Toad had also been the man behind the Young Women's Health Protection Act*—the spanking new law to make sure that every American school girl got a mandatory vaccination to protect her against sexually transmitted HPV, the virus that could cause cervical cancer. Sure, the usual dinosaurs had objected for the usual reasons. So he'd slung his influence and made sure the bill tossed a few hundred million more at abstinence education. Bingo! Both sides were winners once again. And Ted O'Day, of course, would be the biggest winner of all—thanks to his campaign contributors in the pharmaceutical industry.

Yes, that was the way things got done in Washington. "And why not?" Ted often told talk-show hosts and fawning journalists. "That way, the whole country wins every time."

The Toad toweled off his face, looked himself in the mirror again, and smiled his big professional campaign smile. "You're a good man," he said, "if I do say so myself." And with the satisfaction of knowing his country became a better place with each moment he lived, he prepared for another day of serving the people.

———————————

Away from the offices of the U.S. House, in a discreet (though in these politically correct days, non-smoky) restaurant in Georgetown, The Representative of The Agri-Tech Industrial Coalition waited. He waited like a man who is used to waiting for the powerful. He waited like a man who knew the game and agreed to act like a supplicant while really working for the master who pulled all strings. He waited like a man who knows he's being forced to wait to show him his lowly place in the world, but who is all the while sitting there contentedly plotting world takeover.

And he waited for the man who walked in the door.

A few heads turned to notice Toad O'Day as he lumbered in from the stormy night. The man was obviously sloshed—within and without. But this being that sort of place, everyone quickly pretended not to watch him, while nevertheless noting exactly whom he'd be meeting. The word would be all over town by morning, but no one would speak outside the Club—the inner circles of government and media—because all had their own chips in the same game. All had their own secrets they wanted kept. So they would keep secrets for The Toad.

The Representative from Agri-Tech stood respectfully. He even gave a small continental bow, designed to impress aristocracy-worshipping Americans with its European urbanity, as he greeted his quarry.

Yes, the congressman would do. Indeed he would serve Agri-Tech's purposes nicely.

The two men sat. They ate regally. And then, over brandy, they leaned their heads together and they talked.

———————————

Qwai Ching Paine, clear-eyed from meditation, looked into the mirror and saw beyond himself.

Yes, he was aware of the slight, wiry young man standing before the glass. But Paine, youthful student of monkey-fu, was trained to see much more than the obvious.

He turned his inner vision toward Charlotte Carolina. He envisioned her living out many possible lives her choices and her karma might create for her. Sad. So many of her likely paths lead nowhere but to despair and disaster. But there were alternatives ...

He considered the most intriguing of his insights—and how that particular path might be encouraged to unfold with a subtle and well-directed application of monkey-fu. He smiled. Inscrutably.

Yes, he thought. *She needs me.*

Then he admonished himself not to be prideful. He had no ability to see the future, only to perceive potential paths and turnings through the heightened perceptions of monkey-fu. He had no ability to magically change lives, only to ... hint and encourage toward certain courses of action, certain potential outcomes.

Beyond the mirror, Qwai Ching perceived the Hilltop Hermitage, high above the town of Hardyville. He could smell the honeysuckle and hear the memory of June bees. But thinking of the hermitage where he had received his training made him homesick, and even a young monkey-fu student knows how to shift his focus from the comforts of home. He had a path to walk. That path was here in the real world.

But which turning should he choose next? Which branch in his own road would take him on the path most true to his *dharma*—his duty, his personal truth?

He gazed once more into the mirror, past his lean Amer-Asian face, and into the depths of his own eyes.

And in the darkness of his eyes he saw that dark young man, Tonio Carolina. Charlotte's son. Yes, the path to the future—many futures—lay through Tonio. He would touch Tonio like a stone touches a pond, sending out many ripples before sinking into darkness.

———————————

* The Young Women's Health Protection Act is fictional. However, it mirrors real-world state, federal, and international programs, which at the time this article was published (2007), were gradually moving toward making vaccinations against HPV mandatory for girls as young as nine years—and extending the requirement to boys, even though no studies existed to show that the vaccine was either safe or effective for them.

Later, the effort faltered when a number of girls around the world had serious, adverse reactions to the vaccine (some died) and when "ties" were revealed between the drug makers and certain politicians who were pushing the plan. Later, one of the scientists who developed an anti-HPV vaccine pointed out that the risks of the shot outweighed its benefits.

Nevertheless, requiring an increasing number and variety of vaccines, at increasingly younger ages, remains a problem—both a political one and potentially a health problem. I take no position on whether any specific new vaccine is useful or healthful. I do take issue with medicine being imposed by, mandated by, or funded by government. And everyone should be watchful lest too many more politicians become "wholly owned subsidiaries" of the pharmaceutical industry.

Chapter 2
The Game Afoot

"It's just a test, Tonio," shrugged Baron, clumping out of Alexander Hamilton High School, past the metal detector, the RFID-card reader, and the security cameras and down the steps. "It doesn't even count toward our grades. So what's the big deal?"

"The big deal," said the rangy, scowling dark boy beside him, "is that it's a Pentagon test. The Armed Services Vocational Aptitude Battery. Didn't you hear those two teachers call it that when they were whispering about it in the hall? They were ordered to tell us it's just a regular career-planning test. But it's the ASVAB. ASS-VAB. And I don't want anything to do with the military. So I don't think I should have to take the test."

"Yeah, so? They're not gonna make you do anything afterward. If your scores look right for the military, maybe they'll pitch you harder than everybody else. But they're not gonna draft you."

"Yet. They're not gonna draft us yet," Tonio corrected. "But what about next year? Or the year after that? They make us register for the draft, don't they? Why do they keep doing that if they're never going to draft us?"

"Well, take the test and lie about stuff. Make it look like you're such a psycho submoron they wouldn't want you anyway. Make it look like you couldn't do anything better than sit in the dirt and pick your nose."

"Look," said Tonio, whirling around and forcing his friend to a halt, "This is wrong. We shouldn't have to take a test for the Pentagon's databases—and that's all it's really for. But this isn't some ... some ... some dictatorship! This isn't the Galactic Blanking Order. This is America. The school shouldn't make us do it."

"Yeah. But take a mental mail delivery, bonehead. The school *can* make us do it. They're *gonna* make us do it. And we got no say. So quit bitchin'. It's only gonna get you in trouble. And if you get in trouble, that means I'm in trouble, even if I didn't do anything. Just because everybody knows I'm your friend."

They passed a pair of campus resource officers, dumping the contents of a student's backpack onto the hood of their squad car. Baron went on, "So forget it, okay? Take the test. Give fake answers. Or tell the truth but just use your scores for college entry. They won't draft you. I promise. You don't have to get your butt blown off by an IED in Upsnortistan or Iranomania unless you sign up to. So please ... shut the bleep up."

Tonio shook his dark head in frustration and wheeled back out of his best friend's way. The two strode down the sidewalk together in thudding anger.

As they passed, Qwai Ching Paine, waiting unnoticed beneath the barely budding cherry tree, gazed inscrutably after them.

The Triumph Stratocycle darted from the clouds. It buzzed toward the domed settlement like a determined bee. In the cockpit, Darkboy hunched over the controls—watching his holographic readouts and at the same time watching the sky for patrollers of the Galactic Order.

There. On the ground. A torch. The drop point. Darkboy tapped the controller to head for the beacon and—bam!—in that instant a cruiser of the Health Enforcement Agency exploded into view on his right.

He dodged. That was the one thing he could do well. Use cunning. Use speed. Maneuverability. The Triumph was small, lightly armed, and vulnerable. The Order cruiser had bigger power, longer range, and all the guns. But it could not dart like a hummingbird in atmosphere. Darkboy could.

Still, the federation cruiser lumbered in relentless pursuit, swinging around in a wide arc and closing once again.

He had to lure the agents away from the drop point. He knew that. His mission had ceased to be delivery of illegal pharmaceuticals and contraband lipids. Even if it killed him, his job was now to keep the cruiser occupied long enough for the groundies to make their escape. They were, after all, innocent farmers and villagers and his future partners in trade, should he survive. So ... keep the cruiser occupied. Be killed if that's how it came down—or kill it.

Could a little Stratocycle really kill a government cruiser? Darkboy didn't know. But he could try.

Darkboy and the Triumph dodged and this time looped, doing the unexpected. Instead of merely dodging out of the cruiser's path, they did a 180—a turn that took them zooming straight past the cruiser's guns. But they had a trick up their sleeve.

Darkboy flipped a protective cover and flipped the switch below. Now, throwing out multiple ersatz heat signals, they appeared to the cruiser's sensors—and to its automated weaponry—to be everywhere at once. The computer-controlled guns of the cruiser didn't know where to aim. So they fired everywhere at once—everywhere except where the

Stratocycle appeared. Zow—right up the cruiser's backside! He pulled in behind the lumbering beast, directly into its blind spot.

Ya gotta love federation design. Contracted to the highest-bribing bidder.

The cruiser began another ponderous move, with Darkboy clinging annoyingly to its tail until he had it pointed in the direction he wanted it to go. The cruiser couldn't see him, but its automated projections told it he had to be there ... somewhere. So he maneuvered. And the cruiser, all unknowing, did his bidding. When it was aimed where he wanted it to go, he darted ahead of it again. Once again, explosions from its automatic weaponry popped around him, thumping in his ears and in his blood.

And he lead-footed past the ship's vast bulk and got that cruiser to follow ... and led it ...

Right into a whole waiting nest of Angels. The Outlaw band of Stratocycles came out of the clouds and flew straight at that cruiser, stinging like rabid wasps, sleek laser-flame guns melting metal. And down that fearsome cruiser began to spiral ...

"Nice move, Man," Baron said, pushing himself back from his own game console. He stretched and rotated stiff shoulders.

"Nice move, GUYS," Tonio Carolina, aka Darkboy, amended. He looked above the monitors and bowed heads of the warehouse-sized LAN party. A few glazed-but-grinning faces looked back at him. A fist pumped air. It had been great teamwork: Tonio and the Helios Angels crew. There would be some partying tonight. That move ran up points for all the Angels and added to Darkboy's "cunning" tally.

"I need some Bawls," Baron yawned. "And some exercise for my sore ass. Want to come take a break?"

"Nope," Tonio replied, returning to watching the cyberskies. "I'm plotting my next move. I'm gonna make that delivery tonight without losing any groundies. You watch."

"Y'know, for somebody who's against the military, you sure are good at the sort of stuff they like."

"I'm not against the military. My dad was military. So was his dad. I'm against BS. You seen the way they're promoting that test? Like it's about sunshine and puppy dogs. Their web site's got, like, happy dancing jumping people all over it. They try to hide that it's military. It's dishonest. And it's a set-up for the draft, I'm tellin' you."

"Yeah. But on Monday, no matter what, we're both gonna be in there taking it. Or you can cut school. Or get 'sick.' One or the other."

On the computer screen, Darkboy shot out a few nearby drones. Easy stuff. "Not me," Tonio said, as if making a decision. "Monday morning I'm going in there, and I'm going to stand right up in front of the teacher, and say, 'Go .... yourself.'"

"You're nuts."

"Maybe. But that's what I'm going to do. Walk in there and say 'no way.'"

"Oh man. Oh man, you are gonna make things hell for yourself and anybody dumb enough to be friends with you. Do you know that?"

Darkboy hunched down and prepared to make a run on the alternate landing zone.

———————————————

Around 2:00 a.m. the brain starts shutting down and even the most Xtreme caffeine, sugar, or Bawls Guarana emergency measures may fail.

Darting in for a try at the alternative landing site, Darkboy felt a presence over him. He played on, zigzagging through an aerial mine-field around the game's territorial capital. A mine-field could be pretty good territory for a tiny, maneuverable craft smuggling modest things.

"Agility is the underdog's Overmind," a voice spoke softly over his shoulder.

Not sure the comment was meant for him—or what it meant—Darkboy dodged onward. He used his tailwind to whip two of the mines together behind him. They exploded with a satisfying boom.

"And stealth is the power of the powerless. Darkboy shapes darkness into advantage."

"I am the MAN!" Darkboy agreed, not looking up to see which of his allies or opponents in the game might be standing behind him, babbling middle-of-the-night nonsense. He zagged, dropped below the mine field and immediately made another 180, traveling away from the capital at dizzyingly low altitude. Any Ordergoons searching for him would start looking in the opposite direction.

"The enemy is perilous, but inflexible. Do you confront him on his own terms?"

"No way. Can't you see, man? Stealth. Speed. Moves. Smarts." Well away from any pursuers, he dodged through the walls of a canyon, its walls too narrow for Ordercraft to follow. Zoomed past the first beacon—a decoy beacon meant only to fool any smaller pursuers—and bulleted in for the hidden cargo drop. At the last second, lights flared up from the ground, a welcoming circle. He hit the drop button. Right on target—again.

"Ah," said the impassive voice, "the young man moves from darkness into the light. And finds friends in narrow straits."

"Who the hell are you?" Tonio finally asked, turning. But there was no one there. Tonio logged off and sank back in his chair. Weird. Most definitely weird. He took a couple of deep breaths, finally feeling his exhaustion.

And then, out of nowhere, an idea began to form. "Yeah ... brilliant. That would be brilliant."

———————————————

"So," said Baron, returning with a half-empty bottle of Bawls and a bag of chips, "tell me you're sitting there looking so whacked because reality finally smacked you in the face about the test."

Tonio looked around again as his friend dropped into the chair in front of his console. "Did you just see that guy who was standing here?" he asked.

"Uh ... no. What guy?"

"He ... never mind. But you're right. About reality, I mean. I'm not going to show up Monday morning and refuse to take the test."

"Thank you, God." Baron rolled his eyes heavenward. "Thank you, thank you, thank you."

"I'm gonna show up on Monday morning and the *whole senior class* is going to refuse to take the test."

"No. I didn't hear that. You didn't just say what you just said."

"You heard me. The whole senior class. Is going to refuse. To take the test."

"Yeah. Right. And what crazy genius is gonna pull off this superhuman stunt?"

"Two crazy geniuses. Me. And you."

Chapter 3
Tactics

The Toad considered the bill lying on his desk. It bore the name of a credibly bland Midwestern congressman as sponsor—the sort of cornpone country boy who would be a believable sponsor for an agriculture bill. Of course, like so many other bills making their way through Congress, this one had been written by some faceless drone in an industry group or government bureau. Congressmen merely put their names to the work of interested parties, often not even bothering to read "their" bills.

Custom needs—custom laws; that's how the game is played.

The case for this particular bill had been presented to The Toad in that discreet Georgetown bistro by the representative of The Agri-Tech Industry Coalition. It had been presented along with certain other considerations. Rep. Ted O'Day, the Great Centrist, smiled as he thought of those considerations. Some of them were now waiting for him in an Austrian bearer account.

The bill's title was "The Food Supply Health and Security Act." The few colleagues paying any attention were already calling it "A Chip in Every Chicken."*

The bill took the "voluntary" National Animal Identification System and made it mandatory—for every hobby farm, everybody with a goat tethered in the yard, every horse in every stable, every 4H animal in the nation. Every animal would not just have to be registered and reported to the government every time it was moved anywhere. That was old news. Now it would now have to be injected with a radio-frequency ID (RFID) chip and electronically tracked anywhere it went.

The language was a masterpiece of indirection. Anyone other than an insider might not recognize that it let giant factory farms and poultry processors register their animals in huge batches, one chip per shipment. The family farmer, on the other hand, would have to chip every sow, piglet, lamb, ram, ewe, chick, duck, rooster, goose, mare, stallion, foal ... everything but the mice in the barn.

The Toad chuckled. If the Agri-Tech Coalition, a Frankenstein marriage of the Radio-Frequency ID chip industry and big ag, could have figured out a way to make family farmers chip their mice, they'd have included that, too.

The day of the family farmer would soon be over. "And good riddance," thought Rep. Ted O'Day, city born, city bred. Animals on small farms were the most likely to spread disease. So the Agri-Tech lobbyist had assured him. Big producers, on the other hand, took the latest, most scientific precautions and had the healthiest animals. So if this bill drove little rubes off their farms and ranches, well, so be it. Those rednecks were standing in the way of progress, anyway.

"Now," Toad thought, "it's time for a little 'I'll scratch your back, you scratch mine' to get this baby through the Agriculture Committee."

Or no ... on second thought, maybe he'd feed it through the Homeland Security Committee. After all the bill protected a vital national interest (not to mention his own vital interests). He knew that his counterpart in the Senate—whom rumor said had also had an agreeable meeting with the Agri-Tech representative—was considering similar options for the Senate version of the bill. And homeland security ... while Congress could go either way on a mere ag bill, homeland security ... now that was sacred. Oppose a homeland security measure and you were ...

Yes, that was it. The legislation would be promoted as "vital to our national food security." Homeland Security Committee it was, then.

DYK mon tst wl put u ina Pntagon db?
wn2 gt draftd? taK d tst.
wnt Obam 2 snd u 2 Afganistan? taK d tst.
U dnt hav 2 taK d tst. dey cnt mak u taK d tst.
Pass d wrd. Pass d wrd. Pass d wrd.

The text messages scrolled along on computer and cellphone screens. Facebook postings and email began carrying the word. It was still only Saturday morning and Tonio Carolina and his friend Baron, slightly glazed from their all-night LAN party, were busy.

"If they ever find out I helped you ..." Baron groaned.

"Don't worry. They won't. If you want to go in Monday morning and take the test, go. I won't stop you. But ... well, thanks for helping."

"You owe me. Big time."

"I owe you. Now keep working."

While Baron sent messages from his cellphone and laptop, Tonio's own fingers were busy Googling. He'd learned some stuff already.

Like that the test was voluntary. The school was going to make them take it, but no law said they had to—even though that's what their teachers were telling them.

Like that the school was going to turn over every, single test result to the Department of Defense. Even the results of students who had already opted out of having their results shared. (Unless the school chose something called "Option 8"; even if they did that the students themselves had no choice what happened to their data.)

Like that the test was pretty useless for career placement and that its real goal, as stated in the Pentagon's own manuals, was to provide "pre-qualified leads" for recruiters.

Like that if the school was really interested in giving students the best possible career aptitude test, there were better choices —ones that wouldn't put everybody in a Pentagon computer.

"Posters," Tonio called over his shoulder to Baron as the boys worked intently. "Who do we know that can make posters and signs for people to carry?"

An hour later, two art-geek girls from the junior class were taking their assignments, then heading to the craft store for posterboard and the hardware store for sticks.

"Who were those freaks?" Tonio's sister Paris (formerly Jennifer) sniffed, dragging herself out of bed at 1:00 p.m., just as the art students left on their errands. "Your new girl-friends? Eeew."

"Better them than you, Britney-Clone," snorted Baron. The two boys kept on working.

> mEt mon. AM O/side d skool 2 Rsist d tst.
> shO ^ mon. AM W protest syns.
> Hell no, we won't go N2 d Pntagon db. Join us. Rsist.
> no govt snoop tst. Rsist Rsist Rsist.

The messages went out. The replies came in—everything from "IL B W/U mon. a.m." to ... well, something that can't be translated in a family story but that certainly meant "No thanks, Tonio, you jerkface."

"Uh ... maybe we won't get the whole senior class," Tonio admitted, reading one of the latter sorts of messages.

Charlotte poked her head into the bedroom briefly. Those boys. They were always so intense about their computers.

"What are you working on, boys?"

"Oh, just stuff. Usual."

Charlotte paused, hoping for elaboration. None came. "Well, I just thought I'd check in and see if you boys needed anything. Jennifer and I are going shopping, then I'll be dropping her off at her counseling appointment. And after that I'll ..."

"Sure, Mom. Don't need anything. Bye."

She paused in the doorway, thinking there must be something else to say. But the impenetrable wall of the boys' e-ttention thwarted her. She really would have a talk with Tonio later. A good talk. Find out what was occupying him so much, these days. Maybe go somewhere special with him. But ...

"MOM!" shrilled Jennifer. "If we don't get there, somebody else might buy that sweater. If somebody's bought my sweater, I'll never speak to you again. I swear. I won't."

"Okay, Jennifer. Coming. I'm coming."

Charlotte fled. Tonio and Baron exchanged eye-rolling glances. "dat wmn mizd d clu-train," Baron typed to his friend.

"ey, she's my mom," Tonio typed back with a shrug. The two friends went back to work.

Sunday night. Baron, Tonio, and their ever-growing crew of helpers had done all they could. Almost.

"What's missing?" Tonio asked the seven students sprawled exhausted but excited-looking around his bedroom. "What haven't we considered?"

Everybody looked around at the signs and banners stacked in the corner of Tonio's room. "Nothing, I think," somebody said.

"It's showtime," agreed one of the boys.

"Showtime," Tonio mused. "Oh. Wait. Showtime. Baron, toss me my cell."

He punched buttons.

"Karen," he spoke into the phone. "Your sister's a reporter, right? ... Well tell her if she shows up at Hamilton High tomorrow at 8:00 a.m. there'll be a good story for her ... Yeah, I know her boss decides what stories to cover. But tell her he'll like this one. Tell her it's a good one. Free speech and stuff like that. No. A secret. Top secret. We don't want the school to know in advance. But really good ... Yeah ... Okay ... I know, I know. No guarantees.

"But listen, this is really important. So tell her if she shows up ..." He looked over at his exhausted friend, "I'll get Baron's oldest brother ... you know, the lawyer? ... the good-lookin' one? ... to buy her dinner at the Lobster Shoppe. Baron guarantees it."

Baron, sitting on Tonio's bed, fell backward with a thump. "Oh god. Just shoot me right now," he moaned.

And so it happened that on the following Monday morning, as Tonio, his friends, and about two dozen supporters turned up outside Alexander Hamilton High School with picket signs, Qwai Ching Paine stood near the CYACorp entrance, watching Charlotte Carolina struggle with her cigarettes and her keys.

Thus it was that, while Tonio Carolina was talking with young local reporter, Heather Ames-Becker, on the sidewalk just outside school property, his mother was blissfully unaware that her son was about to become both a local celebrity and a royal pain in the backside to school and Pentagon officials.

And thus it also was that, while Charlotte Carolina struggled to stay alert, watching the clock until the blessed relief of her 10:00 a.m. coffee break, Tonio was being dragged into the school admin office.

But thus it also was that, thanks to the weekend's preparations, and the leafleting and on-the-spot picketing, about one third of the senior class at Alexander Hamilton High School—including a certain young man named Baron—decided they didn't want to take the Armed Services Vocational Aptitude Battery, at least until they knew a lot more about the test and what might be done with their scores.

And thus it further was that the test scheduled for that morning was postponed.

The school principal told hustling young Heather Ames-Becker, (who would soon get a long hoped-for date with a certain young lawyer) "We will re-schedule the ASVAB after our students have received a better understanding of the vital importance of this test to their careers here at Hamilton High as well as their careers in the larger world."

But Charlotte Carolina knew none of this all morning as she struggled to stay alert and pretend interest in her work. She still knew none of it as she settled herself into the last remaining table at Starbucks that noon to drink her double-shot caffeinated lunch. Tired and tense from her morning's labors, she ignored the insistent shouts of the cellphone in her purse. Whatever it was could wait.

She had her head down, skimming an article in the *Post* about the dire threat to homeland security from vulnerable and diseased food animals on shamefully unregulated, outdated family farms, when she felt, more than saw, a presence across from her at the small round table.

She looked up. Another patron smiled politely and gestured with a hand that held a sleeved paper cup, communicating wordlessly: *Tables full. May I sit here?*

She shrugged and waved a hand at the chair opposite. Then she lowered her head again and set her whole body to send the message, Go ahead and sit there, but don't imagine I'm going to chitty-chat with some stranger. *I'm busy reading this vital news story.*

She hated sharing tables. Just hated it. But at least her unwanted companion was the silent type. She turned the page and pretended to be engrossed in another article about how the Selective Service was planning to test the draft system, but that really, everybody involved assured the reporter and the readers, nobody in government—well, almost nobody—was even thinking about actually drafting anybody or even planning for such an event. Thank heaven. The thought of Tonio ... or for that matter, Jennifer ... being dragged off to ...

Then a soft, steady voice came from across the table.

"The universe within is reborn amid chaos," it said.

She looked up, scowling at the slender, odd-looking young man across from her. He smiled. Inscrutably. His eyes were like deep wells. Darnit, were crazy street people infiltrating Starbucks now?

---

* The Food Supply Health and Security Act is fictional. However, it follows from the provisions of the National Animal Identification System (NAIS), which is now being sneakily implemented by bureaucratic fiat. After outraged protests, NAIS has been switched from mandatory to "voluntary"—for the moment.

Like Toad O'Day's fictional bill, NAIS does demand that family farmers meet more stringent requirements than enormous agri-businesses. It does require all animals within its system to be registered and reported upon every time they leave their registered location. While NAIS will be completely ineffective in curbing diseases like mad cow, it creates absurdities like expecting horse owners to report every trail ride to some level of government. Do not expect the "voluntary" status of NAIS to last. That status is already deceptive and the pressure is on for even the smallest family farmers to comply with a system that will make their way of life impossible.

Although the protest depicted in this story is fictional, it was inspired by a real incident.

Chapter 4
Wheels and Webs

"The universe within is reborn amid chaos." Qwai Ching Paine spoke, then waited politely for Charlotte Carolina to respond.

It didn't require the heightened perceptions of a monkey-fu student to see what was going on in her mind as she looked up, scowled, and struggled toward a response. *Oh Lord. Some schizoid street person wants to ruin my lunch hour. What am I going to do? Do I tell him to buzz off? Ignore him?*

Qwai smiled. "When life plays new song, wise woman learns to dance."

"What?" Charlotte grimaced. Then realizing she'd just opened a conversational door for some Hare Krishna or other sort of fanatic to wedge his sandal into, she looked down and tried desperately to pretend total absorption in her copy of the Post, "I'm sorry," she said, eyes averted. "I'm very busy."

"The son rises," Qwai informed her.

She glanced at him, uncomfortably. Then she rose and fumbled to fold up her uncooperating copy of the *Post.* "Um, I'm sorry," she said, kicking herself inwardly for her weak-kneed habit of apologizing to annoying strangers, "but I was just leaving and anyway I already have my own church so ..."

"*Your* son rises," Qwai corrected, taking a sip from his paper cup, then wincing slightly as though he'd never before tasted a double-shot latte with peppermint flavoring and didn't exactly approve. "And opens perception's gates for dancing woman."

My son? She paused in the midst of stuffing the newspaper into her bag. Is this actually about ME? No. Couldn't be. Nonsense.

Qwai recalled a mid-night conversation, a game, an aerial pirate called Darkboy finding his way to a hidden drop site, a signal light illuminating the darkness of a narrow canyon. "Will you," he asked, "befriend bold spirit who travels from darkness into light?"

"What are you talking about?"

Qwai smiled and tried once more to make himself understood. "In narrow strait, hardest choice opens widest horizons," he said, "And lonely heart tells the way."

"Oh, give me a break," she groaned. As she swung around to leave the table and get away from the loon, her purse knocked over her Starbucks cup, spilling sticky brown liquid across the table and onto her skirt. "Oh, darn. Darnit. Damn." She grabbed for a napkin and began ineffectually blotting at the mess dripping from her hem onto her nylons. At that moment, her cellphone began to bleat again.

Qwai stood and offered her a perfectly mundane tissue from his pocket. "Change strives to touch dancing woman," he noted.

Grabbing the tissue, blotting, she barked, "What on earth are you talking about? And can't you see I'm too busy for this kind of nonsense?"

Qwai shook his head ruefully. Sometimes it was hard, practicing true monkey-fu in traditional inscrutable fashion. "I'd check your cellphone if I were you," he sighed, reverting to his native Americanese. "You're getting an important message."

When she looked up from her dabbing and wiping, the strange young man was gone and the cellphone was cheerily chirping that yet another voice message demanded her attention. "Lord," she prayed silently, "for once let it be good news."

———————————

"Suspended? Suspended! Do you have any idea how it felt to get a call from your school telling me you'd been suspended???"

Charlotte's right hand snapped angrily toward Tonio as her white-knuckled left gripped the steering wheel. Tonio, slumped in the passenger seat, gazed out the window.

"Do you even begin to comprehend what an idiot I felt like, telling my boss I had to leave for the afternoon—in the middle of his big project—to pick up my son who was stirring up so much trouble his school couldn't put up with him any more?"

Tonio said nothing.

"Your sister, I might have expected trouble from. But you, Tonio. I thought I could rely on you. I thought you were the responsible one. How could you? How dare you do this to me ... to your teachers ... to the principal ... to ...?"

Tonio's fist clenched around the strap of his backpack. "What I did," he muttered, "was right. It's the school that's wrong."

Charlotte's face turned redder than before. For a moment she was at a loss for words. "Look," she finally muttered through clenched teeth. "I have had a crappy day. Everything went wrong at work. Some lunatic practically monopolized my whole lunch hour spouting incoherent nonsense at me. Then I discover I've got about six messages from your dean's office, telling me ..."

How did that lunatic know the phone messages were important? A little voice fluttered, trying to penetrate her anger. But for the moment Charlotte Carolina, mother on a mission, was in no mood to consider the implications of lunchtime lunacy. "What am I supposed to do with you for the next two weeks? If you think you're just going to sit around the house eating Doritos through your whole suspension, Tonio, you've got another think coming. I'm going to ... You're going to ..."

"Mom. I don't care. Whatever you want. Do whatever you want. Just leave me alone, okay?"

"... And when you go back to school," she insisted, ignoring him, "you are going to take that test. The school says you have to, and what the school tells you to do is the reasonable thing to do. They know better than you what's best for everyone. Do you understand?"

They drove homeward insulated by a large, heavy silence.

That night, tossing in a tangle of blankets and sheets at 2:00 a.m., Charlotte discovered that, among her host of troubling thoughts, she couldn't get her encounter with The Lunatic (as she was beginning to think of him, in capital letters) out of her mind. Of course he was just another crazy person. The world was full of them these days. But his strange phrases ran though her consciousness like an irritating pop song that wouldn't leave her alone.

She finally got up and wrote down every statement she could remember. Then she looked at what she'd scribbled: "learn to dance," "befriend ... travels from darkness into light," "lonely heart tells the way." Nonsense. Absolute utter, worthless, mental nonsense. She flung the notepad disgustedly into the nightstand drawer and slammed the drawer shut.

Still, she thought as she laid back down for another attempt at sleep, that strange guy did seem to know something. Weird. She'd ask Tonio—next time they were on speaking terms—if he knew a sort of vaguely Chinese looking guy who talked funny. Because it did seem the man knew—or at least knew something about—Tonio. She eventually struggled back to sleep and dreamed the dreams of every single parent who's in over her head.

And the days droned by.

The Toad entered yet another non-smoky, but still somehow covert-looking little bistro. He paused just inside the door, partly to let his eyes adjust, partly to ensure that he was seen by the kind of people you saw in places where the dinner tab for two was $600, and dinner was not the most costly thing to be purchased.

That, too, was the game. Nefarious purpose? Never mind. The kind of people who dined here were the kind for whom nefariousness was their world. Each had a little something on the other. Each dangled hints about his latest "compromises"—which were also his latest boastful scores. But no one was at risk. Because people in this shadowy legislative world observed a kind of *omerta*—a code of silence—the Mafia could hardly match.

Toad spotted The Representative of The Agri-Tech Industrial Coalition, rising respectfully from a table in the back, even giving a stiff little from-the-waist bow like the illegitimate son of a two-bit Continental prince. The man might make a pose of being, as they said in the olden days, "above his station." But he was ... useful (as the growing balance in Toad's new Austrian bank account showed).

So Toad was happy to report that he in turn was being useful in herding the "Chip in Every Chicken" bill through the mazes of committee and through the minds of That Great Unthinking Herd known as Washington Correspondents—who, after all, considered themselves too sophisticated to give close scrutiny to something as dreary and dull as a farm bill ...

———————————

Certainly in record time, Toad's current favorite horse in the big legislative betting race was galloping out of the subcommittee gate.

And as the bill to put family farms out of business—and spy on the few that might be left—silently slid through the full Homeland Security Committee on greased skids, Tonio Carolina returned to school.

He returned on the very day the rescheduled ASVAB was to be given.

Thanks to the hard, diligent work he'd done on his two weeks off, this time more than half the senior class either stayed home or joined him and his friend Baron outside the school with picket signs. This time, with a little help from a grateful local reporter Heather Ames-Becker and the lure of a major free-speech confrontation, satellite trucks showed up.

And this time, Tonio got himself busted by cops and hauled summarily to jail, right in front of CNN, NPR, and Fox News, for demonstrating without a permit, disturbing the peace, and resisting arrest.

Chapter 5
Arrested Development

"Bail!" Charlotte ranted. "You made me make bail for you! Never in my life did I think a respectable person like me would have to make bail for one of my own children. How could you do this to me?! Even your father wouldn't have ..."

As the door between the dismal jail and the only slightly more friendly county administration center swung closed behind them, Tonio tried to shut his mother's harangue out of his head, which was already aching from the noise and cold and the disinfectant-over-vomit smell of the jail.

"I don't want to hear any more about how bad my father was, okay?" Tonio snapped. "And I didn't do anything *to you*. I did something I thought was right. And still think is right. Will you cut it out? Please?"

They stepped out the courthouse door onto the street. At that moment, three reporters descended on them.

"Tonio, what made you decide to lead the protest?"

"Tonio, what will you do if a judge orders you to take the test?"

"Ms. Carolina, as his mother, what do you think of the stand your son has taken?"

Tonio stopped and began a rapid-fire set of answers. About the test being voluntary. About Pentagon databases. About dishonest and abusive recruiting practices. In a daze, Charlotte noticed dimly that he seemed very well prepared. And articulate. But ... in a cause that was all wrong, at a time that was even worse.

Charlotte stared at the reporters like a spotlighted deer. Then, panicking, she grabbed Tonio's arm in both her fists and tried to drag him toward the car as he continued to spout claims and statistics back toward the reporters.

Even sitting at his office desk, Rep. "Toad" O'Day gave the impression of a man in motion. He was watching CNN with part of his attention, initialing a stack of memos with another, and with a third part of his mind, trying to figure out how to work this Internet thing on the computer his aides insisted he keep on his desk.

It's pointless trying to understand technology. Of that he was sure. But this afternoon he felt motivated. At their first meeting, The Representative from Agri-Tech had given him a bank book for a numbered bearer account, a phone number in Austria, and something called a URL that supposedly would let him check on the amounts being added to that new bank account. The Toad was peering at all that URL gobbledygook, trying to figure out where the heck you were supposed to type whatever.

At that moment, a ruckus from the TV screen caught his attention.

He heard the words "Alexander Hamilton High School" and the name of a town in his own state and district—something that could always attract the good congressman's attention. Still gripping the piece of paper with the incomprehensible tech-scribblings, he gave his full attention to the TV screen.

As he watched, he got mad. And madder. Challenging the Defense Department's skills test. Going on about a few bad apples in the recruiting barrel as if they were typical. Those pipsqueak kids could threaten the whole in-school recruiting program if the noise they were making got out of hand. *His* in-school recruiting program. The compromise he worked so hard on. And naturally a protest like this was just the kind of thing a bunch of bleeding-heart journalists would sink their teeth into and not let go of. Damn.

Then ... wait a second. A smart man could make lemonade out of this lemon. Maybe even give a little extra help to some generous donors, too, if he handled it right. Donors who would be very, very grateful for services performed. Wouldn't hurt his public image any, either. Lemonade. Yeah ...

His chief aide appeared at the side of his desk 10 seconds after The Toad mashed the buzzer with his broad thumb.

"Alexander Hamilton High School," The Toad barked. He named the town. "Who do I know there?"

The aide consulted his remarkable mental Rolodex. "Principal. Warren, Alfred B. ... Ah ... your college classmate. Varsity football. Nickname was 'Boots.'"

"Yeah. Yeah. Football team. Sure, I remember. Tackle?"

"Running back."

"Huh. Running back. Doesn't ring any bells. Oh well, doesn't matter. Now. Who do I know in the health department down there?"

"Doctor ..." the aide began, consulting the cranial card-file again.

"Never mind. Never mind," Toad barked. Just get good ol' Boots, whoever the hell he is, on the line. Then be ready to set up a conference call—Boots, Doctor whatever-his-name-is, and me."

A few minutes later, the aide patched the first call through to his boss's office.

"Boots, baby!" grinned Toad O'Day, master of the game. "It's your old buddy Ted. Yeah. Ted O'Day, the Tedster. Hometown boy made good. Nope, no. I ain't joshin' you. It's really me, calling you straight from my desk here in DC, looking out over the Washington Monument. And even better. Alf, my old pal, I'm calling 'cause I think I can do you a little favor." He put his feet up on the desk, enjoying himself hugely.

"You know that scrape you got going on right now? ... Yeah, I know, one troublemaker can spoil the whole barrel ... Well, I got an idea. How would you like some good PR to counter some of the crap you're being handed? Yeah, it's tough, isn't it? But trust your pal here, like you did in the old days on the team. Remember those great running plays we two worked out together? I'll never forget 'em. So. Here's the plan I want us to run with ..."

———————————

"I'm sure everybody here is patriotic," The Toad began, as the applause quieted down and he gazed out over the two thousand students, teachers, and journalists in Hamilton High's vast auditorium.

"Or at least everybody here imagines himself—or herself, no offense to you ladies—to be patriotic. For many years, in wartime and in peace, your government has provided, purely as a public service, with no selfish motive at all, a vocational skills test to enable you young men and women to make your best choices in life. Now some people, right here at this very school, think they know better than ..."

The Toad could give this kind of speech with his brain on autopilot. As he went on about the country's great traditions of military and public service, his eyes scanned the audience. He wondered how many of those troublemaking, test-protesting kids were here. He'd glimpsed a few outside, waving signs, as his limo pulled alongside the auditorium. But it seems ol' "Boots" had done a good job of keeping them out of the building. Good ol' Boots.

And of course, his speech was going to make Boots' life easier—though this talk of the test wasn't meant to be the meat of it.

"Let me tell you about some of the ways your government is keeping you safe right now ..." So Ted's autopilot said, as his mind continued to calculate audience reaction. And the audience ... Man, look at the bazongas on that blonde in the front row. Bet she's the bounciest cheerleader on the squad. He was certain she was giving him a "meet me in the baseball dugout after dark" look. He gave her back just a hint—so nobody else would notice—of his favorite studly smile. The one with the right eyebrow raised just a fraction.

"And your government is going to go right on keeping you safe, right into the future," he orated. Now he gave the speech his full attention. He was getting to the parts that might result in some payback.

"I'm going to tell you about some new bills your leaders are considering. But first ... let me tell you about a pig. Yep. That's right. A pig. I want you to think about this filthy old pig. Laying in dirt. Laying in mud. Laying in some farmer's yard out there in Middle America. Some yard that's never been inspected by a single government agency. Some yard that isn't licensed or subject to sensible health regulations. Some yard that could be harboring every disease known to man ... diseases like mad cow that'll rot your brain right out of your head." He loved this sort of stuff.

"And that pig," he continued, laying it on thick, "that pig out there in that stinking, diseased mud—do you know where he's going to end up? He's going to end up right on your dinner table. I'm tellin' ya, we need to stop that. Now of course I completely support the great American family farm. But it's time to get our food animals into safe, government inspected, clean and scientifically run ..."

Uh oh. Miscalculation. His inner politician told him so. Faces around the auditorium were going blank. They didn't care about some pig out in flyover country. They were suburban kids who believed pork was manufactured and wrapped in plastic in hygienic factories. Kids who thought that nothing but dirt and dreary bible thumpers existed between the Appalachians and the Sierras.

Well, so be it. He'd dropped his hint for the benefit of that particular group of benefactors. The Agri-Tech Coalition, promoters of the "Chip in Every Chicken" animal-registration bill, would be happy. Now he'd better get off this topic. Fast. And get on to something these teenagers would care about: sex. "... and that's why I'm a proud co-sponsor of the Food Health and Security Act," he concluded, "which is now headed for the floor of Congress. But ..."

"... that's not why you came here today, is it? You didn't come to hear about pigs. You came here to hear good news about your own health. I'm talking specifically to you young ladies now. And your parents. And you boys who will someday be husbands and fathers. I'm talking about ..."

Toad O'Day milked the moment for all it was worth. Yep, he was the man who was personally going to save every young woman in this audience from a deadly fate.

———

"And I'm here to announce, in the name of your future health, and in the name of empowering you young people to make solid decisions, that I have arranged for Alexander Hamilton High School and Alexander Hamilton Middle School to be the first in the nation to be able to say that every girl—every, single last healthy girl here—has been vaccinated against the deadly, sexually transmitted HPV virus.

"Up to now, this vital vaccine has been costly and in short supply. Under the Young Women's Health Protection Act, which just became law, your government is changing that. A federally funded program to vaccinate every girl in America from age nine up will go national within two years. But starting this month, you will have the honor and satisfaction of being the first ..."

Charlotte pushed the remote button to change the channels. The smiling face of The Toad was replaced by a huckster, waving a gadget into the air. "Just $29.99!!!" flashed on the screen. She was glad she'd watched the coverage of Rep. O'Day's speech—at her own kids' school, no less. But enough, thank you.

That announcement, she thought, *... about the girls being vaccinated against a sexually transmitted virus ... well, that's a little troubling. I mean, what about Jennifer?*

Of course Jennifer wasn't sexually active yet. At 14 for a nice, middle-class girl that would be out of the question. So she simply didn't need the shots. That wasn't the big thing, though. Ever since she was a baby, Jen had been sickly with one thing after another. Auto-immune problems. And Charlotte knew from a mother's own experience a fact that drug manufacturers' studies somehow rarely showed: that whenever foreign chemicals were injected into Jennifer's veins, her health problems were likely to flare up dramatically, then settle back into a chronically worsening state.

Why take a vaccine she doesn't need and could at least avoid for a few more years? Give her body time to condition itself. Give her mind some time to make decisions.

Of course, the school and the health department would have a form or something to get Jennifer out of the program. Just check the right box, sign it, and that situation would be taken care of.

Thank heaven. Charlotte sighed and let that particular worry go. After a whole lifetime of being one sort of trouble or another, for once Jennifer wasn't going to be the one causing the flare-ups.

But then ... then Charlotte knew she'd have to look herself in the mirror and figure out what to do about Tonio. Or rather with this strange, defiant boy who had suddenly replaced her Boy Scout of a son. Is he going to be expelled from school for good? Will he flunk? Will he end up serving a sentence? And all over some pointless stubbornness! It makes no sense at all.

He should just do what the school tells him. They're experts. They know more than some 17-year-old boy.

All she knew was that she'd better solve Tonio's problems for him pretty quick. The strain of dealing with them was taking a toll on her work. Her boss—never exactly her best friend—was noticing. The tensions were killing her. Tearing up her life. Hitting her nerves like hammers.

The phone rang. Again. She let the answering machine pick it up. "Ms. Carolina? Marlise Abruzzio, *Times Tribune*. Is it true that your son ...?"

Charlotte balled up her fists. She screamed in total frustration. Then she snatched up the phone and hurled it into the big mirror hanging over the couch. Cracks ran everywhere and shards of silvery glass rained down upon the upholstery.

Chapter 6
Sex and Motherhood

"What do you mean, they won't let you out of the vaccination program?" Charlotte set down the dish of Cherry Garcia ice cream she'd been eating—a comfort food neither her body nor her budget could afford, but that her jangled nerves ached for. "Of course they'll let you out of the vaccination program. They have to have provisions for children with allergies or other health problems. They have to have parental consent." She looked up from the recliner chair.

Jennifer ... Paris ... whoever her daughter was this week, stood gazing into the new mirror over the couch. It wasn't as nice a mirror as the one that got accidentally broken last week. The girl twisted a lock of her bronze-streaked hair around her finger and pouted at her image.

"Listen to me, Jennifer. I'm talking to you," Charlotte continued. "I said of course they'll let you out of the vaccination program. For health reasons. And in any case, I won't sign a consent form."

"They said everybody participates. And parents' consent isn't required. That's the law now. And anyhow, I'm *not* a child. And I don't want to get out of it."

"Of course you want to. You know how vaccines sometimes affect you. They say this one's safe. But it's just not worth taking the chance. Not for something you don't need."

"You want me to get cancer?" Jennifer demanded, shifting her mirrored gaze from her own image to her mother's. "It's a shot against cancer, you know."

Now Charlotte thought she understood. "Oh, honey. I think you've misread the situation. First of all, it's a relatively uncommon kind of cancer. The shots don't actually prevent it. Not directly, and perhaps not even at all. And second ... well, you know, the shots actually protect against a virus you get only from ... well ... from having sex. You're still years away from making that decision, honey. So you can't possibly need ..."

She halted abruptly. Something in Jennifer's suddenly tense posture, something furtive in the girl's mirrored expression alarmed her. Mother and daughter met each other's gaze in the mirror.

Jennifer was the first to blink.

"No," Charlotte said. "Don't tell me. I don't want to know."

"Okay, then," Jennifer shrugged defiantly. "I won't. But you don't want me to get *cancer,* do you?" She made a comically ugly face, "Or a bunch of horrible old witchy warts on my you-know-what. Eeew."

"You and Shawn. You've ...?" Charlotte went on, disregarding her own desire not to know.

Jennifer, caught between the guilt of being found out and delight at making her mother squirm, cast an even more defiant look into the silvered glass, straight into her mother's reflected eyes. "Yeah. And me and Jordan before that. So what? Everybody does it. And you don't want me to get *cancer,* right? Or ugly old warts?"

Some moments in a mother's life get carved into the heart. Very slowly. As if by a dull knife. Charlotte knew this was one of those. Her 14-year-old daughter. Her baby Jen ...

Somehow, she found herself clutching the bowl of Cherry Garcia again. The scent of the melting ice cream wafted up. But now instead of tempting her, it was almost nauseating. She carefully set the bowl back down on the end table and this time shoved it away. She took several deep breaths. "Jen. Come over here. Sit down." She waved toward the other big chair, just across the coffee table. "We need to talk."

Jen rolled her eyes, but slouched over to the chair and sunk into it. She picked at an invisible bit of lint on her blouse.

"Jen."

"Paris."

"Jen. Listen to me. Cancer and warts are the least of your worries. What happens if you get pregnant? Have you thought of that?"

"Quit worrying, Mom. I'm on the pill. You know?"

"You're ...? How did you get birth control pills? Did you steal them? Did you take them from a friend's mother or older sister? Did you ...?"

"That's stupid, Mom. I got them the way everybody else does. From a clinic."

"Jennifer."

"Paris."

"Jennifer, you're too young for this. For any of it. For birth control pills. For sexually transmitted diseases. For shots against them. For ..."

Jennifer just shrugged. *So what? It's done.*

"How did you get any doctor to prescribe you pills? At your age? Did you lie about how old you are?"

Jennifer twisted another lock of her hair and frowned at the ends, critical of splits and frizzes.

"How? You tell me or I ground you. And I mean it."

Shrug. "School nurse told me about the clinic. Made the appointment. And everybody knew how old I am. Like I said. I'm not a child. I'm old enough to make my own decisions."

Charlotte had thought she was already as stunned as she could be. Now the dull knife dug further into her heart. *And nobody ever mentioned anything about this to me?* She gulped another deep breath.

"Jen, I want this all to stop. Now. The pills. The sex. The vaccination. None of it's good for you. Not at your age."

"I'll do what I want, Mom. You can't stop me."

"If you won't agree to stop on your own, I really will ground you. I'll ground you until you're in college. I swear I will."

"So I'll sneak out."

"I'll flush your birth-control pills down the toilet."

"I'll get more."

"And I'll flush them down the toilet, too."

"I'll get pregnant, then. So there. Then what'll you think? You can raise your grandbaby while I go out and party. And if I get warts and cancer and herpes all that stuff, too, it'll be your fault. All of it. Your fault."

"Jen ..."

"Get over it, Mom. The school nurse has no problem with it. The clinic has no problem with it. The government has no problem with it. I have no problem with it. What's *your* problem? Are you too stupid to figure it out? The way it is is the way it is—and there's nothing you can do about it."

And Charlotte Carolina, increasingly desperate mother, begged another day off work to deal with her children.

She went to the school nurse at Alexander Hamilton High, who told her, "Mrs. Carolina, your daughter is already sexually active regardless of what you think of it. Be practical. Our job now is to protect her. Birth control pills are part of that. Safe sex is part of that. And now we have the opportunity to save her from a deadly virus—if it's not already too late. If she hasn't already been exposed."

When Charlotte continued to protest that, at the very least, she wanted to wait and learn more before anyone gave her daughter the vaccine, the nurse said, "Mrs. Carolina, experts have determined that this vaccination is perfectly safe. Why don't you just accept the word of people who know more than we do? For the sake of your daughter. And think what a proud example Hamilton High and Hamilton Middle School have been chosen to set for the entire nation. Surely you don't want your family to be the only ones to ruin it for everyone else. Surely you don't want more ... negative focus on your children. I would have thought you'd have had enough of that."

Charlotte went to the county health department whose staff would administer the vaccinations, this time carrying a fat file of Jennifer's medical records and printouts from several Internet vaccine-information sites. "There's a health exemption," she insisted. "I want it for my daughter."

After a cursory perusal: "There's nothing in her records that indicates that this vaccine will be a problem to your daughter."

"But you don't understand," she protested. "See? Here. There may be a connection between ..."

"Ms. Carolina, it's true that there's an exemption in the new federal law for legitimate health problems. But we must caution you: Child Protective Services is very interested in parents who try to deny their children basic health care, like vitally needed vaccinations. We could call CPS and ask them to look into your situation—which we've heard is already quite troubled. But wouldn't you rather listen to reason? Now, extremely knowledgeable people have determined ..."

Toward the end of that desperate day, Charlotte Carolina called the office of Congressman Ted O'Day, whose idea the Hamilton High vaccination program was. A young aide whose name she didn't catch assured her again that experts had determined that the vaccine was perfectly safe. "Ms. Carolina," he said, "Just think how many lives can be saved if other schools follow the example of Alexander Hamilton High and Alexander Hamilton Middle School and ensure that every single girl is protected. Full participation in this initial effort is vital. You don't want to stand in the way of saving thousands of lives, do you?"

But before his comment was finished, Charlotte heard another voice coming through the telephone in the background. It was a familiar voice. One she'd never heard in person, but that she certainly knew from TV. It boomed, from somewhere near the aide's telephone, "Carolina? Carolina? Isn't that the last name of that boy who's making all that trouble for me down there?"

Resignedly, Charlotte dropped the phone back in its cradle. Numb, and with an enormous headache pounding between her eyes, she dragged herself into the bedroom. Her body demanded a long nap—even though she knew she'd only wake up with the same old problems.

Sitting down on the bed, she opened the nightstand drawer and pawed through it for something stronger than aspirin. She pulled out a couple of empty prescription bottles and tossed them aside. Nothing.

Her eyes fastened on the dog-eared notepad on which she'd written down The Lunatic's bizarre words. "Learns to dance," "opens perception's gates," "befriend ... travels from darkness into light," she read. "Hardest choice opens widest horizons." Total nonsense. Pointless garbage. Why'd she even write it all down, let alone save it? *Maybe,* she thought, *I did it just to remind myself that it would be nicer being A Lunatic than to keep fighting a losing battle for sanity while raising teenagers.*

And tomorrow she had to take even more time off for an afternoon appointment with Tonio's lawyer. The throbbing in her head suddenly felt like a jackhammer cracking her skull wide open.

Chapter 7
Awakenings

"Seems they want this over quickly." The lawyer smiled confidently across his desk at Charlotte and Tonio. "Guess someone doesn't like all the publicity you've generated, young man."

When Tonio didn't smile back, the lawyer consulted his notes and cleared his throat to continue.

Charlotte's headache had lasted all night. It finally quieted down to dull thunder shortly before lunch hour. She hoped this meeting would be over soon and this whole mess would be settled so she could get back to work. One more look like that from the boss and...

"They're offering a decent deal," the lawyer said, to Charlotte's relief. "Take the test. Do six months probation. And that's the end of it. Oh, and no more protests. Quite an offer, Tonio, considering the alternative could be a pretty good chunk of time in confinement, even for a juvenile offender."

Charlotte sighed with relief. "Good. What do we have to do? Can we just sign..."

"I want a trial," Tonio interrupted. "No plea bargain."

Charlotte swiveled in her seat and glared at him. "But you have to take the plea bargain! Be sensible! You can't be so selfish as to..."

"Mrs. Carolina," the lawyer gestured her to calm down, then went on to back her point. "You see, Tonio, maybe you don't understand. This is actually a win-win situation for you. You take the test ... but you know, you monkey it all up. Give dumb answers. Lie. Make yourself look like something the Army would never want and the Marine Corps would wipe off their boots. Then you're scot-free. And you've still outfoxed 'em. Now, all we have to do is ..."

"No test. No plea bargain if there's a test in it."

"You are just being stubborn!" Charlotte bellowed, lunging up from her chair and looming over her son. "You are doing this to spite me. Just to be irritating! You will take this plea bargain. And you will take that test! Because I say so!"

Tonio turned to her, expressionless except for some unreadable pain behind his eyes. "You can force me to take the plea bargain, Mom, because I'm underage and can't afford my own lawyer. But you. Can. Not. Make me. Take that test. I won't."

Charlotte drew back her arm to backhand him across the face. For a moment, mother and son froze, locking gazes with each other.

The lawyer made a palms-down quieting gesture, putting Charlotte back into her chair. Then he turned to Tonio. "Do you understand that if you accept this plea bargain then don't take the ASVAB, you'll be in contempt of court? And when you're in contempt of court, there's no telling how long you have to be locked up? As long as the judge wants you in there, you're in there. Now you're a juvenile, so maybe ..."

"I won't take the test. And as long as I can talk, I'm going to tell other kids out there, anywhere the media can reach, that they should ask questions. That they should get true answers about why the government wants 'em to take it. Kids have a right to decide for themselves—based on the facts. That's not unreasonable. Being forced to take a Pentagon test *is*."

They left the office with no agreement—and with Charlotte's head pounding so fiercely she could only spend the afternoon sitting at her desk, pretending to work. Even the occasional beeping of her computer and the footsteps of her co-workers outside her cubicle were enough to induce nausea.

———-

Saturday. But there was no relief. Nobody in the Carolina household was speaking to anybody else. Jen had locked herself in her room, sulking and grounded. Tonio was working silently on his computer, also closed in his room. And Charlotte was just ... distraught. And even that melodramatic Victorian word was inadequate to describe her frantic state. If she could have bromidically torn her hair and beaten her breast, she would have. As is, she did some actual hand-wringing. Along with much consuming of chocolate.

But finally, she could stand only so much. She knocked on Tonio's door and got a mumble in return that at least wasn't, "Go away!" She opened the door wide enough to stick her head in.

"Tonio, can we talk?"

"Don't start in on me again, Mom."

"No, I'm sorry. I won't. This time, I really do want to know why you're doing this thing. I want to understand you."

"It's too late, Mom. You wouldn't. You'd just end up yelling at me like you always do."

"No. This time really, I wouldn't."

"That's what you say, Mom. But that's not what happens. It's always..." he raised his voice in a crude parody, "'Why are you doing this to me you awful boy?' Well, I'm not, Mom. I'm not doing one thing *to you*. What I'm doing and why has absolutely nothing, not one thing at all, to do with you. So it wouldn't interest you. It would bore you because it's not about you. So why bother?"

"But Tonio, I want to ..."

"Forget it, Mom. You're not my friend. You'll never be my friend. I don't expect you to be. Just leave me alone, okay?"

———————————

Saturday night. Charlotte tossed once again in a wretched tangle of sheets and blankets and nightgown. No position was comfortable—nor was any thought. "You're not my friend," she heard her son telling her. "You never will be." She heard herself: *Me, me, me, me, me.*

She thought back on the job she'd done as a mother. And hated herself. Sure, she could blame the schools or Tonio's stubbornness or Jennifer's defiant nature. But the truth was ... well, Tonio was telling the truth. About her. She could blame her absent husband or her own mother and father. She could blame the government, the media, Planned Parenthood, or for that matter the spirits, gnomes, gremlins, fairies, or gods. But it wouldn't change a thing.

It wasn't important that she be Tonio's friend. What was important was for her to be a good mother.

It's your fault, you stupid woman. Your fault. Not just for how much trouble you're having with them. Your fault for your own stupid, worthless life. Your fault for ruining your health with smoking and using pills to get you through the night. Your fault for Cherry Garcia. But most of all, your fault for putting your own kids in second place to your own big, fat ego— your own big, fat ego that isn't even pretty or clever or smart or witty. It's just all blown up with hurt and anger and me, me, me, me, me.

It's all your fault. Every bit of it. And now it's up to you—and you alone—to undo a whole lousy lifetime's worth of stupid damage. No more excuses.

She sat up. The light of the waning gibbous moon streamed in through her window. She hoped it wasn't a bad omen to begin a new venture during the waning moon. (And then wondered from what ancestral peasant memory that superstition arose.) But there was no question. Her life was rotten. Completely rotten. It had to change. Starting now.

But where to begin? What to do? And how to get past all the opposition there was certain to be—opposition from everybody else—from her own kids, the authorities, and not least her own weak self?

She slid the drawer of the nightstand open, drew out the dog-eared old pad, thinking she should write herself some notes, some resolutions, some ideas, something, about how to turn her life and her family around.

But there, on the ratty old pad, were The Lunatic's words: "In narrow strait, hardest choice opens widest horizons." Yeah, tell me about hard choices, she thought. Then she read ...

"Will you befriend bold spirit who travels from darkness into light?"

And it was suddenly perfectly obvious what she needed to do.

———————————

Charlotte and Tonio sat in the conference room at his lawyer's office. It was the only good place she could think of when she called—she could hardly believe she was doing it—her news conference.

"Before I begin," she said, "I want to tell you that I am with my son—not just physically, here today, but in the decision he has made." She knew the next part of her statement would seem cryptic to the reporters. "You also need to know that my daughter Jennifer, who is 14, is not with me. Not in person and not in agreement. But that doesn't matter. I am her mother, and she is not yet mature enough to make certain life-altering decisions for herself. Tonio is.

"So. That said, I guess I'll just tell you what I have to tell you. And then you can ask me and Tonio whatever you want." She took a surprisingly calm breath and continued.

"I've asked you here today to inform you that my son, Tonio Carolina, is not going to take the Pentagon database test. And he's not going to take any plea bargain that requires him to do so. That's his free choice. The school has no right to make a decision that will turn him into a 'prequalified military recruiting lead' if he doesn't choose to be one. Others may make a different choice and that's absolutely fine—for them. But Tonio has a right to his choice, too.

"Furthermore, he's going to go on informing other students that they have a right, and even a duty, to ask questions and get honest, complete answers—about anything and everything that affects their future and their well-being. And you know what? He's right to do so. One hundred percent right. If he gets put in juvie or jail, well, then I'll carry on his work of informing other students. And their parents. Especially concerned mothers.

"In fact, I may just form a group against this test—and against other aspects of using schools full of captive students as military recruitment centers. Mothers Against Militarized Education. MAME. What do you think of that?"

The reporters made a pretty respectable hubbub. Camera operators crept in closer and pencils rushed over paper. A few journalists started to call their questions.

Charlotte could hardly even believe she was saying these things. She was no anti-war activist, no leftist get-out-in-the streets woman, no little-old-lady-in-tennis-shoes. She was just an ordinary mother. And a patriot. And a person who'd always trusted her leaders. Yet, something within continued sweeping her along.

"That's not all I'm going to do," Charlotte went on smoothly. "I've also asked you here to tell you that my daughter is not going to receive the anti-HPV vaccine at her school. If at a more mature age she chooses to be sexually active and to receive the vaccine, that's entirely her business. Any young adult should be free to make those choices.

"But there is no casually contagious disease involved. Nothing you can get from sitting next to a stranger on a plane or in a restaurant. It is not a plague spread by rats or dirty handkerchiefs. The disease in question is entirely avoidable to those who wish to avoid it. Because of that, the government has no business trying to force anybody to get pharmaceutical protection from it." She took a quick sip of water and went on.

"The particular vaccine we're addressing may have its place in the world. It may be good medicine for responsible women—and perhaps men—to choose once more questions are answered. But in high school and middle school students, HPV could be controlled by behavior—by 14 year olds and 16 year olds not having sex. Neither Representative Ted O'Day nor any county or school bureaucrat is going to tell me that I have to allow them to put some problematic and unnecessary substance into my daughter's body. And that is that. Period. Do you have any questions?"

Charlotte felt her face flushing. Even two days earlier, she would never have imagined saying such things in public. Now here she was and her statements felt ... right. Awkward. Foreign. But right. And all because of Saturday night and Sunday morning. And one Lunatic.

The morning after Tonio's dismissal of her, when she had looked into the mirror of her own mind and despised what she saw, Charlotte had knocked on Tonio's door. Once again she had found him at his computer, this time in his pajamas. But this time, she had arrived bearing cups of hot chocolate topped with melted marshmallows. Pulling up a chair next to him, she said ...

"Show me some of these web sites you've been looking at, Tonio. The ones about that test. And explain to me. What's true? What's false? What makes you so determined?"

She would never forget his first words—not exactly high-minded—as he took her to the first site on his cyber-tour. "You see these jumping morons?" he said pointing to photos of ecstatic, leaping young people on the Pentagon's ASVAB website.* "Well think about in-stead if they were getting blown sky high by roadside bombs. Because, Mom, that's what this test is about. And that's the only reason the government wants us to take it. Not for career aptitude. Not because they are giving it to us as a public service. That's just the cover story."

"For kids who want to go into the military ... the test is okay. But Mom, they're conning the rest of us. Just to get us into a database and send recruiters after us."

He went on to show her many things. And she looked at other web sites on her own, in late evenings at the old family computer, or in unobserved (she hoped) moments on her job at CYACorp. And the more she looked, the wider open her eyes became. She would never see her government in the same way again.

And now she was here at—believe it or not—a press conference. While there weren't quite as many reporters as there had been just after Tonio's arrest, there was still a respect-able number. They loved her when she was, as they saw it, 'anti-military.' But after her comments about the mandatory vaccine, most of them were now staring awkwardly at her.

She knew what had happened. In the time it took to utter a handful of sentences, Tonio's Crusading Left-Wing Hero Mom was replaced by Jennifer's Right-Wing Nutjob Mom, the sort of crazy who thinks vaccinations pollute our precious bodily fluids and doesn't want her daughter having sex until she's 30 and married.

The reporters' questions were thereafter a mix of ardent curiosity about Tonio's stance, polite avoidance of any discussion of what they regarded as wing-nut issues, and a marked desire to get this conference over with. A few, however, couldn't resist tossing out snide questions like, "Do you think girls should wear chastity belts?" or "Do you believe the Arabs are behind the plot to fluoridate our drinking water?" And a few even asked some-thing like real questions about both Tonio's and Jennifer's situations.

Half an hour later, it was over. For good or ill, it was done.

Charlotte staggered away from the little press conference, leaning on Tonio's arm, as exhausted as she'd ever felt. She knew the news coverage might be disastrous. But she didn't care. She had said what she had to say to begin getting right with her kids. And herself.

That's all that mattered.

———————————

* The site Tonio referred to was: http://www.asvabprogram.com/. At that time, it featured graphics of young people leaping into the air with big grins on their faces. As of 2010, the visuals have been toned down, but the site still positions the ASVAB as a general "career-exploration program." One secondary page notes that the test was developed by the Department of Defense. But nowhere on that site is the full name of the test (Armed Services Vocational Assessment Battery) given. Nor is it stated anywhere that taking the test will subject students to sometimes intense military recruiting pressures.

Chapter 8
What Goes Around

"And on a lighter note," chirped the chipper news-reader to her onscreen partner, "You remember that high school boy who raised such a fuss about taking a school test? Well, now his mother has made the news, too; she says her daughter can't have a vaccination that would protect her against cancer. And she says she's willing to go to jail to prevent it."

The co-anchor shook his blow-dried head ruefully. He chuckled, "Boy, that's one family I wouldn't want to mess with. Sounds like the whole bunch of 'em enjoy fighting like Tasmanian devils. Cousins of Jeff Foxworthy by any chance?" The lovely and lissome onscreen pair shared a bright-toothed chuckle.

Charlotte looked at Tonio, sitting next to her on the sofa, and rolled her eyes. She aimed the remote at the TV as if it were a handgun. She poked the button. But not before Jennifer, wandering from her bedroom into the kitchen, heard the report.

"Mommmmmmm!" she wailed. "How could you do this to me? I've never been so embarrassed in my whole life!"

Charlotte and Tonio both turned. Charlotte considered her complaining daughter. Guiltily, she realized she'd heard that tone of voice and that phrase all too often—and not from Jennifer. "Kid,", she announced, "suck it up. Things are going to get a whole lot tougher before they're done." She bit the end off a carrot stick for emphasis. "Just remember, whatever happens in the future—and lots of things are likely to happen—I still love you."

Jennifer thumped back into her room, slammed the door, and threw herself dramatically onto the bed with a groan of grief and bed-springs that could be heard clear into the living room.

The media coverage hadn't been totally catastrophic. One local TV station had quoted Charlotte saying, "Representative O'Day and school officials don't seem to understand: You can't make up for forcing people to do one thing by turning around and forcing them to do another. It's the forcing that's the problem in the first place."

One newspaper had almost entirely accurately reported her other best moment from the news conference: "How strange. Kids can't legally take a sip of beer until they're 21. They can't hold real jobs until they're 16. They can't sign contracts until they're 18. We tell them what to think, not how to think. We tell them personal responsibility is years in their future. Then we turn around and say, 'Hey, you teenagers: Have sex! Have babies! It's your decision! Join the military! Kill and be killed! It's as if we're trying to keep them babies in their minds, but turn them into 30-year-olds in their bodies. Does that make sense to anybody? Because it doesn't to me."

But good or bad, what was done was done. The question now was what to do next, now that she'd made such a dramatic declaration of her change of ways? She took a nibble of cauliflower, pulled a little face, and put the offending veggie back into the dish. Some of this "healthy change" stuff was going to take getting used to. But by damn, she wasn't going back.

She had one idea to put in motion. She wasn't exactly sure how, but she thought maybe she had the resources at least to begin the job.

"Tonio," she said, in the TV-less, Jenniferless silence, "You know, that Representative O'Day, he's the one behind all this—what's happening to both you and Jennifer. He's the one who brokered the deal to put recruiters into schools and he's the brains, if you can call it that, behind getting nine-year-old girls vaccinated for sexually transmitted diseases."

"I guess. Yeah. He's one of the people for sure."

"Well, he's the one who stuck his nose in when he gave that speech at the high school."

"Yeah ... So ...?"

"I think it's time to try to cut that busybody nose right off that fat ugly face. Who do you know who's really good at research on the computer?"

And Qwai Ching Paine gazed deeply into the mirror—or rather, into the glassy eye of a television set—and saw that monkey-fu continued to work its mysteries. He was humbled by his "leaf on the wind" role in the great chi flow.

All was as he had hoped when he first cast the stone of monkey-fu into the stagnant pond of the Carolina family. But—he was astonished to see—the power of an aroused and indignant Charlotte Carolina had potential to be more like a tsunami than a stone's watery ripple.

He smiled. Yes, once again he did so inscrutably. For all his humble failings as a monkey-fu student, at least he was getting good at inscrutability discipline.

It appeared that Charlotte Carolina was going to do far more than he ever hoped when he first stepped into her life.

Perhaps he could help her a little farther along her path. And help her make the world better, one congressman at a time.

––––––––––––

Charlotte didn't know much about research on the computer. But she did know that her employer, CYACorp had a lot of government contracts and did a lot of lobbying. And corporate headquarters was in Toad O'Day's district. Surely, she thought, somewhere there's a 2 and a 2 to be added up to 4, and it just might be somewhere in CYACorp files.

So while Tonio and friends delved deeper electronically, she used just a little more of her employer's time to search a little further into filing cabinets when she placed folders there. And she used a little more of her employer's time to read emails from her boss's boss (who had so very kindly left login data where anybody bringing coffee into his office could see it).

In the next few days, Charlotte occasionally had a passing thought. Several of them, actually. *Who is this person doing this? It can't possibly be me. and If I get caught ... no, I'm not even going to think about that. But if I get caught ...*

After a handful of days, with a little help from some of Tonio's angry hacker friends, Charlotte had before her a stack of information about Rep. Ted "Toad" O'Day far bigger than she would have imagined.

Unfortunately it didn't amount to much. The stack of printouts consisted mostly of carefully altered "official" biographies. Puff pieces about his fabulous family life. PR statements. There were a number of critical news stories and a few unconfirmed but highly believable rumors. She had dug out some routine correspondence between CYACorp officials, or their lobbyists, and the representative's office. But ... despite the thickness of the stack, the actual evidence of any wrongdoing on the Toad's part was all very thin.

And ditch-water dull to read through, Charlotte thought as she sat in the dim light at her home computer desk one midnight. Still, she had to keep reading, keep digging. That man was trying to hurt both her kids. And that, a mother simply couldn't tolerate.

She slugged another dose of coffee, turned to the next sheet of paper, visited the next web site. She was going to find out everything there was to know about Toad O'Day.

––––––––––––

Finally, one of her filing-cabinet forays at CYACorp struck pay-dirt. With "pay" and "dirt" both perfectly appropriate terms. The photocopied note was vague and short. It didn't come right out and say, "Thank you for doing tat. In exchange, here's tit." But it was close.

Dear Ted,

I hope you and your companions enjoyed your visit to Parrot Cay. Just remember, I'm always glad to be of personal service in any way. And of course you can count on me to be among your most steadfast campaign supporters.

The letter was on personal stationery and signed by the president of CYACorp.

Charlotte went back to her desk and looked up Parrot Cay. Hm. Not bad. The private Caribbean island resort billed itself as one of the most exclusive and expensive in the world. It featured not only luxury resort accommodations, but privately owned beach houses for the very rich.

Why would the president of CYACorp host Toad O'Day and "companions" there? (And who, she wondered, were the married legislator's "companions"?)

Then she made her way over to THOMAS, the Library of Congress' web site that covered all legislation, proposed, in progress, recent, past, and present. That was a site she'd never even heard of a few weeks ago. Now she was so familiar with it she needed to go there only to refresh her memory about a particular bill she had already noted.

Yep. That 2,000 page appropriations bill that contained a quiet little page with a special multi-million-dollar, multi-year project for CYACorp got the Good Congressman's vote, and his helping hand, *just three weeks after the date of the letter.*

She had him. It seemed like a small thing. But if it wasn't a smoking gun, it was at least a gun with gunpowder residue around the muzzle. Tit for tat.

Sliding the filing-cabinet drawer closed, Charlotte put a lid on her elation. Her co-workers should only see the usual bleak old Charlotte Carolina, hunched grudgingly over her work, half asleep. But she was so thrilled by the hunt—and by this glimpse of success—that she didn't think she'd ever sleep again.

With the photocopy hidden deep inside a file of field reports from the sales staff, she casually ambled into the copy room and ran off the letter along with a load of routine expense accounts and appointment memos. Just as casually, as if she had carelessly forgotten something in the file room, she slipped the original of the letter back into its old place.

At her desk, she furtively folded her new copy into a small square and tucked it into the bottom of her purse.

She wasn't sure what she'd do with it. She wasn't sure whether one little letter hinting at a tit-for-tat arrangement would be enough. But she'd get it to one of those reporters she'd just met. One of the serious ones. She wasn't sure who, just yet. But she was absolutely, certainly sure that nothing was going to stop her.

At that instant, the phone on her desk shrieked.

"Mrs. Carolina?" The woman's voice sounded odd—both self-righteous and apologetic at the same time, as if two people were inhabiting the same body. "This is the school nurse at Alexander Hamilton High School. I'm calling to inform you that your daughter, Jennifer, is on her way to the hospital. The ambulance just ..."

"What?!"

"... on her way to the hospital. She apparently had an ... well, you see, you must understand, it wasn't the school's fault. It was no one's fault. No one could have predicted. It was ..."

"Shut up!" Charlotte barked. "Shut the"—she interjected an obscenity that had never before parted her lips—"UP! Just tell me what happened and what hospital. And don't say one other word!"

Chapter 9
Shock

Her daughter was alive. That was all she knew. How bad off, she had no idea.

"Anaphylaxis," the very young doctor in the blue scrubs began to explain. "A severe allergic reaction which, among other things, causes the airway to swell shut. Rare but possible with exposure to certain foods, chemicals, and ..."

"Vaccinations," Charlotte finished. Though she could almost feel her blood pressure swelling within every vein and artery, she noted, too, how surprisingly focused she felt. Not her old frantic self.

"Yes, vaccinations. There's nothing in the research to indicate that this particular vaccination is unsafe. Sometimes these things strike out of the blue. A person develops a sensitivity to a particular allergen used in formulating the vaccine."

"I know all about the research on this particular vaccination," Charlotte said, trying not to sound as if she were blaming the doctor. But she'd been doing her homework—and had the sleepless nights and bags under her eyes to show for it. "And I know what anaphylaxis is. What I don't know is how my daughter is. Is she going to be okay? Did you counteract the shock quickly enough?"

"She's going to be fine," said an older doctor, coming to the young one's rescue. This veteran ER physician arriving on the scene took Charlotte by the arm and guided her to a chair. The senior doctor pierced her young colleague with a "why didn't you tell her that in the first place?" glare.

The newly arrived doctor continued, "The school staff, health department nurse, and paramedics took appropriate emergency measures. By the time they got her here, she was stabilized. We have her on an intravenous drip of corticosteroids and are monitoring her vital signs—which, rest assured, are improving. We do want to keep her overnight. But we expect no further problems."

"They gave her that HPV shot against my express wishes."

The doctor looked down at the PDA on which she kept her notes. "Perhaps. I couldn't say. They tell us Jennifer simply got in line for the vaccination and health department staff administered it. Serious reactions to vaccines are rare, Mrs. Carolina. Even given Jennifer's complex medical history, no one could have anticipated a life-threatening reaction."

I did, thought Charlotte. *Maybe not this exactly, but ...* She decided she'd take that up with the school and the health department later. And—indirectly—she'd take the matter up with a certain over-eager congressman. *Not the doctors' fault,* she reminded herself. *Stay calm. Stay polite.*

"When can I see Jennifer?"

"Now, if you like."

Jennifer was propped up on a bed in a curtained alcove. She was red-faced and surrounded by the detritus of life-saving efforts just past. A technician bustled around, wheeling a mobile blood-pressure unit out to some now more-urgent patient.

Her daughter looked so small to Charlotte. So fragile. She wanted to rush to her and embrace her. But the IV drip and Jennifer's own attitude held her back. The girl turned her head away as soon as Charlotte pushed past the curtain. Wouldn't even look at her own mother.

For a moment, Charlotte had no idea what to say to her own daughter. So, wordlessly, she stepped to the bedside and simply laid her hand over Jennifer's. The girl still didn't look at her.

"Jennifer," she began. Then she realized the girl wasn't avoiding her eyes out of hostility, but because she was crying.

"Jennifer," she began again, "how are you feeling, baby?"

Jennifer turned to look at her, tears streaming abundantly. "Mom? I'm so sorry, Mom. I just wanted to get the shots so I wouldn't get cancer. Don't be mad at me."

"It's not the time for mad, Jen. I'm just relieved you're okay."

"Mom? You said you'd love me no matter what. Did you mean it? Did you really mean it? Mom, I'm so sorry!"

And reaching around and through the maze of medical equipment, Charlotte hugged her daughter while both wept tears of relief.

But secretly Charlotte thought to herself, *Jennifer, you are so totally grounded.*

Unlike the secretive tête-à-têtes between Toad O'Day and The Representative of the Agri-Tech Coalition, Charlotte's meeting with the reporter from the Tribune wasn't held in any exclusive bistro. Just a grubby newspaper office. She had come as yet another of the cranks and case-pleaders hoping for the august attention of The Media. She claimed to have evidence of The Toad's vile corruption.

The *Tribune* wasn't exactly known for its investigative journalism. It wasn't even a very important paper. But Charlotte had already developed an unwelcome "mother on a crusade" reputation with the more important media. Despite its shortcomings, The *Tribune* had one big advantage. It was the first semi-serious media outlet with a reporter willing to hear her out.

She slid her small, well-culled stack of key documents across the journalist's chaotic desk, the CYACorp president's letter on top. She explained the trail of evidence, carefully, step-by-step.

"All I want is for somebody with better connections, better information sources, to follow up this lead and see what else there is to see. Who all was on the island with O'Day? How much did CYACorp spend on the trip? Is there any evidence of specific agreements being made? I mean ... you can see that CYACorp did O'Day an expensive—and pretty hush-hush—favor. Why would ..."

"Charlotte," said the harried reporter, "This is thin. You're asking the *Tribune*—you're asking me—to follow a trail that's most likely not going to lead anywhere."

"But it's clear from the letter and the bill passed just weeks—weeks!— later that something crooked had to be going on. You can see that, can't you?"

The reporter sighed and briefly wished for the days when his kind could have whiskey and cheap cigars at their desks. "It's not enough. You're claiming that one of the most powerful men in Congress, one of the most well-connected men in the country, is basically taking bribes. But where's your smoking gun?"

"I don't mean to offend you, but isn't it your job to find things like that? I thought I was helping by bringing you a clue."

This was going to take a lot of patience. "Charlotte, my job is to get the news my editor assigns me. My job is to report the truth, but without offending the advertisers. My job is to keep my job when a lot of young journalism students would like to take it from me and the newspaper business is rapidly going to hell. My job is not to offend the corporate powers-that-be who own this newspaper and who therefore own a certain part of my anatomy. Charlotte, what you have here is suspicious. I grant you that. But I could probably look for the rest of my life and not find the smoking gun that proves your claims. Understood?"

"I understand perfectly." Charlotte put out her hand. "Give me my papers back, please. I know that man is dirty and I'll take my information elsewhere. There are bloggers out there who dig for this sort of information. The whole Internet is out there. I'll put up a web site of my own if I have to, I'll ..."

The reporter thought again of whiskey, beautiful smooth, calming whiskey. "I'll tell you what," he conceded. "I'll make some calls. I'll check with some people I know. I'll see if I can find anything behind this."

Charlotte beamed.

"But don't get your hopes up. Okay?"

The following Friday afternoon, after discussing it with Tonio and Jennifer, Charlotte Carolina took off work two hours early. She went to the administration office at Alexander Hamilton High School. She sat down with Alfred "Boots" Warren, school principal and old football buddy of one Rep. Toad O'Day.

She said, "Heaven knows why, but my son Tonio would like you to lift the new suspension you imposed after his arrest. He would like to return to school and graduate with his class."

"Fine," Good Old Boots beamed, leaning back in his high-backed chair. "Whenever he's ready to take the ASVAB, he's welcome back."

"No, Mr. Warren. You don't understand. He would like to return to school and graduate with his friends. But unless you lift the requirement that all seniors take the test, he has agreed that home-schooling would be preferable. We've already begun making the preparations the state requires. So. Either you make the test optional and inform all students that they can refuse to take it without consequences, or I withdraw my son from your care, effective immediately."

"And what will you do if the court orders Tonio to take the ASVAB?"

She gazed at him with frank innocence. "Why, Mr. Warren, Tonio and I already said, right out on TV, what we'd do. Taking the test—and having Tonio place so much knowledge about himself in a military database—is not even open to discussion."

She went on, "My daughter Jennifer has also agreed to alternative schooling. I'm here to withdraw her from your school as well. Immediately. She won't be returning for any reason." She didn't mention that Jennifer's reluctant agreement had been obtained only after Charlotte had pointed out that home-schooling or a Catholic girls' school were the only alternatives to being grounded until snowball fights were regularly conducted in Hades. (The gentle reunion in the hospital hadn't solved the host of underlying problems.)

Charlotte had no idea how she was going to swing the schooling options, what with having a full-time job and no money. Tonio was one thing. Jennifer ... well, she'd figure out how to handle Jennifer. She'd just have to. All she knew was that the kid wasn't going to stay here, of all places. Not after all they'd done to her.

"Mrs. Carolina ..."

She could see the calculator running behind the principal's eyes as he tried to frame an argument. Every student withdrawn took thousands of tax dollars out of his operating budget.

"No, you don't have a thing to say to me, Mr. Warren. Whatever it is, I don't want to hear it. I came here only as a courtesy, to tell you what I have to tell you. Jennifer is not coming back here. Ever. And Tonio will return to finish out the school year only if you remove the ASVAB testing requirement and make it simply optional for those students who—after being fully informed of its nature—still want to take it.

"Anything else you have to say," she finished, rising and turning toward the door, "you can say to my lawyer."

Chapter 10
Outside Chances

Charlotte Carolina, scared but exhilarated, faced herself in the mirror and barely recognized the woman she saw. Sure, the face and body were the same (though maybe, just maybe, the effects of all those carrot sticks and rice cakes were beginning to show). But the woman behind those eyes? No, definitely not the person she was a month or two ago.

Not the same woman, not the same life, not the same household.

Two kids not returning to school. And what on earth to do with them? One still facing legal charges. The other—Charlotte could be sure—hell-bent on getting into serious mischief despite her brief moment of repentance.

Everything was turned upside down.

And then there was Charlotte herself. Crusading media mom. Muckraking, whistle-blowing wannabe. Home-schooling mother? *Oh my Lord, how will I ever manage that?* she thought as she stood before the mirror preparing for Monday miseries to come.

Yet as she gave herself one last check before leaving for the office, she discovered that she didn't regret a thing. Not one thing.

"Tonio, look out for your sister today," she said, stopping at her son's bedroom door. "I've told her she'll get to go to the mall on Friday if she solves all her math problems, finishes that essay on *The Chocolate War,* and reads *Animal Farm.* Maybe you could quiz her a little?"

She didn't like setting brother up over sister. That wasn't likely to lead to anything good. Worse, what would she do if brother ended up in jail or juvie? But for the moment, she wasn't sure how else to manage.

"Mom," Tonio sighed, "I've got stuff to do, too, you know."

"Just bear with me a few days. I'll work out something better, I promise. In the meantime, I really appreciate you helping out."

"Well," Tonio said with a wry grin, "Since you made my bail and all, I guess I can do it. Just this once. Just for you."

Mother and son exchanged smiles as she headed for the front door and another wonderful day in the gray cubicles of CYACorp.

Charlotte didn't realize that solutions to her dilemmas were about to arrive in the classic "good news/bad news" fashion.

The phone on her desk shrilled, shattering her computer-induced daze.

"Mrs. Carolina." It was Tonio's lawyer. "I have an interesting development to report. All charges against Tonio have been dropped." She could almost hear him smiling through the little holes in the telephone headset. But for a moment, she was too bemused to absorb the news.

"Dropped?"

"All three charges. Dropped."

"Well ... that's great. That's wonderful! But ... why? I thought we were in for ..."

"I know. I thought so, too. A long fight and possible time in juvenile detention, at the very least. Not to mention a court order to take the ASVAB. But ... your son's in the clear."

"What happened?"

"Now don't take this for gospel because it's only courthouse scuttlebutt. But seems that somebody contacted somebody, who contacted somebody. Bottom line is that the somebody in question really didn't want Tonio's case getting more publicity. That somebody, who is apparently well-placed in DC, didn't want a lot of publicity about schools being used for military recruiting, or about Alexander Hamilton High forcing boys and girls into a Pentagon database. He figured maybe the Pentagon would be better off if this whole thing just quieted down and died away."

"Really."

"Like I say, just courthouse scuttlebutt. But the name O'Day was mentioned. Thought you'd like to know."

Charlotte thanked the lawyer, hung up, and was just beginning to absorb the good news when the bad-news shoe dropped.

"Charlotte," her stern-faced supervisor said, stopping at the entrance to her cube. "You're wanted in Human Resources."

"HR? What for?"

"You're wanted in HR. Just go."

Suddenly chilled, she rose silently and made her way through the vast gray maze toward what she felt sure was to be an ominous fate.

Half an hour later a security guard escorted her out the grand glass doors of CYACorp. In one hand, she lugged a plastic bag of personal possessions from her cube. In the other she clutched her purse, which contained a two-week severance check.

Pale and still trembling, she wasn't sure exactly what had happened. "Security violations." Yes, she'd committed those. "Unauthorized computer access." Yes, she was guilty. But why hadn't the HR manager looked her in the eye? Something more. She was sure there was something more not being said.

The guard escorted her all the way to her car, waited as she got in, then watched as she drove out of the parking lot. She didn't really want to try to make her way through traffic in such an emotional state. She wanted to sit a moment behind the wheel and catch her breath. But the guard's eyes were relentless upon her. The heel of his hand rested casually, yet threateningly, on his gun. So she drove.

She drove about a block. Then she pulled into the parking lot of another business, shut off the engine, and sat there shaking. She craved a cigarette. Really, really, really needed a cigarette. Desperately. *Surely a girl should be able to have just one smoke at a time like this, even if she is trying to reform.*

Spotting a C-store down the block, she eased herself from behind the wheel of the Taurus and started to pace rapidly toward filtered Winstons and relief.

The early spring afternoon was sunny, unseasonably warm. The trees lining the road were filled with songbirds. It didn't take long before Charlotte began to slow and to look around her. Though cars and SUVs whizzed by, the air still managed to hold a tang of blossoms.

She stopped. *It's Monday afternoon and I'm not trapped in a little gray box. Monday afternoon and I don't have to go to work tomorrow. Monday afternoon and the sun is shining. Monday afternoon and I can go home and be with my kids. And help them with their lessons. Monday afternoon and no matter what the future holds, right now, at this moment, my life belongs to nobody but me.* She couldn't remember the last time she could have said any such thing.

Charlotte Carolina stood still in the sunshine for a long, calm moment, breathing deep. Her spirit swelled until she thought it would burst out of her on stereotypical white-dove wings.

She turned away from her frantic errand and strode with head high toward her car—and home.

She had just one regret. The *Tribune* reporter blew her off. Had he ever made any of the calls he promised? Maybe he had. And maybe, she thought, that's what got me fired. Maybe, because of his inquiries, somebody figured out that Charlotte Carolina, crusading mother, was digging for dirt on one of her betters. Maybe that better—using his cozy connections to certain people at CYACorp—had engineered her dismissal.

She'd probably never know. After all, she really had committed all those violations they accused her of. But the reporter's last words to her had been, "Forget it. You tried. I tried. But even if you were right, lady, it wouldn't have made any difference."

Nevertheless, life went on.

Spring was glorious and summer stretched temptingly ahead. True, there was no justice for the powerful. True, there was no money for the powerless. But unemployment was enough to keep the Carolina family scraping by. For now. And, really, it was a pretty good thing, being home with the kids. "School" turned into visits to museums and excursions to historic sites, or sometimes just into family discussions or even making repairs together on the old Taurus. Yeah, sometimes "discussions" turned into temperamental outbursts from the ever-volatile Jennifer. But overall, life was surprisingly peaceful.

And the lawyer—not Tonio's criminal lawyer, but the tort lawyer she had threatened the school principal with—said that the school, the health department, or the National Vaccine Injury Compensation Program (imagine; there really is such a thing!) was likely to settle soon enough for Jennifer's vaccination catastrophe.

Charlotte would have to find other work. Soon. But for the moment, life was good. It was wonderful being part of the kids' lives again. And being part of her own life.

"Hey, how about we all take a trip together?" she suggested one day. "Just drive. We'll pack our own food. Camp out. See some pretty scenery. We can't spend a lot, but maybe we can have some adventures."

"Sure," Tonio agreed instantly.

"Do we *hafta?*" Jennifer moaned.

What Charlotte didn't tell the kids—not right out, anyhow—was that once they left on their trip she didn't want to come back home—at least not any longer than it took to pack the family's few most important possessions. She didn't want to come "home" to Toad O'Day's district. No place could possibly be "home" where schools were military recruiting centers and teenagers were encouraged to take license without taking responsibility. So while the kids packed for a vacation road trip, Charlotte cleaned their little rental house as though she never planned to live in it again.

One afternoon, sorting through the junk in her nightstand, she came across the dog-eared notepad with The Lunatic's ravings on it. But of course, in light of all that had happened, they didn't seem like ravings any more. They all made a certain sort of weird sense. Hard choices. Learning to dance. Being a friend moving from darkness to light. They all made sense, that is, except the crazy man's next-to-last comment, which still seemed like ... well, the raving of a crazy man.

She threw the notepad away with all the other accumulation of a life she wanted to leave behind.

Then one day, while she was busy cleaning out the last of the clutter from the last of the closets, the doorbell rang.

At first she didn't recognize the slight, wiry young man who stood on her doorstep. And why should she? She had seen him only once, and that was many months ago. He smiled, bowed slightly, and held out a thick padded envelope. Only when he spoke did she make the connection.

"Angry woman brings truth," he said, doing his best to be inscrutable. "Toad in sheep's clothing will be brought low by ewe in polyester."

"What?" she gasped.

Qwai Ching Paine gave a little sigh. There was so much he still had to learn about the properly inscrutable practice of monkey-fu. He was beginning to realize that watching all those old Charlie Chan movies was a terrible mistake. "Oh heck," he said, "Just look at what's in the envelope. You'll know what to do. I'm sure you will." And while Charlotte stood sputtering and staring down at the thick package in her hand, he slipped away.

She never even got a chance to thank him for helping to change her life—though in fact, she was about to be more grateful than ever to Her Very Own Lunatic.

───────────

"Here," Charlotte said to the *Tribune* reporter as she once again sat across from him. She thrust a paper-wrapped package across his grubby desk.

"Whiskey?" he said, unwrapping it.

"Irish," Charlotte said, "I thought you needed it. I'm not sure why. Don't worry, it's not a bribe. I really came to bring you this." She handed across Qwai's padded envelope. "I made copies of everything," she added. "So if you don't do anything with it, someone else—maybe one of those young reporters who wants your job or maybe one of those muckraking bloggers—will."

The reporter spilled the envelope's contents out amid his desktop clutter. Mini-CDs and photocopies of documents spread out before him. He began to paw through them.

"What is this?" He dug some more. He examined a copy of what appeared to be a bank record. Now his world-weary eyes began to light up. "Where did you get this? Who gave it to you?"

"I'm not going to tell you. But if you listen to those discs you'll hear two voices. Two men. They sound like they're meeting in a restaurant or maybe a bar. More than one meeting. One of the voices belongs to our friend Toad O'Day. The other ... well, it belongs to a man I think I've met—though when I met him he sounded ... a little different than he does on those discs.

"Listen. Read. Then do whatever you want with the stuff. But frankly, I don't care any more. I'm leaving. No matter what you do—or don't do—I'm ridding myself of Toad O'Day and all his works."

As she departed, the reporter was inserting the first of the mini-CDs into his computer. The voices of Toad O'Day and The Representative from the Agri-Tech Industrial Coalition soon rose over the subdued murmur of a discreet Georgetown bistro. The voices eventually discussed a certain bill to force RFID chips into farm animals in exchange for certain favors. The voices began to make their way into history.

The Carolina family drove. And drove. At first, they rambled aimlessly, visiting state parks and historic sites. Then they drove along, discussing history. Tonio, who'd been doing his homework, had a lot to say. Jennifer mostly sulked in the back seat, occasionally uttering complaints about her absolutely unendurable boredom.

Eventually, without conscious intent, they turned westward. Still driving aimlessly, they headed over the Appalachians and toward the Mississippi. Then they ventured farther, to where corn-belt green yielded to prairie-grass yellow. Eventually, the Rockies rose in the distance.

When talk ran out, they tuned in the radio. That was fine in the crowded east. There was a lot to hear. But out there in the yellow and brown lands, radio pickings are slim. You can take your choice, mostly, between "cryin', dyin', and goin' home" music or biblical exhortations. It takes a lot of frequency-scanning to hear anything else.

Jennifer was in the front seat one day doing some heavy channel-flipping when a fragment of a news report flashed by: "... his party colleagues are said to be pressuring him to resign amid the growing scandal ..."

Jennifer poked the scan button in futile search for her kind of music.

"Wait! Wait!" Charlotte cried. "Go back. Find that news report again!" With a groan and a roll of her eyes, Jennifer complied.

"It appears that the scandal may even spread into the Senate," the news voice continued, "where the food security bill was equally heavily promoted by ..." static interrupted the broadcast and it took an hour before they found another station broadcasting the news. But then as they neared Denver, it seemed every station was talking about nothing else.

"... The Agri-Tech Coalition denies any involvement ..."

"... the embattled Rep. O'Day denied ..."

"... what pansy-livered moron thought it would be a bright idea to microchip itty-bitty chickens?" (This from a famous commentator noted for performing with half his drug-addled brain tied behind his back. He neglected to mention that he had recently supported the "Chip in Every Chicken" bill, declaring it "absolutely vital to our homeland security" and proclaiming that "anybody who doesn't think so should be hanged as a traitor.")

And from NPR: "... Of course the Food Security Act is, to quote the House majority leader, 'Dead, dead, dead. And I mean dead.' After this, every congressman is running as fast as possible away from any association with the tainted legislation. For an analysis of how this development will affect the poor, minorities, and women, we go to ..."

The Carolinas spent the night camping high up in a mountain pass between Cheyenne and Laramie, Wyoming, under a silent, starlit sky.

In the morning they drove into Laramie and treated themselves to a rare restaurant breakfast. In the restaurant they borrowed a crumpled copy of the Casper *Star-Tribune* left by an earlier diner.

O'DAY RESIGNS

the 72-point headline screamed.

FBI OPENS CRIMINAL INVESTIGATION

Charlotte smiled. There went the Great Centrist. The Toad was getting skewered.

Somehow, she was not at all surprised when she turned to a small boxed item on the second page that asked: "MYSTERY: WAS AUSTRIAN BANK ACCOUNT BOGUS?" The story went on to say that an unnamed inside source hinted that while Ted O'Day might have believed he was taking a bribe in the form of money deposited to a private Austrian bearer account, in fact, the bank account and its sources of verification appeared to have been the work of a mysterious team of forgers and hackers.

"Was O'Day caught in a sting? And if so, who stung him?" the gossipy article asked. "Authorities are still trying to locate the young Asian man seen meeting with O'Day in several Washington locations. On recordings purported to be of these meetings, the man meeting with O'Day claims to be a representative of the Agri-Tech Coalition. But that coalition continues to deny ..."

Charlotte was serenely sure they'd never find the mysterious young Asian.

———-

Tonio was at the wheel as they drove up through Casper then hit the stretch of sagebrush locals call "the longest road in Wyoming." In a state known for endless miles of nothing, they'd struck the nothingest of all. After Tonio nearly fell asleep at the wheel from boredom, Charlotte took over the driving chore.

Jen kept her companions awake complaining. Charlotte tuned out the girl's words, but felt perversely grateful for the noise. It kept her alert. Well, at least half alert.

After several more hours driving through nothingness and sagebrush, one of Jen's remarks penetrated Charlotte's weariness.

"Gawd, look at that. They even have stupid names in this stupid place. What kind of idiot would come up with a name like ...?"

"What did you say?" Charlotte turned to look back at her daughter.

"I didn't say anything. I just saw a stupid sign that said something about some stupid, boring, dumb place called ..."

"Lonelyheart Pass." Charlotte said, wonderingly. And at last, the penultimate words of The Lunatic—whom she now knew to be the cagiest lunatic in the whole, wide world—made sense to her.

"And lonely heart tells the way."

Charlotte shoved the transmission into reverse and backed down the middle of the empty Wyoming highway until she could see the sign for herself. Lonelyheart Pass. The arrow pointed toward a ragged ridge of mountains. The prospect looked utterly forbidding.

Yeah, she thought. That's good. She turned the wheel and headed up the narrow two-lane highway that soon began to twist and turn through a field of boulders. She didn't know where she was going. But she knew that somewhere, up there beyond that pass, was her family's destiny.

UNDER SEIGE

In which we experience the continuing traumatic transformation of Hardyville
(The events in this story take place immediately after The Coup)

Chapter 1
The Mysterious Driveway

Spring slouched into Hardyville, reluctant and truculent. The cheery banners of our departed do-gooders still fluttered from lampposts, but March gales ("In like a lion; out like a lion," as they say around here) had shredded them. Their frays and rips reflected the tattered state of Hardyville itself.

The mayor and city council had been gone for weeks. City hall was just a hole in the ground. Even the buckets of tar and bags of feathers had been put away.

But there was no evading the fact; after its nearly fatal bout of government, Hardyville would never be the same. That was bad. And that was good.

The bad was some of the new people. Displaced city types still expected their potholes to be filled and their neighbors taxed to pay for it. But worse was the fearsome realization among us old-timers that Hardyville—good old isolated, independent Hardyville—wasn't immune from the modern disease of "do unto others simply because you have the power."

Hardyvillians, new and old, were mere humans. Not saints.

We now tip-toed around, figuratively speaking. We didn't trust our neighbors. We didn't quite trust ourselves. We squabbled about the futile task of "putting things back the way they were before."

Of course, that was like repairing Humpty Dumpty.

Some parts of the old Hardyville were simply missing. And I don't just mean city hall. What about Dora-the-Yalie? She had ridden off in the Toyota Prius of ex-councilman Dan White and hadn't been seen since. Carty muttered, "Good riddance. She was a twit, anyway." But she was our twit, I thought sadly. Not to mention our conscience. I missed her.

Still, some changes were positive—and those also involved new people. Besides the good old Goodins with their second-hand store, several other newcomers had opened businesses. Liberty Avenue and Freedom Way were coming to life like never before.

The owners of the Bon Mot ice cream parlor were busy preparing for the warm season. They had gotten through the winter competing with the Hog Trough to see who could sell the best coffee and pastries at the best price.

Charlotte Carolina, newly arrived in town when government hit (poor thing), bought the smashed remnants of Sassy Frassy's All-Natural Hemp Boutique for next to nothing. With the help of her hardworking son, sulking daughter, and a repentant Young Curmudgeon, she put the place back together. She was now busily selling controversial hemp washcloths and wallets with the air of a lifelong churchwoman who, for reasons unclear even to herself, has taken up the harlot's trade.

There was also Bark's Tavern, out on the north edge of town, where Walt-the-Barkeep presided over nights of music and dancin' like Hardyville had never seen.

There were still a few gaps. Pickle's Groce Mart was nothing but a shell, the political Pickles having fled along with the rest of our tin-pot dictators and their corrupt clans. As he had done throughout the long sales-tax boycott, old cowboy Nat Lyons continued to operate an impromptu grocery store from a corner of one of his horse barns. But that lay many miles west of town.

Pickle's hadn't exactly been what you'd call a health-food store. This far off the beaten path, the produce truck doesn't make many stops. Especially when the local idea of a "vegetable" is a can of cold baked beans. Nat's was the same at first. Cans. Boxes. A few specialty items. But "fresh" was just another word in the dictionary between French fries and Froot Loops. It was discouraging to trudge that far out of town for such a dismal, badly presented selection of alleged foods.

Then one day, I walked into Nat's Grocery Barn and ... *lo and behold!* ... a few feet from his industrial metal shelves and brown corrugated box grocery "displays" was a long wooden bin, divided into segments and bathed in appetizing light. Over it, fine sprays periodically rained down upon ... fresh, beautiful veggies!

"Organic" said the hand-calligraphed signs. "Earth-friendly."

"Nat?" I squeaked. "You ...?"

Nat, who'd come up to my shoulder while I gawped, shuffled his feet. "You like it, Claire?" he said. And I'd have sworn I saw him blush.

"Of course I like it!" I cried, rushing up to the nearest bin and picking out a ripe melon. "But it's not like you. I mean ..." I dashed to the next bin. Carrots! And the next, crispy fresh red-leaf lettuce without a sign of the liquid black rot standard at Pickle's. And ... "Nat," I said, picking up another vegetable and waving it vigorously in his face, "Arugula, Nat? Organic arugula???"

"Thought some variety might be good," he mumbled, busying himself straightening up one of the little recycled cardboard price signs.

Try as I might, I couldn't get Nat to reveal where those miracle vegetables came from, or how they happened to be in those bins in his store. He wouldn't tell anybody. And of course, we all nagged him about it for weeks.

And who, you might ask, would buy arugula in Hardyville? Well, ask away. Many of the newcomers seemed to find it to their taste. Janelle at the new and gentrified Hogge Trough Grille and Feede gave it a try (though I understand that large batches of salad had to be thrown out that evening).

But Hardyvillians, old and new, weren't Nat's only customers. While browsing the growing grocery selection, which soon included bins of bulk grains and spices, we found ourselves shopping beside a whole new class of people.

Some of them wore Birkenstocks. And peasant skirts. And natural-fiber hand-woven ponchos. They weren't Hardyville's late, unlamented political Birkenstockers. But their kissin' cousins.

Now normally—normally, I stress—this wouldn't have been any big deal. If people can't tolerate peaceful differences between them and their neighbors, then what good is freedom? But as Debra, my friend from the real world, put it, Hardyville at this moment was a little like the U.S. right after 9-11. We'd been smacked (by our former government) and we were jumpy about getting smacked again. Suspicious of anyone who might even think about wanting to think about controlling and taxing us.

So we shopped at Nat's among these mysterious strangers, silent and uneasy. We didn't know—or particularly care—where they came from. All we hoped is that they wouldn't show up in town and start trying to run things. And to our relief they didn't. In fact, they appeared to want no more to do with old Hardyvillians than we wanted to do with them.

But where they went, when they toted home their woven hemp tote bags colored with all natural vegetable dyes, nobody knew, at first. They didn't go to Hardyville itself. So ... where?

And then one day Marty Harbibi solved two mysteries at once: where Nat's organic produce was coming from and where the new people in the peasant garb were going.

Do you remember the mysterious new driveway I spotted while returning from the Hilltop Hermitage last summer? Well, up there is where the peasant-people went. And down from that driveway the produce came. Marty saw it for himself. The driveway was just a mile or so uphill from Nat's gate (that's rubbing shoulders in Hardyville terms). Marty was out plinking in the badlands one day when he saw several hybrid cars and old beater Saabs go up. He also saw Nat's truck come down, riding low on its springs from all the gourds and strawberries and tomatoes loaded in the back.

152

Fresh produce? Enough of it to sell? Grown in Hardy County's sand and sagebrush? No way! Or only in a pretty darned impressive greenhouse.

"Them hippies couldn't afford big, fancy greenhouses up there," Marty insisted.

"Dunno," Carty sneered. "Might be their mamas and daddies give 'em a lot of money. And them veg'tables is comin' outa there. Can't deny that."

But if somebody had built anything big up there at the end of that mysterious driveway, wouldn't some Hardyville hardware store or jack-of-all-trades have gotten some work out of the project? And most assuredly, we had not.

"The Driveway Place," as everybody shorthanded it, became the hot topic around the Hog Trough's big, round table. Come to think of it, it was probably also the hot topic at the Hell-in-a-Handbasket Saloon, Bark's Tavern, the Ladies' Gun Club, and the private rooms at Miss Fitz's Academy. Well, maybe not the private rooms at Miss Fitz's where people were ... er, otherwise occupied.

Still ... nobody wanted to venture up that driveway to see what was really going on. Us in our Carhartts. Them in their 100 percent sustainably grown no-harm-to-the-rainforest whatevers. Ne'er the twain shall meet. Once in a while, a few of them would come shop at Sassy Frassy's. Or they might stop in and inform the owners of the Bon Mot that ice cream savagely exploits helpless members of the bovine species. But our narrow gazes followed them everywhere they went around town. And they mostly conducted their business then skedaddled.

But curiosity, though it may kill cats, is life's breath to human beings. Finally, egged on by the others, Bob-the-Nerd and I got in his battered Honda one day and headed up there to say our howdies to the new neighbors. We got chosen, I do believe, because (again in the words of Carty), "You two are about as strange as they are in y'r own ways. B'sides, if them Gaia-lovin' airheads give any trouble, you two are less likely to shoot 'em than some of us."

Carty had a point there. So off Bob and I went, more than a little apprehensive about what we might encounter out there in the vast emptiness, so far from town.

Chapter 2
A Fight

"Hey! You can't bring those up here!"

Uh oh. We'd barely gotten out of Bob's Honda and our visit to the Mysterious Driveway Place was already going wrong. The skinny young man who rounded the corner of a building to greet us pointed at our sidearms. The look on his face said we were lepers who'd forgotten to ring our little warning bells and shout "Unclean!"

"Violence," he informed us, puffing himself up bravely as he approached, "is against our principles."

Bob and I looked around to see who was getting violent. We didn't see a hostile-looking soul. Meanwhile, the young man in the stone-washed jeans and Huarache sandals continued to glare at sweet old peaceable us.

"Um. Well. Hello to you, too," I stammered. I know. I shouldn't have been surprised by the young man's reaction. But in Hardyville, carrying a sidearm is so much a part of life that we forget the rest of the world finds it scary.

"Bob?" I asked under my breath, "What do you think we should do?"

"Sorry," Bob-the-Nerd said to the young man. "Your property, your rules. If you have a firearms storage area, we'll ...?" Somehow, this remark upset the young man even more. Now, several other young men and women began to gather around him. Others, we noticed, came out of the buildings but—seeing our armament—hung back.

"... we'll ... uh, how about we just lock the guns in my trunk? Is that okay with you, Claire? Is that okay with you ...?" He left a verbal space for the young man to introduce himself. Who'd ever have thought geeky Bob would be the diplomat?

"Thomas," said the young man. "And yes. Thank you. Please lock the guns away. Then you can tell us what you want."

Bob and I both unbuckled our holsters, moving slowly so as not to alarm the deer-like starers off at the margins. By tacit agreement, neither of us mentioned our concealed back-up pieces. When the visible hardware rested in the locked trunk, Thomas, still standing stiffly without so much as extending a hand to shake, asked, "Now, may I ask who you are and why you're here?"

Bob and I offered names and hands, which Thomas and one or two of the others gingerly accepted. You could almost see their efforts not to wipe the contagion of us off afterward. Nat Lyons traded with these people? Hard to believe.

"We just wanted to meet the new neighbors," I said. "We're from down in Hardyville, but we've seen some of you at Nat's Grocery Barn and thought it was time to say hello."

Their tightly wound springs still didn't relax.

"And," I went on, "If you're the people who grow those fantastic veggies, I want to say thanks and congratulate you. It's wonderful to have healthy, locally grown produce." Yes, that was pride and the beginning of smiles I saw on their faces. "And maybe you could even give us a little tour of your operation?"

It took a while. But eventually they decided we couldn't shoot them and weren't going to bite them. Thomas and a couple of the others agreed to show us around. It really was quite an operation. Quite a place, actually.

It was a weird combination of do-it-yourself primitiveness and "Boy, somebody spent a whole lot of money up here."

The housing—must have been enough for 20 or 30 people at least—was mostly earth-ship and similar, built into hillsides. Picture Hobbiton from Jackson's film version of *Fellowship of the Ring* and well, take away all the pretty green and flowers, add a lot of rocks and dirt, and you've pretty much got it. Some of the 20-to-30 were still working collaboratively on one of the last of the houses, sweating like honest men and women in the sun. Even a handful of little kids were helping out and having fun rolling recycled tires into place so the most sturdy adults could pound dirt into them to create the earthship walls.

But the very scale of the thing spoke of impressive funding.

Judging by the location of their wind farm they held a lot of land. And yes, I did say wind farm, not just one old high-in-the-sky propeller like a lot of Hardy County ranchers have. They had a whole miniature wind farm that was on a hilltop some considerable distance away. They said yes, they really did own that much land. Actually, they didn't say "own." I think it was "are entrusted with." Anyhow, the wiring alone needed to bring the power from that wind farm into the homestead area must have been pricey, even if they did dig the ditches and run all the conduit themselves.

Wind power was only part of their energy system. Several big solar arrays stood on trackers that followed the sun, and those arrays sent power into several very expensive DC-to-AC inverter/chargers and a tremendous bank of batteries. But, they said, they'd gotten the batteries as surplus inventory of a struggling company and saved a ton on them.

The biggest feature of The Driveway Place—which Bob and I now learned was the Emma Goldman Arts Co-op and Biodiverse Living Center—was its greenhouses. Talk about vast. Yeah. Vast. Their huge, hand-built native stone bases were set a few feet into the earth, but their walls and tops gathered the sun—with artful shades to block the burning heat of summer and coatings to retain heat in winter. And in those greenhouses, they grew ... everything. It was awesome. Everything.

And they used heirloom seeds, in defiance of all the big agri-businesses that are trying to force the entire world to buy their hastily created, imperfectly tested genetically altered product. They planted heirloom. They saved heirloom. They told us they contributed heirloom to other organizations and small farmers.

After showing us most everything, I noticed they carefully led us around the perimeter of the last and largest greenhouse (avoiding giving us any glimpse inside) to display their modest attempt at a fruit-and-nut orchard downslope.

Well, good luck with an orchard in this climate and soil, I thought. But I had to admit they were doing everything right. A homemade irrigation system carried water by gravity-feed from a cistern the size of a small city water tank down to the trees, which sat in wide catch-basins. Vast screens (are you getting tired of me saying "vast," here?) kept deer and other destructive beasties at bay while still letting in light.

Definitely an impressive place. You know, maybe we were fools to avoid these people, I thought. They had a lot of skills and knowledge that fit right in with Hardyville. Heck, they know a lot more about solar and wind power than some of us townies who've been spoiled by the small coal-fired generating plant in the next valley north. We might be able to get along with these neighbors. Well, except for the ninnyhammer attitude toward firearms. But that could change, in time.

I was feeling optimistic.

Silly me.

Only one thing The Emma Goldman Arts Co-op and Biodiverse Living Center seriously lacked (aside from any sign of "arts" that is). And Bob, of course, was the first to spot it. Or not spot it. No telephones. No computers. No communications technology at all.

"Not even Windows Vista?" Bob squeaked when he realized that the piles of paper heaped around the various little offices and work stations were the form of communications between the co-op and the outside world. "No Internet? No LAN? No wireless? Not even something as primitive as a sneaker net?"

After his moment of shock, Bob spotted the vast void of potential. His inner geek sparked to life. As Hardyville's one-and-only vendor of all things computerish, he darn near pranced with excitement. "You know, I could set you up with wireless," he enthused. "And you've got a half-dozen perfect places for a satellite dish. And even if all you could afford is old machines, I could help you get started by installing Ubuntu ..."

Poor Bob was so busy waving his arms around and mentally building their brand-new computer system that he couldn't see what I saw. Thomas's expression darkened. He glared at Bob. Then at me. The other two young men pulled back like snails into their shells. Maybe we should have brought those leper bells, after all.

"Technology," Thomas Pronounced (with capital-P and all), "is the manifestation and propagation of corporate neo-Fascism. Computers are an assault weapon that kills the mind instead of the body."

Bob froze, dumbfounded. Thomas went on. "You and people like you threaten the life of this very community, in fact the planet herself, with your materialistic, globalized ..."

Before he could go on too much longer in that vein, Bob pulled himself up to the full grandeur of his 5'7" and 125 pounds and Proclaimed right back, "And people like you are complete &^%$#ing ignoramuses. You don't know what you're talking about. You use all this computerized energy-generation technology, then you have the brass to say computers are evil? There's no such thing as a tool that's evil all by itself. Not a computer, not a fire-arm, not a &^%$#ing hammer or a brick or an Internet, you half-assed, bigoted ..."

"Guys. Guys!" I pleaded. But it was too late. Mr. Violence is Against Our Principles and Mr. Bantam-Weight Computer Geek bristled at each other, about to come to blows.

Then...

"What's happening here? What's going on, Thomas?" We all stopped. We all turned. The same voice, now just a little incredulous, piped, "Bob ...? Claire ...?"

And there stood Dora-the-Yalie with a pencil behind her ear, a sheaf of file folders in her hand, and a very authoritative frown on her face.

Chapter 3
Hardy County Discovery

"Dora!" I cried—and rushed to embrace her. Thomas and Bob backed off from their argument. The frown faded from Dora-the-Yalie's face as she set down her clipboard and opened her arms for a hug.

"What are ...?" I almost asked, "What are you doing here?" But of course Dora would be here. Where else would she be, assuming she hadn't hot-footed it back to the civilities of New Haven or snuggled herself down in the lefty comforts of Boulder, Boston, or Berkeley? Naturally she'd be at the Emma Goldman Arts Co-op and Biodiverse Living Center.

"But really," I exclaimed, "what are you doing here—clipboard and pencil behind the ear and all? Do you run this place?"

"Nobody runs this place, Claire," Dora corrected, her tone suggesting I'd just praised Dick Cheney at a meeting of militant mothers of Iraq-War dead. "It's an experiment in pure community empowerment. But I do help keep track of the size of the crop and its eventual destinations. Thus the pencil."

She plucked it from behind her ear and laid it down next to her clipboard on a nearby recycled barnwood table (never mind that the "primitive" wood was probably a pricey commodity trucked in from a yuppie auction house in Vermont on a semi-truck whose emissions wiped out entire species of adorable polar fauna with every mile).

Bob had come up by then. He refrained from hugging, but seemed boyishly glad to see Dora, as well. He grinned, "Your friend Carty sends you greetings. Or would have, if he'd have known."

"Oh, I'm sure." Dora rolled her eyes.

"Yeah, well maybe he did add a few words like 'twit' and 'airhead liberal' to the greeting. But you know, from Carty, that's still pretty good." We all laughed. But then the questions tumbled out. We were dying to know more about her, about the co-op, and about what became of ex-councilman Dan White, in whose Toyota Prius and company she had fled Hardyville last winter.

She gave answers as best she could, though our questions outran her energy.

158

Finally, I had to ask it. I had to blurt the one question my mother taught me polite young ladies never ask: "Who's paying for all this, Dora? There must be at least a couple million dollars invested here."

"And none of it spent in Hardyville," Bob pointed out.

"Yes, well," Dora stammered. "Um ... Hardyville was charging a sales tax at the time building got underway. With the Republic of Montana only a few miles up the road with no sales tax ... um ...." Um indeed. An interesting little footnote to our former town governators' assertions that their new tax would "help" the town. Then she found her courage. "Besides, Hardyville hasn't exactly been friendly territory. Downright hostile, I'd say. We don't owe the town any business, do we?"

For a second, it looked as if another fight was about to cloud over and produce lightning. I was hoping, instead, to find a way back to the question I so itchily wanted answered. Then Bob, looking through the windows for any possible way out of conflict, spotted the one place Thomas had avoided showing us and asked what in other places might have proved to be an even more impolite question: "So what's in that huge greenhouse that those other idiots didn't want us to see?"

"C'mon," smiled Dora. "I'll show you."

Thomas scowled. But she assured him, "It's okay. We can trust these people."

Meanwhile, far away in Mordor-On-the-Potomac ...

Deep in the bowels of A Nameless Federal Agency (ANFA), a statistical analyst shoved his glasses up his acne-pocked nose and adjusted the ink-stained pocket protector over his heart. He hunched just inside his boss's door, tremulously waiting to be recognized.

"What is it?" the Big Man finally boomed. Not The Big Man, of course; but the Big Man below The Big Man who answered to the Really Big Man—who was actually, due to political correctness, a Hispanic-surnamed woman of African-Irish descent who walked with a limp. Anyhow, the quaking analyst approached the Pretty High Up the Hierarchy of the Great Apes guy, laid a stack of printouts on a corner of the Big Man's vast continent of a desk, and began mumbling an explanation.

"Well, you see, sir. Um. I requested this meeting because I have a sort of oddball little hobby. I mean ... not really a hobby exactly, because of course I'd do that only on my personal time. This is work-related. But it's a special curiosity of mine, sir, and I hope you don't mind me having a special curiosity, do you? It makes the work go a little more ... er, what I mean to say is ..."

"If you mean to say something, say it."

"Um. Well, sir. Yes. Sorry, sir. It's just that it takes a little explaining how I found what I'm about to show you and why it's so important."

"Explain then. But keep it short. Or I won't be listening."

"Oh, sir. Not meaning to be presumptuous, but I think once you grasp the importance of what I discovered, you *will* be listening."

The Big Man leaned back into the embrace of his Big Chair and waved a hand, telling the analyst to continue. He'd have chomped on a fat, unlighted cigar, had such items not become cause for dismissal, triggers for mental-health counseling, and roadblocks in the way of a future run for Congress.

"So. You see, I have this hob ... interest in the statistics of some of the country's least populated regions. Other analysts prefer the demographics of metropolitan statistical areas—busy, busy, busy, you see. But I've always enjoyed places where things move at a slower pace. The truly fascinating statistics stand out a little more against such background, you know?"

The Big Boss apparently didn't know. Or care. He flapped his hand more impatiently.

But now the analyst was not to be hurried. He had hit his stride, gained his confidence, and was beyond intimidation. He knew that he—obscure, unimportant little he, who drank exactly 1.75 cups of coffee before the morning's first coffee break, and knew the precise value of the 1918 Curtiss Jenny stamp (both the inverted and the correctly printed versions, used, unused, and hinged)—was about to make the kind of governmental history that the Big Man, no matter what his eventual career, could never dream of. After his initial stumbles, he was going to make the most of his moment in the sun.

"Um ... as I was saying. Statistics. The number of board-feet of lumber produced in Granite County, Montana, in June 2003. The average age of married women in Durango, Colorado, vs. the average age of single men of Finnish descent in Naselle, Washington. You understand. Intriguing. Highly amusing. But also potentially valuable to the right federal agency. Never know when something new needs regulating, or some new group can be found to be eligible for a subsidy or a social program, right? Ahem.

"Well ... several years ago, I detected the largest statistical empty space I'd ever seen within the bounds of the fifty states. Statistically speaking, nothing was coming out of that area. I mean nothing. No records on the number of chickens processed in the third quarter of 1999. No gross adjusted income figures for Latina females over the age of 40. No applications for social security by retiring Caucasian men with 12th-grade educations. In fact ... no applications for social security at all. No applications for food stamps, no federal contracts, no grant proposals, no federally subsidized student loans, no applications for federal employment, nothing. Not even a single income-tax return! Imagine that! And this

160

is a large area, too, sir. Three thousand six hundred and one point two-four square miles, in total.

"At first I thought perhaps I'd stumbled upon a federally designated wilderness area. Nothing else could possibly account for such a total absence of statistical data. But even a wilderness area has its managers and its data on wildlife, climate, and what-not. I checked, nevertheless. And checked. And checked. This area is simply one vast statistical and reporting void. Sir, it's as if the United States of America has a hole in the middle, sixty miles long and wide. It simply doesn't exist."

The Big Man chomped on his even more non-existent cigar and looked both impatient and intrigued. "So what? So what?" he demanded. "Get to the point."

"Well, sir, in part that is the point. As you know, sir, federal agencies always require new markets to serve. Otherwise, they reach a saturation level and their growth stagnates. Can't have our valuable federal agencies stagnating, now can we? Three thousand six hundred and one point two-four square miles must certainly have within it much to tax, regulate, and … um, service. But with nothing and no activity there, no apparent natural resources, no communities to join in partnership with, no roads to maintain, no military bases, no meth labs to eradicate, with no one asking for Washington's help … well, you see the problem. No 'entry point,' so to speak, by which federal assistance and enlightened management could reach the area."

"Hmmph," said the Big Man.

"Until, sir, my research brought me this."

The analyst—no, now let's give him the capital letters he has so richly earned in the hearts of his fellow bureaucrats and the field personnel of all expansive agencies everywhere—The Analyst—whipped a single photocopy from his stack of many on the desk. He did it with flair. With insouciance. With élan. Even with a Cyrano-style panache he hadn't previously known himself capable of. He spun it to face the Big Man and launched it on a zephyr of air across the vast mahogany terrain.

The Big Man leaned forward. He looked down. He regarded the document so dramatically presented.

It was a request, dated the previous year, for federal aid for a local police force. Perfectly routine. It had been duly signed and submitted in triplicate by the legitimately constituted government of the municipality in question. Exactly according to procedure. It had been approved and the requested funds and equipment dispatched without further consideration. No doubt the paper had then been stamped, filed, and forgotten—until The Analyst and his mind-bendingly dull hobby turned it up again.

But it was from a town right in the middle of the three thousand six hundred and one point two-four square miles.

A town called Hardyville.

The Big Man leaned further over his continental desk. He beamed across at the analyst (who felt himself shrinking back to lower-case as he stood pinned in the boss's gaze). The smile curved The Big Man's lips almost to his ears. Somehow, though, it never reached his eyes, which remained as calculating as the wheels of a slot machine

"Hardyville, eh? Sounds as if that berg—and its thirty-six hundred square miles—needs our help. Good work ... er, Howard."

"Harold, sir. It's Harold Perkins. Harold F. Perkin ..."

"Yeah. Thanks, Howard. ANFA sincerely appreciates your efforts."

The Big Man reached out both arms and pulled the stack of printouts toward his chest. "Don't worry. I'll take it from here."

"And here," Dora announced, opening a door in the bermed west side of the giant greenhouse, "Is our most important crop."

The herbal aroma would have been unmistakable if we'd have been blindfolded. With eyes wide open in marvel, Bob and I entered a towering jungle of *Cannabis sativa* and more squat, broad-leafed, but equally fragrant *Cannabis indica* hybrids.

"Medical marijuana. Home grown and distributed to dispensaries throughout the west."

And soon to become the target for the first direct federal "help" ever provided to Hardy County.

Chapter 4
Big Men

"So that's what pays for all this land and development!" Bob hooted, picking up the impoliteness banner right where I had dropped it and soldiering boldly on. He and I stood amid the co-op's green sea of cannabis and simply boggled.

"Oh, no!" Dora insisted, recoiling from the word 'development'—and something else. "No. This is not our profit center," she said, sounding more like the Yale grad than like the Earth Mother of a commune.

"This is our mission." Oh. Maybe I spoke too soon on that Earth Mother thing.

"We don't sell our medical cannabis," she insisted. "We give it away."

I looked around, astonished. "But this must be worth ... I mean, if it were on TV it would be at least that week's 'world's biggest ever' bust. You give all this bounty away?"

"Yes. To ease pain, ease nausea, ease muscle spasms and other sufferings. To try to make the world the kind of place we'd like to live in. And for public consciousness-raising."

"Holeee!" What do you say to somebody who's just told you they're giving away millions of dollars worth of anything, just to make the world—in their view—a kinder place? I couldn't think of a worthy word.

Given that no noble sentiments immediately bubbled to my lips, I continued the impoliteness campaign, instead. "C'mon then. Who pays for all this now that we know it costs you even more than we realized? Who? Whose daddy has the big bux? Which communista shed his prep-school blazer to play hippie anarchist bum with you?"

"It's not like that. Really it's not, Claire. Most of these people are dirt-poor idealists. Maybe they came from the families of college professors or book editors. But nobody here is just playing in a parent's big sandbox."

"How, then? Foundation grants? A rich benefactor to causes? What?"

"I shouldn't say. At my level I shouldn't even know. But I've heard it's the latter."

"Names. Give me names." I noted the mention of 'my level' and made a mental note that these folks sounded fairly elitist and hierarchical for members of the equalité, fraternité set.

"Claire, really. Don't you think you're taking this too far? Haven't you ever heard the expression 'MYOB'? As in *mind your own business?"*

"Sorry. You're right. It's just that ... well, Dora, c'mon. People like us—even people like you—don't get to rub shoulders with this kind of money in most of our lifetimes—the kind of money it took to establish this place. Now here it is, all that money being used to fund organic kumquats and medical dope? Honestly, Dora, this is more than private business. This is a *story*."

She snorted at my writerly instincts, not (in my humble opinion) valuing them anywhere near enough.

While I'd been badgering poor Dora, Bob had wandered off to one side of the greenhouse, where another native-stone and trucked-in-from-exotic-locales "natural" wood counter held packages—quaintly brown-paper wrapped and ready to go. These were no anonymously bromidic brown-paper wrappers, though. These were old-timey unbleached paper bags with a little cellophane window for viewing the product. They were sealed at the top with a cute sticker in the shape of a cannabis leaf. They had a Ye Olde Fashioned kind of label. And a brand name. And an address.

Goldman's Golden Medicinal Blend. Hardyville, USA.

Hardyville. They had put our hidden home's name on packages for all the world to see. King-sized packages of an herb illegal in all the imperial realm surrounding us.

"You're mad," I gasped. "You're stark, ranting, chained to the wall in a straight-jacket with a Hannibal Lecter-style face-mask on you mad. Even Carty couldn't imagine you could do anything like this. Putting your location on packages of cannabis??? That you ship out into the real world???"

"But Claire ..."

"Mad. Hearing little voices in your head telling you to take the guns to the post office today mad. Voting for Republicans or Democrats mad. Syphilis eating out the vitals of your brain mad."

"Claire, stop it. It's not that bad. Cannabis is legal here in Hardy County. It's legal where we're sending it to help people. It's plain to every thinking person now that it should be legal everywhere, at least for life-saving, pain-relieving uses. It's okay. The time is right for us. What could possibly go wrong?"

I stared at her in disbelief. Could she have really lived in Hardyville almost as long as I have and not know exactly what could go wrong? I pierced her brain with the sharpness of my incredulity.

Defiantly, she met my gaze. For all of five seconds. Then she turned away.

"Well ... I know," she agreed, weakening under the hypodermic needle of my scorn. "I admit I disagreed with that particular decision. Some of these people are a little too starry-eyed. Just a little. But they have good intentions."

Yeah. And we all know where *those* lead, don't we?

Meanwhile, back in Mordor-On-the-Potomac...

In the fetid bowels of A Nameless Federal Agency (ANFA), the Big Man lounged in his Big Chair, perusing a pile of paperwork. Very pleased with his own master detective skills. Oh yes, and mildly grateful to that groveling little underling, the statistical analyst, who had delivered the paperwork. Such people had their uses, he supposed.

Though he couldn't have a big, aromatic cigar in the office, he could still sneak in a bottle of Tullamore Dew. He held up a glass of the golden liquid, roiled it in the light, and was mightily pleased with life.

Through his own wits, the Big Man had discovered 3600 unexploited and unimproved square miles over which, for the moment, he held a wholly imaginary, yet theoretically kingly power. The potency lay dormant within the pile of paper before him.

Question was, what to do with all that power?

Pass the information upward to his own boss? Not a chance! That move just led to a whole chain of Big Men. He knew those ruthless bastards would take credit for his own discovery. He didn't even give a serious minute's thought to passing the secret of the missing 3600 square miles out west up the food chain to the big sharks.

No, this pile of paperwork was an unequaled bargaining tool. Nobody had held this much bargaining power in Washington since Jefferson's big land buy or Seward's Folly. And look how those moves had turned out. The thing to do was use this power. Very gradually, and very wisely. To shepherd it. To let a little out here and there, when it most benefited him.

The trick was not to try to control the land or its people like a king or lord of old. That was ... well, old hat. Unthinkable, too, when the entire might of the American Empire already surrounded the terrain in question. And besides, it was unnecessary. Control didn't reside in holding a territory in your fist. Not in the modern world of realpolitik. It resided in *influence*.

Sooner or later everyone in Washington would know about this Hardyville berg and its still-mysterious surroundings. Every agency and directorate would swoop in like vultures over hoof-and-mouth-diseased cows. That was inevitable. But for a limited, strategic time, the advantage—and all the advantages of that advantage—would be his alone.

True, this nameless little hole in the country wasn't even remotely the size of Jefferson's Louisiana Purchase or Seward's Alaska. But things had changed since those days. Now, land wasn't so free-and-easy plentiful.

Mineral wealth could be precious—especially if the markets could be manipulated—or regulated—strategically. And government ... now there was the big change. Government didn't just give land away anymore, or sell it on the cheap to any member of the riff-raff as they had before the twentieth century. Government *managed* land. And all its resources. Forever and ever. Managed it with a growing alphabet soup of agencies and regulations. Same with people. Management. That was the key.

Yes, forget the crude old methods of conquest. Times are more sophisticated now.

Who were these people, these Hardyvillians? Hicks, obviously—even if somebody in their city government was literate enough to write a grant application. Dust-brained cowboys who probably didn't care about anything but getting drunk and laid on a Saturday night. Their inbred children would be in desperate need of government schooling, no doubt with a heavy dose of special education. These townspeople would be easy pickings except for one thing. One big thing.

All those cretinous cowboys, all those descendants of people too stupid to make it in the oil fields of Oklahoma or the wheat fields of North Dakota, had guns. They *always* had guns.

Lots and lots and lots of guns.

Which didn't mean Washington couldn't kick the crap out of them. It just meant moving slowly. Surreptitiously. Ease in until it felt like you'd always been there—and they couldn't live without you. Give them equal but unpredictable doses of raw power and velvet-gloved kindness. Tell them even the rough part of the power is "for their own good."

Then all those guns would stay harmlessly in the closet. Even while the cowboys' lives were put under micromanagement. Just don't target the guns directly. That irritates the cowboys. And it's so unnecessary when all you really have to do is disarm their minds.

The Big Man pondered the many, many agencies that could have use for information about 3600 un-taxed, un-regulated, un-aided, un-mined, un-managed, un-schooled, un-plucked, un-dependent miles. The many agencies he could benefit while benefiting himself.

Some agencies gain power by giving. That is, they give away others' money while retaining a fat 2/3 share for themselves. Others gain power by taking. That is, they take homes, land, vehicles, and bank accounts in the various wars-on-this-or-that and pocket the profits without criminal charges or the messiness of trials. Both givers and takers were needed for control. You just had to be wise in introducing the balance.

Some strategists would advise first offering benefits. But people who aren't frightened aren't impressed by the good government can do. They don't need saving until you give them something to be saved from. These city fathers had already emerged from their historic obscurity to cry for help—for training and equipment for cops. They had the beginnings of fear. Good. Now, goose up the fear, then be the only power around both strong and humanitarian enough to fight the menace *du jour.*

As John Wayne once said in the days of Vietnam, "If you've got them by the balls, their hearts and minds will follow."

He glanced at the map that showed a couple of low-travel state highways generally disappearing into the rocky hills of a basin-and-range area in the northwest Rockies. Funny nobody had ever questioned that before. He looked at the satellite photos, which showed, much more clearly, an odd-looking little town at the intersection of those now-you-see-them-now-you-don't highways. Funniest-looking little town he'd ever seen, come to think of it. But still, it was fundamentally a town like any other in the west, with bars and feed stores on the main street. With outlying ranches, some more prosperous than not.

Needing the iron fist before the velvet glove, it was only natural the Big Man thought of three agencies—or rather, ambitious heads of agencies who might be willing the help an earnest man on his way to the top. The IRS. The Bureau of Alcohol, Tobacco, Firearms, Explosives and What-not. And the Drug Enforcement Administration. Surely, the pickings for all three should be good in this Hardyville place.

But the Big Man reminded himself: Leave guns alone this time. And the IRS ... well, they'd be in business forever. But the monster of the moment—the one the rubes of Hardyville needed saving from even if they didn't know it yet—was Evil Drugs. Drugs. Seducing your children and causing people of those races you no longer openly admit are dangerously inferior to run amuck in the streets. Drugs. As exemplified by snaggle-toothed homicidal villains building meth labs next to your daughter's nursery school. Yes, that was the one to take best advantage of, right here and right now.

And surely out there in that 3600 nearly empty square miles there was some field of ditchweed growing unnoticed on some rancher's roadside. Grab the multi-million dollar ranch of a snobby eccentric. Or a pot grow in the cellar of some illegal Mexican immigrant. The locals would just read the newspaper—if they were even that literate—and tell themselves they were sure glad it was only "people like that" who got in trouble. Still, they'd understand on a gut level that trouble can be delivered to any door, on any night.

Get them good and scared. Then reach out the benevolent helping hand.

Yes, the DEA should be first to get in on the 3600 square miles of fresh pickings. But first, he'd send some scouts of his own in for a confidential look-around.

The Big Man gazed around at his walls full of plaques. He beamed, picturing a far grander office and a bustling, obsequious staff that never contradicted his opinion. Maybe ... Just maybe the idea of a career in the U.S. House of Representatives wasn't aiming high enough. No, not for a man of his talents. Nowhere near high enough.

He picked up the phone. It's too bad, from a writer's point of view, that it was the modern kind, with buttons, instead of an old rotary like a character in a Hitchcock film might dial. Because the appropriate expression here is: wheels began to turn. And wheels within wheels.

Chapter 5
Beneath the Wheel

In Mordor-on-the-Potomac, ponderous wheels began to grind. At first they churned as slowly as the monster gears controlling the gates of Middle-Earth's most hellish domain. But instead of Sauron's reeks and seeps, these wheels churned through the suffocating tar of bureaucracy.

But however slowly they moved, they rolled toward Hardyville, discovered by the outside world at last.

The Big Man knew there was no way he could send employees of A Nameless Federal Agency (ANFA) to investigate this Hardyville berg on his agency food-chain authority. No, he dare not tip his hand. He had to keep knowledge of these 3600 unplucked square miles as close to his shirt as a handful of aces. Besides, even if he disguised the trip as a fact-finding mission about the condition of Asian-American women in the gaming industry or the growth of wheat-worm (was there such a thing as "wheat-worm"?) at latitudes north of Aurora, Colorado, getting budget approval would take forever. So no, this was not going to be an official mission.

With future returns in view, the Big Man put up his own money (though he did manage to get reimbursed for a thousand dollars of it as per diem for attending a non-existent multi-agency conference on the demographics of the grandchildren of Norwegian immigrants in Bemidji, Minnesota). He sent his brother-in-law, his darling baby sister (wife of said in-law), and their brood of tax deductions on a paid vacation in the West.

Brother-in-Law was no slouch. He might not be able to hold a job for more than a month. But if there were drugs or any other sort of trouble to be found in this Hardyville place, or anywhere in that giant statistical hole in the country (that hole that was surely filled with things crying out to be regulated, taxed, controlled, and banned), Bro-in-Law would find them—and be right in the middle of them.

The investment paid off.

On the vast plain of the Big Man's desk now lay an empty brown paper sack. It had a little window for viewing the (former) contents. The aroma of cannabis still wafted from its little paper pores. And for the second time the Big Man looked upon his desk and encountered the name Hardyville.

He should have considered—he really should have—that the kind of place where people are comfortable with putting their logo and location on a half-pound sack of weed is going to be ... well, a little unusual to deal with. But if he gave any thought to that at all, he merely snorted, "What a pack of idiots."

"Idiots" was perhaps true of the naive product distributors in question. But that begs the question. The Big Man did not understand that people in Hardyville, and by tradition its 3600 square-mile surroundings, think just a hair of a tad differently than most of the folks who reside within the governmental tumor metastasizing through the nation around them. And that different thinking is not so much a matter of degree, but of kind.

On the other hand ... as you and I know, Hardyville was changing. So maybe the Big Man was right to be cavalier.

Regardless, the wheels of power now began to break loose and turn somewhat faster. The Big Man turned to his ambitious acquaintance high atop the Drug Enforcement Administration. At a meeting in the DEA man's office, he showed him the bag—but did not as yet reveal any of his closely-held secrets about Hardyville's location and importance. He explained broadly what his chemically loquacious in-law had discovered—about an isolated but obviously profitable drug-growing commune in the west, a little town miles away just waking out of a long economic snooze. A whole lot of nothing.

"The place has no government to speak of," he explained to his DEA counterpart (thinking, Hm. Suppose he might someday be a possibility to share my ticket as VP?) "All they've got is a sheriff. Couple of deputies. But their SWAT team was disbanded after some sort of incompetence. They don't even have a mayor or a county manager. The drug dealers are left-wing anti-corporate types—peace, love, and no guns—and the townies can't stand them. It's a pushover. And my confidential informant ..." (He liked that term, having heard it on cop shows.) " ... tells me we could be talking another 'world's biggest-ever pot bust.'"

The DEA man scrutinized his own "confidential informant"—the Big Man from ANFA sitting across the desk. *What the hell did ANFA stand for, anyhow?* the DEA man wondered. *And what did it do, again?* He never could remember. Even after someone told him, ANFA's mission could somehow never stay in his head for long.

Oh well. No matter. The man now sitting in his office, an acquaintance from dozens of blindingly dull think-tank evenings, might be from some damn-near nameless nothing of an agency. But it was an agency that controlled a lot of data. And the guy was smart. Very smart. *Hm,* the DEA man thought, *Might someday be a possible VP on my ticket.*

"Bust of the week," he shrugged, waving negligently toward the dozens of news photos and clippings on his walls. At least half a dozen of them trumpeted biggest-ever" busts of the last 30 years. "Useful. But that's old news. How much do you think there is in asset forfeiture?"

No, thought the Big Man, scrutinizing Mr. DEA anew. *Too ambitious. Too dangerous. He'd be my assistant secretary of Agriculture. At most.*

The Big Man from ANFA began to dole out snippets of information, making sure to share enough to be useful but hold back plenty for the future. Without a word being uttered on the topic, he also made sure he guaranteed himself both public anonymity and plenty of buzz within the DEA about being some unspecified sort of good and useful friend to the Drug War. A political ally to be counted on.

And soon enough, the two anonymous bureaucrats had their agreement.

And once again, the wheels, freed of their burrs and their clogs of chaff, began to speed their turning. Now they spun at the velocity and with the weight of ... oh, let's say a tank's tread.

From many states and from a variety of lesser agencies, the federal anti-drug task force (although darned near big enough to be an invasion force) coalesced. From several directions, it prepared to converge on Hardy County. And specifically, to converge on the hapless, unarmed, and unprepared Emma Goldman Arts Co-op and Biodiverse Living Center.

Grim-faced men arrived at airports in Billings and Salt Lake City, fresh from eastern headquarters. They supervised the offloading of crates of gear. From National Guard armories in Casper and Cheyenne came armored personnel carriers and covered trucks bringing portable security barriers, tents, and communications gear.

On the roads, the HumVees rolled. Helicopters took to the skies to move to bases closer to the target.

Dynamic entry teams adjusted new HellStorm goggles and pondered their selection of riot shields and body armor. Recon teams and snipers packed their Ghillie suits. Men and women of the DEA, the Bureau of Land Management, and yes, even the National Park Service (believe it or not even the BLM and the National Park Service have armed-response units) cleaned their MP5 machine guns and zeroed their "deadly, long-range bolt-action sniper rifles" (which were, in this instance, actually deadly, long-range bolt-action sniper rifles).

But despite all the armor and weaponry, the first incursion into Hardy County was so covert nobody would even have recognized it as an invasion.

Around dusk one silent April evening, the first covert-action teams violated the borders of Hardy County, high up in the unpopulated mountains, unobserved. Down toward the red-rock valley they rolled in a convoy of anonymous, and innocuous-looking Jeeps and off-road vehicles, turning off road before reaching The Mysterious Driveway of the commune. Looking for all the world like innocent varmint hunters or plinkers (their serious gear stowed away in lockers in the backs of the vehicles), they deployed in a vast irregular circle for "Operation Firestorm" and began securing a perimeter on the hilltops around the far reaches of the Emma Goldman Arts Co-op and Biodiverse Living Center.

Then they waited.

Under cover of darkness, the more identifiable components of the operation began to move into place. By midnight, the rest of the teams and their support personnel were set up, blocking the long driveway that gave the only conventional vehicle access to the cannabis grow. The sleeping communards, their children, and even their dogs had no idea of the powers that were massing against them, down near the highway, too far away for them to see or hear.

Everything was in readiness before 1:00 a.m.—Zero Hour. The teams merely awaited the signal that was to come from command headquarters. Command HQ, in turn, awaited a signal from Washington.

The media were in place, too. Blow-dried throngs shivered in the spring cold and cast around in vain for an all-night latte stand, finding only tumbleweed and spiky greasewood bushes. They cracked lame jokes about the 30 mile-per-hour winds whipping sand across the sagebrush. ("No wonder nobody lives out here; they've all blown away.") But secretly many among the media worried that the winds would ruin their polished appearance and therefore their chances for advancement. While ambitious others speculated that the gale might help them appear more adventurous and therefore earn them plum assignments in future wars and picturesque disasters. Most didn't even know why they were there. But when the DEA hints "biggest ever" ... reporters follow, even if that means following into the biggest of Earth's many stinking armpits.

They all waited, network satellite trucks side-by-side with armored personnel carriers.

They waited a few hundred yards from the highway on which, at that hour, a lone car or a lonesome semi-truck passed infrequently. Invisible in the dark, the heavily armored teams and the heavily starched journalists shivered and joked, and awaited word to launch the assault on the compound.

But they were not quite as invisible as they intended.

———————————

Higher up, where the highway wound out of the cover of the pines and plunged into country marked by dark clumps of juniper and silvery clumps of sage, one of those lone cars, a veggie-diesel special, running somewhere close to empty, rounded a rock outcrop and began coasting downhill. Its road-weary driver didn't notice anything out of the ordinary. But suddenly one of the passengers in the back cried out:

"Whoa! Stop, man! Go back. Go back!"

The driver glanced toward the back seat, annoyed. Sleepy fellow passengers looked up groggily. They all glared at the speaker, a plump young man with a feeble fuzz of beard and a tee shirt that read "Official Anti-Globalist Slogan."

"What do you mean, go back?" the driver demanded. We don't have enough fuel to go back anywhere. Why?"

"Just back to that last turn!" insisted the young man, whose name was, to his eternal horror, Jasper F. (for Feldspar) Clarke. "I saw something."

"Yeah, well there's lots of something to see," muttered one of the others.

"Or lots of nothing."

"I'm serious. Go back. Just a few yards." As an afterthought (whose reasons even he didn't quite understand at the time) he added: "And douse the headlights."

The driver rolled his eyes at Jasper in the mirror. But he slowed, put the car in reverse, and slapped the lever, reducing the headlamps to parking lights. Car, road, and high desert disappeared into darkness. Through memory, feel, and the feeble glow remaining, the driver guided the car to a stop in a miniscule view turnout at the curve Jasper indicated.

All was darkness. Or was it?

"Over there," Jasper pointed.

For a moment, the other three saw nothing. Just the usual waning moon rising over the usual windblown desert bleakness. Then their eyes adjusted. Below, down where they knew the road to their very own home turned off from the highway, the four members of the Emma Goldman Arts Co-op and Biodiverse Living Center, returning from a round of travels that included a planning session for the Black Hills Hemp Hoe Down and a rousing riot against free trade in Chicago, caught the glint of moonlight—outlining dozens of vehicles and half a dozen trailers and temporary structures in silver.

The young men might have looked down their noses at modern communications technologies and disdained all the products of corporate globalism. But they were products of the TV age, nevertheless. They knew exactly what they were witnessing.

"Oh crap," said the driver.

———————————

At 1:54 a.m., precisely 54 minutes after the signal to launch Operation Firestorm was scheduled to arrive from Washington, an unlikely band of brothers staggered into Hardyville. Their feet were numbed from the cold. They were beat from walking several miles after the corn and peanuts powering their engine gave out.

They didn't look quite like themselves. Cowboy hats or baseball caps anchored their windblown hair (most of which had been hurriedly tucked up under the hats to disguise its length and in one case disguise its distinctly violet color). Their tee shirts were turned inside out, but if you looked closely you could still read, backwards, a couple of the slogans: "Meat is dead" and "Think globally. Act anti-globally." They shivered in the cold as they stumbled through the door of the Hell-in-a-Handbasket Saloon, one of the few businesses in town open at that dark hour.

"You've got to help us!" one of them cried to the handful of weary drunks and the one alert bartender behind the counter. "Our friends are in terrible trouble!"

The drunks barely raised bleary eyes. What little attention they gave the young men was less than friendly. Despite the cowboy-hat and backwards tee-shirt disguises, it was clear the young men who'd just flung themselves into the saloon were rather strange strangers.

The barkeep—Carty, subbing for his friend, who owned the joint but was off for a few days attending an advanced defensive shotgun course—finished swabbing a wet ring off the counter with a rag, wadded up a cocktail napkin and shot it into a wastebasket 10 feet away. He sized the newcomers up, quickly seeing past the native headgear and inside-out shirts. Then he leaned forward.

Resting his fists on the counter, muscles bulging, he loomed his big bald self over the scared-witless boys and drawled, "Okaaaay. So why is it now, exactly, that you think we should help you?"

Chapter 6
Minutemen

"Why should we help them?" I snapped, incredulous that anyone could doubt. "Why should we help them??? Because if what they say is true, feds—*feds!*—have invaded Hardy County! For the first time in history. Don't you get that? This isn't just a risk to them out there at the commune. This is a catastrophe for freedom!"

Marty Harbibi, the twit who provoked my swivet, snorted as he raised his cup of coffee. Janelle had opened the Hog Trough as a command center when word arrived in the middle of the night that feds had crossed our borders. But very darned few of us were sitting around sipping. We awaited word, awaited action. We were not just there to jawbone, despite a few people's (e.g. Marty's) inclinations.

We knew we had to act. And act against the most militant power on the entire globe—the U.S. government. The tension was almost unbearable.

"Yeah, yeah," Marty said. "I understand we gotta get rid of the feds. Sure. But hey ... first let 'em clean up a little trash for us." He rolled his eyes in the direction of the four scared communards, huddling at a corner table of the Hog Trough, trying to get warm after their mid-night dash through the desert to plead for our aid.

I wanted to leap across the room and throttle the idiot. Instead, I clenched my teeth and checked my silent cell phone once again, as if staring at it could force it to ring.

Fortunately, Marty Harbibi wasn't Hardyville. He wasn't even supposed to be here. Only the Minutemen and the communications crew (Bob-the-Nerd, Janelle, and yours truly) had been alerted. Others, like Marty, heard something and came for the show. The Bible doesn't make note of it, but it should: "The yammerheads will always be with thee."

No matter. Carty and four dozen Minutemen—Hardyville's version of a rapid-response team—had rushed to collect the heavy-duty militia weapons from the back room of Goodins' second-hand store. They added the weapons to their own impressive arsenal and sped toward the Emma Goldman Arts Co-op and Biodiverse Living Center in a pickup-truck convoy. They'd been on the road 15 minutes and must have been halfway to their destination, still not knowing exactly what the sit-rep was and therefore what plan they should follow.

Nobody knew anything beyond what the four shivering young men had told us. And all they knew, from creeping by on the highway hoping not to be spotted as the neo-hippie anarchist dope growers that they were, was that a small army of fed and state officers was blocking the driveway to their home.

We awaited a call from Nat, whose ranch bordered the commune. First to be alerted, 80-something Nat was out there on horseback right now, crossing silently overland, avoiding roads, trying to scope out the extent of the fed operation.

His report would determine what everybody did next. Who we would call. How many. What actions aroused Hardyvillians should take in the face of this unparalleled threat. It was like waiting for an asteroid to strike. The few of us left in the restaurant were numb from shock, tense with fear, blazing with anger, but most of all we were doing that truly horrible thing ... waiting. It brought out the worst in us.

We couldn't even warn those poor saps out there at the commune what was about to hit them. Cell phones? Ha! Not even a landline on the place. And if, heaven forbid, they had already been hit, they couldn't get word to us. Them and their damned disdain for 'the corrupting influence of technology'!

Damn Marty, damn the communards, but above all, damn the invading forces of unfreedom! I itched for action. Not the fighting kind. No, I dreaded that just as much as Marty no doubt did. Just give me some way to be useful. Give me any excuse to get out of Marty's presence and do something. Anything other than being stuck here.

Hey, wait a minute... Janelle had to man the Hog Trough's landline, and the coffee pots, at the Hog Trough. Bob had to stay connected to the wifi network. But I ...

I snatched up my cell phone. I could take Nat's call anywhere. At least anywhere a cell tower could find me.

"C'mon," I said to the four shell-shocked boys. "I think the Rocket Scientist has some veggie diesel at his place. We'll get a can of the stuff, take you to your car, then you can drive back out to the highway with me. We'll join up with Carty. We may need your help knowing who's who and what's going on." All four looked terrified at the prospect of going anywhere near the feds.

At that moment, the phone buzzed in my hand.

I looked at the clock. It was past 3:00 a.m. I punched the green button.

"Is this damn thing working?" Nat's voice crackled through the device. A cell phone had been foisted upon him, all unwilling, some months ago, after Hardyville's first government crisis. But he had never used it until now. "Did I push the right buttons?"

"Yes, Nat. Yes. I hear you. Now please. What do you see?"

"Nothin'."

"What???"

"Nothin'. There's a whole lotta people and 'nough equipment to invade a country, for sure. But all just millin' around like they're waitin' for a bus. Some of their sniper teams look to have fallen asleep."

What the hell was going on out there?

───────────────

"What the hell's going on out there??!!"

The field commander of Operation Firestorm, awaiting the official signal for action, had finally gotten his phone call from Washington. It came at 1:23 a.m. But it wasn't the expected go-ahead. The voice on the line boomed with the fury of a bureaucrat scorned.

The call was—though the field commander didn't know it—the last in a series that roused some Very Important Sleepers in Mordor-on-the-Potomac before reaching out and punching him.

First, the U.S. Secretary of State called the Attorney General and demanded, "What is this I hear about your drug people planning to raid some ... some commune or something out west?" (If you wonder how the Secretary of State knew, go read the footnote to this chapter.)

After hearing what his State Department colleague had to say, the Attorney General called his subordinate, the DEA Man, and barked, "Did you do any investigation? Do you have any idea who owns that place out there?"

"Of course," mumbled DEA Man. Some outfit called ... Anarchaos Holdings. We got the information from their corporate filings. We've already initiated the forfeiture actions based on ..."

"Well, let me tell you something you evidently didn't bother to learn ..."

And once he had been thoroughly pummeled by his boss, the DEA Man called the Big Man from A Nameless Federal Agency (ANFA)—the one who had given him the dope on this "biggest-ever" pot bust as a career-making prize. The Big Man, startled out of sleep and slapped in the ear by the voice on the phone, didn't call anybody. Except his cardiologist.

But the DEA Man kept making calls. Ultimately, he reached the cold, tired, wired, bored, impatient field commander for Operation Firestorm, shivering in the icy winds in the middle of some point-of-nowhere called Hardy County.

The DEA Man screamed at his subordinate. "You nincompoop! Did you do any homework before you decided to go ahead with your scheme?"

"I decided? My scheme? Hey, wait a ..."

"Anarchaos Holdings. If you'd traced that back through three layers of holding companies and a Belize-based lawyer, you'd have avoided the mess you've just plunged us into."

"What I just plunged who into? Damnit, you approved...! I've been freezing my butt off out here waiting for your ..." The field commander took a breath. He understood perfectly well that he was already screwed—already the designated fall guy for an operation which, for unknown reasons, had become a fiasco before it even began. Now it was a matter of finding out just how screwed he was.

"What the hell. What are you actually trying to tell me? Who owns Anarchaos Holdings that makes it such a big deal?"

"Jorge Delaval."

"Who?" Momentarily, the name didn't register.

The DEA Man sounded it out, as if teaching a slightly retarded child: "Hor-hay. Del-La-Val."

Then it penetrated the field commander's brain. And dropped like a boulder into his stomach. "Oh sh ...!"

Jorge Delaval. His face was in the newspapers at least once a week. Maybe not the important papers like the *Hardyville Independent* ("All the News and Sometimes Even Spelled Right"), but little rags like the *Post* and the *Times* and *USA Today*. Maybe his name wasn't spoken much on radio station HRDY, featuring whatever anybody showed up to play from their personal collection of old 78s, 33s, and 45 RPMs. But on NPR and CNN he was a household word.

Jorge Delaval. Citizen of the world. Heir to one of Europe's most mysterious fortunes, which he enlarged every day. If he wasn't appearing at the coronation of a decadent European monarch, he was romancing Italy's prima ballerina on his liner-sized yacht. If he wasn't on his yacht, you could be sure he was attending a U.N. conference on the global economy. Or meeting with the gnomes at Davos.

When not in Davos, or the Hague, or Zurich, or Monte Carlo, or Dubai, he could be seen indulging in his favorite hobby. No, not polo. Not baccarat. Not foreign currency manipulation (although he did find that mildly diverting). No, Jorge Delaval's hobby was improving the world. Everywhere people suffered, the Delaval fortune eased pain. Delaval funded AIDs relief in Africa, tsunami relief in Malaysia, poverty relief in Mississippi. Lately he had branched out into long-term world-saving causes, like funding heirloom seed banks to preserve mankind's historic foodstocks against careless depredations of agri-biz.

Millions considered the man a living treasure.

178

Delaval had one other cause that (some people thought) tarnished his halo. Specifically, he funded U.S. state-level initiatives to decriminalize cannabis.

First, he intended to see cannabis made legal for medical use. Then for everyone who ever suffered a pain. Eventually, he hoped, the pain of life itself would qualify as reason enough to use cannabis. He was an idealist, a self-appointed benefactor to mankind. That he was also positioning himself to become the Global Cannabis King once the herb was legalized (as he fully expected it to be, quite soon) was simply a minor sidelight. And he believed that. Truly.

Everybody at the DEA would have loved to see Jorge Delaval ground under the hooves of wild horses then dipped into a vat of hyperbolic acid. But to say that the man was untouchable would be like saying the Queen of England is a bit prim. Aside from his personal power and reputation, Delaval owned citizenship in several of those quaint, uniquely European nations that, while small enough to fit into a Texan's back pocket, could, upon a whim, topple banking systems, currencies, and stock markets from Namibia to Newark.

Jorge Delaval was, in short, a one-man international incident waiting to happen.

And the DEA had just triggered it.

———————————————

"So now what?" the field commander grumbled to the DEA Man in D.C. "You're gonna order us to call this off? With half the media in the country at our backs? How are we gonna explain that?"

"No, I'm not telling you to call the operation off. Yet. We've got to buy time. Save face. We've got to think our way out. I'm meeting with State, the General, DHS, and the Federal Reserve in 10 minutes, trying to divert an international crisis—and trying to save everybody's ass. In the meantime: send the helicopters back to base; we may need them to bring in damage control teams. But maintain a physical perimeter and beef up your public relations stance."

"And what the hell is my 'public relations stance' supposed to be?"

The DEA Man thought fast. "It's that ... that you're after the biggest marijuana crop ever grown but that ... they have hostages. Yeah. That's it. Tell the reporters the pot growers are using their children as human shields and they've threatened to blow themselves and the little darlings up if anybody storms the compound. So you can't go in exactly as planned. Tell 'em we're negotiating. That'll buy us some time. That'll buy you some time. Got that?"

"I got it. Loud and clear."

The field commander hung up. Yeah, he got it, all right. He knew his own career was in the toilet, no matter what happened. His first impulse was to storm the line of satellite trucks and blast the wind-blown journalists with a story they'd never forget—the story of

179

one hapless field commander and his innocent men (and women), screwed over by craven agency muckymucks in collusion with international money people. Give them the story of a brave, bold, jut-jawed commander, ready, willing, and more than able to eradicate America's drug problem, but thwarted by cynical power politics.

He had been set up. His career was over. He could do it; he had nothing to lose.

But. He was an agency man. Above all else, he was loyal—even when his bosses weren't loyal to him. He was loyal to the men who relied on him—and relied on budget money provided by Congress. He couldn't put their jobs at risk. In a minute, he'd go over and obediently tell the blow-dried crowd the official story of why the signal to move hadn't come. He'd look them straight in the eye and describe the helpless children in the clutches of the violent, Evil Drug Kingpins. He'd tell them of tense, absolutely crucial, ongoing hostage negotiations. Of precision teamwork. Of lightning-fast, perfectly accurate intra-team communications. Of the DEA's deep concern for the safety of American citizens, especially those most at risk. He'd tell them he was holding off the raid—for now—*for the children.*

And so he did, after he wrestled his temper into control and gave terse word of the new development to his aides. As he spoke to one particularly admiring young reporter, he almost believed himself. Afterward, a cameraman let him look at his image on a monitor. He looked good, he thought. Tired, but resolute. His jaw really did jut nicely.

He looked so resolute on that monitor that, as the light of false dawn glowed over the eastern hills, a thought occurred to him. Maybe, just maybe, since he was going to be hung out to dry for planning this raid, he'd find some way to pull it off, after all. On his own. He'd one-up those wussy mucky-mucks in D.C.

What the hell. Screw Hor-hay Del-La-Val. Screw all the damn foreigners. And screw the bosses and their limp-wristed political objections. He had a job to do. He had the men and equipment to do it. He had a career to salvage. He'd pull the raid off, somehow. Then the media would cheer him so loudly that nobody in Washington would dare speak a word against him. Congress would be so impressed they'd double the agency's budget.

Ha. Instead of standing around here, accepting a set-up that doomed his career, he'd find a believable reason to act and probably even end up with a promotion.

He didn't know just how he'd do it. But suddenly making this raid work for him and his men seemed like the best damned idea he'd had all day. *Just give me a few hours sleep and a head-to-head with some of my best people. I'll show those desk-bound wimps what a real man can do.*

He handed temporary command to his second, instructing him to hold for now, and headed for one of the tents to grab some zees.

Up on the hill, out of sight, the residents of the Emma Goldman Arts Co-op and Biodiverse Living Center also slept on, unaware.

Dog tired, grating with frustration, and focused on their now-unapproachable target, the exhausted men and women of the DEA-led multi-agency task force failed to notice that they, too, were gradually being surrounded. Just as their snipers and guards ringed the hills around the commune, so .50 cal Barretts and Serbus, 20 mm cannon, and other assorted militia weapons were quietly being trucked, packed on horseback, and hand-carried to the ring of hills beyond.

The circle of feds became a circle within a circle, surrounded by the men and weaponry of Hardyville.

FOOTNOTE: If you wonder how the U.S. Secretary of State got the news in the middle of the night, it came to him, indirectly, from an indignant little statistical analyst in some agency whose name and mission the Secretary could never afterward remember. The analyst heard about the planned raid through a file clerk at the DEA with whom he played a weekly game of penny-a-point cribbage. The little analyst, whose name was Howard, or maybe Harold something, seemed to feel that, somehow, anything that happened in Hardy County was a personal affront. Therefore, he tapped into his vast databases, uncovered the ownership of the Emma Goldman Arts Co-op and Biodiverse Living Center, and—with the malicious satisfaction of a nobody getting a little of his own back from a Somebody—went on a personal crusade to get the information to Very Important People.

Chapter 7
Between Word and Deed

"Provocation. I'd like to give them provocation," Jasper Feldspar Clarke muttered impotently beside me. We stood at the DEA barricades that separated Jasper from his friends, who were trapped and surrounded within the Emma Goldman Arts Co-op and Biodiverse Living Center.

Provocation, indeed. We had all heard the latest statement delivered by that self-important, faux-military DEA field commander. He told reporters his teams were taking a slow approach—negotiations, rather than a full-force raid—because they didn't want to give the radical criminals up on the hill any provocation to "carry out their threat to blow up themselves and their children."

Blow themselves up, my Aunt Fanny. That bunch up at the commune could barely pool their collective technology skills to light a match. Rigging explosives to blow themselves sky high was ... well, I hardly have to tell you. But then, you know the tactics governments resort to when they're after evil, deadly dope dealers.

But Hardyvillians could have dynamited, sniped, booby-trapped, and fought like real Americans ... sigh. We could have done so much. But you know what we had to do instead?

Wait. Our sniper teams lurked in the hills, disguised in their Ghillie suits and hidden under brush, moving continually, wary of helicopters. Or even satellite spying. Other militiamen impatiently awaited orders. (Our militia may be unorganized. But it's not disorganized.) We alleged communicators, being official noncombatants, could stand right in the open, with nobody knowing what we were up to. So there we were, milling around at the barricades with the blow-dried crowd, awaiting information. Any information. From anybody. Our guys. Or theirs.

Unfortunately, official lies didn't count.

The worst thing that had ever happened in the history of Hardy County was upon us—invasion by tyrants—a violent gang surrounding and planning to attack people who had never hurt a soul (and who had possibly helped many). And we couldn't do a damn thing.

Why didn't we just shoot the bastards now that they'd invaded? Think about it. We shoot. They send in the Army. We shoot. The survivors end up in a protracted guerrilla war. And Hardyville might as well be Baghdad, it'll be so often on the lips of every news anchor. Pretty soon, Hardy County will be a wholly owned subsidiary of Halliburton.

No, our strategy had always been to keep them out through invisibility.

The town's historic invisibility cloak might have worn thin and might be on the verge of tearing through, but it still protected us more than a little. The media variously reported the location of the commune as Montana, Wyoming, or Idaho. Blessedly, neither they nor the DEA teams had even approached Hardyville proper. So we still had at least tatters of our anonymity going for us, and it would be foolish for us to blow those tatters away by ... well, blowing the invaders away "without provocation."

Now that the feds and their media friends were here ... well, whatever we would do—and rest assured, we would do something—had to be done with finesse.

The big question was why the heck were the feds stalling? And how much time did we have?

Like Sergeant Schultz in the old *Hogan's Heroes,* we knew nothing.

————————————

"Is the communications monitoring looking any better, Bob?" I had left Jasper at the barricade and slipped into an inconspicuous Honda parked by the side of the road, where Bob-the-Nerd and a raft of e-gear struggled to get some solid information out of the Babel of fed transmissions.

"Nope," he sighed—then continued tinkering. (We'd never had cause for snooping into other people's communications in Hardyville so nobody was practiced at it.) "I'm sorry. But they're using ..." He went off, describing random frequency-switching and a host of other tricks that They the Rulers have adopted to keep We the People from learning what they're up to. I tuned out the technicalities, understanding only that the feds were about as communicative as Jehovah.

"I don't think I'm going to be able to hack into their official communications," he said finally, leaning back and pushing up the baseball cap that had slid down to his eyeballs. "It's beyond me—at least, beyond anything I can do now."

I thought I just might sit there and have myself a big, hysterical cry. I stared out at the milling raiders and their media followers. I regarded the gathering crowd at the barricade. My gaze trailed up the long, empty driveway winding behind the hill—where surely our communal neighbors, and our old friend Dora, knew by now what deep trouble they were in, even without phones and radios to tell them. I wondered what they were doing up there, what they were saying to each other, whether they were considering surrender in the face of grim odds.

"What on earth are we going to do, Bob?" The question wasn't really for him, but for me. He ignored it and returned to fiddling.

Then after a while, he lifted his head and grinned. "Listen," he said, passing me a tiny ear-bud.

"...groceries," a woman's voice was complaining. "And Thad fell and broke a tooth and you're out there having another of your big adventures and ..."

"We've hit some sort of snag ..." a man interrupted.

"Right. Another 'snag.' There's always a 'snag' that keeps you from getting home, isn't there?"

Still pressing the ear-bud to the side of my head, I looked at Bob—totally confused.

"Who needs official communications?" he grinned. "A dozen of those idiots over there behind the barricades are talking all about it on their cell phones. Anybody can listen in on a cell phone."

I grinned back, high-fived him, and continued eavesdropping.

Eventually, we heard magic words. And terrifying ones.

"Holy shoe leather," Carty whistled, when Bob and I arrived at his command post on Nat's ranch and showed him the scribbles we'd made from our cellular surveilling. "So Delaval's behind that place. That explains a lot."

"Yeah. But there's this, too." Bob pointed further down the page. Carty squinted at my illegible scribbles. Bob continued, "Most of these agents are getting the same disinformation Herr Kommandant Field Commander is shoveling on the media. He's telling his BS story about how Dora and her friends are holding kids hostage and planning to blow the whole place up. They're passing that horse manure to their wives, girlfriends, and boyfriends.

"But near as we can tell, a couple of the Kommandant's close subordinates have the real skinny—that they've been called off until their bosses in Washington can come up with some way of saving their own ... er, faces. The Kommandant ... he's planning something. Planning to do something on his own, and he and his seconds-in-command are talking about it. Claire and I couldn't always tell junk from the real deal in these conversations. But that ..."—he pointed to one particular set of lines again—"well, you know."

Carty read aloud from my sloppy transcription of one cell conversation: "They'll give us 'provocation.' We'll be 'forced' to move. Even the wusses at HQ won't be able to object. Watch the fireworks."

He shook his head. Nat walked in at that moment and Carty passed the sheet of scribbles to him. Nat read. We all wondered what kind of deadly "provocation" the feds might manufacture. And how soon they'd do it. And how deadly the feds' "fireworks" would be.

"Provocation," Nat muttered, with all the power of rage in his old voice. "Provocation. Those poor suckers up there on the hill couldn't provoke a fruit fly."

"Provocation," he muttered again. Then he paused, seeming to be struck by an idea. "Provocation. That's it. *We'll* give the bastards their provocation."

And we all looked at each other—and knew we would do exactly that.

Exactly *what* was another matter. In reality, it took a few hours for a workable scheme to congeal. And some phone calls. And more than a little "wing and a prayer." But afterward it seemed to us all that a fully formed plan had been born in our minds at that very moment.

"Let's roll," Carty ordered.

Leaving the heavy weaponry hidden in brush and rocky caves, and a skeleton crew of fighting Hardyvillians out in the sagebrush, we called as many other Hardyvillians as we could find—and trust—to meet us back at the Hog Trough.

Of course, the usual idiots objected. And to be honest, so did plenty who weren't idiots. The plan—mostly the work of Nat and Carty—was dangerous. Some of us might not survive it.

"It's one thing to go head-to-head with invaders," one of the newly recruited footsoldiers in the Hardyville Militia objected, as assorted Hardyvillians crowded into the back room at the Hog Trough at the hastily convened meeting. (I watched the clock, painfully aware we had no idea when or how the feds would arrange their "provocation." Would they move while we were talking—even though it was still daylight?) "It's another thing to risk our lives ... like that ... to rescue people who think we're scum. I'm all for running the feds out—and the sooner the better. But ..." He punched a finger at the paper on which Nat had drawn a sketchy diagram. "That's crazy stuff."

"Yeah," agreed another Hardyville militiaman, "We'll get rid of the feds. Somehow. But them gun-hating hippies are on their own. No reason we should risk our lives for them."

"Dora's up there," Nat reminded everyone, as if that simple fact answered every objection.

Bob added, "And the communers aren't doing anything to hurt anybody, don't forget. While the feds are."

"If we don't put ourselves on the line to defend unpopular people," I said, "then who's going to defend us?" I didn't have to add that we might need defending perilously soon.

"And we have been invaded," Carty reminded them. "Tyrants are on our sovereign territory. We're not just 'helping the hippies.' By doing this right instead of attacking the feds head-on and foolishly, we're giving ourselves the best chance to stay free. More than that. We—you and I, the people of Hardyville—have been given the responsibility of defending the last bastion of freedom within these united States. It might not be what we'd wish. No one wants to face hard days and hard choices. But now is our chance to rise for freedom's sake."

Everybody looked down at their copies of Nat's sketchy diagram. To some of us, it was the most terrifying thing we'd ever seen. Were abstractions like sovereignty and freedom worth such risk?

"I'll do it." It was the voice of Tonio Carolina—the new kid in town, just 17. "I don't want to lose Hardyville after we just found it." His mother Charlotte grasped at his sleeve and opened her mouth to object. Then, seeing his resolute expression, she halted. Her boy was becoming his own man.

"I'll help," volunteered Christian Goodin, even younger, and Tonio's boon companion. His father, Will, looked at him proudly and nodded his head: I'm with you.

"Me, too," squeaked Jasper Feldspar Clarke. The Emma Goldman communard came to the meeting clinging to my side in fear of all things Hardyville. But he insisted he had more of a stake in the plans than anybody. Everybody stared at him as he spoke up—this weak-chinned kid who looked ready to hurl, but who was willing to do what some of them were not. "And I'll carry a gun. Just like the rest of you." Some snickered.

He felt the need to explain. "My dad was a rock-hound. He taught me to shoot rattlesnakes when I was six years old." He added, as if making a shameful, but necessary, admission, "I've even hunted prairie dog." He hung his head, unable to face the stares.

Watching teenagers and a chubby pacifist volunteer for duty that terrified them prompted some older, sterner militiamen to contemplate their boots or fingernails in shame. Pretty soon, Carty and Nat had a full complement of volunteers for every duty—including the most nightmarish.

"Those old mine tunnels are unstable," Carty admitted, nodding toward the diagrams everybody held. "We don't know their condition. Even Nat's not sure exactly where they run any more. His drawing's only guesswork. We're not gonna be havin' one minute of fun, I don't need to tell you. But the fact is simple: Overland is out; too heavily patrolled. We have to go underground to the commune and bring those people out. Through those old mine tunnels. Now. Tonight. Before the feds can concoct their 'provocation' to Wacoize the commune."

"And then," Marty Harbibi offered from the back of the room, quavering as he tried to sound bold and insouciant, "we'll give them fireworks. Right?"

Chapter 8
Hardyville Underground

I'd rather not write about those hours in the tunnels. We burrowed into the earth—using old and unstable mine runs opened by earlier burrowers. The earlier burrowers, a hundred years and more ago, had been looking for silver. Ours was a less profitable aim.

We struggled to make our way from the far reaches of Nat's ranch to a vent shaft somewhere near—we hoped—the commune's homes and greenhouses. From his boyhood adventures (involving a larger-than-usual quotient of "Hey, I'll bet you can't beat the speeding train" kind of dares), Nat recalled the ancient mines, cut a bare generation after Hezekiah Lyons and Sean Brendan McCarty founded Hardyville.

Some of the mine openings were on Nat's land and he knew those well. But where they went, and what condition they might be in ... that was another matter.

Nat remembered one vent shaft deep in a dimly recalled tunnel that opened next to a certain rock outcrop. The outcrop bore a petroglyph, left by wandering Indian tribes long ago. If Nat remembered right—if—it might be on the hillside just below the commune.

A lot of ifs. A lot of maybes.

Exactly where Nat's rock was in all that vast nothing, we didn't know. Was Nat remembering correctly at all? How could he be sure that a certain hill with a certain rock was really the same hill where the Emma Goldman Arts Co-op and Biodiverse Living Center now stood? And even if that certain rock was really somewhere near the commune, would we have to run half a mile after emerging from the ground, with DEA snipers and night-vision equipment trained on us? Or would the gods who watch over daredevils and fools allow us to surface somewhere near dwellings, where we might creep unobserved toward the targets of our rescue? Jasper Clarke, who walked—and sometimes crawled or slithered—alongside me through the man-made caves remembered no petroglyphs from his months on the property. But then, he wasn't exactly the casual ramble-through-the-sagebrush type. So we still had hope.

It was our only hope, really. So what do you do? You take it.

Concerns about where we would arrive were only an afterthought. The big question: With these crumbling mine shafts would we arrive *anywhere at all?* (Any of you who think it's just a bit too convenient for these miles of old tunnels to appear in this location in this story probably can't picture how terrifyingly inconvenient these tunnels really were.)

LED lights on our heads, flashlights in our hands, and spare batteries in our pockets or backpacks, we entered the tunnel complex standing tall. The opening of the shaft was cut horizontally into the bottom of a hill in a far corner of Nat's ranch and was more than high enough to accommodate the biggest of us. There was a lot of bravado in our walks. Now that we'd decided to do it, none of us wanted to show how scared we were.

I would have given anything to beg off. Going underground, into the grave-dark, into the domain of the rats, the bats and the crawly things (and perhaps large, hairy, big-toothed mammalian things) well ... I'd have rather attended a Hillary Clinton fundraiser.

But as the various assignments of what we began to call Operation Santa were parceled out, it became clear that the job of tunnel rat was—this is going to sound strange—women's work. And work for young boys.

Women's work because if those gods were favorable, we wouldn't be involved in any fighting. We in the tunnels would "merely" conduct a rescue. Women's work because small people were more versatile for this part of the action than bruisers with shoulders like tanks. Women's work, Carty said, because women were needed to steady men who might be inclined to panic. In front of women, they wouldn't dare.

And it was young boy's work because ... well, who else would get a thrill from delving into old, collapsing tunnels, having no idea where, or if, they'll surface? The same kind of people who think it's amusing to try to reach the railroad crossing before the freight train. Or who are frequently known to die just after uttering the words, "Hey, watch this!" Boys.

We walked. At first. Then a side tunnel Nat said he *thought* was the right one was so damaged we had to crawl over the rubble hills at its opening.

Nat led the tunnel-rat party, feigning confidence. He went first, being the only one of us who *might* know what he was doing. With him went Carty.

Yes, Carty was the commander of all parts of Operation Santa, our General Eisenhower. It might seem risky, even stupid, for him to be out of touch, underground, during crucial deployment and decision-making for an operation that had other aspects than this tunnel-crawl. I suppose every theory of modern warfare would dictate that he'd stay somewhere behind the lines, overseeing all, giving orders, and keeping his own backside safe.

But there were plenty of good Hardyvillians out there on the hills, ready and able to make decisions. Carty's final orders of the operation would depend on what happened right around that hoped-for vent shaft. So that's where the big decision maker needed to be. Besides, if we came out of the earth in some sagebrush exile a thousand yards from the commune, Carty would be there to help us fight our way to the people we hoped to rescue.

Besides, I think he just wanted to do what commanders used to do in the days before We the People let them get away with riding desks far from the action. He wanted to show us he'd do the hardest, scariest job to earn our respect. So there he went, ahead of the pack with Nat.

First we walked. Then we crawled. Then we waited in tense terror as the stronger men cleared an earth-fall blocking our path. Would the roof hold, as they pulled the fallen boulders and dirt from underneath it? The old mine timbers were remarkably stable in our dry climate. Nevertheless, many were bowed and cracked. A few hung like the shards of a compound fracture. Under those, we faced belly-scraping rubble-crawls. Even with gloves and kneepads (which some of us had thought to bring from our shooting kits) it was painful.

But worse was the claustrophobic fear.

I felt the weight of the unstable rock, bulging inward from every direction, under unimaginable pressures. I thought of the land, ever moving (even if on a geologic time scale). I thought of wandering lost without a horizon. Down here, there was no east, no west—none that we could feel or see. What if we took a wrong turning and were submerged for days? (Never mind the Day-Glo markings Nat sprayed on the wall with each turning. Never mind the feel-our-way blazes, carved with a pocketknife into old timbers, that accompanied them.) I thought of the unbearable pitch of the darkness, should we be trapped and our lights fail. I thought of mine disasters and earthquakes...

But I said I didn't want to write about that.

I'll make this short. Carty was right about the "women's work." At the very moment I was about to start screaming uncontrollably from claustrophobia, Marty Harbibi (the next ahead of the 30 mine-crawlers) let out a whimper. Then another. As we crawled from a single-file tight spot into a wider area, I saw that he was shaking and breathing in gulping, hyperventilating gasps. The man was about to shatter into a million pieces.

I considered putting my arm around him and giving him comfort. It was the kind, womanly thing to do and it would have uplifted my own morale, perhaps more than Marty's. But behind me, Jasper Clarke—who we all expected would have become a babbling baby half an hour ago—was pale and grim, but soldiering on. So I did my assigned "women's work" in a different way. I leaned forward until my LED headlamp bumped Marty's skull. Then I whispered, "Hey, Marty. The broad and the wimp can take it. Why not you—wuss?"

Marty shot me a foul look. But he straightened his back and trudged on. In a moment, I could hear his raspy breath smoothing.

And lo and behold, after several horror films worth of fear, a faint scattering of moonlight sprinkled onto our path. We stumbled ahead—and soon we could see Nat and Carty's faces, barely gray in the dappled light of the outside world.

They were standing under a vent shaft.

Had our mouths been moist enough to manage it (and if Carty hadn't sternly cautioned us about making unnecessary sounds near the vent), we'd have cheered.

We doused our lights. We didn't know how much radiance we might be shining to the outside.

Lord. Don't even ask me to think about that moment of dousing. Those tiny spots of moonlight were no more than fireflies in the pitch, illuminating bare inches. Turning off our lights plunged us into the dreaded grave-darkness until our eyes adjusted and we gratefully embraced the comfort of seeing shadows within the shadows once again.

Tonio Carolina and Christian Goodin—skinny boys—began hammering rungs into the old vent shaft, which was just wide enough to accommodate one worker climbing hand-over-hand, then swinging a mallet. First they balanced on the shoulders of other volunteers as they hammered their makeshift iron rungs. Ultimately, they had to stand on the lower rungs to hammer the higher ones, still taking turns. All the while we didn't have the slightest idea whether this was even the right vent shaft. Or, if it was the right one, whether we were too far from the commune or too close to the feds—so close they might hear us and send a greeting party. For all some of us knew, we weren't even in Hardy County anymore.

The hammering reverberated so loudly that I almost hoped we weren't in the county—at least not that part of the county occupied by DEA ears or sensing gear.

Christian finally reached the top, pushed his hand up, and found himself touching the old rotted boards of some cover that had been laid above the vent shaft, probably to prevent cattle from stumbling in. Through those gaps the moonlight had fallen.

With effort, bracing his feet hard against the newly planted rungs, pushing upward with all his miniature might, Christian shifted the old cover away. Gouts of sandy dirt showered on everyone near the vent shaft. Slowly, Christian raised himself through the opening and looked around.

"Outcrop," he whispered back down the tunnel. The rest of us suppressed a cheer as word filtered back to us that Christian had spotted a ridge of rock.

"But no petroglyph. At least not that I can see from here." As that whisper filtered back to us, our spirits sank as quickly as they'd just risen.

"Go ahead out. But stay low," said Carty.

Christian pulled himself out of the tunnel onto his belly. He slithered a few yards to the left, so he told us later. Then he slithered a few yards to the right, looking around the small rock outcrop.

Then a voice at the top of the tunnel called softly, but triumphantly, downward: "I see Thunderbird. On the outcrop. And I see buildings. About 50 yards."

Fifty yards. It was a long way to be exposed. But at least the gods weren't playing their worst tricks on us. We were at the commune.

Carty and two of the militiamen slithered out of the tunnel next, creeping around the rock outcrop with their rifles and their night-vision goggles.

Then it was Jasper's turn. Lucky Jasper to escape the tunnels so early. Poor Jasper; he would be the first to run and creep and dodge across that 50-yard No Man's Land because he knew the locations of everything in the commune. He was the one they'd recognize and not fear. He had a better chance than any of us to get his friends to go along with the rescue plan.

He and Carty crept off together, weaving through the sagebrush, avoiding the low, unpredictable patches of prickly pear, grateful for the dense, wide junipers that could give them real concealment from any watchers in the surrounding hills.

And the rest of us waited, deep in the dark, with only that nearly-invisible ribbon of moonlight to encourage our hope.

———

I wonder if the trek, exposed to snipers' eyes in the moonlight, felt as long to Carty and Jasper as the hours in the tunnels. But no one must have been watching in that sleeping hour. On they crept, apparently undetected.

Beneath the last juniper of No Man's Land and the complex of buildings, Carty and Jasper paused, crouching low. Carty got his bearings as Jasper pointed out landmarks. Greenhouses on the left. Earth-shelter dwellings on the right. A pump-house and a power shed between us and them. The two gazed around. Everything was silent and still. Not even a dog stirred.

Taking a deep breath, Carty and Jasper stepped out of the brush, upright and walking as slowly and calmly as if they were communards going about routine business. If there were night-enhanced eyes on them, they hoped at least that their calm matter-of-factness might give a sniper pause. Maybe they were just communards who'd been out for a secret smoke or a tryst.

They approached the first dwelling.

The commune being a pot farm, I'd like to tell you that Jasper tapped on the door and called, "Hey, let me in! It's Jasper!" and someone on the inside had at least the passing thought to reply, ala Cheech and Chong, "No, man. Jasper's not here." But that's not what happened. Before they could knock, a voice whispered out of the darkness:

"Over here!"

Carty and Jasper dropped to a crouch (although it might be more accurate to say that Jasper fell into an attempted crouch). Carty raised his Bushmaster and scanned the clearing.

"This way!" the voice cried more insistently. And a pale arm waved from the doorway of the second dwelling.

They strolled—going back to faux casual—toward the doorway—where arms reached out of darkness to pull them into the lightless structure.

"Jasper, my man!" "You're back!" "They didn't bust you—thank God!" A dozen or more voices greeted the returning communard. Jasper found himself dragged into the center of the room, victim of a serial hug. Even the commune's dogs, brought inside to avoid notorious paramilitary puppy-killers, leaped and yipped about him. No one approached Carty, who stood just inside the doorway. Only one voice addressed him.

"Well it's about time," Dora snapped. "Where've you been?"

Before Carty could frame choice words to describe where we had been, Dora came forward and explained. "I promised them Hardyville would come for us. But some of my friends here ..." she waved her arm in a gesture that included, most emphatically, the scowling countenance of former Hardyville city councilman and Dora's current main squeeze, Dan White—"... didn't believe me. They wanted to surrender. But I got everybody to agree to stay dressed, ready, and gathered in two houses to wait for you, just for tonight. So here you are—*finally.*"

"Jeezus you're an arrogant broad," Carty said.

"And you are a hyper-macho chauvinist pig," she shot back. Then she wrapped her arms around his neck, pulled his sand-dusted head down, and gave him—right in front of Dan White and all the rest of the world—one big, huge, sloppy, and (given the urgent need for split-second timing in Operation Santa) obscenely extended kiss.

Chapter 9
Showtime

Dora unlocked her lips from Carty's and stepped away. Carty stood shock-still, imitating an ox that's just been whacked across the forehead with a copy of the U.S. tax code and hasn't figured out it's dead yet.

Dora finally had to break the silence. Snapping to a parody of attention she asked, "Well, Heroic Rescuer, what do you have in mind for us?"

When Carty explained, there were groans. But—his old self again now—he cut off all objections: "Two choices. You can stay here, whine, and get Waco-ed. Or you can get to work."

Blank faces queried other blank faces in the dark. Fear crossed paths with doubt. In the end, though, what choice did they have? The response was the same when Carty, Dora, and Jasper appeared in the second dwelling where the rest of the communards hid and started doling out assignments there. Anything was better than idly waiting for disaster or walking down the hill, surrendering, and facing decades in a federal prison.

But the next stage of the rescue was going to involve some 60 people—the communards and we tunnel-rats—moving at will around the complex. And what about those prying eyes? If even one sniper spotted the proposed goings-on, the jig, as they say, was up. No hostile watcher could mistake what we were about to do for "casual activity." We had to hide from their eyes.

Carty pulled a cell phone out of a pocket in his tactical vest. He drew its batteries from another pocket and inserted them. Punched in a one-word text message and selected a pre-set list of numbers to zap to. Poked send. He waited to make sure the call was well-launched. Then he switched off and removed the batteries.

"SHOWTIME," the message read.

On a hillside nearly a mile southwest of the commune—across the highway, over a wide arroyo, down a slope of loose shale—and far away from where Carty and company were up to nefarious good deeds—a Hardyville militiaman reached into his vest and pulled out a cell phone that silently buzzed the arrival of a message. He punched buttons. Read words on the tiny lighted screen. Raised his shooter's earmuffs onto his ears, as did the three fellow militiamen waiting invisibly among the boulders nearby. He nodded as he signaled thumbs up.

Will Goodin, who had—surprisingly for a city man—become one of Hardyville's best benchrest shooters, rotated his shoulders, inhaled deeply, then lowered himself to gaze through the long-range night-vision scope of the .50 BMG Barrett that had rested all those months in the back room of his store. He took another quiet breath or two while focusing on his target. The combination of the night scope and invisible infrared "illumination"— a.k.a. heat—made the target stand out against the cool hillside. Will's confidence took over. He let out one breath halfway and smoothly compressed the trigger.

The night exploded. Across an ancient river valley, now a dry moonscape of sand, rock, scrub, and cactus, five booms reverberated in succession as five isolated benchrest shooters took their shots. Answering them, from the bases of the even more distant hills, thundered five tremendous explosions.

Each explosion triggered a second series of explosions, so close-paced only someone listening carefully would realize they weren't one solid blast. Five fireballs bloomed into the night, all in a chain, making a ruby-and-gold necklace at the base of otherwise empty hills.

It was merely Tannerite going kaboom. Pretty innocuous stuff. All sound and fury, very little destructive power. Quite a bit of Tannerite, actually. And okay, I admit, it was Tannerite augmented by a few sticks of volatile old dynamite. So there was quite a bit of sound and fury coming from a spot very far away from the Emma Goldman Arts Co-op and Bio-diverse Living Center. There was not much else, though, unless you count one sagebrush bush that caught fire and burned brightly for a while.

But the DEA and friends didn't know that. All they knew was that something nasty was happening. In a place they hadn't been paying attention to.

As the boom rolled across the landscape Herr Kommandante of the DEA rolled—almost literally—out of his cot. The guards on duty were already shouting at each other or calling into their radios: "What the hell ...?" "It came from over there." "No, wait a minute! I heard heavy-weapons fire south-southwest first!" "No way. It was east. Had to be. Behind that row of hills ..."

Sleep-disoriented Herr Kommandante experienced another weird moment of believing his own lies. Could those commune people have actually blown themselves up, as he had told the media they threatened to do? But no way. All intel said they were as passive as babies.

Fully clothed already, he launched himself out of his tent and into the chilly night. By the time he reached the command post, aides and guards had agreed: the noise and flash had come from the southwest, far from the Emma Goldman Arts Co-op and Biodiverse Living Center (a.k.a. "World's Largest-Ever (would-be) Pot Bust of the Week"). The glow of fireballs and smoke still lit the horizon, though the explosion sites themselves were hidden from view.

He cast his eyes up the commune's driveway. It curved away into the night, silent and dark, revealing none of its secrets. "All posts report in," he demanded to his second. The aide relayed the request, and from the hills encircling the commune came ten reports of "all quiet" at their locations and on the commune's hill.

Damn bosses, the DEA field commander thought, as his teams gathered around him, watching him for orders and looking antsy. Damn them, sending the choppers back! The muckymucks left him operating on a shoestring—or more likely dangling from his own hangman's noose—as the diplomats in Zurich, Liechtenstein, and D.C. figured out how to get out of the political stewpot.

From the moment he'd hatched his plan to create a provocation to raid the commune—a plan he hadn't yet had time to implement—he'd known he'd have to move against the target without the choppers. He could work with that. What he hadn't imagined was this: explosions in a completely different direction. Drawing off what was left of his strength. Damndoubledamn. He could really use those choppers now to chase after those fireballs.

He glanced uneasily toward the media vans, where rumpled reporters were awakening, in that ready-for-action way that only doctors and journalists can manage. Their faces echoed those of his men. Anxious. Eager. Questioning. Respectful—but also ready to judge him. Hero? Or scapegoat? Which would they make him when this was all over?

He glanced at the scattering of silent citizens standing by the road, outside the barricades, even at this hour. Their faces were blank, unreadable. Some looked eager. Some hostile. But they'd all be witnesses if he screwed up. He felt his future career in the agency—or anywhere outside of the Lower Podunkville Police Department—slipping away even further if he didn't do this right. *Is it a real incident out there? Or a diversion? But who would set up a diversion? The locals can't give a crap about these dope-dealing hippies. And we've got all the hippies surrounded and trapped. Anyway, even if it is a diversion, I have to...*

"Squads Two and Three," he ordered. "I'm pulling half my sharpshooters from the perimeter and giving them to you, just in case you run into something you can't solve up close and personal. Investigate and report. Engage if provoked."

As half his team members loaded up and started rumbling overland toward the smoky remnants of the explosions (and as nearly 3/4 of the media vans raced after them, as if satellite trucks were capable of navigating sagebrush), Herr Kommandante again glared up the driveway in frustration. He wanted those pacifist, dope-sucking weenies up there. He wanted them bad. Wanted them now. But explosions a mile away in the wrong direction aren't enough excuse to raid. The nine black-robed Nazgul in D.C. would never buy it. This wasn't his provocation. At least, not yet. He needed something more, and he was working on that.

He turned his attention back toward the smudgy southwestern horizon.

Huddled in the darkness outside one of the commune buildings, Carty had observed the explosions with a tight smile barely cracking his face. Now he heard the roar of heavy vehicles lumbering away. And saw the reflected glow, from the rocky valley beyond, of their retreating headlights.

Again, he quietly drew his cell phone and its batteries from separate pockets in his tactical vest. Again he assembled, hit buttons, typed a one-word text message, and launched the message toward multiple recipients.

"APPLAUSE," the message said.

"APPLAUSE" set in motion another series of militia actions. Swiftly, silently, Hardyville teams in the hills started moving in on that half of the federal snipers and spotters still posted around the perimeter of the commune. This—aside from the tunnels—was the trickiest part of the operation. Just one fed alerted too soon could ruin the entire operation. We had to be very discreet.

"APPLAUSE" also sent our diversionary explosives team further into the hills—stashing their .50 BMGs among the rocks and swapping them for a variety of rifles and handguns, from .308s and 7.62x39s to little, silenced .22s.

There was more. But for now Carty, as he twisted his wrist to check the watch he wore on the palm side, was more immediately concerned about what the Emma Goldman communards and we tunnel rats—still waiting in the old mine shafts—would do. The other operations were in solid, trustworthy hands. The commune rescue was in his.

Down in the tunnels we had felt and heard the explosions. Trust me; you do not enjoy feeling the earth quake when you're crouched in a 150-year-old collapsing silver mine. But we knew it meant we'd be moving in minutes.

Those minutes stretched on for a long, long time. We waited below. Christian Goodin, still crouching by the rock outcrop at the mouth of the vent, awaited Carty's signal.

There it came. A wave, no more than shadow against shadow. But repeated.

Christian stuck his head into the shaft and nodded to Nat, who stood at the bottom.

"Let's roll," Nat whispered, with a fatalistic sigh. (Let's roll. I was coming to hate that expression.)

Grateful tunnel rats swarmed up ladders into what seemed glaringly bright moonlight, though in truth the moon was no more than a little lemon slice in the sky. Damning discretion and hoping our fellow townspeople had taken care of that small sniper problem, we moved with, as they say, all deliberate speed, toward the buildings. There, the blinking, shell-shocked communards emerged and stared at us as though we were an apparition born of some drug far stronger than cannabis.

But Carty, Nat, and Jasper as a sort of impromptu Captain of the Communards kept them, and us, moving. And move we did. As fast as we possibly could. We had an impossible task to perform. But if Herr Kommandante had something to prove to himself for his own sake and the world's perception, so did we. We had to prove that Hardyville could not only beat an unconstitutional, tyrannical, invading government, but also that we are such a formidable opponent that it's better never again to touch us.

And so we hustled—every dirt-smeared tunnel rat, every Birkenstock-wearing idealist, every 100-percent-all-natural-sustainably-grown-cotton-diaper-wearing toddler, every man, woman, and dog of us. We hustled.

Chapter 10
Applause

Tunnel rats and communards traced their way back and forth across the sandy ground of the Emma Goldman Arts Co-op and Biodiverse Living Center. Since we didn't immediately get Horiuchied, and since HumVees didn't soon swarm up the driveway toward us, I assumed with relief that our townsmen had taken out the snipers. That meant that the first part of the rescue operation, at least, had a chance.

Taken out. What an impersonal, military term. Like collateral damage, if we had to face what being taken out really meant, we'd have a hard time living with ourselves. These people, these feds, threatening though they were, had done no more than trespass up to now. To take them out seemed a violation of our precious non-aggression principle. Or even worse, of the time-honored Code of Hardyville.

I wish I could tell you that our hill-crawling militia teams simply ... oh, slipped a Hollywood-style mickey into the canteens of the snipers. You know, one of those tasteless, odorless, harmless poisons that tidily make people fall asleep without the slightest hint of an ill-effect. Or I wish I could say they shot them with diligently calculated doses of animal tranquilizers, then simply carried them away, bound in the softest of ropes. Then, when the snipers were fully recovered and feeling full of vim, I wish I could tell you that our townsmen released them all at the top of the pass that unofficially defines the western—and most isolated—border of Hardy County. Released them to be free as doves after learning the error of their ways. Released them naked. Into the snow. Without food. And released them only after a tort action on behalf of their victims stripped them lawfully of every possession they ever owned or ever might own.

I really do wish I could tell you that's how Hardyville took them out. But rest assured, they got took.

And at the commune, we hustled.

———————————

More than a mile to the southwest, over the highway and through many a radiator-busting, tire-puncturing obstacle, our explosives teams—having stashed their .50 BMGs among the rocks and traded them for lighter, more portable weaponry—were on the run. Nimble men, on foot or navigating ATVs over familiar Saturday-afternoon playgrounds, they led the federal squads onward—across more arroyos, through more scraping, sticking, prickling greasewood, over more rocks.

They had made sure to be seen a few hundred yards beyond the fireballs, where they fired a few random shots and took off. The feds had followed like politicians after money.

A graveyard of major-media satellite trucks and yuppie SUVs had been left behind, scattered randomly across the landscape, spinning wheels in sand or with juniper branches tangled in their transmissions. Blonde girl reporters stood by the trucks, weeping in pain and frustration as blond boy reporters, equally mired, chivalrously pulled prickly pear spines out of their female competitors' open-toed shoes. The media hadn't come prepared for a chase like this.

On the fly, the leader of Squad Two reported in, informing Herr Kommandante they were chasing a small gang that appeared to be drug runners. (Where they got that idea, we're not sure. I guess when you're a drug warrior, every American looks like a drug-crazed criminal instead of what we really were—well-armed, all-American guerrilla fighters.) Bumping over a field of half-buried boulders and trying to hear with his headphones jolting up and down on his ears, Squad Two leader didn't especially notice that the transmission was beginning to break up. These were, after all, not real soldiers used to operating in guerilla wars. They were just ... donut eaters wearing soldier suits and carrying cool-looking weapons.

And the hills were getting closer together until, if you'd noticed in the dark, they began to look more like the mouth of a narrow canyon.

I wish I could say that thing about animal tranquilizers and Hollywood mickey finns again. But this time, the Hardyville Militia didn't even need them. Just block the only exit, put our own sharpshooters up in the rim, and the thing is pretty much done. By then, only one lone indy photojournalist in his own well-beaten Jeep was still keeping pace. It was chance and good luck that he later managed to get the only photos of what happened once the fed patrols sped into the trap of the canyon. His pictures were dark and full of vague blurs. There really wasn't that much to see. In the glorious tradition of journalists everywhere, he wrote all the details wrong, besides.

In the canyon, Squad Two and Squad Three commanders, along with the accompanying head of the sniper detachment, called frantically on radios, and then on cell phones, that weren't paying any attention to them, thanks to the narrow, rocky declivity rising around them. Above and around them, Hardyville closed in.

The last of us tunnel rats dropped the last burden into the mine's vent and scrambled down after. We were utterly exhausted. We'd been operating on adrenaline so long that only now did our bodies and minds finally get hit with the overload. But we'd made it. We were all in the tunnels—rats, communards, kids, dogs—and thousands of "rescued" pot plants of all sizes and shapes. Not to mention brown sacks stuffed full of product. Harvested bud still in the drying process. And processing equipment still sparkly with resin from prime bud.

We had just removed all (we hoped) of the evidence that justified the fed raid. Now, when Herr Kommandante finally came up with his "provocation" and sent his troops crashing into the commune, he'd be in hotter water than ever for attacking a peaceful agricultural experiment.

All that—and all the people—had made it into the underground tunnels. Everybody was with us but Carty. And Marty and Jasper.

Carty, of course, because he had other duties that required him to remain out there. Marty and Jasper...?

"C'mon, Mr. Harbibi," Jasper rasped. "C'mon. You can do it!" They crouched together in the shelter of the rock outcrop near the vent's portal into the real world. Marty gasped and gulped sobs of air.

"I can't. No way. Never. I'm never going. Down ... there. Again. No."

"You have to, Mr. Harbibi. You just have to ..."

Jasper desperately looked around. Carty was running at them in a low crouch, "Move it, &^%$#@!!" he ordered. But even faced with The Carty, the hyperventilating Marty didn't budge.

"I'll die if I have to go down there! I'll have a heart attack. The rocks will fall on me. I'll suffoc ..."

"Jeezus, shut him UP!" ordered Carty. Jasper clasped a hand over Marty's wailing mouth.

Then Carty looked back toward the now completely abandoned commune and saw a much bigger problem than Marty.

A trail. Winding through the moonlight and the sandy soil. Not just a trail of our footsteps. That would have been bad enough. The real problem was what was mixed with our footprints.

It was a trail of cannabis leaves and broken buds, of dark organic soils, of occasional cracked bits of ceramic pot or residue of peat potting cups. A trail of wheel ruts from where we'd steered garden carts, of parallel skids from where we'd dragged pallets of potted plants. The trail unwound from the big greenhouse straight to the mouth of the mine's vent—where we had carried each cannabis plant for the last hour, from the tiniest rooted cutting to the most towering sativa hybrid in its black earth.

The plants were in the tunnels beyond us. But would all our work be for nothing? Against the dead tan sands of our native soil, we'd left the remnants of a tropical jungle—and possibly the remnants of a now futile Operation Santa.

"&^%$#@," Carty muttered.

He looked around. All was still quiet—but wouldn't be for long. How the hell to erase this giant neon arrow pointing from greenhouse to tunnel? Part of it would soon be obliterated, anyhow. But he needed to get rid of it all, guaranteed, to avoid discovery. But how to get rid of any of it? *Impossible! Some operation commander I am.* Carty battered himself. *&^%$#@. No brains.*

He glanced at Jasper, still clasping Marty's face. Jasper had spotted the problem, too. It was that obvious, even in the dark. He looked stricken. Terrified. As if doom had followed him with a personal thundercloud.

Carty turned from Jasper and Marty and regarded the trail again. He made a scuff mark or two with his foot, right where he stood, trying to obliterate the incriminating trail. No good. He snapped off a small broom of sagebrush and scuffled that in the dirt. Black soil blended with sand. Wheel ruts softened. Better. If he could just start at the greenhouse and if he could...

"I'll do it," a voice behind him quavered. "I'll stay and cover the trail."

Carty glanced back at Jasper's white face. "It might not work."

"I know. But it'll be better than it is now."

"You'll need to start out there—in the open near the greenhouse to keep them from heading in this direction once the raid starts. Not here in the brush. You might not have time to finish."

"I know."

Neither of them wanted to consider the implications of not finishing. Either for Jasper or the operation.

Jasper—still holding Marty like a ventriloquist's dummy—turned Marty's wooden head toward the trail, then nudged him to pay attention.

Marty's eyes widened.

"Look, Mr. Harbibi. Now there's something you can do besides go back into the tunnels."

Marty nodded numbly.

"Go!" Carty ordered as he faded down the hill himself, heading for a rendezvous in the dark. At least he didn't say, "Let's roll." We'd all be rolling too soon, anyhow.

More endless minutes passed. The rat pack in the tunnels didn't know what was going on. In a way, we were out of it. We'd done our part. We'd gotten communards and crops underground. Now those unreliable gods were in charge again. There was nothing more we could do except wait. Wait and emerge back out of the vent shaft if the fates were with us and we defeated our adversaries. Or leave the plants stashed where they were and make a desperate run through the labyrinth to Nat's ranch if the feds discovered our trail.

Each rat was assigned a communard to comfort, and if necessary, to guide. We were probably as terrified as they. But now we were the bold rescuers being strong for the rescuees. I clutched the arm of a skinny young woman I couldn't see in the dark, and she clung to me, making my claustrophobia even worse. Down the tunnels, babies whimpered. And grownups, too.

Wait and emerge if our guys above beat the feds. Wait and escape through the mines to Nat's ranch if something went wrong. There was one other possibility we all understood but didn't dare utter—the possibility that the tunnels would collapse and we'd all die when ...

Ka-boom! The earth rocked. The earth rolled. The earth jerked like an attack dog hitting the end of its leash. No distant thunder this time. This time we were smack in the middle of the thunderhead with the lightning storm cracking all around us.

Dirt and small rocks rained down upon the cannabis plants and on our arms and faces. Screams shrieked through the tunnels—but mostly unheard amid the ear-splitting thunder and concussion. We hunched down. We grabbed our ears, ducked our heads, tried to make ourselves small. And all the while we knew that 16 or 20 feet of earth over our heads was no friendlier than if it had been 200. Either way, planet Earth held enough gravity to crush us to nothing.

And then the rocking stopped. And all we could hear was the ringing in our ears. But we rats and our charges were still alive.

And over our heads—well, 50-some yards from over our heads—the feds now had their "provocation" to raid the commune. Our pyrotechnics crew had promised they'd do it as gently as they could, for our sakes and the sake of the rest of the commune. They assured us their blast would not have the power to collapse the tunnels. Probably. Maybe. Most likely. It hadn't felt very damned gentle. But it was done. And there we were with all our parts intact.

Aboveground, the formerly cannabis-containing greenhouse had gone up exactly on time, thanks to our guys. Now, no doubt, it burned as brightly as a beacon, calling to Herr Kommandante and what was left of his raiders.

It was an act of strategic property destruction we hoped our communal neighbors would forgive.

"Sniper teams! Sniper teams! Report in!" The DEA field commander barked into his radio. Beyond the curve of the commune's mysterious driveway, the fireball bloomed, close enough that he could hear its roar, see its red-gold top, and hear its rubble raining down. But exactly what was going on up there at the commune, he didn't know. (He had another moment of unreality, wondering once again if his lies about the communards blowing themselves up had magically become true.)

"Sniper teams! Report!"

Silence. Of course. Our hill-crawlers had taken care of that. Herr Kommandante had no "eyes" to tell him what was going on up on Commune Hill.

"&^%$#@" muttered the commander. He had already been trying to raise his away teams, Squads Two and Three, and getting nothing but the silence of the box canyon where we had them trapped. Now this. He darted his eyes toward the few remaining journalists, those who hadn't chased the original explosions. They leaned forward like wolves about to hunt. He could almost see them sniffing the scent of blood in the air. "&^%$#@," he cursed again. He didn't know what was going on, but this time he knew for sure he was screwed. Even the lower Podunkville P.D. wouldn't hire him after this fiasco.

Well what the hell. *If you gotta get raped, might as well enjoy it,* he thought, without a twinge at his own grossness.

He got on the horn to his boss, the DEA Man, waking him out of dreams of world domination.

"What the &^%$#@!" growled the DEA Man. "I just got back from the latest try at working this out with Delaval's people and the ambassadors of about six European countries. What are you doing waking me up at this ...?"

"Forget 'working it out,'" Herr Kommandante snarled. "Forget politics. This is it. This is the real thing. The compound is burning. I don't know why. And I can't raise my sniper teams." He decided not to mention also having lost half the rest of his people to a now-obvious ruse.

"Listen up," Herr Kommandante barked to his startled boss. "I am going in. I am taking my teams up there. Those hippie anarchists can blow themselves to powder for all I care. Hor-Hay Del-La-Val can kiss my ... But I am not going to let anybody destroy the evidence for my big pot bust. You get me backup—stat. You get me a medical team with tactical EMTs. And choppers. I want my choppers back. More. I want a gunship. I want evacuation. And I want everything here within half an hour; I don't care if you have to carry them personally on your back from Denver or Salt Lake City. Get off your damn politics and get me what I need to do my job!"

He punched the disconnect button. It wasn't as satisfying as a good old-fashioned receiver slam. He flung the phone into the dirt.

In Mordor-on-the-Potomac, the startled DEA Man stared at the phone receiver as if it were a rattlesnake that had just slithered into his bed and nibbled his earlobe.

At the foot of the mysterious driveway, Herr Kommandante marshalled most of his remaining team and the blood-sniffing wolves of the media. He dispatched four of those precious few agents into the dark, to the first sniper position in the hills, with another "investigate and report" order—maddeningly aware that his forces were draining away in drips and floods.

Then, clad in enough armor to make them twins of Imperial Stormtroopers, his depleted teams lumbered into armored personnel carriers and ground their way—at last—toward the commune.

It wasn't the way any sane commander would have chosen. Only enough personnel for a frontal assault. Not even enough to prevent an escape to the rear. An unknown situation in the surrounding hills. Unknown dangers to himself and his men from all that godawful empty landscape. But by God, it was the last chance to save his World's Biggest Pot Bust and his career, and he was taking it.

NOTE: This chapter is dedicated to Robert Crichton, author of one of the world's most delightful novels, *The Secret of Santa Vittoria*. I ... um, borrowed an element or two from him for this part of the story.

Chapter 11

Encore

Marty and Jasper were still in the open when the armored personnel carriers of the multi-jurisdictional task force rumbled up Commune Hill and hove into view.

They were that close to the edge of the clearing and the more brushy, more safe reaches near the mine shaft. But not close enough. With their frantic sweeping and some help from the disintegrating greenhouse (whose initial effects they'd dodged by ducking behind a power shed), they'd almost obliterated the most visible portions of our cannabis trail. Almost done what was necessary to make our escape thoroughly mysterious.

But for Marty and Jasper, time had run out.

Because of what happened next, many Hardyvillians later said Carty deliberately set those two up as human decoys. Some claim he did it to gain a little time or a small tactical advantage that Operation Santa didn't really need. Others are convinced Carty had an even darker, more cynical motive. Still others say he did only what he had to do. Carty himself kept silent, so judge for yourself.

As the growl of engines rounded the last curve, Marty and Jasper, silhouetted in the glow of the blown, burning greenhouse, started a crouching dash in the direction of the mine tunnel. Nobody knows which one of them realized they had to do something smarter—for us—and braver—for them. But at the last minute, as the beam of a headlight swept past, one suddenly dodged in another direction and the other followed. Instead of running toward the tunnel, they bolted—as well as two out-of-shape and pot-bellied people could bolt—at an angle that carried them a good 90 degrees away from our hiding place.

Now they had nowhere to run, except downhill into the dubious concealment of hillside rocks and flora—where movement could be seen easily from above. And in the fireglow and headlight glare, they had been spotted.

Herr Kommandante had intended to go slow, stay inside his armored vehicle, and check things out first. He intended to dispatch a dynamic entry team to bust into the remaining buildings, subdue the occupants, put them under arrest, then use the earth-bermed dwellings for cover against whatever might be out there in the hills—whatever caused his snipers to go silent.

But two running miscreants were too much temptation. Imperial Stormtroopers clattered out of the vehicles and into the night.

A spotlight swung, sweeping after the fleeing pair. Fire erupted from half dozen MP5 machine guns and a handful of semi-auto carbines. Thirty-round magazines emptied. Brass rang on flying brass, then on broken glass. Tactical reloads ratcheted and snapped. A few more bursts. Then...

Silence.

"Cease fire," Herr Kommandante ordered redundantly. He stepped to the edge of the clearing, peered down the hillside, and tried to distinguish any shape of moving or dead bodies down in the brush. Nothing. One way or another, nothing.

"Check it out," he nodded to four of his men. Then he and the rest of his stormtroopers seemed to remember, belatedly, that they were standing bareass-naked (except for 50 pounds of armor, of course, but that wouldn't help them against rifle fire) in the middle of an Uncontrolled Situation, lit up by the burning greenhouse and their own vehicle lights. Somewhere around them 30 or 40 people had to be hiding in these houses. In the hills beyond, God only knew what unknown threat lurked. He had to get back on plan and enter those buildings.

After a huddle in the cover between two armored vehicles, the teams grabbed battering rams and went to work.

"DEA! Open up!"

"I said, 'Open up!' you &^%$er &^%$ers!"

The thud of the battering rams accompanied their shouts. Wood splintered. Glass shattered. More foul shouts erupted as they burst into the Earthship houses, expecting criminals.

Then ... puzzlement.

Herr Kommandante crept from building to building after his baffled men. Not a soul stirred anywhere, other than those he'd brought with him. All around them hung that endless, empty, eerie silence.

Inside the vacant Earthship houses, task force members slunk down below the window-walls and waited for orders. Or for something. What the hell were they supposed to do? A body pumped with adrenaline and ready for action can't just crouch in the shadows.

But that's what they did for some very long minutes, waiting for an attack, looking around for any sign of trapdoors or hidden rooms.

———————————

After a while, when no sign of a threat emerged and they realized the criminals were truly ... gone, the DEA teams crept cautiously across the clearing and flung open the doors

207

of the remaining greenhouses. No pot. Mere garden-variety vegetables grew there, or lay on their sides under glass shattered when our pyrotechnicians sent the pot-house sky high.

Finally, feeling both more puzzled at this *Mary Celeste* of a compound and more confident that, whatever else was going on, nothing was about to attack them, they stood up and turned their attention to the remains of the big ruined greenhouse whose destruction had brought them here. That, of course, had to be the real scene of the crime. That, of course, was where the precious evidence for the World's Biggest Pot Bust of the Week would be found, despite anybody's amateur attempts to obliterate it.

The drug-sniffing dogs bounded from the personnel carriers. They burst out eagerly, nearly pulling their handlers off their feet. Then ... confusion. The dogs dashed randomly, sniffing, whining, sniffing, whining, sniffing, pawing, alerting up a storm. But what was there to alert to? The ground itself? The charred wood timbers? The very air?

No matter where they rushed, in ever widening circles around the obliterated greenhouse, the dogs alerted—but to everything. And therefore to nothing.

"Is it possible this could have wiped out every trace of the plants?" the commander asked a handler, indicating the still-smoldering bits of rubble.

"No. There'd be something." The handler pointed. "Like ... look here. Here's a potting table that survived, there on its side. Look, there's dirt. Broken pots. If there were plants around when the place blew, there'd still be ... well, some trace. Something."

The handlers and their sensory-overloaded dogs continued to circle in confusion.

The commander walked away from the milling men and dogs. He squatted where he could see his four men, still beating the brush for the fleeing dopers—or their bodies. Someplace out there in all that darkness, there had to be one hell of a lot of people and a whole forest of pot plants. It didn't seem possible they could all disappear like that. But it had to be. He raised his visor and pulled on his night-vision goggles. But if some Birnam Wood of cannabis and pot growers was out there, he couldn't see it, even under IR.

Down in the junipers on the opposite side of Commune Hill from which Marty and Jasper had fled, Carty did that trick with his cell phone again. He and his handpicked Hardyville Minutemen—the expert teams who had "taken out" the fed snipers—had waited a long time in the shadows. They had waited unmoving through the feds' gunfire at Marty and Jasper. They had done nothing because doing nothing was a vital part of Operation Santa. But now was the moment to do something.

This time Carty's text message read, "ENCORE."

After he sent it, he waved a signal and the Minutemen around him began creeping silently up the hill, approaching the earth-sheltered rears of the dwellings.

At the barricades, outside the DEA base camp, near one of the few remaining media vans (now staffed only by sleepy technicians), another cell phone buzzed. Another message arrived.

Moments later, a battered red Dodge pickup truck rattled its way down the highway and turned in at the driveway. That is, it tried to turn in. But its drunken driver, the Young Curmudgeon (who in this case was only pseudo-drunken; he had a job to do and took it seriously), missed the roadway and jolted to a halt with one wheel hanging over a ditch.

"Hey," Mudge slurred with beery friendliness, waving at the five remaining *federales* nervously manning the barricades. "Hey guys! C'n ya help me out over here?"

Metal shrieked on metal as he pushed his door wide and stumbled out—revealing an untidy pile of plastic-wrapped packages on the passenger seat.

Most of the packages contained baking soda. A few had enough oregano to season all Italy—thanks to Nat and his grocery store.

But the DEA agents didn't know that.

It was that "politicians-to-money" thing again. Drug warriors to drugs. Drawing guns and stumbling all over themselves and each other, the last agents at the barricades swarmed Mudge.

And every single "civilian" at the barricades—plus a few who'd been bedded down in and behind cars—mostly women, kids, and old people—pulled sidearms and swarmed them.

Not a journalist was in sight. Only the media techs stood witness. By then, although they didn't know what we were up to, they thought whatever was happening was pretty clever. Even amusing. Techies tend to be natural libertarians, anyhow. And our friends at the barricades had been working on them, feeding them coffee and discontent. By the end of that night several of the techs abandoned their vans and their pet journalists and defected permanently to Hardyville. There was nobody to report the incident at the barricades to the outside world.

As to the agents that our "civilians" captured at the barricades ... just tell yourself that old Hollywood mickey finn story again. Of course we wouldn't harm them. Technically, they were only trespassers, even if they were everybody-else's-business minders with felonious intent.

The drug dogs and handlers still circled on the hilltop, keeping one eye out for a threat that seemed more abstract at every moment. Members of the media, emerging cautiously from the relative safety of the armored personnel carriers, poked into the rubble or stuck their heads into the silent, empty dwellings. Herr Kommandante still crouched at the edge of the clearing, scanning fruitlessly.

He whipped off the clumsy night-vision goggles and looked out into the unaugmented darkness. Nothing.

Yet he felt, at that very moment, a chill so deep it nearly turned his spine into an icicle. Yeah, the whole situation was creepy. Had been creepy all along. The whole setup was chill-inducing. But at that instant, something prickled an extra added creepiness, right at the back of his neck and down to a certain body part that abruptly puckered like a prune.

Why, how, he didn't know. But suddenly he was certain that the very silence of this place, the very fact that he and his men weren't being shot at from the hills, was one very damn bad sign. The worst kind of sign. Every minute that went by without somebody taking pot shots at them put them in that much more trouble. He didn't know how. But he knew it down to his bones and sphincter.

He leaped to his feet and wheeled back toward the ruined greenhouse, just as a media contingent rallied itself to descend on him with video cameras and notepads outstretched, the question "What the hell ...?" in their eyes.

"Take cover!" he screamed. "Take cover!"

Take cover from what? Confused journalists and raiders alike stopped in their tracks. Take cover from whom?

"For God's sake, get DOWN! TAKE COVER!!!" Herr Kommandante screamed, waving as he ran toward them.

At that moment, shots rang out. Shots boomed, cracked, zipped, spat, and ka-chinged as bullets struck rock and metal. Shots seemed to come from everywhere—and nowhere.

Shots zinged off the sides of armored personnel carriers as journalists and raiders alike hit the dirt. Raiders inched under vehicles and rubble piles, looking around for something to shoot back at. A few fired, randomly.

Caught in the open, still far from concealment, Herr Kommandante dropped to a crouch, shouldered his MP5, and swiveled, seeking a target, chillingly aware that he was a target.

But again ... silence. Weird silence. The shooting stopped and the silence went on. And on. He looked around. Nobody screaming. Nobody bleeding. It was as if all that gunfire had only been to say, "We're here."

He looked beyond the pile of quaking journalists, to a pile of rubble in front of one of the vehicles. If he could reach there...

Still holding his MP5 in firing position, he flopped onto his belly and elbows and began inching toward cover.

Smack! Dirt kicked up in his face as a bullet hit the ground in front of him. He inched backwards. Bullets smacked the dirt at his feet. He froze. They—whoever they were—weren't going to let him move. A couple of his men fired in the direction of the muzzle flashes. But there was nothing there to hit.

From another direction altogether boomed a voice: "If you wanna die, keep firing. Don't make no difference to us."

It was a fact. The DEA teams were in a lighted clearing, some of them completely in the open. The shooters and the voice were above, on the rooftops, in darkness, sheltered by the berms of the housetops. Unless they exposed themselves by firing again, there was no way to retaliate. And even then, there was no way to retaliate without getting well-exposed butts blown off.

The multi-jurisdictional federal task force, led by the mighty, politically untouchable DEA, had been beaten by a bunch of yokels that nobody could even see.

"Throw your weapons out," Carty ordered. "Throw them in the middle of the clearing where we can see them. You! Down there on the hillside!" he shouted to the four agents who had been after Jasper and Marty, "Throw your weapons and walk up. Nice and slow. With hands in the air."

A clatter as the first firearms hit the dirt. Herr Kommandante flexed his sweating palms around his MP5. He couldn't give up like this. Not like this. Not on his face in the dirt, beaten by invisible tricksters. He was the government. He was the federal...

Then he realized that a sound had been growing on him.

He dared to raise his head imperceptibly. He listened. *Yes!* It was the thump of helicopter rotors. The helicopter was distant yet, and out of sight. But it was his miracle.

The cavalry had arrived.

They'd done it. By God, the bosses had done it. D.C. had actually gotten him a chopper. He couldn't believe it. His demand on the phone to his boss had been sheer bravado—the gesture of a man going down in flames.

But now here they were ... backup! He raised his head further and started to chuckle. All around him, he could feel the slight stir of his cowed men noticing, shifting slightly, readying for hope. The clatter of thrown weapons ceased before it had hardly begun. They hung on to what they had. He started to raise his body from the ground.

Psst! Another shot spit dirt into Herr Kommandante's eyes. He flattened.

"Stay down on your ugly face," Carty ordered, implacably. "And I told ya—throw those weapons out. All of 'em. Or die. Your choice."

Despite the promise of aerial backup, this confident command voice booming through the night rattled the raiders. More machine guns, carbines, sidearms, and even a few tactical knives landed with a clatter on the growing pile.

"No, you idiots!" Herr Kommandante screamed, watching his men surrender around him. "Don't you hear it? They're coming. Our guys are going to blow these yokels off this hilltop!" He laughed again, edging into hysteria. "We've won!"

Carty let him laugh for a while then called over the increasing roar, "Sorry, Mister. But that chopper? It ain't yours."

Herr Kommandante looked into the sky, where a civilian Bell JetRanger abruptly burst into a halo of spotlights as it descended. It was white. It had a company logo on its side, with a prominent red cross hastily taped over that.

As it hovered, the once-and-never-again DEA field commander flung away his MP5 and, as ordered, laid his face in the Hardy County dirt.

The chopper set down. Blue-clad medical personnel burst from its doors. After a word from Carty, and led by a handful of Hardyville militiamen, paramedics hustled down the hill after Jasper and Marty.

Carty and his hand-picked crew of Hardyville Minutemen made their way down from the rooftops and finished the job of rounding up the last members of the task force and their leader. You can think about that humane catch-and-release program again.

Operation Santa, the first battle fought by the Hardyville Militia in nearly 200 years, concluded with a pair of surprises.

The danger past, and the invading *federales* under control, a distinguished older gentleman with a silver aura of hair shining in the spotlights stepped out of the helicopter and gazed around for the first time at the sacred ground of Hardy County. You could tell, even before he emerged fully and spoke in his elegant Castilian accent, that he was continental down to his manicured fingertips.

No, he wasn't Jorge Delaval. That would just be too, too *deus ex machina,* wouldn't it? It was merely Delaval's chief aide, Alejandro Verdugo Serrano. Carty stepped up to shake his hand. As the rats and communards emerged dazedly from the tunnels, so did Nat, who approached the chopper as if he'd been expecting this visitor all along. Serrano accepted Nat's dirty paw with diplomatic aplomb and a radiantly gracious smile. When Dora hobbled up on work-sore legs, Serrano bowed low over her brown, broken-nailed hand.

The second surprise came with sorrow.

One of the paramedics rushed back up the hill to retrieve more supplies from the helicopter. In answer to Carty's question, he paused long enough to say, "The older man. He's dead. I'm sorry. The young woman ... seriously wounded. Very seriously. But still alive."

Carty gaped after the paramedic. *Young woman?*

Claire Wolfe

THE DEAL WITH THE DEVIL

In which Hardyville and the outside world come to terms with each other and the Carolina family desperately attempts to come to terms with itself

Chapter 1
New Era

I have a confession. When we ran the invading feds out of Hardyville, I implied that we committed large acts of all-American carnage—but committed them "off-stage," so to speak. You probably thought I was just being discreet. Actually, I misled you. Strictly by accident, of course.

The truth is: No feds were harmed in the making of that story.

We really did—as I mused—capture the invaders and gently release all but a handful of them at the top of the mountain pass that defines the western border of our happy anarchy. We set the majority of them free and waved goodbye. After, of course, stripping them naked. Not to mention confiscating their weapons, ID, credit cards, cell phones, and available cash.

Consider that divestiture their fine for trespassing, making threats, and blowing up the cannabis-growing greenhouse at the Emma Goldman Arts Co-op and Biodiverse Living Center. (Yes, I know *we* blew up the greenhouse. But it was entirely their fault that we needed to.)

There was still snow up there in those passes. And below-freezing temperatures—although not enough to hurt much more than their dignities and maybe a few small protruding parts. Toesies and such.

Our aim, remember, wasn't to make war with the unconstitutional United States government—and end up getting Iraqed or Vietnamed. Our aim was to persuade the feds that it's best to leave Hardyville, Hardy County, and Hardyvillians, alone.

If that disappoints you, I'll tell you something else: We did keep five of the fed shock troops captive—Herr Kommandante, whose federal ID said he was named John Davis Melvin, and the four paramilitaries who had so unquestioningly obeyed his orders to gun down the fleeing Marty and Jasper. I can never keep the names of those four henchmen straight. Call them War, Pestilence, Famine, and Death, if you like. More about their fate later. I assure you that while it won't be bloody, it will be effective—as both restitution and retribution.

Sigh. But how do you restore (which is what "restitution" implies) a lost life?

Marty Harbibi was gone. Never more would his opinions burst like particularly gaseous farts into the air of the Hog Trough Grill and Feed. Never again would someone in Hardyville know everything there was to know about every possible subject, even subjects he had never heard of before. No, we couldn't say we missed him. We're more honest than that. But he died a hero. And most of us were kind of sorry when his widow—herself named Mardi Harbibi—decided to cremate him and requested no public fuss. It would have been difficult to compose, let alone deliver with a straight face, a respectful eulogy.

Actually, given Mrs. Harbibi's nature and the quality of their relationship, we considered it a relief she didn't feed Marty's carcass to the Harbibi hogs. In fact, we were all rather amazed that she hadn't fed him to the hogs years ago. Without waiting for him to die.

But I'm rambling. There's so much to tell you about the aftermath of our brush with the forces of Mordor-on-the-Potomac that I scarcely know where to begin.

You probably want to know about Jasper ... or whatever we should call her now. Yes, what about Jasper Feldspar Clarke? Another hero. A volunteer who put himself ... I'm sorry ... herself at risk to save friends and save Operation Santa.

She's still in the hospital, still touch and go. I don't know her history—though I'm sure it's an intriguing one. What I do know is that by laying her life on the line for both Hardyville and the Emma Goldman Arts Co-op and Biodiverse Living Center she helped forge bonds between two groups that had previously been at odds.

After the feds were driven out and the rubble settled, members of the two very diverse communities began to trust each other. At least a little. As had happened earlier between old timers and new residents of the town proper, we woke up to the realization that we had more in common than out-of-common with our counter-cultural neighbors up the road.

A shared enemy can do wonders to unite uneasy neighbors.

Next thing we knew, Nat and Dora had partnered up. They leased the old Pickle's Groce Mart building, and re-opened Nat's makeshift grocery store on a grand scale. This time it had not only veggies from the commune, but also communard workers as well as townies. This time it was not just a grocery store, but much more.

"Lyons and Yale Good Foods" soon sprawled into the vacant lot where city hall once stood. It became a grand, free-spreading food market, farmers' market, flea-market, flower fair, and collection of makeshift sidewalk food and craft vendors, which grew as other enterprising Hardyvillians, new and old, joined the party.

Dora's boyfriend, former city councilman Dan White, kept the books for the grocery—and kept an eye on his lady. Of Dora and Carty's passionate lip-lock on the night of Operation Santa, there was—for the moment—no further trace. They went right back to ignoring each other, leaving the town gossips sputtering with unanswered questions.

217

But now we come to the real crux of the matter. Hardyvillians and communards had a common enemy—and now a common friend. Or did we?

Was Jorge Delaval a friend to Hardyville? Now there's a question for you.

And here's an even bigger question: What will happen to us, now that Big Men—both in government and out of it—have discovered Hardy County?

We locals pulled off Operation Santa, driving the feds away, on our own. But the aftermath—and our future—now hung on the hasty agreement Nat had made with Delaval Enterprises. No longer was our old "invisibility cloak" (made up of our remote, forbidding terrain and our centuries of stubborn silence) enough to protect us from the ravages of two-bit tinhorn rulers and self-appointed nannies. Some Big Man in Washington, D.C., had learned about us and made us a target. Now dozens, maybe hundreds, maybe thousands of Sauron's minions had their eyes on Hardyville.

We needed the protection of the powerful against the powerful. Now Delaval, who could bring down small countries and major currencies with a single call to his financial managers, was solidifying a deal with little Hardyville. Nat had offered him a trade. His protection for ... the greatest thing Hardyville has to offer.

Yeah, I know. Little guys have, in the past, made bargains with powerful allies. And the deals haven't worked out so well—at least not for those "protected" or "aided." Just ask the Irish who long ago invited the Normans and the Anglo-Saxons in. A millennium later, they're only now beginning to recover from their "protectors."

Be that as it may, here's the deal in rough form: When Nat patiently phoned his way up the Delaval organization food chain in the hours before Operation Santa, he offered that international billionaire and his friends something precious: an off-shore haven (very far off-shore in our case, being a good thousand miles from any ocean) more pure than Switzerland or the Caymans or Andorra or the Bahamas combined.

Hardyville: Land of no taxes. Land of solid, non-inflating money. Land of total financial (and many other kinds of) privacy. Land where your honest earnings are your own and nobody else's to seize or control. Land where, if you're just trying to live, you'll be left alone. Forever and ever, world without end, amen.

If the Delaval billions and influence would protect us, we'd work with him and his friends to make all this available for their purposes.

Surely, Delaval already knew something about Hardy power; why else would he situate his medical cannabis operation here? But Nat—on no authority but his own—offered to lay the Full Hardy at Delaval's feet: "You and your billionaire pals need a haven within America for the coming hard times. It's all well and good to have places you can go in Thailand or Singapore. But you need someplace *here,* in North America, which up to now you don't really have. You need a place to weather the storm and a base from which to rebuild. It's hiding here right under your nose. You help us preserve it and we'll show you all the ways it can serve you."

Nat said all that—though no doubt in more crusty, cowboyish terms.

The verbal agreement had been sketchy. And wildly unofficial. Now Alejandro Serrano, Delaval's envoy, was here to turn the sketch into ... well, a drawing. A blueprint. After that, Serrano would depart and a long-term Delaval project manager would be sent in. It would take time for the full edifice to emerge.

And what would Hardyville look like when the last brushstroke was painted or the last brick of the agreement was laid? We, the Hardyville *hoi polloi,* faced a representative of the billionaires of Europe and beyond and hoped—perhaps not with perfect confidence—that when all was done, we'd still be a hidden, rural, simple place for ordinary, self-sufficient, cussed, do-it-ourselfing, doing-it-our-own-way people, even as we provided offshore services for the Delaval cabal.

Yes, we'd made a deal with the devil. Those with the power to protect also have the power—and often the will—to destroy. Even without ill will, moneyed men could ruin us. We knew that.

Picture Hardyville being transformed into Monte Carlo or Las Vegas or even Aspen or Jackson Hole. Picture our vast cattle ranches disappearing under the foundations of the pricey houses of the rich and the dismal McMansions of their mid-level enterprise managers. Picture the humble little wood and brick store facades of Liberty Avenue and Freedom Way being torn down for shiny high-rises. Picture our independent souls yielding to a promise of "prosperity" that meant ultimately that we'd get to become the housekeepers and wait-persons for the truly prosperous. That we'd be mere cogs, where once we spun the wheel.

We pictured it. And were very, very scared. Some said we'd have been better off facing wave after wave of feds on our own than risking such a fate.

But most of us thought it was worth the risk when the alternative was being transformed into Baghdad.

And we hoped, we really did, that the stubborn, principled, cussed, durable, centuries-old, heat-forged Hardyville Way was strong enough to prevail over darned near anything.

We'd soon find out.

But first, we had some plain, simple Hardy County justice to dispense. Which our five fed prisoners were determined to make not so simple.

Chapter 2
Justice

For every crime, there is at least one victim. No victim, no crime.

And no nonsense, please, about how victimless "crimes" cause some amorphous non-entity called society to do all the real suffering. I've never met "society," and neither have you. Nor will we ever. Down that path of reasoning, the path in which "society" has more rights than individuals, lies the total control state.

Okay, I admit it. I'm going to launch into a lecture. I hate that when other writers do it. I try to avoid it. But sometimes ... well, that's the way it has to be.

I'll keep it short—and I hope unboring. But it's the groundwork for the events that follow. In fact, it's the groundwork of Hardyville itself—a little town where things aren't quite perfect but are frequently better than in the real world.

No victim, no crime. When you have an act of aggression and a victim, you need justice. If justice can't be delivered by the intended victim on the spot, then you need Procedures. On the other hand, when you have neither aggression nor victim, then *laissez faire*. It's a simple principle. It's bedrock under our feet.

Of course people who make up a society—or a neighborhood, or a community—suffer when criminals rampage. But "society" also suffers when individuals don't have refrigerators. Or shoes. Or when they abuse their health. That doesn't mean some government should take over Amana or Whirlpool, establish a Commissariat of Cobblery (and a five-year plan for ending the inevitably-worsening shoe shortage), or order people to eat right, stop smoking, and wear their galoshes when it rains.

Right?

In fact, people suffer their very worst griefs when governments decide to get a wee bit too involved in their lives. Ask anybody who had to live with Mao or Stalin or Hitler or Pol Pot. If that's too large a scale for you, ask anybody who's been "helped" by an IRS auditor or an ATF agent.

At a slight angle from this, I want to point out two facts that would appear blatantly self-evident to everybody if you were creating a justice system from scratch and some bright young graduate student piped up, "Hey, I know! Let's have the government run it!"

Fact the first: In a government-run justice system like the one you have out there in the real world, any person who's actually been injured is about the last one to be "made whole," as the expression goes. People who've been robbed don't get their money back through prosecution of the criminal. People who've been maimed don't get compensation unless they bring a separate private case for it (and are very, very lucky). People who've been raped often just get raped again by attorneys and have nothing in the end but more pain. Sure, there are now itty-bitty token restitution programs attached like barnacles to the tax-funded "just us" system. But the government regards itself (a.k.a. "society" again) as the primary victim. Which is, frankly, dopey.

Fact the second: If you had offended Microsoft, how would you feel if you had to be dragged into a court whose building was owned by Microsoft, whose officials, right down to the all-powerful judge, were paid by Microsoft, whose jury received their little *per diem* from Microsoft, whose rules were entirely determined by Microsoft, and where even your own attorney was considered an "officer of the (Microsoft) court"? Would you think you were getting a fair trial? Oh, c'mon. People would be rolling around the floor laughing at such a ridiculous idea. Yet that's what we face if we're on the receiving end of "The State vs. John Doe" or "California vs. Mary Jones."

And that's only the *beginning* of the legal game that gets played. Matters get worse from there.

It's no wonder (and shouldn't be a point of pride) that 95 percent of all cases (or more!) in some jurisdictions go in the government's favor. And that most defendants plea bargain—giving up their right to a defense and their right against self-incrimination.

That high conviction rate isn't a sign that cops always arrest the right people or that prosecutors operate with nearly perfect skill. It's mostly just a setup in which terrified and sometimes pure-as-snow-innocent people get caught.

But the setup is a profitable one for the lawyering industry, the law-spewing industry (aka every legislature in the land), the prosecuting-and-judging industry, and the relatively new (but thriving) prison-industrial complex out there in the real world.

There's only one good thing you can say about all this. The relatively small number of true, hard-core psycho or career criminals who get arrested and end up in prison are prevented from plying their trade on random innocents while they're locked up. They have to wait until they get back out.

But at the same time, millions of non-violent "offenders" have their lives ruined and their families shattered (a great method for producing future criminals and for beefing up the public-assistance rolls). And the real purposes of justice—to make the victim whole, discourage people from harming each other, and even give the offender a chance to re-establish his honor within the community by doing the right thing—are pretty much cast aside.

Anyway, that's the lecture, whole and entire. In Hardyville, no victim, no crime. Bedrock principle.

And in Hardyville, there is no government—not any more, you betcha—to be victim, prosecutor, and profiteer. No "Hardyville vs. John Doe" and certainly no "Hardyville vs. two pounds of hamburger" or "The City vs. a pocketful of cash" as you'll find beyond our red-rock valley walls.

The upshot: In Hardyville, things work a lot better. But still, way far from perfect. I'm not going to pretend Hardyville is Libertopia. There is no perfect when you're dealing with human beings.

Thanks for bearing with me. Lecture all done. This time I really mean it.

So there we were. We had five genuine bad guys on our hands. Murderers. Top of the Hardyville Most Unwanted list: Gang leader John Davis Melvin (formerly referred to in these pages as Herr Kommandante of the DEA's multi-jurisdictional taskforce)—boss of an illegal party of armed, paramilitary invaders. Then there were his four henchmen who had obeyed orders to shoot at fleeing men (correct that — fleeing persons). Call them War, Famine, Pestilence, and Death or whatever else you feel like calling them.

Marty Harbibi. Jasper Feldspar Clarke. *Those* are victims, without a doubt; no fuzzy-wuzzy "society" about it. Justice, without a doubt, had to follow. And unlike the earlier episode with the Goodins and our local SWATters, mere pocket change from the offenders would not be sufficient recompense.

The five malefactors enjoyed sub-deluxe accommodations in the Hardyville jail, watched over by our good old familiar non-tax-paid sheriff and his two deputies, Tomas Castenon and Emin Borgo. The feds' not-so-terribly-vile durance was covered by a fund established for just such purposes by the coalition of Hardy County arbitration agencies.

And yes, those *federales* really were treated decently, other than being a mite crowded. Neither the Code of Hardyville nor the personal code of Hardyvillians allows anything like the tortures and deprivations of Abu Ghraib or Guantanamo Bay. Not even for the most difficult prisoners.

And I tell you, those guys were real pests.

Problems, problems, problems they caused us. Having arrived in the county in the middle of the night, Bent on Nefarious Purposes, none of the five had signed an arbitration-services agreement, as is common for residents in these parts. Even after somebody explained to them that justice proceeded here via mediation and agreement between trespasser and victim (or surviving family members thereof), they smugly refused to select an arbitration service. They thought their refusal to sign on with an arbitration firm would foil us. And for a while, they were right.

Justice did not move forward.

Guess they expected that their government would swoop in any minute, extradite them, and move their case to federal court—where we all know exactly what sort of justice the government's own agents get for killing members of the *hoi polloi*—a paid vacation (aka "administrative leave") followed by complete exoneration.

Little did they know that Hardyville was never going to allow that.

And so they waited. Of course the sheriff allowed them to call in attorneys. But can you picture how a real-world legaloid would encounter Hardyville? We have few attorneys here and none of them handle what you in the real world might think of as criminal cases. We have skilled mediators, hired by the parties to any dispute, or employed (freelance) by the arbitration services. They help ease disputants toward a solution. We have forensics experts we can call on. People like that. But with nothing but the Code of Hardyville, the Golden Rule, and whatever general laws private associations and individuals came up with for the smoother running of daily life, what would a D.C. attorney do here?

Invoke the "fine print"? What fine print?

The D.C. attorneys were, I believe, trying to research exactly what kind of jurisdiction Hardyville is supposed to be—whether that be a state or county or federal occupation zone. If they managed to discover that they could declare our local laws void and thrust us into some familiar—and badly broken!—system, they no doubt figured their system would rule and we would rue the day we ever tangled with them.

And that worried us. You can imagine how that worried us. Even though we were pretty sure we couldn't legitimately be wedged into any of their legalisms.

But in such things as case law and the nature of Hardyville's justice system (a justice system which, from their blinkered perspective, appeared to be missing entirely), the fancy Washington attorneys made no headway. They simply did not, and given their deeply held biases, could not, understand us.

Still, the eager law boys and girls had the limitless resources of an aroused federal government at their disposal. And they were looking at us in ways we (brother, this is understating the case) did not like. That meant we had to turn to Delaval's representative. Post haste. Rapidly. And lickety-split.

Now. How to get Delaval to agree to continue to use his money and connections to keep government off us while not losing our low-key rural souls to Delaval himself?

In that we were at least momentarily in luck.

Alejandro Serrano, Jorge Delaval's personal envoy, embraced Hardyville with remarkable aplomb, considering he was far more used to the spas and metropoli of Europe. He never once looked down on us from the height of his urbane, silver-haired eminence. With the old-school manners of one raised to believe that the nobility are privileged to serve the people, he acted toward us as though we were his equals. A good sign. A great sign.

He and Nat appeared not only to have a productive rapport with each other when they met with the other major Hardyville property holders to hash out the details of an agreement. They also had a jolly good time together after midnight at Bark's Tavern or the Hell-in-a-Handbasket Saloon. It took the bartenders a while to find the delicate liqueurs Serrano preferred. Or the vintage Bordeaux. But pretty soon, he was drinking those alongside regular old Moose Drool beer, and he and Nat were just like a couple of the guys.

Basically, Nat acted as negotiator-in-chief for the largest of Hardyville's landowners, who are the people who basically counted the most in the negotiation with the Delaval interests. Oh, we would all have some sort of say at some point. But nope, Hardyville is not a democracy.

We heard lots of reports on what the landowners were negotiating. Even though they were perfectly open about what they were up to, the property owners and Serrano became the subject of much rumor and gossip (especially since Dora and Carty weren't supplying enough of that particular commodity at the moment).

We heard hopeful news emerging, some of it even true. We were relieved when we got the announcement that all parties had agreed on a clause that anyone actively attempting to implement any tax of any shape, kind, size, or degree of toxicity, could be shot on sight by any self-responsible resident of Hardy County.

That was a good start. Serrano seemed to find it a particularly amusing clause.

We were happy and more than a little relieved when we watched the negotiators (because everyone wandered in and out of the meetings and occasionally even offered an opinion) hammer out the clause that said the Delaval organization would issue an immediate "cease and desist" message to federal attorneys and researchers looking into the exact nature and location of Hardyville. The rumor about Nat and Serrano's midnight-at-the-bar negotiations said the Delavals would use, as their "stick," a threat to make a demonstration of how very, very precisely they could drop the U.S. dollar against every major currency on any given day.

So while our captives were certainly entitled, as per the Bill of Rights, to have "counsel," their fancy-pantsy political law-twistificators would soon be scrambling, as far as their wrong-headed legal educations could take them, to understand Hardyville's native, and very sensible, justice system. We would not be dragged into any "jurisdiction" of theirs.

The Delaval people and their international mega-billions would stand between us and the intrusions of federal and state governments. But what sort of "us" lay in our future?

Agreements are only paper. The U.S. government once made infamous agreements with the people they found living near these parts. But a single gold strike could blow those agreements right in the natives' faces. Paper? What paper? Federal troops would just ride right over paper treaties with the natives.

That was our position, a century and more later. We were the bow-armed red man, facing the infamous might of the Washingtonian power-grabbing government. We just had to count on our bows being a little more high tech, and the Delaval "non-government" being more benign than the feds.

Serrano ... well, most of us would have loved to keep Serrano as Delaval's personal project manager in Hardyville. But he was merely a globe-hopping envoy. He made the basic agreements, but others would come in to "develop" Hardyville as a haven.

That very word ... "develop."... Ugh. Well, you know. The communards weren't the only ones who found that word ominous.

Eventually, though, it had to be. While our five prisoners were still sneering down their noses at the rubes' jail and the rubes' crude justice system, confident that they'd be sprung momentarily and that the rubes would swiftly be made to pay for their uppitiness, Alejandro Verdugo Serrano concluded Delaval's agreement with Hardyville. He delivered it by private-satellite uplink and teleconferencing with his boss. Soon thereafter, he prepared to fly away with signatures from both sides. And—blessedly—he began the process that called off the feds.

But then, he left us.

Dozens of us trooped out to the airport with him one blue day in May, and gathered 'round to see him off. He gave us all a jaunty, but somehow dignified, wave, bowed low over a feminine hand or two, and departed.

Two weeks later, after Serrano and Delaval had quietly made their choice of permanent on-site project manager, and shared their private aims for us, and discussed their secret strategies with the new man, nearly the same number caravanned to the airport again to meet the man the Delaval organization had chosen to live among us.

Where Serrano had merited a dedicated Delaval helicopter, his successor flew commercial—via the one tiny puddle-jumper that touches down in Hardyville every couple of days (when the ice isn't too slick or there aren't too many steers on the runway).

As he unfolded his lankiness from the hatch-like door of the Cessna, we could see he was of a different breed than Serrano. Younger, with bare touches of silver at the temple, he was satin-haired, pale skinned—and the very picture (as nearly every swooning female in the crowd probably pegged him) of the roguish Latin Lover.

We thought some relationships in Hardyville were doomed—soon to be left behind, along with many angry men and (eventually) weeping, love-shocked women, in the wake of this middle-aged Valentino.

Of Hardyville's larger doom, we remained unsure. We were too busy taking in the D'Anconian magnificence of Delaval's new man. Especially we of the female persuasion.

We were collectively struck in the heart when a beautiful young woman not much above half his age stepped out of the plane behind him. Females for yards around were speechless with disappointment. Except, apparently, one.

Charlotte Carolina, at the rear of the crowdlet, suddenly shoved herself into the backs of her neighbors. She lunged, clearly without conscious intent, toward the figure now stepping from the plane and carefully ducking to avoid the propeller.

"You pig!" she cried. "How dare you turn up here?!"

Chapter 3
Monkey-Fu, Too?

Our new arrival—and our future friend or foe—was Charlotte's roving ex-husband, Gael Carolina.

Some of us suspected another instance of monkey-fu at work. The coincidence (if that's what it was) seemed too great. Conspiracy theorists speculated on the recent whereabouts of that wandering young monk from the Hilltop Hermitage, Qwai Ching Paine. Señor Carolina himself, who claimed no encounters with zen-babbling strangers, explained more simply how he happened to end up in this obscure corner of the world.

"It was I who persuaded Señor Delaval to finance an independent cannabis farm in Hardy County. I learned about this place in emails from my son, Antonio. When opportunity arose for Delaval Enterprises to forge closer bonds with the fine people of your land, who more natural than I to help forge them—I who already have such loving bonds here?"

And he embraced his worshipful son (who looked just like him in that raw, unfinished teenaged way) and his daughter (who looked a lot more interested in the hairdo and fashions of the Audrey Tautou double accompanying her father).

But those who heard Gael Carolina make that statement, on that June day at the airport, couldn't help but notice that the word "fine"—as in "fine people of your land"—didn't sound quite as genuine and genial as it might have on the lips of his predecessor, the envoy Alejandro Verdugo Serrano. It sounded, in fact, distinctly sardonic. Like the tone of a man who found himself among the most red-necked of rubes. A man who thought he just might make his career by molding our weak Hardyville clay into exactly what we didn't want to be: Monte Carlo, U.S.A.—a place more fitting his ambitions and reputation.

We looked at each other uneasily, began to treat Señor Carolina with kid gloves, and once the dust of his arrival had settled, rushed to Charlotte's store to get the scoop on this Latin stranger.

You can imagine what Charlotte's scoop was full of.

"Wild adventurer. Couldn't bear to stay put to raise his own kids—his own kids! He barely contacted them for ten years—too busy exploring for gold in the Amazon or sailing the Mediterranean with a sailboat full of ... *women* on somebody else's money." We could picture the epithet she'd wanted to utter instead of "women." The picture contained champagne, cocaine, and much nakedness.

"But of course, they adore him," Charlotte ranted on, nodding at a photo of her children on the counter. "Wouldn't you know it? I work my behind off getting them through everything from scraped knees to their surprises about birth-control pills. And that just makes me a bad guy. Look at them fawning on him—on that man who barely could remember to send child support, let alone Christmas or birthday presents! And here sits terrible, rotten mom ..."

Charlotte's rants interested those with a taste for gossip, and broke even more hearts among those smitten with Gael Carolina's continental sleek looks. They could now add "Byronic adventurer" and "dangerous man" to his résumé of attractions. But none of this driftwood of his private life helped us really understand the man whose opinions and ambitions would determine our fate.

He and his ... girlfriend? wife? administrative assistant? mistress? hitchhiker? (no one was saying) ... settled into the old Pickle residence, the entire political clan having fled the town. The Pickle Manse was the nearest thing we had to decadent European splendor. The Delavalians moved in, then proceeded to keep their own counsel.

There were meetings, of course. And many tours of this and that. Señor Carolina visited Doc's amazing drug store, the One Unattractive Tourist Attraction, the Den of Iniquity casino, and (strictly for professional purposes, of course), Miss Fitz's Young Ladies Academy, where even those rather jaded and experienced girls' hearts beat a little faster in his presence.

He even visited the Federal Five and had some talks with the murderous members of the multi-jurisdictional task force, who still languished in jail as their attorneys tried to figure out the arcana of the Hardyville justice system. (Hint: Our system was too simple for their overly complexicated habits.)

But most of all, our new arrival had long meetings with the owners of Hardyville's banks and was given a cautious overview of how our money system works.

Don't worry; I won't give you that lecture—the big one on how money works. Suffice to say that our money system works much more steadily than, say, the Federal Reserve system, albeit on a pretty small scale until now.

It was money, and banking, that interested Señor Carolina most. That was Hardyville's prime virtue in the eyes of the Delavalistas—their money flowing in, their money flowing out, money safe within, money kept private from entry until exit. And that we could give them. Numbered accounts safer than the Swiss. Bearer books better than Austria's. More security than the Cayman Islands. For Hardy County was not a signatory to any international banking treaty. And until just a couple of weeks ago, Hardyville had never been under the evil eye of the IRS, the Department of Homeland Security, or the "know your customer" law.

Our bankers mostly did know their customers, of course. But only because they'd gone to school with good old Joe or Mary since ... well, the Hardyville equivalent of going to school, that is. Shooting tin cans together. Stuff like that. But even then, when it came to what Joe or Mary had in an account, our bankers couldn't have had their records pried open with the biggest crowbar in any government arsenal. Nor did they consider it their business what Joe and Mary did with their money—as long as they weren't taking any obvious Mafia payoffs to perform hits on inconvenient, but otherwise innocent, people.

That Señor Carolina appreciated. It was the rest of Hardyville he didn't appear to like.

"Quaint." "Outdated." "Eccentric." "Amusing." The epithets uttered by the man on his various tours mounted up. Oh, it's true he let truth-telling words like those slip only very occasionally, amid pleasant nods, polite questions, and keep-his-own-counsel answers. But we were getting the message.

"Quaint," my Aunt Fanny.

Carolina didn't grok that, to work as it does, Hardyville has to be what it is. Start building high-rise hotel-casinos and pretty soon you have to have politicians to run things. Next thing you know they're making you get licenses for every move you make and taxing you for every breath you take (idealistic paper agreements not withstanding). The temptation to sell their power, or give it to buddies from the country club or the political party quickly overwhelms what tiny grain of a conscience such people began with.

Start putting up high-rises and advertising Hardyville (even discreetly within the billionaire network) as place to live and enjoy the cosmopolitan pleasures ... and Hardyville is useless to you. Hardyville is dead.

I mean, what do you think happened to the whole U.S.? Yeah, the country started out with less-than-Hardyvillian principles—neither chattel slavery nor a powerful federal state are tools for creating liberty. But what happened after that was that the country became more urban than rural. People who've never had to dig their own ditches or rely on their neighbors for sustenance after a crop-killing storm rarely "get" freedom to the bones—even those few who still get it, intellectually.

They do not get that the best of life—and the deepest of freedom—lies on the other side of overcoming risk and peril: in Hardyville.

Gael Carolina certainly didn't get it.

While Señor Carolina, often with one of his children or Mlle. Audrey/Mirabelle (or whoever she really was) on his arm, made his rounds—and his plans—chaos erupted in the other Carolina household, that of Charlotte and the kids Tonio, 18, and Jen, 15 going on 25.

"I don't have to put up with you!"

Jen turned her back on Charlotte with a flounce. She stomped a couple of paces to frown at herself in a mirror—a constant occupation, these days.

"You do have to put up with me," Charlotte barked. "And you will have to put up with me. Because I support you. I put the chocolate syrup on your ice cream. I buy that ghastly shade of purple for your lips. And as long as I do, you will have to put up with me. And obey me."

"Not for long, I don't! 'Cause in this place—even if it is a stupid place in every other way, full of people who could compete in an uglification geekathon—I can leave home any time I want. They say I don't have to wait 'til I'm 18."

Charlotte sighed. She had known Jen would discover that fact, sooner rather than later; there is no arbitrary "age of majority" in Hardy County. Now that the day had arrived, and the information had sprouted in Jen's muddy little brain, Charlotte didn't know whether to be horrified or relieved. *My baby—threatening to leave home! This poisonous little pest I'd like to strangle with my bare hands—promising to leave me in peace!*

"No, you can't leave home any time you want," she explained wearily, treading a dangerous line. "You can leave when you're capable of supporting yourself or when you can, on your own, find some other family willing to support you. That's the rule around here, girl. And you're still a long way from either. Leave without making some provision for yourself and, no, they won't throw you in jail. But nobody's likely even to help you. And remember, if you leave home I'm not under any obligation to take you back or assume responsibility for your screwups."

"Oh, yeah? Well, you watch me. I'll get myself a job. I'll make lots of money and get myself an apartment. I'll move in with somebody else, if I can think of anybody I can stand in this stupid town. Or ... or I'll move in with Dad and Mirabelle. Yeah! That's what I'll do."

"Mirabelle? So that's what that woman's called?" Somehow, hearing the name of her most recent replacement, spoken aloud, made the entire situation that much more outrageous. "Mirabelle. Boy, isn't that just a perfect name for a tramp?" Charlotte snapped. "'Mirabelle, baby, come over here and massage my toes.' 'Mirabelle, you look so good in that lacy peignoir, darling.' Is that the kind of life you want to lead, Jennifer? Is it? Is it really?"

She realized seconds too late that she'd just painted a picture of Jen's idea of heaven.

Jen squinted into the mirror. *Is that a new zit? Ohcrap.* Her eyes then darted to her mother's. "Yeah. That's how I want to live. And in this place you can't stop me. And don't forget, I'm not Jen. I'm Rosamund now. Dad says it was his mother's name." Jen smiled maliciously. *"She* was from Spain," she added, as if being from the mere U.S.A. could be an unforgivable character flaw. "I'm Rosamund Madeleine Carolina, daughter of Gael Roberto Carolina—from Madrid. That's in Spain, too. And I won't have to put up with you much longer."

Charlotte resigned herself to the reality. Jennifer was going to do something stupid. Stupid. Stupid. Breathtakingly stupid. There was no halting the girl. Charlotte had an inkling, from what she already knew of the community, that Hardyville reality was going to slap Señorita Rosamund right across her fresh, if slightly pimpled, teenage face. After that, she'd be home safe and sound within a week. But nobody could be sure. On the other hand, her baby Jennifer could end up pregnant, drug-addicted, AIDS-wracked, and in the gutter.

But then, girls in the real world ended up pregnant, drug-addicted, AIDS-wracked, and in the gutter—and that was with all those laws and controls supposedly designed to prevent it. *What can a mother do?*

Sigh. All Charlotte could do is let go of control.

Let go of control when the day came, that is. In the meantime: "Dishes, young lady. And after that, you'll tell me what you've learned this week about Hardy County geography and geology. You can start your globe-hopping life as Rosamund ... or Rosalinda ... or Rosecrucia or whoever ... tomorrow. But for today you're still my dependent daughter. Now, get in there and wash those pots and pans."

Jen slouched toward the kitchen, dragging leaden chains of adolescent disdain and ennui. Charlotte plopped onto the couch. *I thought things would be better here. Isn't that the way it's supposed to work? You change your attitudes and lifestyle, and life improves? Isn't that the way it works in every self-help book? So why is life still so miserable? The shop is good. The kids seemed better for a while. But Jennifer's still Jennifer. God forbid. And now that damned man turns up here, messing with their heads. Even Tonio ...*

"Hey, Mom!" her son called, plunging through the front door, all angles and energy. "Guess what? Dad offered me a summer job with him and Delaval Enterprises! And he says if I want, he'll send me to college in Paris. Isn't that cool? I sure wish you liked him better, Mom. I think he's the greatest!"

Yeah, he's the greatest, all right. The greatest damn trouble-stirrer I've ever met in my whole sorry life. Charlotte bit her lip and said nothing.

Chapter 4

Interruptions

It will not do. This preposterous place simply will not do.

Gael Carolina sat in the study of the former Pickle Manse—now temporary headquarters for Delaval Enterprises' Hardy County operations—and studied his notes. He had been aware, when he requested the position of project manager, that Hardyville was somewhere sunsetward of the middle of nowhere. He had, perhaps, expected miles of sagebrush and a heavy dose of Wild Westness. He had known the place was unusual; its very unusualness was what attracted his and Delaval's interest in the first place.

But this! This was ridiculous.

People walking in off the streets and buying opium or hashish at Doc's Drug store! Surely, a civilized place couldn't allow that. A few discreet lines of cocaine among adults, fine. Sharing a mellow smoke in the privacy of one's own home. Having representatives who grow one's own crop in some out-of-the-way location. But storefront displays of such substances? Uncivilized!

Miss Fitz's Academy for Young Ladies? It was a good thing he had investigated that before making the humiliating blunder of promising Jennifer he'd pay her tuition there! Again, a discreet out-call service for the traveling businessman ... fine. Having one's own mistress ... of course. But an open walk-in trade? Outlandish. Unseemly. How can one hope to attract the finer sort of visitor with that going on?

And guns! Guns everywhere—and not just in the hands of bodyguards or carried quietly in purse or pocket. These people bore every imaginable sort of weaponry as if it were some primitive badge of honor. Submachine guns in pickup-truck racks, .50 calibers mounted on their rooftops, sidearms as big as cannons strapped to their hips.

It was embarrassing. Not to mention intimidating. And surely most repellent to well-heeled European visitors who were coming for the banking ... and who would later come for the exclusive clubs and casinos, the nearby skiing, and the private high-level conferences. Can you imagine their faces when they saw gangs of rowdy teenage cowboys with Kel-Tecs slung insouciantly over their shoulders? Heavens, what a thought!

But Gael Carolina was not one to let obstacles stand in his way.

He swept aside his notes about how things *are* in Hardyville. Better to concentrate energies on what should be. A few clicks of a mouse took him to the web site of a world-famous architect, known for his stylish high-rises.

If the princes of Europe could build the grandeur of Monte Carlo on a cramped plot of land barely wide enough to stage a soccer match ... if a mere gangster could conceive and give birth to Las Vegas in an unpromising desert oasis ... surely Gael Roberto Carolina could father a playland for the wealthy, even given such an unpromising patch of mother earth. But first...

Riiiiing.

The shrilling of the phone down the hallway didn't, at first, interrupt him. Mirabelle took care of such things. But this time, after a moment's pause, she tapped on the door of his study.

"Darling," she called, using English, their most fluent, if not quite perfect, shared language. "I think you must talk with these people."

"Who?"

She opened the door a crack. "May I enter?"

He sighed and clicked to minimize the browser. His computer screen now showed only his favorite wallpaper—a portrait of himself on a yacht, raising a crystal goblet with a buxom redhead, most definitely not the raven-tressed Mirabelle. Her eyes flicked to the photo, and away again, as she approached. Her face remained carefully neutral.

"It is very odd," she said. "They are the attorneys calling. From Washington. They ask for your help."

"Attorneys?"

"For the five federal agents in the jail."

"And they want my help? Why should they want *my* help?"

"I don't know. They say no one else will do what they need."

Generally, the wheels of justice turn much faster in Hardyville than elsewhere. But due to various technicalities, the case of the DEA Five seemed only to be spinning its wheels in mud. Thick, tenacious, knee-deep mud. The mud the locals not-so-fondly refer to as "tiger poop."

We blamed the delays on the attorneys, who kept looking for things like courthouses, judges, precedents, and such, long after they should have figured out that's not how things are done here. They blamed it on our stubborn, cussed backwardness.

And perhaps we gave them reason.

"They won't do what?" Gael Carolina chuckled into the phone, after hearing out the puzzled travel planner from the big D.C. law firm.

"Rent us hotel rooms. Or temporary office space. No one will. We've even tried booking rooms at a bed and breakfast and cabins on a dude ranch. No one will have us. The nearest accommodations we can find are 200 miles away, and that won't do."

"Surely rooms here can't be that booked up. This *fine*"—he said *fine* in that sardonic way again—"community doesn't exactly teem with life. You must be mistaken."

"No. Seriously. It's not that everyone is booked. It's that they don't want us."

That was true ... and not true.

Plenty of business owners would have been glad to rent rooms to the Devil, had he shown up with a retinue of purple demons and a wad of cash. Homeowners who wanted to see justice move ahead might have cleaned out their children's rooms, held their noses, and invited the D.C. legal-ators to sleep in Spider-Man bunk beds and share their macaroni and cheese for free.

It wasn't the attorneys we didn't accept. It was their money. Or their lack of money. Federal Reserve Notes? Paper? Vouchers? Chits? Scrip? Purchase orders guaranteeing payment of only more paper?

Surely you jest.

The distinction was one the minions of Mordor-on-the-Potomac would never understand—until it was too late. That they never tried to understand us—on our own terms—was their gravest fault.

"I'd like to help you," Gael Carolina told the travel planner. "But you can't seriously expect me to. Appearances ..." he gave a small, refined shudder. "I cannot be perceived as being on your side, you know. And in truth I am not on your side—or the other. In this legal case, Delaval Enterprises must remain a neutral ..."

"I understand, Señor Carolina," explained the travel planner. "But the situation is dire. Only one individual is willing to offer accommodation. And to accept would be unthinkable. We hoped that you, as one of the few civilized individuals on site would ..."

"I don't understand? Unthinkable?"

"Yes. We received a call from one person, offering to put our attorneys up in the bunk house at a ranch a few miles outside of town."

"Well, then. It may be primitive, but I'm sure you can arrange some comforts. I would be glad to discreetly supply ..."

"No. No. You really don't understand. The person offering to house our legal staff is Mrs. Harbibi. The widow of the man our clients are accused of murdering."

And she meant it, too. Anything to get this legal show on the road. She had even promised to let them sweep for bugs everyday. And to feed them her best beans and pork. The faster things moved, as she saw it, the faster she might get some goodies to compensate her for the loss of her late unloved loved one.

Gael Carolina shook his head in bemusement as he hung up the phone and clicked the architect's site back onto the computer screen. This was indeed the strangest place. But thus it was, sometimes, with isolated communities before their development. Such folkways would eventually fade.

He clicked through a gallery of the famous architect's drawings and structures. Although he couldn't have distinguished post-modern from deconstructionist by name, he sought a certain look. Free-form, yet grand. Sophisticated, yet amusing. Yes, he could envision a building like that one rising at the intersection of Liberty Avenue and Freedom Way (which would perhaps someday be renamed Delaval Boulevard and Via Carolina).

He would, in fact...

This time the doorbell clanged, disrupting his train of thought. Mirabelle's footsteps receded doorward. There were murmurs in the hallway, followed by a clumsy thump. And once again, Mirabelle's light tap on his door.

"Yes? What is it?" he snapped.

"May I enter?"

"Can't you deal with whatever it is?"

"No."

He sighed. "All right then, if you must. Enter." Again, he minimized the architect's website, leaving only himself and the redhead beaming outward. Mirabelle eased herself inside the door and closed it, casting a worried glance back down the hall just before the latch gave its solid, brassy thunk.

"It's your daughter," she said without preamble. "She has arrived with a suitcase and a backpack."

"Damn. What has that woman done to upset her now?" The question was rhetorical. Gael looked at the pile of work on the broad desk that once contained the entire mayoral burden of Hardyville. "Well, whatever it is, they'll just have to deal with it on their own. I'm too busy. Tell her ..."

"Gael. She is your daughter. I cannot tell her. You must."

He pushed back in his chair and ran his fingers through his sleek black hair. Another sigh. "You're right. Send her in. But whatever you do, leave that suitcase and backpack by the door. It's one thing to visit with my children again. But we can't have a young girl ..."

Mirabelle cast her eyes toward the door and made a shshing gesture. "Please," she begged.

"Oh, all right. I'll handle it nicely."

Mirabelle slipped away, leaving the door ajar. He stood, ready to be resolute. Seconds later, Jennifer burst in.

"Oh, Daddy! Daddy!" she cried, flinging herself into his arms. "Thank God you're here. I couldn't stand it at Mom's house one more minute! She's just awful. A witch. She's horrible and mean. But that's over now. I'm here and you're here and it's going to be wonderful, living with you and Mirabelle!"

Against his best intentions, Gael found himself awkwardly patting his daughter's back. He looked over her shoulder at Mirabelle, standing beside Jennifer's pathetic heap of possessions in the hallway. He shook his head. But the gesture, instead of conveying the "no" he had intended, was full of fatherly, if still reluctant, resignation.

Chapter 5
Trials and Tribulations

The fancy D.C. attorneys ended up living in the Harbibi bunkhouse for the duration. As promised, they swept for bugs every day—and not only the electronic kind. They dined on the finest of pork and beans. And after brief private preliminaries between them and several of Hardyville's arbitration services, they were chauffeured to the Hardyville One-Plex (site of the soon-to-be main arbitration proceedings) every day in various compartments of Mrs. Harbibi's crew-cab pickup. Everyone rode in silence to avoid giving away any strategies on either side.

And Jen Carolina, in her pursuit of shortcuts to self-responsible adulthood, ended up in the toilet.

On the toilet, actually—the cracked pink one next to the statue of the Drunken Cowboy. She had been living in her father's house only a week or so when it happened.

"And what exactly do you make of this?"

Gael Carolina thrust the opal necklace into his daughter's tear-stained face. "If you didn't steal it, how did it end up inside your pillow slip?"

Jen shook her head wildly, beseeching first Gael, then Mirabelle, whose necklace it was. "I didn't take it! I swear I didn't take it! I don't know how it got there!"

Mirabelle shook her head sadly and turned away. In the few days Jennifer had lived with them, a number of minor items had gone missing. A decorative abalone-shell comb for pinning up long hair (which neither she nor Jen had). A gold-lace shawl. A roll of minor coins. Small things. Often pretty things. Not terribly useful things.

And at first, it was impossible to suspect Jen. Not only was she so pathetically eager to please—bringing them cups of tea, making her bed every morning without fail, and adoringly aping Mirabelle's every style choice. She was ... well, she was rarely out of their sight. If Gael was in his study, Jen was looking over his shoulder, asking questions. If Mirabelle was at her mirror, Jennifer was there, probing her about her make-up, her origins,

237

and which clothing designers were most popular in France and Italy. She worshipped them both and was so eager to be part of their lives. Perhaps the items were just misplaced.

Still, it was undeniable. Things went missing. And now a necklace of semi-precious stones had turned up, hidden in Jen's bed.

"I didn't!" She pleaded, mascara and eye-liner beginning to trickle down her face in twin streams of black and purple. "It wasn't me!"

But her cries were of no avail. The evidence was undeniable.

"We gave you a roof over your head, young lady," Gael reminded her sternly. "We took you in when your own mother didn't want you. I indulged your whims. Mirabelle and I tolerated your clinginess. And this is how you repay us?" He shook the necklace in his fist. Jennifer merely sobbed in choking gulps.

"Get out!" Gael ordered. "Pack your things and get out of my house. Now." Mirabelle turned back in silent concern. She reached toward Gael's arm as if to protest so much imperiousness. But he shot her a stern glance and she withdrew her hand.

"But where ..." Jen sobbed " ... will I go? I don't have any place."

"Go back to your mother. Move in with a friend. I don't care. Your dishonorable behavior merits nothing from me. Just pack and go. Mirabelle, please escort Jennifer to her room and make sure she takes only her own possessions. Then show her the door."

The streets of Hardyville aren't exactly mean—unless you consider piercing winds, baking sun, and gritty red dust in every cranny of your skin or clothing to be perils. But to a 15-year-old girl without a home or family, our streets are plenty unfriendly. Jen walked a block from the Pickle Manse and flung herself down on a curb to get her emotions under control. And to try to figure out what do.

Where could she go? No way ... no way was she crawling back to her mother Charlotte to put up with a bunch of "I told you sos" and piles of dirty dishes to wash. But what else? It's not like she'd made any friends in this ugly Nowhereland. *They're all a bunch of dorks. Every one of them. I wouldn't stay with any one of them if I was dying in the gutter.*

Everybody had betrayed her, anyhow. Everybody was against her. She'd tried her best to be good and look what they'd done to her. *They hate me. Everybody thinks I'm terrible no matter how hard I try to be good!*

Jen burst into renewed sobs. She sat hunched on the curb a long, long time, not even trying to put herself together again. It was a neighborhood street. Hardly anybody passed. There were few to notice. Fewer to care. The sun, beating down on her head when she was bounced out of her father's house, began to swing toward the western horizon before her sobs settled into quiet despair.

Eventually, noticing an empty feeling in the pit of her guts, she stood, smoothed her rumpled clothing, and began to wander toward what little downtown there was. Outside the Hog Trough, she dug into her pockets. Not enough there even for a hamburger. She was about to cross the street in search of a candy bar when a message board outside the Hell-in-a-Handbasket Saloon caught her eye. Bits of paper fluttered from the board, some protected by plastic slip-cases, others slowly tearing apart in the breeze.

"Pick up truck. For parts." "Babysitter needed. Must be mature and have references." "4 SALE: home-baked cakes and cookies." "Wanted: someone to mow and weed." The papers fluttered, white and yellow and blue, fresh and grubby, ungrammatically hand-lettered or impeccably produced on computer. Around the outside of the board were more permanent ads for local businesses. Jen scanned those until one in particular jumped out at her.

A light went on in her brain. Sort of a strobe light, actually, with overtones of ultraviolet.

Yeah, she thought, with a bitter rictus of a smile. *That's what I'll do. I'll show them all. I'll earn my own living. But they won't like it and it'll be their fault. All their fault.*

She began to trudge northward out of town.

Miss Fitz escorted the bedraggled child into the parlor (in her profession, one preferred "parlor" to "office," even though the function was strictly business). The pathetic adolescent with the puffy, purple-streaked face had tried so hard not to look awed as she entered the gilt-and-velvet realm of the Young Ladies Academy. She had tried not to stare at the young ladies in their beautiful gowns. She had done her valiant best not to look terrified by the men sitting in the downstairs bar, each getting acquainted with a girl or two.

But Miss Fitz had seen a little of everything in her life. She might not have recognized who she had in front of her. But she recognized *what.*

The girl sank onto a Victorian fainting couch in the parlor, slouched back against the elaborately flocked red-and-gold wallpaper, and dropped her few tatty possessions with a thump.

"And your name again is ...?" Miss Fitz asked.

"Tiffany Devine." Jennifer was finished forever being Rosamund Carolina. Never again, after Dad and Mom's betrayals would she use their family names. "Tiffany Marisol Devine," she added. (Spanish remained appealingly exotic.)

"Well, Tiffany, can you tell me why you're here?"

"I want a job. You know. As one of your *ladies.*"

Jen felt Miss Fitz's eyes assessing her from her spiked and dirty hair to her pink tights and combat boots. She self-consciously shuffled her legs to hide a hole in the tights.

"And how old are you?"

"Eighteen."

Miss Fitz waited patiently.

"Okay, I'm 16," she lied, more plausibly. "But I know in this town my age doesn't matter. I'm grown up as long as I can earn my own living, okay? I know that, so don't tell me otherwise, 'cause it's a lie if you do. I'm 16 and I can do this kind of work."

"And what, if I may ask, leads you to want to choose this profession?"

Jen felt a momentary loss for words. Why else would anybody choose this kind of work? "Well," she said, as if she were stating the perfectly obvious, "I've done it ... you know, *it* ... lots of times. And I know all about birth control and stuff. I haven't got any diseases or anything. Besides, I'm not qualified for anything else. But I can lay on my back or do, you know, whatever ..."

"Thank you," Miss Fitz waved a delicate hand. "That will be sufficient." She glanced at Jen's grubby suitcase. "Miss ... Devine, do you have a home you can go to? Family?"

Jen stiffened. "That's none of your business."

"True," Miss Fitz conceded. "It's not. I ask only out of concern."

"You don't have to be concerned about me. Just give me a job."

"Now that, I fear, I'm certainly not going to do."

"But why? You can't refuse to hire me just because I'm young. I already told you, I know my rights and ..."

"Please, young woman. Hear me out. I can and *do* refuse to hire 16 year olds. Routinely. Local custom on hiring is just that—custom. I have my own policies. To interview for a job at the Young Ladies Academy, a woman must have reached the age of 22 or, if she is younger, have been self-supporting for at least two years. This profession, to practice it well, requires a certain amount of maturity, inner strength, and independence."

Jen's face fell—and her whole body slumped even further.

"So I'm sorry; you would not qualify on that basis alone. But if you'd like the truth, Tiffany—or whatever your name may actually be—contrary to certain opinions, this profession also requires a lively, engaging personality and an adventurous intelligence. You, on the other hand, appear to have the personality of a barracuda with an entire mouthful of abscessed teeth."

With a growl, Jen lurched to her feet, fumbling for her suitcase and backpack.

"But I'll be glad to call your family or a friend for you, and even ask one of my young ladies to drive you home if ..."

But by then, Jen was storming down the plush-carpeted stairs and shoving through the oak-and-leaded-glass doors of the academy into the chilling evening sun.

And thus it was that Nat Lyons found the former Jennifer Paris Rosamund Tiffany Marisol Devine Carolina, back in Hardyville, slumped on the cracked pink toilet next to the statue of the Drunken Cowboy. The toilet was all that remained of our former city government. It served as an apt symbol of all that remained of Jen's hopes. After the piercing summer day, the bleak desert night was descending on them both.

Nat spotted her after making a delivery of home-baked items to the new Lyons and Yale Good Foods Store. He was heading back to his ranch after a long day of trying to be both grocer and cowboy. But recognizing Jen and the deep dejection only a 15-year-old can feel, he parked his truck and stopped to talk.

And thus it was that Jennifer Carolina got her first shot at becoming, in the eyes and customs of Hardyville, a self-responsible adult. After hearing her story—and her heartfelt denials about the opal necklace—soft-hearted Nat gave Jennifer a job stocking shelves at the Good Foods market. With the job came a small paycheck—very small—and a cot in the storeroom. That first night, he also threw in the bonus of a hot microwaved dinner, for which the weary Jennifer was so grateful she didn't even bother to complain—yet—that the offered pay was below minimum wage.

She gobbled her dinner, then collapsed onto the cot fully clothed and slept the sleep of only slightly sullied innocence.

But Nat took care to warn all employees to empty every last dime out of their cash drawers at night and make sure both the office and the storeroom were locked. Jennifer could leave the building via the back door after the store was closed. She could use the facilities, including the small break room/kitchen off the storeroom. But no way could she roam the rest of the building, cadging apples, candy bars, or cash.

Warnings given, Nat then quietly called Charlotte Carolina and told her that her daughter was safe and sound—but probably best left alone for now.

The next morning, the D.C. attorneys finally managed to spring the DEA Five from the discomforts of Hardyville's jail-built-for-one. There was no great trick to it; all the miscreants had to do was sign agreements to participate in, and abide by, arbitration—with the Harbibi interests now and with Jasper Feldspar Clarke and friends later, if the additional victims so chose.

The miscreants also had to select either constant electronic monitoring (yes, we do that here—only for violent aggressors who haven't yet made restitution) or a 24-hour-a-day escort of armed citizens, paid for by the miscreants themselves.

They opted for the electronics, whose signals Bob-the-Nerd fed onto a public web site for all to view. Then we gave them—as a bonus, *gratis,* but strictly for our own interests—that armed citizen's guard. Our watchers remained at a discreet distance, but within effective firing range, should the need arise.

Staying within range was pretty easy, since the prisoners were moved from the cozy discomforts of the jail to the cozy discomforts of the Harbibi bunkhouse, where they doubled up with their attorneys while Mrs. Harbibi doubled the quantity of beans and pork in the pot.

And soon the arbitration was ready to "go live."

Chapter 6
Arbitration

The arbitration between Mrs. Harbibi and the "Federal Five"—presumed murderers of her late, unlamented (but nevertheless fairly-useful-around-a-hog-farm) husband—was ready to commence.

But were the attorneys, the culprits, and the few media types who'd managed to find their way into town ready for Hardyville justice? Most of the media crowd was still wandering around Montana, Wyoming, and Idaho (where they imagined Hardyville to be), looking for a place on a map that contained a county seat and a courthouse—none of which would anyone find here. But a bold handful of media types were wandering our town, dazed and confused.

The Young Curmudgeon and a conspiracy of hard-core bar-hoppers invited the reporters out to Bark's Tavern as the arbitration got rolling. Some of Miss Fitz's young ladies awaited them there and kept them too busy to realize events were about to roll. Instead of coverage of Hardyville's non-trial of the century, they got uncoverage. The young lady reporters ... well let's just say that some of Carty's buff young militiamen can do a pretty good Brad Pitt when they have a mind to.

So all those living, breathing, blow-dried threats to our privacy were, shall we say, otherwise occupied as things got under way.

Those of us with nothing better to do were assembled in the Hardyville One-Plex, the only building big enough to hold this particular attraction. We hunkered down in our seats, clutching tubs of popcorn, Swedish Fish, and bags of Extreme Sour Patch candies, and got ready to enjoy the show.

At stage right sat Mardi Harbibi, the grieving widow (no doubt holding an onion in that handkerchief she pressed to her weepy eyes). With her were two members of Acme Arbitrations and Mediations, the company with whom she had a contract for services. Stage left, a considerably larger crowd jostled for space—five culprits, five attorneys, and the two local arbitrators who'd agreed to serve as their consultants. Center stage sat a citizens' panel of seven volunteers, which the arbitrators for both sides had chosen randomly out of the phone book and asked to serve. The panel wasn't customary in ordinary arbitration cases. But this was a Big Event and nobody wanted any doubts about the integrity of the process.

The panel's job was to time the proceedings, making sure both sides got the same amount of time, and to decide any questions that might arise concerning procedural fairness— whether one side was kicking mud on the other's cowboy boots, so to speak. If the arbitrating parties couldn't agree on a decision about something—up to and including the final settlement—the panel would also function as a jury.

("Where's the judge?" you might ask. But that would be silly. What kind of bizarre legal system would put godlike power into the hands of any one individual, let alone some guy who is both a lawyer and a politician?)

Meanwhile, Carty and his Minutemen were on the rooftops and in the mountain passes, manning the Barretts and Serbus and such in case the federales decided to try to pluck their agents from the clutches of us ungovernable savages. Sure, the agreement the feds had made with the billionaire Delaval interests told the whole U.S. government, "Trespass and the dollar will drop like Bill Clinton's drawers." But we figured better safe than sorry.

So far, so good, though. The Minutemen sat idle at their guns. Even the feds were acting like civilized human beings for a change.

Civilized, yes. But still misguided. The fed attorneys—the poor, muddled, overpaid legal "experts"—just couldn't bring themselves to get it. Among other things, they were still trying to argue "jurisdiction." They nattered about moving the case to federal court under some bizarre interpretation of the Constitution's supremacy clause. And the poor local arbitration teams had to explain over and over again that "jurisdiction" had nothing to do with it.

"Your clients killed Mr. Harbibi and therefore they have to settle with Mrs. Harbibi for her loss," Samuel Webster of Acme Arbitrations and Mediations explained for the umpteenth time. "Those are the facts, and only those facts are relevant. We don't know anything about 'jurisdiction,' here. This is between Mrs. Harbibi, John Davis Melvin, and ..." he tried to remember the names of his four subordinates. It's so much easier just to call them War, Pestilence, Famine, and Death. "Government's got nothing to do with it," he shrugged. "Offending party, offended party. They decide responsibility and work out a settlement. Simple."

But of course the federal attorneys weren't in the business of accepting simplicity. They piped up to protest:

"The death occurred in the course of legitimate enforcement of federal law. Therefore ..."

Members of every Hardyville arbitration service—on stage and in the audience—sighed. Daniel Adams, one of the consulting arbitrators for the Fed Five, gasped, horrorstruck. He tugged at the sleeve of the lead attorney, shook his head frantically, and whispered something. The citizens' panel scribbled notes. Samuel Webster smiled at Mrs. Harbibi. It was a money smile. No doubt Daniel Adams informed the attorneys of the perils—not to mention the complete uselessness—of using words like "legitimate" and "federal" together in a Hardyville sentence.

The proceedings proceeded.

They proceeded despite the fed attorneys, who expected their clients to have to enter a plea, expected some invisible judge to rule on pre-trial motions, and expected somebody, somewhere, somehow to provide them with the number of some statute or another their clients were accused of violating. But none of that was to be. Nor were there any bailiffs—just armed Hardyvillians. Nor any state to press its case. None of that stuff.

"We just sort of sit down and talk it out," Daniel Adams, their consultant, had explained in advance. "You know, check whatever information either side wants to produce—and it's entirely up to them what they want to present, it being their own limited time and all. Then all put our heads together and agree on who did what and what to do about it."

"You people expect us to agree our clients are guilty?" one of them was overheard to bark.

"Well, no. Not guilty, per se," Adams explained. "But responsible. After all, who the hell else was out there that night, shooting at Marty? Nobody around here's gonna believe it was the standard 'bushy-haired stranger.' We've all seen the ballistics report and the medical examiner's conclusions, right? You know who did it. We know who did it. If you had evidence it really *was* a bushy-haired stranger you'd have dragged it out by now, wouldn't you?"

"But we don't have to prove our clients aren't guilty."

"Right, right," Adams explained, growing frustrated. "Like I said, not guilty, per se. Just responsible."

After that, the fed attorneys kept Dan Adams and his associate around because they'd signed a contract. But I don't think they listened to 'em much.

Sometimes the attorneys were reasonable in their desire to make things unsimple. After all, each federal attorney had a responsibility to just one of the culprits. When they began to realize their united federal front wasn't going to hold up, then it became in their best interest to protect their own guy—and damn the rest, if need be.

As forensics and ballistics guys—local, from the Big City, and elsewhere—paraded to the stage on that morning to answer questions about their crucial, but excruciatingly boring, information (which both sides had already studied exhaustively), factions soon appeared at the federal table.

"The evidence shows that my client, Pestilence, did not fire the shot that ..."

"My client, John Davis Melvin, did not give an illegal order to ..."

"My client, Death, was acting strictly under orders from John Davis Melvin ..."

"My client, Famine, fired only after the decedent pulled a weapon ..."

"My client, War, was not present, as the evidence clearly indicates, when Death and Famine fired upon Mr. Harbibi."

We had to give 'em points: Being individually responsible, the Federal Five were entitled to individual defenses if they wanted 'em. And the less culpable ones and their attorneys soon wanted 'em badly. So they started pointing fingers at the more culpable.

The facts were pretty darned clear. Once their attorneys' procedural ploys failed, those from whom the facts looked more favorable were willing to jettison their co-conspirators.

Eventually, War and Pestilence—who had fired weapons but hadn't actually hit Marty (they might have to account to Jasper in a later arbitration)—begged to have their arbitrations separated from those of Death, Famine, and Melvin.

Death had fired Marty's fatal shots. Famine had hit Marty a couple of times with shots he might have survived. And Melvin, of course, had given the orders for his guys to gun down fleeing men.

In the way of arbitrations everywhere (and very unlike real-world trials), the proceedings proceeded into the evening. Mudge and friends kept drinking the reporters under the table. And under the bed. And half the population of Hardy County wandered into that theater where the proceedings were going on at some time or another—although a few stalked out after realizing the One-Plex wasn't going to show them the latest installment of Harry Potter.

The idea of dividing into two or more separate arbitrations was a scary development for the hog-farming side of the dispute. Not for the Widow Harbibi herself. But for her hired arbitrators.

When War and Pestilence asked to go it alone in a separate proceeding, Samuel Webster and his Acme colleague, sitting beside Mardi Harbibi, blanched.

Now, I mentioned that the citizens' panel up there on the stage was present to determine issues of fairness that the arbitrators might get stuck on. This was one. You see, Acme wasn't getting paid by the hour. They were simply spending the premiums the Harbibis had paid them for a bunch of years—and those premiums had never been structured around a murder case, let alone two or three or four separate murder cases. Far from it, Acme had

246

never expected to arbitrate anything hotter than a question of whether an old oak tree was on Joe's property or Marty's.

"Fair" to Acme meant getting things over with quickly. Do understand, they wanted to do as well as possible for their clients. That, after all, is their best advertisement for getting more clients. But they wanted to do it efficiently, too.

"Fair" to the other side might have meant drawing things out as long as possible (except for the fact that each side had an equal and pre-determined limit of time to work with and didn't dare squander it). But "fair" certainly meant each culprit had a right to have his individual culpritude considered on its own lack of merits.

So the citizens' panel called an hour's halt and went off to consider what "fair" in this instance might really be.

When they came back, they said that "fair" meant having as many as five different arbitrations, if that's what individual justice required.

Samuel Webster might have blanched again at hearing that costly bit of news. But he had anticipated what was coming. During the panel's recess, he had taken Mardi Harbibi to dinner at the Hog Trough, got her liquored up and, in a desperate effort to forestall the worst (from his viewpoint) possible outcome, talked her into extending a settlement offer to the Five Feds:

$50,000 in restitution from John Davis Melvin for giving the orders and leading the invasion.

$25,000 in restitution from Death for firing the fatal shots.

$10,000 in restitution from Famine for firing shots that weren't fatal but didn't exactly make Marty Harbibi's day.

And $2,000 apiece in restitution from War and Pestilence for being lousy shots who missed Marty altogether.

After the break, the Harbibi side handed their written proposal to the federal side, then stepped back to wait.

The feds and their attorneys gazed at the offer in disbelief. A total of $89,000? They whispered at each other, urgently. Only $89,000? Heck, a D.C. legal team could spend that much on photocopies on a good afternoon. They could run up bills for mochas and lattes that would be higher than that!

Here they'd been expecting ... well, surely they hadn't known what to expect from these strange people in these strange proceedings in this strange place. But something in the range of millions of dollars in fines, or maybe hanging from a lonesome tree at dawn. Something like that, for sure. But $89,000?

"Um, well," Dan Adams, arbitration consultant for the feds, started to explain. But nobody was listening.

Leaping at the chance to get free for mere pocket change (which they were sure their federal bosses would pay), War and Pestilence demanded that their attorneys accept the offer. Now!

Death and Famine followed.

"Really," said Dan Adams. "I recommend you give this more thought."

"Are you kidding?" Famine snarked. "It'll cost more than $89,000 in legal fees just for the lawyers to think about it. If that's all these rubes believe one dead guy is worth, I'm takin' it. I'll put my share on my credit card and be out of this hellhole tomorrow."

Even John Davis Melvin, aggrieved at being held more accountable than the actual shooters but not wanting his men to think he'd turned into a total moron, ordered his attorney to agree to the terms. All he asked, in addition, was a stipulation that he was "not admitting guilt."

As if anybody in Hardyville gave a damn what he admitted.

"Admit any old thing or not," Mrs. Harbibi told Samuel Webster. "Admit he's the Virgin Mary. Don't admit he's got ugly toes. I don't care. As long as I get what's coming to me."

So each of the Federal Five agreed, in a howling hurricane of haste, to settle.

And thus all the federales missed the implications of a teeny, tiny bit of fine print Dan Adams had probably been trying to point out. That teeny, tiny and truly quite innocent bit of print said: "...in lawful money."

You think they'd have gotten it, back when nobody in town would so much as rent a room to them. But those smart, super-educated attorneys never did get a clue. They never did understand Hardyville or anything that it's built on. Not until it was way too late.

"Lawful money" isn't a paper receipt for goods that aren't ever going to be delivered. "Lawful money" isn't a promissory note for a promise that's never going to be kept.

And that, of course, is all those federals had: paper.

Sure, we accepted paper for transactions in Hardyville. But only as a convenient token for the gold, silver or (depending on the wishes of the transactors) other commodity actually being used as a medium of exchange.

And those federals—they didn't have one dime's worth of lawful money between them. Matter of fact, even if they had tons of gold, silver, pork bellies, old Beatles records, or something else Hardyvillians might have recognized as being of value, they wouldn't have had it lawfully because they got every dime they ever had by stealing.

248

And that's why nobody would rent those attorneys a room or sell them a meal when they came to town. That's how they ended up on Mrs. Harbibi's charity in her bug-infested bunkhouse. And that's why the Federal Five and their smart out-of-town boys made just the slightest little bit of a mistake when they lined up so fast to sign that agreement.

I wish I'd have seen their faces when they realized how they'd been outfoxed.

But by then Death, Famine, War, Pestilence, and Melvin were right where Mrs. Harbibi wanted them: Back in her bunkhouse, under guard, being instructed on how they would work off their debt. Instructed by the Widow Harbibi herself. Whose profound, if wholly manufactured, grief for her Dear Departed was matched only by the amount of work he left undone and the Annie Wilkes-like charm of her personality.

I told you once that the Hardyville justice system isn't perfect. It really wasn't structured to deal with murderers (of which we have very few and, face it, those are customarily shot to death by their prospective victims, which somewhat forestalls the need to bring them to arbitration). I'm sure that dedicated patriots of Libertopia would look down their noses at the process I just described.

Nevertheless, there's a certain poetic justice for freedom lovers in the fact that this particular group of federal agents would now be feeding the hogs.

Oh, and did I mention that, since our money hasn't had 95 percent of its value inflated away like the money of certain snaky and unreliable governments ... $50,000, or even $2,000 takes a long, long, really very, very long time to work off?

———————————

The Fed Five did get one break, though. A few days after the settlement, Jasper wrote from her Billings hospital bed to say she wasn't going to take War, Pestilence, or Melvin to arbitration. She didn't want anything more from any of the feds, despite everything they had done to her.

"All I want is peace on earth," she wrote.

Well, good luck on that, Jasper. Unfortunately, as the Federal Five waded into the slop for the very first time, we weren't exactly having peace in Hardyville.

Chapter 7
Crime and Punishment

You'd think—you'd hope—that with the Federal Five up to their knees in pig poop on the Widow Harbibi's ranch, Hardyville could settle into a nice, peaceful period. We could maybe take our time to get to know our new neighbors and help rebuild the blown-up greenhouse out at the Emma Goldman Arts Co-op and Biodiverse Living Center.

And we definitely were moving in that direction. (Meanwhile, in the absence of sufficient facilities at the co-op, nearly every house in Hardyville held a small crop of medical cannabis plants; the herbaceous aroma drifted throughout the town.)

You'd also think we could take the time to keep an even closer and more wary eye on the activities of Señor Gael Roberto Carolina, who continued to inspect our humble town with a gaze that seemed only to build high-rise hotels and calculate figures containing many zeros. And yes, we did keep our eyes on him. That was easy. He was quite visible around the town, often with the beautiful Mirabelle on his arm and son Tonio devotedly at hand.

But both our dawning peacefulness and our most rightful wariness got rudely interrupted by, of all things, a crime spree.

No, I'm not talking serial killings, rapes, daring daylight bank robberies, or attempts to impose taxes. Nothing as heinous as that.

The crimes were petty. Little pilferings. Minor evidences of trespass here and there. Petty vandalisms. The kind of thing your communities in the real world might take for granted, but rarely happen here in property-respecting Hardyville.

The blooms were nastily nipped off the nasturtiums that the owners of the Bon Mot ice cream parlor had so painstakingly coaxed into life (against long desert odds) to beautify their patio.

A delicate beaded bag, Victorian vintage, disappeared from its case at Goodins' Second Time Around.

Grouchy, who usually had eyes only for the gun side of Grouchy's Guns & Liquor, noticed one day that a few pint bottles of Captain Morgan's Rum and sloe gin seemed to have walked off his shelves.

And one evening a visiting tourist returned to her car after a restroom stop, only to discover her purse open on the seat and her cash gone. It was only $45 and change. But still.

Most of the crimes, other than the shoplifting, happened at night when no one was around to see. And these were hardly the sorts of deeds for which you'd hire a security guard or sit up all night with a shotgun. So they went mostly unreported and thoroughly unsolved.

They were simply disturbing. And not respectful.

Ah, yes. I see you already have a suspect. Who in Hardyville best falls into the category of "not respectful"?

Well, of course there's the Young Curmudgeon. But he wouldn't be likely to steal a Victorian lady's delicately beaded reticule, now would he?

No. Those who were already in on the Gossip Net suspected—naturally—Jennifer Carolina.

Jennifer Paris Rosamund Tiffany-Wannabe Carolina labored grubbily by day stocking the shelves of Lyons and Yale Good Foods. By night she slept, unsupervised—and in her own sorry opinion unloved, unappreciated, unwanted, and woefully underpaid—on a cot in the back room of the store.

One day brother Tonio, on errands for their mother, rounded the end of an aisle and found Jennifer kneeling there, stacking family-sized cans of tomato soup. He watched her grasp each can as though it were a Sisyphean boulder, lift it with a sigh from its corrugated container and, with vast, ponderous, long-suffering effort, slowly set one atop another on the bottom shelf.

"Hey, Jen."

She heaved a larger sigh and put the can she was lifting back into the box. "Hiii, Tonio ..." she said in her best Marvin the Paranoid Android tone.

"I heard you were working here now."

"Yeah. I'm working. And they aren't paying me aaaanything."

"Nothing?"

"Well, like not enough to actually *buy* anything. I'm thinking I should, like, report them to somebody or something. It's not even minimum wage."

"I don't think they have minimum wage around here."

"Yeah. I know. And it's not faaaair."

"Well, the way I heard it, things could have been worse for you."

She glared at him.

251

At that moment, Dora-the-Yalie poked her golden head around the other end of the aisle, waved, and called "Hey, Tonio! Good to see you!" She shot a significant glance at the soup boxes sitting in front of Jen, but kept going without another word.

"Ugly old bat," Jen muttered, grudgingly stacking one more can, then stopping as soon as Dora was safely out of sight.

"Dora? Ugly? Old? You're kidding."

"Well, she's mean, anyway. But not as mean as the other one. That wrinkly old man." She crumpled her face in an imitation of lines and toothlessness.

"You mean Nat Lyons? You mean the guy who rescued you off the toilet and gave you a job and a place to stay?"

She blushed. "He shouldn't have told people that. See? That's mean. Besides, he makes me sleep on a cot. A stiff, smelly old cot."

Tonio sighed. Better to change the subject. Or maybe just step out of Jen's river of venom. He scanned a shelf across the aisle, grabbed a package of pasta, and started away. "Well, see you later, okay?"

"Have you talked to Dad?"

"What?"

"I said 'have you talked to Dad?'"

"Yeah. A lot, actually." Tonio took a few steps back. He knew he shouldn't say it, but he couldn't quite help himself. "He's going to give me a job with Delaval Enterprises. Later this month, he says, as soon as the budget comes through. And he's going to help me apply to colleges ... in Europe."

Jennifer scowled and turned away. Fiercely, she thumped several fistfuls of cans down on the shelf. "I bet he doesn't," she muttered as Tonio started to turn away again.

That made him mad. He strode back to his sister's side. Glancing around to make sure nobody was watching, he hissed, "Look, Jen, just because you screwed up and made him mad enough to throw you out doesn't mean he's a bad guy. He's been darned good to me. When are you going to get a clue and realize you're responsible for your own behavior? When are you going to realize that things you do have consequences?"

"Things like what?"

"You know what."

"I didn't steal that necklace from Mirabelle. I didn't."

"Yeah. Sure, Jennifer. You didn't steal the necklace. You didn't rob that lady's purse. You didn't kill all the flowers at the Bon Mot. You haven't ..."

"I didn't steal that necklace!" Jen shouted. Then she looked around guiltily. When nobody appeared at either end of the aisle she repeated in a stage whisper, "I didn't."

Tonio sighed. "Yeah. Okay, okay. You didn't. Sure. See you later, Jen."

She scowled after him. "You know," she called, "if everybody already thinks I'm bad, there's no point in being good."

Tonio just kept walking.

———————

If everybody already thinks you're bad, there's no point in being good.

One morning, Dora drove into the parking lot at Lyons and Yale Good Foods and discovered that the filigree grille over the back window of the office had been bashed in with a rock. The grille had been more decorative than protective, in any case. The window behind the grille lay in shards, some in the dirt and pavement outside, more on the floor within.

As early-rising store workers arrived, they peered into the office and onto a scene of destruction. It would be wrong to call the destruction "mindless." Someone put a lot of thought into it. Filing cabinets lay on their sides, papers scattered everywhere. The culprit had smashed desk drawers and strewn their contents everywhere. Copier ink defaced the sofa and chairs. Words not mentionable in a family story were carved deep into desks and drywall.

The intruder had tried—and failed—to smash open the store's safe. But as Dora, Nat, and the representatives of their insurance company sorted through the mess, they discovered a petty-cash box and a lot of personal effects missing.

I should probably try to create a little suspense about whodunit. But what's the use? Jen Carolina's fingerprints were—literally—all over the crime (despite her many sloppy attempts to wipe them out). So were her footprints—in the dirt below the window, in the ink on the floor, and in inky blots down the walls where she had climbed out and headed back to the storeroom.

The insurance company investigator traced her trail from the back door of her storeroom-bedroom, through the window and back again. And Nat and Dora found a few missing items—though not the cash box—hidden near Jen's cot, behind crates of paper towels.

Jen herself hadn't even tried to make an escape. She was right there, snoring, with depleted bottles of rum and gin shattered around her cot, when the nastiest of our two sheriff's deputies, Emin Borgo, handcuffed her and dragged her off to jail.

"Good riddance," Dora snarled, as Borgo strong-armed the hangover-stricken, pea-soup-faced girl past the store's employees. Everyone watched as Borgo thrust Jen into the back of his squad car. The way she looked, he'd probably have a nasty cleanup job to do by the time he drove her the few blocks to the Hardyville jail.

Surveying the damage, the usually kind-hearted Dora grumbled to Nat. "Stupid. Not just destructive. But stupid. I mean, I understand why you felt we had to give her a chance, Nat.

253

But ..." she gazed at the landscape of ruin and hatred "... the girl isn't just vindictive, destructive, and a complete unforgivable ingrate. She's hopelessly stupid—doing all this, then curling up to sleep on the crime scene like a baby who's tired after playing."

Nat, looked around, even more wearily. It was hard enough, running a horse ranch and a store, too. And doing it all when you were well past eight decades. Nothing could make an old man ready for this.

"Don't worry, Dora," he sighed. "If you and the others 'll do the cleanin', I'll gladly give Jennifer Carolina 'zactly the lesson she's asking for."

Chapter 8
Just Desserts

"Technic'ly," said Nat, "she's adult."

"But ..."

The old cowboy raised his hand in a halting gesture. "But you know an' I know she's about as un-adult as can be, right?"

Charlotte Carolina nodded and blew her runny nose. Her face was puffed up with tears over her daughter Jennifer's latest antics and plight. The girl had been released after a few hours from the Hardyville jail and was presently moaning in hung-over agony in her old bedroom. But the hangover wasn't the worst of Jen's troubles.

"She's only 15!" Charlotte wailed.

"Right," Nat nodded. "Old 'nuff to know better, but not old 'nuff to have figured it out. An' that's why I come to you. Here's what I pr'pose."

Nat explained his plan for Jennifer to make restitution for the destruction she'd wrought on the office of Lyons and Yale Good Foods and the theft of the still-missing cash box.

"But ..." Charlotte objected again.

"Thing is, Mrs. Carolina, your daughter's adult. I c'n take her to arbitration without askin' ya. But I am askin' you. Askin' you to help me out here—and help your daughter out, too. 'Cause this is a better deal than what she's gonna end up with if we have t' go through 'proceedin's.'"

Charlotte dabbed at her runny eyes. "It doesn't make any sense!" she protested.

"It does, I promise. Mebbe ya just don't see it yet. But it does. Will ya go along with me? Or at least not get in the way?"

When Charlotte still hesitated, Nat added, "I promise if it doesn't work out, we'll stop and go back to the conventional way. All right?"

Wearily, Charlotte sniffed. And nodded.

Claire Wolfe

"Technic'ly, she's adult," Nat began, sitting in another, grander room, across a wide desk from an elegant, silken-haired man. "I could take her t' arbitration without askin' ya. But ..."

"Will your proposal save my family from drawn-out public exposure and disgrace?" Gael Carolina demanded. He hadn't asked to hear the details.

"Oh yeah. That it will. No public proceedin's at all. It'll just be between Jennifer and me, officially representin' Lyons and Yale Good Foods."

"And you will not expect me to pay for the girl's wrongdoings?"

"Nope. That'd be the last thing I'd want."

"By all means, then," nodded Señor Carolina, turning back to his computer screen, discreetly signaling the end of the very brief meeting. "The girl is incorrigible. I wash my hands of her. If you can obtain her agreement to your plan, good luck to you."

Jennifer, still pale and shaky, stared at the piece of paper in her lap, which spelled out Nat's proposed terms of restitution. She seemed to have trouble focusing her eyes on it.

"This is stupid!" she finally sneered, looking first at her mother, then Nat. "I don't have to do it. I'd rather go back to jail."

"Can't," said Nat. "No point in jus' puttin' ya in a cage, costin' everybody money when you could be makin' some use of y'rself."

"Well then I want to go to ... what do you call it? Like those federal agents did. Arbation. Whatever."

"Oh? So you got the money t' do that? Where'd ya get it—from our cash box?"

"Sweetie," Charlotte said, "I already told you, being new here, we don't have an arbitration policy in force. We'd have to pay by the hour and ..."

"Oh yeah. And I'm not worth it. I know."

Before the conversation had a chance to degenerate into the sort only a mother and teenage daughter could endure, Nat spoke up.

"Girl," he said, casting a silencing glance at Charlotte, "It's like this. We wouldn't have to pay anythin'. Your mom wouldn't be obligated to pay a silver dime. You'd have to pay the whole cost of 'arbation.' Y'rself. 'Cause you made yourself a grown-up when you left home and took a job. And that would be f'r starters. Lesseee ..." He took a much-folded scrap of adding-machine tape from his pocket. "The 'nsurance company says it'll be $55 to fix the walls an' $97 for new carpet an' ... this is all Hardyville money, too, ya know. Not fed'ral money. So you c'n multiply it all by 20 or so to get figures that might sound more realistic where you come from. An' gotta replace the whole desk, which is ..."

Jen sat there and listened until he got to the still-missing cash box.

"... which had, far as we c'n recall, about six months worth o' your pay in it. And how 'zactly do you plan to pay all that back when nobody in their right mind's gonna hire you for anything until—and unless—you make good?"

"All right!" Jennifer finally shrieked, "I'll do it! I'll do it! Give me a pen and I'll sign this stupid thing!"

Charlotte winced as she watched her 15-year-old daughter sign away the next full year of her life. As a mother, she still couldn't accept the wisdom of Nat's plan. Some of it made sense. Yes, the part about Jennifer working and living on Nat's horse ranch for a year without pay ... that made a certain tough-love kind of logic. The girl would be away from temptations. And who knows? Jennifer might even learn some responsibility, caring for horses. But...

"C'mon," Nat ordered, unfolding his old bones from the armchair and reaching out to Jennifer for the signed piece of paper. "I'm gonna deliver you to the shootin' range right now. Got an instructor, one o' Carty's men, already on standby. Then I'll run your stuff up to the old trailer on my place. Carty's man'll bring you up after your lesson and I'll show you your job."

Charlotte bit her lip. She couldn't imagine what was to be gained ... in fact to a mother it seemed hopelessly illogical ... for Nat to make that second part of the proposal. And it certainly didn't help him or his store to recoup their losses. Far from it. It was merely strange. Perhaps dangerously so.

As Jennifer slouched after Nat without a backward glance at her mother, Charlotte looked down at her copy of the agreement and re-read the part that troubled her.

> I, Jennifer Carolina, further agree to take four hours of shooting lessons per week for the next year with an instructor or instructors of Nat Lyons' choice, and at Mr. Lyons' expense.
>
> Furthermore, I agree to obey all firearms safety rules at all times and to practice regularly until I become fully proficient (according to the standards of the Hardyville Gun Club) at the defensive use of pistol, rifle, and shotgun.
>
> Should I fail to keep any portion of this agreement, I will reimburse Mr. Lyons for the full cost of all training, as well as my room and board while at his ranch. Furthermore, if I fail to keep any portion of this agreement, I will repay Lyons and Yale Good Foods, in lawful money, all losses I caused while vandalizing and burglarizing their office.

> If I complete this agreement, at the end of one year, I will be considered to have paid my debt in full. Further, I will be allowed to keep the cash box I stole from Lyons and Yale and all its contents.

Charlotte blew her nose again. Why in the world would anybody take an out-of-control, hell-bent for trouble girl like Jennifer and arm her, on top of everything else? As if the girl didn't already have enough ways to cause problems to herself and everybody around her.

Charlotte shuddered. But she was at the end of her emotional and financial rope. And so was Jennifer. With Nat offering to pay for all this, rather than demanding to be paid ... well, what else was there to do?

———————————

Meanwhile, as Jennifer Carolina glumly trudged into exile at Nat's ranch 30 long, isolated miles west of town, several interesting developments were taking place at another ranch, much closer in.

Out at the Harbibi hog operation, John Davis Melvin (formerly Herr Kommandante of the federal raid on the Emma Goldman Arts Co-op and Biodiverse Living Center, now hog-feeder-in-chief among the Federal Five) and the grieving Widow Harbibi showed signs of becoming An Item. Or so said the rumor from those who'd seen them out-and-about in the big crew-cab pickup truck. Without seatbelt laws to separate them, the two had been frequently spotted snuggled together as cozy as a pair of puppies as they rumbled down the highways and back roads. One gossip even reported seeing them (and I'm sorry, this is a truly unappetizing thought) snogging in a corner booth at the Hog Trough Grill and Feed. Mrs. Harbibi was heard to giggle girlishly as Melvin whispered sweet nothings over plates of fried chicken.

Yet another rumor said that Mrs. Harbibi might be in the process of selling out.

"Selling out" in what sense, some of us wondered.

Chapter 9
Selling Out

To tell you the truth, even though a lot of us suspected Gael Carolina's intentions right from the start, we weren't as worried as we should have been. After all, how could he build those hotel-casinos of his imagination unless someone would sell the Delaval organization the land to do it?

And can you imagine any Hardyvillian selling out for that?

Unfortunately, we didn't have to *imagine* any Hardyvillian selling out for that. We just relied on the evidence that smacked us between our very own eyes.

One day while making a delivery of fresh bread and muffins to the little shop at the airport, Dora spotted Gael Carolina and the lovely Mirabelle greeting an arriving visitor. The visitor ducked out the door of the prop-driven puddle-jumper that touches down in Hardyville, shook hands, and disappeared behind the tinted glass windows of Señor Carolina's leased SUV.

But not before Dora got a good look at him.

"His face looked familiar," she told Nat afterward. "But I couldn't place it. I'd never seen him in person before. I was sure of that. So how could I recognize him? But then ..."

Dora handed Nat a color page printed from a web site—a man's formal portrait inset into a larger photo of a famous building. It was the face of an architect, known for being more flamboyant than his works. The very architect whose works had fueled Gael Carolina's web-surfing dreams.

"I've seen him on PBS documentaries," she explained when Nat cocked an eye at her, clearly wondering what kind of person went around recognizing architects.

The Famous Architect was around town for several days, always in the company of Gael Carolina. They spent hours out at the Harbibi ranch.

The gossip—and the worry—went into high gear.

Some of us tried to get information out of Mardi, the Grieving Widow Harbibi—a challenging task in the best of times. "Information" tended to come out of her in the form of loud complaints. But now ... well, she was too busy snuggling and snogging with her head work-boy, former fed task force leader, John Davis Melvin. She had no eyes, mind, or time for anything else—other than some obvious real-estate deal making.

We wondered what the heck was going on. But wonder was all we could do.

But speaking of snogging, or someone who would rather be ...

Jennifer Carolina, with channels of sweat and dirt streaking her face, clutched a Charter Arms Bulldog .44 special. She pointed it vaguely in the direction of a man-shaped target, arms wobbling, elbows sagging. Beneath her tinted safety glasses and the brim of a very unattractive baseball cap, Jen's eyes shifted from the target to the twenty-something young man standing next to her.

He'd be hot if he wasn't so damned bossy.

The instructor, chosen by Nat and Carty, was named Brad Downey (Brad McCarty Downey, of Hardyville's toughest clan, a fact of which Jennifer was blissfully unaware). He looked a bit like another, more famous Brad, only younger. But bossy?

"Get those arms up. Pay attention. On the count of three, give me a controlled pair to center of mass, followed by a single shot to the head. And remember—front sight."

Jen heaved another of her much-practiced sighs, adjusted her arms imperceptibly and, before Brad had reached the count of two, slammed her eyes shut and flinched off one round that thudded into the berm two feet left of the target, followed by another high and to the right. The little .44 kicked twice into her limp wrists and arms. No third shot was forthcoming.

"Ow!" she whimpered. With her finger still wrapped around the trigger, she lowered the gun and, still clutching it in her hand, rubbed at her left elbow.

"Finger off the trigger!"

"Oh, all right. Yeah, yeah, finger off the trigger. Big deal." She sighed again and prepared to slouch back into her rounded version of an isosceles stance, ready to attempt the belated head shot.

But Brad put his hand out. "The gun. Give it to me. Open the action and hand it to me."

"Does this mean we're done?"

"Open the action and hand me the weapon."

She complied, fumbling. He ejected the unspent rounds and empty brass and holstered the firearm.

"Now. Off the line." He grasped her firmly by the upper arm and led her, not gently, to the shooting benches. The benches sat under the dubious shade of a tin roof, where the temperature was a mere 90 instead of 95.

Jen flung herself flat onto one of the tables. But Brad ordered, "UP!"

"Up? Up? C'mon. Isn't there some law that says you have to give me breaks, like every hour or something?"

"UP!"

She dragged herself into a sitting position.

"Jeff Cooper's four safety rules," Brad said. "Give them to me. In order."

"We did that yesterday. We did that already today."

"The four rules. In order."

"This is BS. I'm not some baby, memorizing my ABCs. I know the rules and I don't care who stupid old Jeff Cooper was. I just made one tiny mistake, okay? You want me to say I'm sorry, then I'm sorry. But you don't have to keep hammering on me."

"Okay. That's it. Your shooting lessons are finished. I'll drive you back to your mother's house and you can pay Mr. Lyons back for everything you stole and damaged."

"No! That's not fair! Wait a minute ..."

"Oh, you don't want to have to pay back all that money? Okay then. The rules. In order. And if I ask you 100 times, you give them to me 100 times, without complaint. And you don't just say them, okay? You live and breathe them. Because the rules might save your life. Or mine. Get it?"

"I get it, I get it."

Fifteen minutes later, after considerable prompting and discussion of the whys and wherefores, Jennifer succeeded in stating, and apparently even understanding, all four basic rules of safe firearms handling. Brad gave her a thumbs-up, handed her the Bulldog, action open, and stood to return to the firing line.

Oh good. For my reward I get to go back out in the sun and get skin cancer while blasting my arms out of their sockets.

"Um, could we, like, wait a minute?" she asked (carefully keeping her finger off the trigger and the barrel pointed down and downrange). "I really do need a break."

He sat back down beside her as she carefully laid down the gun. They both swigged from their sports bottles of warm water and gazed silently toward the horizon.

Again, her eyes scanned him behind her shades. Blond. Muscular. Great profile. Yeah, definitely not bad. For a bully. But she had to admit to herself, even his toughness was kind of cute. Maybe a strong guy could be interesting ...

"You know," she said after a moment, "We could finish this lesson tomorrow. Maybe we could just ... you know, spend some time getting to know each other today."

"Why would I want to get to know you?"

Taken aback (guys always wanted to get to know her), she didn't know how to respond. After swigging down more water, she decided on the direct approach. She gave him her

261

best seductive smile, hoping it wasn't too marred by sweat, dirt, and sunburn. She leaned forward so the neck of her shirt gaped open.

"Well, if you want to be that way about it ... there's lots of things we can do that'll be more fun than giving me boring old shooting lessons. I could do something nice for you."

Brad regarded her stoically. Then he stood up, walked over to the next bench, where two backpacks of equipment rested. He rummaged in one until he came up with a plastic-wrapped package about six inches square. With a small flourish, he tossed the package straight into Jennifer's lap. It landed softly, almost weightlessly.

Jen looked from Brad's impassive face to the package, confused. She picked the package up and squeezed it. It was soft. "What's this?"

"Knee pads. You'll need them for what you're going to do."

"Knee pads?" Jen gulped. "You don't really think I need ..."

"Oh, yes you do need knee pads," Brad grinned evilly. "I'm gonna put you through some shooting exercises that are going to make you wish you had not just knee pads, but full body armor. Now. Back out on the line. Pronto."

That night at sunset, Jen slouched on the hard metal steps of the dusty travel trailer Nat had provided, far from his ranch house. Far from everything. She felt as sore, as dirty, and as alone as she'd ever been. Her whole life was a waste of time. It was nothing but feeding stupid horses all morning, shooting stupid guns all afternoon, shoveling stupid horse poop all evening, then sleeping in a creaky trailer a million miles from civilization, without a single person to talk to. She sniffed, then reminded herself, *Not that there's anybody I'd want to talk to, anyhow.*

Jen sat on the steps as they grew cooler, watching the sun sink, just like her life, into the haze.

A coyote howled, very near. *Oh my god, a wolf!* Jen fled into the trailer, slamming the door behind her, and burying her face in her pillow.

Had any girl ever suffered so much?

"Dad," said Tonio, after being invited into his father's elegantly wood-paneled study, "can I talk to you?"

"Of course. Always." Gael waved toward a comfortable armchair.

"Well ... this is kind of hard."

"But I'm your father. You can trust me with anything that's troubling you."

"Then ... Dad, people are starting to worry about what you and Mr. Delaval are planning to do to Hardyville. I'm starting to worry. This place ... it's good the way it is. It doesn't need resorts and stuff. Big buildings. Fancy hotels."

Gael chuckled gently, "Tonio, I appreciate your concern. But forgive me, you're hardly an expert in urban planning."

"Yeah, I know. But you see, Hardyville, it's ... well, Dad, Hardyville needs to be the way it is. That's what makes it Hardyville. If you try to change it instead of just using what's good about it, you might wreck ..."

"Tonio, Tonio, please. I assure you I have everyone's best interests at heart. Including yours. Once you understand my vision, you'll understand how wonderful certain changes will be, how beneficial to everyone. You'll be proud to be the son of the man who created ..."

"Dad, please don't do it."

"Son, someday you'll thank me."

Tonio took a breath. He recognized finality when he heard it. Now things got even harder. "Dad. You promised me a job with you and Delaval. And ... well, I don't want you to think I'm not grateful. But can't take a job with you. I can't help you do the stuff you want to do."

Gael leaned back in his chair, a hard glint momentarily passing across his eyes. He regarded his son critically. "Your mother did say you're a young man who sticks to his principles. I suppose that is to be commended. Very well, then. I presume you have other opportunities?"

"No. Nothing yet," Tonio admitted. He didn't want to tell his father how it worried and depressed him, to give up a job prospect with Delaval not knowing what, if anything, else might come along. Tiny Hardyville wasn't exactly big on opportunities. "Also ... about your offer to send me to college ...?" He colored, reluctant to raise the issue under the circumstances.

"Ah." Gael understood. "You're worried I won't keep my promise. But of course, Tonio, that offer still stands. By all means, continue to gather applications. One day soon you and I will discuss your options. I assure you I am as concerned as you are about your education and your future."

"Thanks, Dad. I really appreciate it."

Gael smiled as his son departed, then returned to reviewing a selection of rough architectural sketches spread across his broad walnut desktop.

Chapter 10
Confrontations

The timer buzzed. Jennifer Carolina whipped her arms down from the classic "stick-em-up" surrender position, spun on the ball of her left foot, drew, and confronted three targets. She had done this classic "El Presidente" drill at least 50 times, day after day. Every single time, she had stumbled or fumbled or flinched or forgot to do some part of the exercise.

But this time was different. She felt it the moment she began to turn, and felt it even more strongly as she drew the Charter Arms Bulldog from its holster.

Blam! Blam! Two to center of mass in the first bad guy. Blam! Blam! Two to center of mass in one of his companions. The gun bucked in her hands, then right back on target, as if of its own will. She kept on shooting. Ejected. Slammed in five more cartridges with a speedloader. Shot some more. Reloaded. Shot. A 12-shot drill was rough with a five-shot revolver. But this ... it was smooth.

When she lowered her firearm and looked, she saw 12 holes, right where they ought to be.

"Sweet," Brad nodded.

But Jennifer didn't need an instructor's approval. She felt her hands and body in a whole new way. She felt herself in a whole new way ... a person who could do something, and do it right. The energy coursed through her like nothing she'd ever felt before in all her life.

Nat pulled his pick-up truck into a space near the statue of the Drunken Cowboy. With the gait of a man who's been on horseback all his 80+ years, and the determination of a man riding to the rescue, he headed toward the miniature patio outside the Bon Mot ice cream parlor, where Gael Carolina was indulging Tonio and Mirabelle in summer treats. They looked up as Nat came storming at them.

"Like to talk t' you. Alone," Nat told the startled man, without preliminaries. "Soon."

"And what is this regarding?"

"Land. Money."

Gael glanced uneasily at his companions. "I am quite busy this week," he said. "But perhaps next week I can ..."

"Sooner."

"I'm very sorry, Mr. Lyons. But time does not ..."

"T'day."

Gael's face clouded, his voice hardened, "I will not be ordered ..."

"Yeah? Well, mebbe it's true I won't be orderin' you. But a coupla guys named Serrano and Delaval might."

"What are you talking about?"

Nat glanced apologetically at Mirabelle and Tonio. "Jus' this," he said. "I called Serrano. He said you got no budget for buyin' land, no auth'rization f'r buildin' hotels or whatever it is y'r up to. He said all you got's a salary and *per diem* and th' job of makin' recommendations before Delaval gives you a budget for hirin' anybody or buildin' anything."

Neither man saw the dismay that creased Tonio's face. Mirabelle sat with her head down, delicately toying with the rose petals atop her sundae.

"Mr. Lyons," Gael riposted smoothly, "You don't seem to practice what you preach. My private business is mine. And I assure you," he added, scanning the faces of Tonio and Mirabelle as if assuring them more than Nat, "that I am doing my research and making my recommendations in a manner fully satisfactory to my employers. Nothing in my agreement with the Delaval organization forbids me from making my own strictly private investments on the side as long as they don't interfere with Mr. Delaval's interests. Which they do not."

Nat had played enough poker to know a bluff when he saw one. "We'll let Delaval decide that. What I wanna know is where's the money comin' from? Where'd you get the kinda cash to make an offer on the Harbibi operation? Where'd you get the kinda cash to be bringin' some arch'tect in and plannin' God knows what?"

Señor Carolina rose smoothly from his chair and glared imperiously upon Nat. "Mr. Lyons. That is none of your business. This entire conversation is an act of hypocrisy on your part. You and your fellow townspeople puff yourselves up with pride over your so-called 'freedoms'—which you then squander in idleness and license. Your utter lack of rules serves only to corrupt, as my daughter's pathetic example demonstrates. When someone finally comes along with the intention of using those freedoms productively, you respond with ignorant scorn and mistrust.

"And now ..." he inhaled deeply, " ... now you show your true nature by demanding to know the very things you claim are no one's business—how I earn my income and on what I choose to spend it. Mrs. Harbibi, might I remind you, is voluntarily negotiating to sell her

265

land and I am not forcing anyone to comply with my plans and hopes of improving this wretched, inbred, congenitally deficient dust-bowl of a town. I am, in short, embodying precisely the values you claim to cherish. And I will continue to do so regardless of what anyone—anyone—else thinks of the matter. Now, good day, sir."

He motioned for Mirabelle and Tonio, threw a handful of silver coins onto the table, and strode away. Mirabelle meekly left her melting sundae and followed. Tonio stood, then hesitated, looking after his retreating father, then at Nat. His normally dark complexion had the pallor of vanilla ice cream.

"I'm sorry, boy," Nat told him. "Shouldn'ta done that in front of ya."

"I ... yeah. Probably not. But that's okay, Mr. Lyons. I'm glad I heard it. I'm not upset with you." He paused as if he wanted to say more, then thought better of it and started after his father.

Nat put out a gently restraining arm and halted Tonio. "Another thing. Diff'rent subject. Y'r sister's doin' real good out there at the range. Think mebbe it's time to put her in with a group o' kids. You int'rested in takin' an intermediate shooting class?"

"I don't have ..."

"At my expense. My treat."

Tonio brightened. "Are you sure? Really?" Nat nodded. "Heck, yeah, Mr. Lyons. Just tell me when and I'll be there."

Nat and Brad went around town over the next few days, choosing teenagers and a few younger kids to share Jen's shooting classes.

Nat also had a few other talks.

He talked with Charlotte Carolina, who confirmed what he already guessed. "That man? Have millions of dollars—or even thousands of Hardyville dollars—of his own? Don't kid me! He's always liked living big, but on other people's funds. Anything he ever got of his own, he squandered. Trust me, this I know. Investors? Maybe. But who? I have no idea."

He talked with the Grieving Widow Harbibi, who unwrapped herself from the arms of John Davis Melvin long enough to say, "None of your business. I'm just tired of hogs and hog slop and think I might like to ... oh, take a sea cruise. Visit Paris. Live a little, you know?" She giggled grotesquely.

He talked with Marlene McCarty Lyons, his third cousin twice removed, who works at Hardyville Land and Title. "Now, Nat, you know I can't disclose anything about a pending real-estate sale. You're naughty even to ask." Then she excused herself to answer a question at the front counter—and carefully left a file folder opened on her desk.

He talked with Bob-the-Nerd, "The offer on the Harbibi place is coming from something called 'Paradise Unlimited,'" Nat told Hardyville's one-and-only true computer whiz. "Incorporated in the Bahamas. No officers or stockholders named. Carolina has power of attorney, but no other known connection. What c'n ya find out?"

Bob shook his head. "Probably not much, Nat. This isn't a job you and I have the resources for, not with it being overseas. Anyhow, Carolina's right in a way. I don't like what's going on any more than you do, but it's not really our business, is it?"

Nat glared at him. "Peaceful private business is private business. Agreed. Now, what if it turns out this isn't?"

"Isn't what?"

"Peaceful. Or private. Do you think it is? D'you smell roses? Or fertilizer?"

"Okay, I'll see what I can find out."

The Hardyville gossip network kept churning, as news of Nat's conversation with Serrano got around.

Thirty miles west of Hardyville, Jennifer Carolina knew none of it. After caring for Nat's horses and taking her shooting lessons she sat outside her trailer every evening, alone but beginning to feel a little different about it.

Some evenings she even tried reading the books somebody had left in the trailer. Reading wasn't her thing, but there were no video games, no Internet, no cell phones. Then, in a compartment under her bed she discovered a handful of nature guides.

She liked to listen to the coyotes—and now she knew they were coyotes, not wolves. She started carrying the nature guides to identify animals she could hear scampering or slithering through the sagebrush. Pretty soon, the suburban girl who would recently have been hard pressed to tell a skunk from a black-and-white kitty was able to identify sage grouse, pronghorns, two kinds of deer, and at least five different varieties of snakes, mostly poisonous.

She wasn't so worried about the snakes; Nat now trusted her to carry her holstered firearm everywhere around the ranch. He gave her a box of snakeshot. In fact, he turned out not to be such an awful old man. He loaned her a Leatherman multi-tool for odd jobs. He showed her how to groom and saddle a horse. Offered to teach her to ride, which she said she'd think about.

The horses ... they were crazy wild animals, as far as Jen was concerned. More easily spooked than white-tailed deer. More likely to strike than rattlesnakes. Their hooves, teeth, and unstable brains scared her. But one four-month old buckskin colt, long-legged and gangly, took a mysterious liking to her. Though reluctant to stray far from Mama, it watched her devotedly and increasingly yielded to temptation to follow her almost everywhere she went. Despite her doubts about all things equine, the colt's affection felt good. It was the only affection she'd had in a long, long time.

"What's its name?" she asked Nat one day as she hung on the bars of his round pen, watching the old man longeing a yearling. The colt stood beside her, nudging her pockets in search of treats.

"Haven't got around to givin' it one yet."

"Can I name him?"

Nat shrugged, then smiled. "Sure. Go 'head." The colt had had a registered name almost from birth, but no harm letting it have a call name of Jen's choice.

"Bulldog," she grinned. "His name is Bulldog."

Jen was alone one morning, feeding buckets of oats to the horses, when catastrophe struck.

Bulldog squealed, snorted. He began to toss his head wildly, for no apparent reason. Then he took off in a crazed, leaping gallop toward the far end of the pasture, then back. All the while he snorted and blew, flinging his head from side to side and up and down.

The nearby horses began to prance, sideways and back, sideways and back. Some reared. They threw their heads, up, down, up, down. Some of them, too, began to gallop wildly across the pasture, as if on some kind of contact high from Bulldog. In seconds, every horse in the pasture went completely insane.

Heedless of where they were running, they nearly collided with the barbed-wire fence, then wheeled and thundered back in a herd—straight at Jennifer.

Faster than she knew she could leap, slicing the palm of her hand on a barb, Jen flew over the nearest fenceline, out of the path of the maddened animals. They charged the fence, flinging dust and pebbles into her face, then at the last second before impaling themselves, they wheeled away as one and rampaged in the other direction.

Adrenaline pumping so hard she didn't feel the blood or the pain of the slash, Jen crouched on the safe side of the fence. She felt panicked—not understanding what was going on, not knowing what to do. She turned toward the ranch house, but she knew Nat wasn't there. Nobody could explain. Nobody could help.

Up and down the crazed animals charged, squealing and tossing their heads ceaselessly. Then, at the far end of the pasture, within striking distance of the barbed-wire fence, Bulldog quit running and began to buck, fragile legs flying out at random.

Jen cried out, "NO, Bulldog! NO! NO! NO!" and ran along the fenceline toward him, blood spattering from her hand as she frantically tried to wave him away from the wire.

268

But it was too late. Jen saw it as if in slow motion. The colt's spindly foreleg went over the middle wire. His knee hooked around the wire as he came down. Hoof touched ground on the opposite side of the bottom wire. One wire sliced into the front of his leg, the other into the back. Bulldog squealed and struggled—and the more he fought, the more the wires on either side of his leg sliced. Blood poured. Blood flew. Bulldog squealed and struggled harder than before.

Now Mama rushed to his side and rose to strike at the invisible "predator" that had her son's leg in its jaws.

Jennifer shouted and flung her arms as she ran toward the disaster. She had to get Mama away from the fence, had to do something—something!—before Bulldog broke his own leg or sliced an artery. Something. But what? She was alone. She didn't understand what had happened, why Bulldog, then all the rest of the horses had suddenly gone insane. She had no idea what to do.

Chapter 11
Mortal Dangers

Jennifer rushed toward the flailing colt and his maddened mother, stumbling to a halt just a few feet away. Bulldog tugged backwards against the barbed wire, which cut deeper as he struggled. Mama lunged at the predator fence, threatening to trap her own legs in the wires. Horses screamed. Dust choked. Blood flew.

"Shoo!" Jen shouted and waved ineffectively from the "safe" side of the fence. "Shoo, Mama! Get away!" She didn't know how to help Bulldog, but whatever else, she had to get Mama out of there. "Get away, Mama!" Jennifer thrust herself nearly within striking range, pushing her arms toward the horse. But it was as if she weren't there.

With no idea what else to do, she drew her revolver and, staying as close to the horses as she could, fired straight past Mama's head. The startled horse leaped backward. But not far.

Jen fired again. The .44 bullet zinged past Mama's ears, the smell of gunpowder burned the horse's nostrils. Mama reared and seemed ready to lunge forward again. Oh God, it isn't going to work!

Jen gripped the gun tighter, flexing her sweating, bloody fists around it. She glared over the barrel, her eyes as threatening as the weapon. "Get. Away, Mama. Stay. Away." Mama snorted threateningly and beat the ground with a hoof. But she kept her distance. "Now," Jen told her, more gently but firmly, still keeping her in her sights, "I'm going to help your baby. I'm going to *help*. Okay?"

But when she turned to Bulldog, more panicked than ever after the gunfire, she thought she was likely to faint. Ribbons of flesh flapped over the wire. Bone flashed through blood.

"God help me, God help me!" Jen moaned through her own tears and blood. "I can't do this."

For a second, she considered shooting the little horse; his wounds and his predicament looked hopeless. Then a thousand thoughts went through her mind. Thoughts of how everybody would blame her for screwing up again. Thoughts about giving up. Finally, thoughts about how somebody had to do something ... and there was nobody but herself.

Gun in her left hand pointed at Mama and right arm outstretched, she cautiously approached the terrified colt. "Hey, Bulldog. Hey, Bulldog, it's me. It's okay. Look at me. Look at me, okay?"

The colt still struggled and screamed. But finally, whether from exhaustion or desperation (Jen couldn't tell), it finally focused its wild eyes, first on her face, then on her outstretched palm. Bulldog seemed to yield. His body came to rest, with his abused foreleg still held in the wire. He looked again at her palm.

A treat. Offer him a treat. Casting a wary glance at Mama over her gun sights, she patted at her pockets. Nothing there. Nothing to give. But ... her palm slapped the multi-tool on her belt.

She tried to unsnap its holster and draw it out one-handed. For the first time, she realized she was wounded. Suddenly her hand began to burn and throb. But no time for that. Keeping Mama fixed with a glare as threatening as the gun, she crouched, laid the weapon in the dirt, and worked the Leatherman free.

"Now, just take it easy," she soothed—as much to herself as the horses. "Take it easy. I'm going to help."

Opening the multi-tool, she crept toward the nearest fence post, safely away from the colt's hooves. Snap. She broke through the bottom wire. Then the middle.

"Now don't move, still," she said. "Stay right there."

Going wide to avoid renewed kicking, she crept to the next fence post, on the other side of the trapped colt. Snap. She cut through the two wires. The colt was free but didn't know it yet. And not out of danger. Jen pictured him galloping away, trailing 10-foot strands of barbed wire, tangling in them, going down.

"Good Bulldog. Good Mama. Now stay still." Both horses looked at her, frightened, restive, but no longer crazed. Across the pasture she could see the other horses, gathered in a tight knot, watching, but no longer manic.

"Okay. Now." Jen had no idea what do to next. But she didn't want the horses to know that. She looked around. Something to hold Bulldog. Something to stop his bleeding. Nothing. She looked at herself—and still moving slowly so as not to alarm the horses, but thinking in rapid-fire, she unbuckled her belt, slithered it out of its loops, then stripped off her blouse.

At the motion, both horses pulled back. But Bulldog, still aware of the wires at his legs, didn't try to run. Nor did Mama.

"Good, good," Jen soothed. Terrified, but trying not to show it, she approached Bulldog, eased the belt around his neck and rebuckled it. Now she had him on a makeshift halter and lead. Then she reached down, very cautiously, and peeled the wires away from his feet.

"Now, come with me. C'mon. Just a little ways and I'll give you a treat."

Leaving her gun in the dirt, she led Bulldog, limping, toward the barn, where she got a real halter on him and tied him securely to a ring in the wall. Mama trailed and watched suspiciously, but didn't interfere.

Once the colt was occupied with a cup of oats, she crouched and slowly, carefully, picturing her face being kicked off, bound his ruined leg with her blouse.

Then she ran to the house, smashed in a window, crawled through it, and called Nat at Lyons and Yale Good Foods. Finally, she collapsed on the kitchen floor and cried.

"Mad at you? Hell no!" Nat scoffed as he sat at the table, watching the doctor stitch Jennifer's hand at the kitchen sink. One of Nat's old Pendleton shirts hung loosely over her shoulders to cover her missing blouse. She had insisted the doctor tend to Bulldog first, and hadn't said a word about herself and her fears until that was done.

"Why would I be mad at you? You saved that colt's leg—and maybe his life."

Jennifer sniffled. "But it was my fault and I didn't know what to do and what if I made everything worse and I even broke into your house and ..."

"Oh, girl, stop. From what you described, I'd say what happened was a stingin' fly got up that colt's nose. He was hurt and scared. He couldn't blow it out of his nose and he panicked. Then Mama and every other one of them dumb animals panicked. They're herd beasts. That's what they'll do. It happens, even with all the best bug spray and carefulness in the world. I'm jus' sorry you had to be there alone. But girl, even if you didn't do everything a more experienced person mighta done, you did great with what you had. A reg'lar little heroine."

Jennifer sniffled again, colored, and turned away to watch the doctor work.

"Only regret," Nat added, "is with that gash you won't be shootin' again for a few weeks. And just when Brad and me are gettin' a bunch of kids together for you to take your classes with. Tonio among 'em."

Jen looked up. "Not shoot?" she grinned. "No way. As soon as I can go back out to the pasture and find my gun, I'll be shooting again. So what if it has to be with one hand? And I'll beat Tonio. Left handed I'll beat him. You watch."

And she did.

"Damn, I'm glad I didn't bet money on beating you," Tonio laughed as he and Jennifer sat atop a shooting bench, under the shade of the tin roof, eating lunch. It was cooler today, but they were both sweating. In the distance, the younger kids practiced Mozambique drills under the supervision of Brad and Christian Goodin. "You're getting good."

Jen grinned. "You're not so bad, either."

"Yeah. But you've been practicing more."

"Didn't have much choice, did I?" Jen laughed. "Practicing shooting. Shoveling horse poop. It's my life."

"You don't seem to mind much."

"Nope. It's my job." She plucked a potato chip, offered her brother the bag, then admitted, "Anyhow, I deserved to work hard after what I did. Really, I deserved a lot worse. Out there ..." she nodded toward the real world, "they'd have put me in jail. And I'd have just gotten more screwed up."

"Yeah. It's better here, isn't it?"

"Yeah. Different. Weird. But better once you get used to it."

"Speaking of that, Jen ... have you heard what Dad's up to? What he's trying to do?"

She looked at him, her expression tightening at the mention of the man who threw her out of his house. "I don't hear anything out here. But I have some idea."

"He's trying to change this place. And he can't see that if he changes it, he'll end up ruining it, filling it with exactly the kind of rules and regulations and dumb ideas about 'security' and 'civilized behavior' that are making life out there ..." he, too, nodded toward the mountains dividing Hardy County from the real world "... so bad."

Jen shrugged. "He's going to do whatever he wants. Nobody's going to stop him—unless they kill him or something."

"But where's he getting the money, Jen? If he didn't have the money, he couldn't do it. Nat says it's not Delaval money. And Mom says it's not his own. Where's he getting it?"

Jen shrugged again and took another chip. "There was ... well, I saw something that week I stayed with him and Mirabelle. It isn't much. But it stuck in my mind."

"Yeah?"

"I was on his computer one day ... okay, yeah, I was sneaking, but I was really bored, you know, and looking for something to do. And I saw this whole bunch of emails back and forth. 'Re' this and 're' that. I couldn't read them because they were all ... gobbledegook."

"Encrypted?"

"Yeah. Encrypted. But I could read the headers. And they were all 're, re re' the same subject. I remember this because it sounded so mysterious: 'Contingency Plan: Worst-Case.'"

"Okaaay. But that could be anything. Delaval business. Something personal."

"I'm not finished. All the 'Contingency Plan' email was to and from a dot-gov address."

"Dot-gov? You're sure?"

"Dot-gov. I'm positive."

Chapter 12
Manhood

"Dot-gov?" Gael Carolina sniffed, gazing evenly at Tonio across the plain of his walnut desk. "Of course it's possible I've had some correspondence with people in government as part of my function here. After all, Señor Delaval had to negotiate an arrangement with them—the very arrangement that continues to protect this valley from further federal incursions. So yes, perhaps I've had some dealings with government representatives.

"But," he added, "I don't recall anything specific. I'm sure any contacts I had with 'dot-gov' would have been strictly detail-oriented."

Tonio met his father's gaze, son as steady as father. "I don't believe you," he said.

Their gazes locked in a contest of wills. Then Gael looked out the window, to where a lone cottonwood swayed in the garden. Turning back, he informed his son, "You may not believe me. But you know from experience that you cannot believe your sister—whose self-admitted bad behavior—her snooping—provides the only witness to this alleged correspondence."

"No. She's telling the truth. And you're not."

Gael Carolina's elegant European pallor yielded to angry red. With an effort, he controlled his voice. "I see that this place ... this uncivilized backwater with its primitive ideas ... has corrupted even you. Even my own son, for whom I had such high hopes. Tonio, I urge you to think again about where you place your loyalties and to whom you give your allegiance. I can do much more for you than ..."

"Dad, stuff it." Tonio swept to his feet. "Cut the bull. You're never going to do anything for me. You never planned to do anything for me—not give me a job, not send me to college. Nothing. You've lied to me since you laid eyes on me—and I was stupid enough to buy it. Well, no more. That's it. Screw you."

He strode toward the door of the study and flung it open. But before walking out he paused long enough to say, "But you know what? I'm going to stop you from doing what you're planning. I'm going to stop you if it's the last thing I do."

And he walked down the hallway and out the front door, brushing aside Mirabelle. As he slammed out, Mirabelle exchanged looks with Gael. Hers was filled with anguish. His, unreadable.

———————————

Time passed slowly for Tonio. He knew he should be looking for work, but he felt defeated. He felt like a fool for not seeing through his father right from the start. His stomach churned with the rage of the deceived, with the impotence of a boy who wasn't yet enough of a man to save the things he cared about.

But he wasn't a man. That was just a fact. He didn't know what to do. So the weight of the days lay heavy on him. When not at the range with Jen or giving Charlotte desultory help around the house, he stayed shut in his room. He played video games until he was bored, cramped, and crabby. Then he turned to the old books and movies on his shelves, things he'd had around since he was a kid—anything to escape the frustration.

But there was no escape. The books and movies made him feel worse. So many of them seemed to be about heroes and revenge. *The Count of Monte Cristo. The Scarlet Pimpernel.* Even modern stuff like *V for Vendetta* ... it was all about strong people, making a difference. Instead of giving him an escape route, the stories and movies made him feel more helpless.

He switched to history, reading about the American Revolution and its aftermath. But history hit him just the way the stories did. Those were men. I'm not. People lived in those days. Even a little creep like Aaron Burr knew how to deal with enemies. But me? I'm good for nothing.

Snap out of it, he ordered himself. But he was sunk in despair for days before he thought of a way out.

———————————

"A job?" Nat asked.

"Yeah, a job," Tonio nodded. He stood with Nat beside the old man's pick-up truck, just outside the shooting range. "On your ranch."

"Well ... c'n ya ride?"

"I can learn."

"Rope?"

"I can learn."

"Cook?"

"Little bit."

"Run fence wire?"

"Learn."

"Why the ranch? Why not apply down t' the store. Educated boy like you ..."

"Don't want to live at home. For now, anyway. And Mr. Lyons, I'll work cheap. As cheap as you want. I just need a job that'll let me move away from home—without having to wait until I've saved up a lot of money. That's the thing I need to do right now."

"Somethin' wrong between you and your ma?"

"No. Not that. It's just ... time."

Nat regarded him appraisingly. At that moment Jen came up, now sporting a borrowed Glock 21 on her hip.

"I asked Nat for a job," Tonio said. "On the ranch. So I could live out there."

Jen nodded, as if she'd expected it. "He works his tail off," she assured Nat. "And I could use the company and the help."

"I'll work cheap," Tonio repeated. "And I learn everything. Fast."

Nat shrugged. "Well then we'll give it a try. Be nice to have another Carolina kid out there; they're a good bunch." He grinned at Jennifer, who grinned back.

The two men—for they were both men now—sealed the deal with a handshake.

The following day, in town supposedly to pack his things (over Charlotte's puzzled protestations), Tonio borrowed the family car to run errands. In fact, his only "errand" was to shadow his father. He waited down the block for the man to emerge from the old Pickle Manse, then discreetly followed. He followed as his father made a brief stop at Hardyville Land and Title. He followed as Gael and Mirabelle went into a lawyer's office, followed as Gael waited and Mirabelle went into Lyons and Yale. At their next stop, Tonio finally hit it lucky. They went to a place where he'd have an audience. An audience was crucial for his plan.

At the height of lunch hour, such as it is around Hardyville, Gael and Mirabelle entered the Hog Trough to make a quick purchase of take-out iced lattés. Tonio left his car and followed them in.

There are a lot of ways to walk into a room. Some get you noticed. Some don't. From the moment he flung back the door, Tonio aimed for memorable. The very energy of the door swinging caught attention. Heads raised across the crowded restaurant.

Tonio strode straight to his father. Gael, sensing angry energy behind him, turned, startled. His eyes flicked to the Colt on his son's hip, as if he well understood what Tonio had worked himself up to. But Tonio didn't touch the gun.

Instead, after an endless moment of anticipation, Tonio raised an arm and swung a pair of old work gloves. Empty leather fingers slapped Gael's face.

As if he'd been rehearsing the words for a long time and they were finally ready to explode out of him, Tonio snapped, "Dad ... I challenge you to a duel. To the death."

───────────────

Mirabelle cried out and clutched Gael's arm. Gael started to laugh ... but his mirth died. The room was silent. Deadly silent and serious. He looked at Tonio, taut as a wire before him. He looked at the expectant faces.

Mirabelle, who recognized the seriousness, started to protest, "Tonio, don't ..."

Gael's glance came back to Tonio, cold and imperious. "This is not amusing, young man."

"I didn't do it to be 'amusing.' I challenged you. If you're a man, meet the challenge."

Gael's eyes scanned the diners again. He watched them watching him, awaiting his answer.

"You barbarians," he finally sneered. "You utter barbarians. You actually believe this child can do this, don't you? You and your medieval codes of behavior."

No one responded. Tonio waited. "I'm not a child. I'm an independent man," he said. "And I'm waiting for your answer."

"Preposterous," Gael muttered. "Laughably preposterous. But ... if you insist. He smiled sardonically. "All right, Tonio, I'll play by your romance-novel rules. I accept."

"No!" Mirabelle cried. He brushed off her clinging hand.

"I accept," Gael repeated with a mock-courtly bow. "And in accepting, I embrace your quaint little code duello. That code, as I recall, specifies that the challenged party selects the weapons to be used. Is that not correct?"

Tonio looked around for support. Everyone was silent. Remembering the old books and movies, he realized his father was right. He nodded.

"Well then," Gael continued, waving a dismissive hand at Tonio's Colt. "Since all this amuses you, I'm sure you'll be even more amused by my choice of weaponry. I choose ... rapiers."

"Rapiers?" Tonio croaked, baffled.

One of Carty's Minutemen rose from a nearby table and came to Tonio's side. "A sword," he murmured in the young man's ear. "Your dad wants to fight you with swords."

Chapter 13
Challenging Fate

The silence in the Hog Trough, as Gael Carolina set the terms of the duel with his son, was profound. Into that silence, Señor Carolina spoke again.

"Yes, with swords," he said, glaring around at the dozens of closed faces, "and to clarify, I do not mean to spar with protected points. I accept Tonio's challenge—to the death. You all believe so deeply in this barbarity that you mis-name 'freedom'? Well then, observe the consequences."

He turned sharply on his heel and strode out of the restaurant. Mirabelle stumbled in his wake, panic-stricken and still trying to clutch at his arm.

As the door slammed behind them, the Hog Trough erupted into hubbub.

It would be a slaughter. Everybody who learned about the duel understood that. We didn't even have to wait for Charlotte Carolina's confirmation that, yes, her ex-husband had studied fencing. Extensively. For years in his youth. And Tonio, of course, knew no more about sword fights than a boy learns watching Zorro.

Yet, Tonio had issued the challenge and Gael had accepted—and it had all been done in public. Their choice. Their right. There could be no doubt.

According to the ancient rules, each man nominated a second—a representative to set time and date and arrange all particulars of the deadly encounter. Before Tonio even had a chance to ask, Carty stepped forward on his behalf. Finding a second must have been harder for Gael Carolina; he'd made few friends in town. But eventually, Carty was contacted by Dermot Harvard Halloran, vice-president of the Second Bank of Hardyville. With an air of apology—that of a lawyer who knows his client is scum but still believes he's entitled to the best possible representation—the rotund little banker began emailing Carty with proposed terms.

Carty stalled. He gathered his Minutemen. He asked everybody: "Do you have any kind of swords? Do you know anything about swordfighting techniques?" His efforts turned up a couple of souvenir Katanas, a pair of slightly bent epees inherited from a grandfather, and a vast crescent-shaped monster with a faux-jeweled hilt whose owner had once belonged to the Society for Creative Anachronism. But absolutely not one person in Hardyville—other than Gael Carolina—knew anything more about sword fighting than the Internet or old Basil Rathbone movies could tell them.

While Tonio, his friend Christian Goodin, and several young men studied films and practiced exhaustively with wooden makeshifts or the wobbly epees, the puddle jumper flew in with a tooled leather case in its cargo hold. The case, exactly the size and shape to hold a pair of swords, disappeared silently within the walls of the Pickle Manse.

Don't imagine that Tonio's mother Charlotte was silent all this time.

"You are not serious. You are not going to do this," she informed Tonio, having driven to Nat's ranch where her son was now boarding in a spare bedroom of the ranch house and learning to wrangle horses. Her hands trembled. Her whole body shook. "I forbid you to do this stupid, stupid, stupid thing!"

"You can't, Mom," Tonio said wearily, pausing with a coil of rope dangling from his hands. Behind him on the other side of a fence, a knot of half-broke horses eyed the rope suspiciously. "I'm sorry. I'm not doing this to hurt you. But you can't forbid me to do anything. I'm an adult now. I earn my own living. I've moved away from home."

"Adult. Adult! Do adults go around fighting with swords like something out of a comic book? Tonio, this is suicide. Don't you understand? Your father isn't going to back out at the last minute or play 'let's pretend.' You're in his way and now he's going to kill you. And you walked right into it. I tell you ..."

"Mom. Somebody has to stop him from ruining Hardyville. And nobody else has figured out how. Can't you see that?"

"And how exactly is getting yourself killed going to stop him from doing anything?"

Tonio shrugged, "I challenged him. I hoped maybe it would ... change his mind or something. Thought maybe it would wake him up. But it didn't. Now I have to do the honorable thing."

"I thought ... I thought," Charlotte gasped, "that when we came over Lonelyheart Pass we were supposed to be heading into a better life. Yet all that we've gotten here is heartbreak and risk. And now this."

"Mom, have you talked to your daughter lately? Have you seen how this place has changed her? And it's changed you and me, Mom. You've got your own store. You're not some fat, unhappy person trapped in a cubicle any more. I've got ..." he swept his hand, with its rope coil around to indicate the mountains and sky. He sighed. "I'm really sorry. And I admit, I'm scared. But safety isn't freedom, Mom. And freedom comes with risk."

"Fire him, Mr. Lyons. Please. Fire him," Charlotte pleaded, as Nat checked an incoming shipment at Lyons and Yale Good Foods. "And throw him out of your house. If he doesn't have a job and he has to come back home, he's not considered an adult, right? He'll have to stop this foolishness."

"Mrs. Carolina," Nat said sadly, "Tonio's one hell of a young man. He's got a future like ... well I wanna live t' a hundred to see what he's gonna do with himself. If there's any clean way to keep him from gettin' killed, I'll do it. Count on that. But ... I'm not gonna yank all the pride an' manhood outa him just t' keep him safe. Y'r a mother. Y'r not gonna understand that. But I can't force a man t' try t' be a boy again. Can't do that."

"My ex-husband is going to slice my son to death with a sword and you're telling me that's perfectly legal?" Charlotte stood at the counter, shaking anew and trying not to scream at the sheriff.

"I'm sorry, Mrs. Carolina. But they're both adults and they entered into the agreement voluntarily. Your son has the choice to back out if he wants to."

"My son has more pride than brains."

"I'm sorry. Dueling is an old tradition. People don't do it much, true. But it's between them if they want to. It's better than shooting each other in a bar fight and maybe hitting random strangers."

Charlotte snapped. "I'll kill Gael before I'll allow him to slaughter my son!"

"If you do, Mrs. Carolina, I'll have to arrest you for murder."

The front door of the Pickle Manse remained closed, despite Charlotte's pounding. Even if she had come to kill her ex-husband (which she had not), she wouldn't have been able to.

When pounding with one fist wouldn't do, she pounded with both, "I know you're in there," she cried, heedless of any listening neighbors. "I know you are, you coward! You and your latest little trophy! Both of you! Both of you should be ashamed of yourselves! Come out and face me!"

But the door remained resolutely closed until she finally wore herself out, turned and trudged away, exhausted.

Charlotte didn't see the curtain that twitched aside, nor the sad, dark, red-rimmed eyes that stared upon her retreating back.

Nat turned to Bob-the-Nerd. "Have you got anythin' yet? Anythin' on the source of the money Carolina's usin' t' buy the Harbibi ranch?"

"Nat, like I told you, this is beyond me. This looks like an offshore corporation owned by another offshore corporation that might be owned by ... who knows? I'm not getting anywhere. And I don't think I'm ever going to get anywhere."

"But we know who's gotta be behind it. We know. It's just a matter o' provin' it."

"Yeah. I know. But we can't prove it, Nat. I can't. So you'd better have some other idea for stopping Gael Carolina and his plans to turn the Harbibi place into a hotel-casino. Because," he sighed, tapping the Toshiba laptop, "it's not going to happen here."

The weeks passed. And the scheduled day for the duel drew closer.

"Tonio," said Jennifer as they both sat atop the sturdy rail of Nat's corral, watching the horses in the lowering sun. A hard-working Thursday was ending. Saturday, at the traditional hour of dawn, Tonio would meet his father on the field of honor. "I know we never got along much. And that was mostly my fault, I guess. But ... well, you're not a bad brother."

Tonio chuckled. "Thanks. You've turned into a halfway decent sister, too."

Jen looked at her hands. "Do you really think ...? I mean, he's our dad. He might not be a very nice person, but do you actually think he'd ... you know?"

"Kill me?"

"Yeah. That."

"I guess we'll find out, won't we?" This time, Tonio's chuckle was bitter.

"In a fair fight, I bet you would win."

"Jen, by the rules, this is a fair fight. And I'm the one who started it."

"Oh, cut it out. You know it's not fair. Tonio ... you can still get out of it. All this 'honor' stuff. I mean, I understand but ..." she started to sob, "b-but I don't want to lose you."

"I don't want to lose me, either," he said, draping a comforting arm over her shoulder. "But there are worse things to lose than life."

Friday, the day before the duel, dawned dusty and hot. Hardyville went about its business in a daze, as if ordinary activities were mere illusion.

Charlotte rose, showered, dressed, and pushed her granola around in its bowl as if the motions of normal life could make tomorrow's reality go away. She hardly had the strength to drag herself around the house. But she forced herself to step into the burning sun, start her car, and drive to the shop. Moving through molasses, she made herself unlock the door

281

of Sassy Frassy's Hemp Boutique. Inside, in the dim coolness, she went through all the proper motions of a business owner, readying her store for a busy day.

But no customers came. Who would want to stand across the counter, handing silver coins to a woman whose son was going to die in a few hours? Three or four acquaintances stopped briefly in the morning to give her a hug. But clearly no one wanted to stay, to buy, to chat, to console. All day, Charlotte moped about the shop alone, fitfully rearranging things on the shelves, flicking imaginary specks of dust off the merchandise.

Finally, all strength drained away, she slumped into her chair behind the counter. Nothing left to do but wait for the hour when she could return home to even more dismal isolation.

A few minutes later, the bell over the door tinged for the first time all afternoon. Charlotte raised her head wearily. For a second, she couldn't see who had arrived, silhouetted in the bright sun of the doorway.

Then she realized who it was. She gathered what small strength she could marshal, rose to her feet and snarled at the intruder, "What the hell do you think you're doing here? Get out. Get out! I said get out!"

Chapter 14
Duel of Wits

These things traditionally happen in misty green clearings, where men in ruffled shirts meet to test their courage—or their hatred and stubborn pride. But verdant glades are hard to come by in Hardyville.

On the morning of the duel, Gael and Tonio Carolina, with their seconds and a hundred jeans-and-boot clad spectators, assembled in an old gravel quarry southwest of town.

Pickup trucks, ranch-dusty SUVs, and even a few passenger cars jammed the entrance and the curving road leading to it. The crowd was heavy with men, this sort of thing not being a woman's sport. But Jennifer was there to support her brother, and a few bolder, hard-bitten women came with their men to show they had the stomach for a real fight.

To one side stood Gael Carolina, rapier lightly in hand, stance springy and elegant. Fifty feet away, Tonio clutched its twin as if it were a two-by-four.

Between them stood their seconds, Carty for Tonio, banker Dermot Harvard Halloran for Gael. Halloran mopped sweat from his jowls with a kerchief as the two men went over the final details. It was still shadowy in the quarry, but the day already had the relentless feel of an end-of-summer scorcher. It would be a day for iced tea and resting in the shade, a day for shooting the bull with buddies or staying inside with air conditioning and a good book.

But one of the men present might never again enjoy such ordinary pleasures.

All was set. Carty stepped back to Tonio's side, Halloran to Gael's. Each second conferred briefly with a dueler. Then father and son took seven steps toward each other. They paused. Gael saluted smoothly, raising his sword in a crisp, vertical line. He seemed to kiss the steel as he bowed toward Tonio. Tonio's clumsy attempt to mirror the gesture brought a mocking glint to his father's eye.

The two lowered their rapiers to horizontal and began...

A horn blared. Into the quarry bucketed a dented pickup truck, rooster-tail of dust soaring behind it. Slowing, it poked its way amid the chaos of parked vehicles. Unable to get closer, it skidded to a halt as a little man flew out, clutching a sheaf of papers.

Nat!

Two shadowed figures remained in the truck's crew seat as Nat hurried forward, cussing all the way.

"Damn, dammit!" he shouted. "Damn cattle drive on the road, or I'd a' got here 15 minutes ago. Everybody stop. Just stop right now!"

Tonio and Gael stepped back, Gael frowning, Tonio confused and trying to hide his sense of momentary reprieve.

Chest heaving, Nat inserted himself between the duelers. He waved their seconds to his side. The three men, Nat and the seconds, whispered at each other. The seconds inspected the papers Nat brought. Then they nodded and faded back as Nat announced loudly to the crowd, "A duel's a matter o' honor, right?"

Everybody, including the combatants, had to nod at that. "Well," Nat went on, waving the papers, "somethin's come up that speaks t' that very thing. Honor, I mean. This needs dealin' with before anybody cuts anybody up here this mornin'."

"I object!" shouted Gael Carolina. "This violates all protocol. This ..."

"Scared, are ya?" Nat demanded, holding up the papers in his fist as though they were a cudgel.

"Of course not."

"Well," said Nat, "mebbe you should be." He then took the crumpled papers in both hands and looked down. "These are emails," he announced to one and all. "Emails to," he paused. "G.R. Carolina. Emails from ..." he read slowly, followed by another pause. He looked up, scanning the crowd, making sure of their attention "somebody named J.B. Johnston at Dee-Oh-Jay dot Gee-Oh-Vee. Dee-Oh-Jay dot Gee-Oh-Vee," he repeated. "That's Department o' Justice, innit? The fed'ral one? Now why d'you suppose this man here would be gettin' and sending all these mails to the fed'ral gummint?"

Nobody spoke. Everybody knew Nat already knew the answer. They were just waiting for the explanation. He was just savoring the moment.

"Subject," he went on, "Contingency Plan: Worst Case."

Jennifer gasped. She and Tonio locked eyes. Everybody else just waited—except for Gael Carolina, who started angrily forward but, to his own evident surprise, was held back by his second. The pudgy banker had materialized at his side as Nat began to read, and now held Carolina gently but firmly by the sword arm.

"There's a bunch o' these emails," Nat told the crowd. "Some to this man here. Some from 'im. Some was written before them fed boys went into arbitration and some after. But the whole thrust of 'em is the same. You can all look if you want. But what it says here, to put it short, is that if Señor Carolina ..." he pronounced it "seen-yor" ... "will help bust the

DEA five out of Hardy County—scot-free, mind you—the fed'ral gummint will partner with him on a hotel-casino."

The crowd murmured angrily.

"Yep, *partner* with him," Nat nodded. "They promise to pay, up front, 'bout a half million paper fed money into his account in the outside world. Down payment, y'see. He'd buy gold with that money and—in the name of some Bahamian outfit called Paradise Unlimited—persuade Mardi Harbibi to sell out to him.

"Then, he'd use that gold—bought with fed'ral tax money—to spring the five feds from their hog sloppin' duties. After that, the paper millions'd roll in, he'd turn it into Hardyville spendin' money, and together him an' the fed'ral gummint would be the first to take advantage of the Delaval organization's new 'management'—that's the word they use, 'management'—of Hardyville.

"The feds," he emphasized, just in case somebody had missed the point, "would start the process of owning and 'managing' all Hardy County. With the seen-yor's help. And linin' the seen-yor's pockets."

"Those bastards!" somebody called. "Those Delaval bastards!"

But Nat waved the increasingly restive crowd into silence. "Nope, nope. Now put the blame where it belongs." He pointed firmly at Gael Carolina. "The seen-yor here is doin' Delaval as dirty as he's doin' us—wantin' t' build a resort with the fedgov as partner. That's not what Delaval signed on for. Nobody wants this thing except Carolina here and the feds."

"Lies!" Gael Carolina shouted. "Absolute lies designed to rouse mob hatred. The money I shall be using—to help improve this blighted community, mind you—is entirely my own. I have received no money from your federal government and made no agreements with them. And anyone who claims otherwise is a liar—and perhaps a forger." He appealed to the crowd.

"Those papers Mr. Lyons is holding—whatever they actually may be—are not my correspondence. They cannot possibly be. Mr. Lyons himself—or some more intelligent conspirator—created them out of whole cloth. They are not mine and I can prove that."

"Yes they are," Jennifer said in a quavering voice, stepping from the crowd. "I saw them on your computer."

"Little liar," he sneered. "You saw nothing. Even if I had written or received such messages, all my business emails are encrypted against prying eyes like yours."

Jennifer looked uncertain. "I only saw the headers," she admitted. "The messages were all scrambled. But ..."

"Yes, you saw the headers. Of unbreakably encrypted messages, which neither you nor anyone else here could possibly have deciphered. You jumped to the worst possible conclusions. And now you and this man ... your employer who did you so many favors in exchange for your collusion in this matter ... have concocted a preposterous ..."

While Gael and Jennifer dueled with words, Nat nodded toward his truck. In response, the two shadowed figures emerged from the crew seat. Emerging separately, one from each side, they reached the front of the truck and clung together as one. Charlotte Carolina, nerve-wracked herself, supported the tremulous Mirabelle, who approached with tears running down her cheeks.

The afternoon before, as Charlotte sat slumped in her chair at Sassy Frassy's, the bell over the door had tinged. When she saw who had invaded her sanctum, she leaped to her feet and shouted, "What the hell do you think you're doing here?"

And Mirabelle had whispered, "I'm here to save your son's life. And my husband's."

Now Mirabelle faced Gael, braced by Charlotte. She looked her husband in the eye and said, "I'm sorry, Gael. I know you'll hate me and I don't blame you. But I gave the messages to Charlotte. And we gave them to Nat."

"But you couldn't possibly break my encryption. None of you could. You haven't the skill ..."

"Yes," Charlotte interrupted as Mirabelle sobbed in her arms. "She could break your encryption. Easily. Really, Gael, it's not very nice to keep an old mistress' photo on your computer as wallpaper. And it's not very wise to use the slut's name as your encryption password."

Gael glared at Mirabelle. "You traitorous bitch."

"I did it only to save your life," Mirabelle cried. "I love you and I don't want you to die!"

"You're not saving my life," snapped Gael. "There's no chance that this arrogant, ill-trained young man-child could ..."

"But Gael, don't you see?" she pleaded. "It's not just him. It's ..." her eyes and gesture took in the entire waiting crowd.

Nat interrupted. "Speakin' of that ... yeah, it's not just Tonio you got a problem with. He beckoned Jennifer forward. When she came to his side, he placed an arm around her. "I think you got some explainin' t' do t' this young lady, don't you?"

"I don't know what you're talking about!"

"You know 'zactly what I'm talking about," said Nat. Charlotte prompted Mirabelle, who pulled a cloth-wrapped bundle from her shoulder bag and handed it to Nat. Nat handed it to Jennifer. Who unwrapped it and stared down in surprise.

She held a decorative abalone-shell comb, a small roll of coins, and a handful of other small items, all wrapped in a gold-lace shawl—items whose disappearance, together with the discovery of an opal necklace under her pillow, became an excuse to throw her out of her father's house.

"I found them in the back of his desk drawer," Mirabelle confessed. "I did not know, Jennifer. I am so sorry."

"You were making a pest of yourself, always looking over my shoulder," Gael shrugged.

What could anyone say? We all stood and stared wondering at a man so craven he'd frame his 15-year-old daughter for theft.

Nat took Mirabelle and Jen gently by the arm and escorted them, with Charlotte, to the edge of the crowd. The three women fell together into a weepy embrace.

Walking back to his place between Gael and Tonio, Nat went on, "Now, Mr. Carolina, time t' do the honorable thing for once—and withdraw. From the duel and from y'r plans for Hardyville."

Gael Carolina must have felt terrifyingly outnumbered at that moment. But he must have realized mob violence wasn't in our makeup. And he still had his pride.

"Any gold I possess is mine," he insisted. "It is not your business how I obtain it. Mrs. Harbibi and I are negotiating voluntarily. Voluntary action. Enterprise. Privacy. Aren't these among the things you claim to prize? And if this young man ..." he flicked the point of his rapier toward Tonio, "believes he can stop me, I'm still more than willing to demonstrate the error of his ways."

Tonio, who had been silent through all this, spoke boldly and with only a slight quaver. "And now that I know what he's really like, I'm more willing than ever to fight him. I hope I kill him."

Nat turned from one to the other. It appeared that the prideful, stubborn Carolinas were determined to battle each other, no matter what anyone said.

The sun swung over the lip of the quarry, glaring into naked, sweating faces.

Nat shrugged in resignation. Carty nodded at Dermot Halloran, who released Gael Carolina's sword arm and stepped aside. Tonio and Gael approached each other again.

"Just one thing before you begin," Carty said calmly, eyes leveling on Gael. "I want you to know that if you kill your son, five minutes later, I'll be the one challenging you."

"And if Carty dies," spoke one of the young Minutemen from the edge of the crowd, "I'll challenge you."

"And me."

"And me."

"And me."

The voices echoed from all over the crowd. First one. Then two at a time. Then three, four, five. The promises flowed through the crowd like a wave. Then, when the pledges stopped, Jennifer pulled free of the embrace of her mother and Mirabelle, turned on her father and promised, "And if you stab every person here to death with your sword, you rotten bastard, then *I'll* challenge you. And no matter what weapon you want to fight with, by then I'll know how to use it as well as you do. And I'll beat you, Dad. I'll beat you into the ground."

You've got to give Gael Carolina this. Rotten bastard he may have been. Sneak he may have been. Double-dealing, child-framing, ruthless monomaniac he may have been. But the man had guts. Even after all that, he still stood defiant, graceful, and poised to strike.

At that moment, another pickup truck rattled into view. The driver, far less urgent than Nat, parked at the back of the line. Driver and passenger emerged from either side and, as Charlotte and Mirabelle had done, merged at the front of the truck.

"Oh yeah, I forgot," said Nat. "I invited Mrs. Harbibi."

Mardi Harbibi simpered toward the gathered crowd in the quarry, hand firmly in hand with John Davis Melvin, formerly Herr Kommandante of the federal multi-jurisdictional task force, now her indentured servant, not to mention her main squeeze. She beamed with smug happiness, barely noticing the drama taking place before her.

But Melvin's face, as he appraised the situation, froze. Still, in the Grieving Widow Harbibi's grip, he had no choice but to advance.

"Well, how nice of you all to wait for us." Mardi Harbibi mugged, thinking herself the object of all attention and perhaps even envy. "Sorry to hold you all up, but we were having a nice little breakfast. Nat, did you say you had something to show me?"

"Yep. That I did." From the stack of rumpled papers he clutched, Nat chose several and offered them to the Widow Harbibi. She released John Davis Melvin's hand to take them, failing to notice that her lover immediately began to back away.

Rough hands grabbed Melvin from behind. Two burly men held him in place.

Mardi silently read. Nat explained, loudly enough for everyone to hear, "Th' details are all there. But th' story is that the seen-yor over there was in cahoots with the fed bosses to keep them murderin' fed'rals from makin' their proper restitution to you."

She glanced up, alarmed, but continued reading.

"And," Nat added (still playing to the audience and seeming quite pleased with himself), "part of the plan was to have ole Melvin here soften you up real good with his attentions and affections so you'd sell out without askin' too many questions."

For a moment, it seemed she hadn't heard. She continued to scan the messages in her hands, flicking from page to page with no visible reaction. The sun climbed imperceptibly higher.

Then the Grieving Widow Harbibi rounded on John Davis Melvin, papers flying, left hand clenching into a fist. She belted him so hard that spectators across the quarry heard his nose break. She'd have done worse, too, except his blood-spattered captors dragged Melvin backwards.

Other hands reached to grab her. But for a fat, middle-aged harridan she was fast. She wriggled out of the grasping hands. She bared her teeth at Melvin. Then, seeing that he was too well protected, she barreled straight at Gael Carolina, roaring like a lioness.

The last anyone saw of them that day, Carolina was backing desperately out of the quarry and between the parked cars, attempting to fend off a crazed and shrieking widow with the point of his sword.

Gael Carolina and John Davis Melvin survived their encounters with Mardi Harbibi. Carolina, a free man, if a dishonest one, slunk back into town just long enough to pack his things and drive out of town alone in his rental car.

He left Mirabelle behind. Rather to everybody's surprise she entered the parade of rejected Carolina wives to join Charlotte in running Sassy Frassy's Hemp Boutique.

Tonio stayed on the ranch working with Nat. Everybody knew he'd leave for college someday, once he'd earned more money. But for the time being, he was happy not to be battling anybody or anything to the death.

Jennifer started spending more time with her mother. You might say they even almost started sort of getting along. But not so well that Jen was willing to surrender her solitary trailer at the ranch, even after Nat said she could.

Jennifer still had doubts about the sanity of horses. But she didn't say no when Nat said one day, "Y'know, that colt Bulldog. He's not likely to 'mount to anything, terrible scars on his leg and all. Prob'ly won't be able to sell him for much. Might be you'd like to keep him?"

On another ranch—a hog farm, really—on the other side of town ... well, you probably don't want to hear about what went on there. It wasn't pretty.

Her arbitration agreement with the Federal Five prevented Mrs. Harbibi from doing any actual physical harm to the men working off their restitution (she paid a hefty penalty for belting John Davis Melvin in the snoot). But did I ever mention that the Grieving Widow had the personality of Hillary Clinton on a bad hair day? And that it takes a long, long, really very, very long time to work off a debt of $50,000 calculated in Hardyville gold dollars?

Then one day, with the first touch of fall in the air, the puddle jumper brought another visitor to Hardyville. A familiar visitor. An old friend.

Alejandro Verdugo Serrano, personal representative of billionaire Jorge Delaval, was welcomed back with pleasure—and a little trepidation. We all liked him. But after the Gael Carolina experience, we were more nervous than ever about the implications of our deal with Delaval Enterprises.

"I apologize profusely," Serrano told us, as a bunch of us gathered in the big meeting room in the back of the Hog Trough. "We made a grave error in our choice of project manager. We believed a man with family ties to your community would be more trustworthy than Señor Carolina proved to be. Alas, both you and Señor Delaval came very close to paying a high price for that error.

"Our arrangement to shield Hardy County from the U.S. government in exchange for your services as a financial haven still applies. We must, however, take more care. Our next candidate for project manager will be a person with deep, deep roots in this community."

His eyes flicked from Nat to Carty to Dora. They rested lightly on the remaining Carolinas and the Goodins. They twinkled at Janelle, the Hog Trough's owner, who circulated among the crowd with her small staff of waitresses, pouring coffee.

"And," he announced with another twinkle, "to ensure harmonious collaboration between Hardyville and the Delaval interests, I personally shall remain here for a portion of every year. I am retiring—semi-retiring—and I shall be seeking to purchase a hunting lodge in your mountains."

"And you and me can bag us some grizzly," Nat grinned.

"Indeed," Serrano smiled. "I have been looking forward to it." Then he paused and resumed in a somber tone, "There is just one thing ... one vital thing ... that remains to be done to secure Hardyville's continued freedom."

His seriousness touched us. We quieted. Some of us put down our coffee cups and leaned forward.

"I believe everyone here intuitively understands what I am about to say," Serrano went on. "Hardyville's greatest threat comes from its random overexposure to the world. This place is a treasure. Yet, however sincerely you wish to convey its spirit to the outside world, that world is unready for what you have to offer. Continued exposure will attract the very people who wish to destroy everything you stand for. You have already seen it. I'm sorry that an outsider must say this. But you know it is true."

He pierced me with a look that was filled with regret, but very firm. I felt other eyes on me. It was almost as though I were being probed and penetrated by people's thoughts.

"You must once again hide Hardyville from the world," Serrano continued. "It is imperative. It may already be too late to undo all the damage, but you must do what you can, and do it now. Hardyville must—for its own sake—disappear anew into the mists of obscurity that once protected it. You must," he said gazing steadily at me, making no pretense of addressing his remarks to the entire assembly, "stop publishing any news of Hardyville."

I sat pinned in his gaze like a still-living butterfly tacked to a display board. The whole room waited for me to say something, perhaps to defend myself and my Hardyville stories. But he was right. What else could I do?

Slowly, silently, I nodded.

Claire Wolfe

About the Author

Claire Wolfe is the author of a number of books including "The Freedom Outlaw's Handbook" and "I Am Not a Number!" She is the co-author, with Aaron Zelman, of the young-adult novel, "RebelFire: Out of the Gray Zone." Claire has been writing for *Backwoods Home Magazine* for many years and is now one of *BHM*'s bloggers. You can read Claire's online observations at www.backwoodshome.com/ClaireWolfe.

She lives in an undisclosed location somewhere in the west with a pack of dogs. (And yes, Hardyville is a real place, even if her stories about it are ever so slightly exaggerated.)

Claire Wolfe

Other titles available from Backwoods Home Magazine

The Best of the First Two Years
A Backwoods Home Anthology—The Third Year
A Backwoods Home Anthology—The Fourth Year
A Backwoods Home Anthology—The Fifth Year
A Backwoods Home Anthology—The Sixth Year
A Backwoods Home Anthology—The Seventh Year
A Backwoods Home Anthology—The Eighth Year
A Backwoods Home Anthology—The Ninth Year
A Backwoods Home Anthology—The Tenth Year
A Backwoods Home Anthology—The Eleventh Year
A Backwoods Home Anthology—The Twelfth Year
A Backwoods Home Anthology—The Thirteenth Year
A Backwoods Home Anthology—The Fourteenth Year
A Backwoods Home Anthology—The Fifteenth Year
A Backwoods Home Anthology—The Sixteenth Year
Emergency Preparedness and Survival Guide
Backwoods Home Cooking
Can America Be Saved From Stupid People
Chickens—a beginner's handbook
Starting Over—Chronicles of a Self-Reliant Woman
Dairy Goats—a beginner's handbook
Self-reliance—Recession-proof your pantry
Making a Living—Creating your own job
Growing and Canning Your Own Food
The Coming American Dictatorship—Parts I-XI